DON'T DOLPHINS CRY AT ALL?

Best Wishes
Lorraine

Geoff Dormer

ORIGINAL WRITING

Cover images
Bottlenose Dolphins cavorting off Red Strand, West Cork, Ireland.
Taken by Dr Nic Slocum of *Whale Watch West Cork*

ISBNS
PARENT : 978-1-78237-040-6
EPUB: 978-1-78237-041-3
MOBI: 978-1-78237-042-0
PDF: 978-1-78237-043-7

A CIP catalogue for this book is available from the National Library.

Published by ORIGINAL WRITING LTD., Dublin, 2012.

Printed by CLONDALKIN GROUP, Glasnevin, Dublin 11

For Geoff who was always our still, small voice of calm.

"My bounty is as boundless as the sea,
My love as deep...for both are infinite."

William Shakespeare

ACKNOWLEDGEMENTS

Joyce & the late Walter Dormer, Geoff's devoted parents.

Terry Dormer, the intrepid brother-in-law.

Sarah, Tom & Paul.

Former teaching colleagues and pupils, Churchfields School, Swindon, Wiltshire, England

John Crown, Oncologist and his team St Vincent's Hospital, Dublin.

Staff in Clara Library for their patience and assistance to Geoff whilst writing this book.

Garrett Bonner and all the talented people at Original Writing

All our loyal friends, especially our dearest friend, Pauline Kelly.

The late Shane Rabbitte and Jimmy Gorry who shared so many wonderful mountaineering and flying trips with Geoff.

Thanks to the readers and all those who seek to bring the joy of reading to the widest audience.

Nic & Wendy Slocum, Whale Watch, West Cork

Contents

My late husband completed 'Don't Dolphins Cry? whilst undergoing chemotherapy in St Vincent's Hospital, Dublin.

Whilst the book may come under the genre of Fantasy/Fiction there are strong links and parallels with a 'real world' of humans. Concerned for the environment, the book seeks both to inform and question Man's effects within the oceans of the world through his unthinking cruelty and his deliberate violence – as seen through imagined sensory abilities of dolphins in the story.

If you expect another 'nice' nature story, you are way of track.

They are unusual dolphins. All capable of telepathy, a few possess magnified mindskills – brought about by exposure to increasing levels of toxins and dumping in their water world – such that they are able to influence and change human perception and behaviour!

Evil exists undersea as well as above surface but the author would rather let the story tell how man is at the root of it, bringing discord to natural harmony.

If you have read William Horwood's 'Duncton Wood' series, you will realise readers purchase books with animals as central characters. They enter worlds in which cardinal sins are committed by creatures other than man. Too often, human minds regard animals as incapable of differentiating good or evil; fairness or foul play. Indeed, any reasoning at all – but readers can and do accept these in print.

An inventiveness of language was necessary to aid a reader's understanding: to appeal on emotional bases; to make clear distinction when dolphin 'speaks' to dolphin, but always in ways they might experience life in sea. Evident, the author liked to think, are attempts to underpin dolphin dialogue with poetic devices to distinguish and reinforce their world. The author chuckled over new 'words'.

Such are differences between the species that fear arises in human characters, humbled before an 'alien' superiority – even the human heroine, 'Maeve', a young Australian student. The author speaks only of the relationship between Maeve and the principal dolphin, 'Gaze', as being founded in love and a kinship of spirit – despite 'Maeve' being manipulated by his frightening powers for general good.

The author believed readers would identify with the dolphin heroes as much as with human counterparts, attracted by the emotional life with which they are endowed. As 'beneficiaries' of interchanges, humans are manipulated by superior minds and fall prey to an instinctive terror of 'a voice in the sea' – evidenced, for example, by 'Rick Dortmann', the Manager of 'Brisbane Dolphinarium'....who turns his dolphin 'stars' free to fin greater freedom and lives comfortably with the ghost of his wife but only 'Gaze' and the reader will understand.

The author tried to make the human characters plausible and derive from varied social backgrounds. The complex mix of humans and dolphins might seem unworkable in reading this submission – but, as any writer would assert, 'I wouldn't write it unless I felt it would be understood'.

The novel is basically in two parts, the first part dealing with the dolphins of 'Wanderer's warmstream waterspace' and covers a sea-world of 'joy/harmony' and 'suffering/cruelty' at the onset of strange effects due to 'pollution' by Man. The author sought to explain that evil does exist beneath the waves but is initiated and compounded by Man's interference.

New 'Visioners' arise. 'Karg', a bottlenose dolphin, keeps captive a female dolphin in 'the Cave of Pleasure' for 'sadistic, sexual self-gratification'. Karg senses another capable of 'Visioning' and seeks to kill him but, under-rating Gaze, Karg loses. In lead up to climactic confrontation with 'Vorg', Karg's son, the author seeks, by imagery and event, to make grave comment on Man, as a hunter, who takes more than most predators regard as necessary or wise. The author endeavoured to cover a whole range of feelings – from panic to pathos and anger to despair – and more the author doesn't mention in the water world of the dolphins of the story. The author hoped the experience would be emotionally satisfying, content informing.

The second part of the book has increasing predominance of human dialogue which patterns and progresses events in the first part. Human relationships are more deeply explored together with the force of 'dolphin influence' upon people.

'Maeve', her family and other people around the fictitious 'Brisbane Dolphinarium' are shown to be 'beneficiaries' as dolphins 'interact' with them. 'Gaze' is shown as shrewd, capable of learning and adapting and, above all, a factor in 'change of human hearts and minds'. A reader will question if Dolphinariums are performing a role which is more than a 'zoo'.

Increasingly, a 'benevolent after-life' intervenes in the form of White Dolphins. These interventions, plus attempts by 'Gaze' to convince Man of a parallel intelligence in the oceans, make, the author hopes, readers question 'attitude and belief' concerning dolphins. Also how Man's activities threaten existence below sea surface as he does above it.

The only sense you can really make of this submission is to read the manuscript for yourself – sense a sea's 'Harsh Messiah' in a young 'Bottlenose'.

The novel takes the challenging leap of moving from a factual and informative base into the realms of a kind of science fiction having its own psychological/sociological reality. Not so distant from a diet of popular television to which viewers, old or young alike, are exposed, the author thought readers would 'tune-in' to language and conceptual constructs quickly. In 'Follow a Wild Dolphin', such a step was left to writers of fiction to take. This author sought to take it.

As an ex-English teacher with 30 years' experience the author believed a market for a novel like this exists in Schools where it would have a role in Language and Literature studies for older students. The author suggested Comprehension, Creative and Formal Writing, Group Oral Work and so on. The author believed these things were possible – possibly in the form of a booklet for teachers. But, the author believed it more important that the manuscript stood up in its own right.

Aside from the above, the author was convinced the book would have a market for mature readers with concerns for environmental issues.

You can't read the author's mind – his 'dolphins' can. You can't alter feeling, perception of memory – the author's 'dolphins' can. You can't span distances between 'now' and 'then' or 'what might have been' or 'might be' – the author's 'dolphins' do….and know the weaknesses of men and injustice which accrues for our world.

FOREWORD

To interweave a story of bottlenose dolphins and humans would be easier if dolphins were portrayed as unequal in status and ability...

Man clings to his vain notion of superiority, desiring despotic dominion above sharers of the 'worldspace'. Indeed, the Christian religion speaks of Adam and Eve as banished from the Garden of Eden and going forth to multiply throughout the Earth - to hold sway above all other creatures. Perhaps the Western religions encourage an attitude and belief of Man's superiority with which some Eastern tenets would be at variance.

No species in world history has had the ability to change the harmonies of co-existence as mankind today. With late conscience, fearful for his own survival, mankind now looks at a world which is far from a mythical Eden. His chemistry and technology debases and violates huge areas of air, land and sea, a world in which he had no creative part. Through recent time, echo distress and suffering from the genocides of whole species - or the prey of man hunted to excesses which wiser predators abhor.

Fiction has a part to play in forming attitudes and beliefs in a reader - of challenging or modifying them. Fiction may also be a means of informing or giving new experience in an imaginative context, but it must always seek to be entertaining. This story seeks to recognise the need to be informative but moves, quite deliberately, beyond the factual base into the realms of fantasy. The author seeks to ensure that a reader will be able to identify with a dolphin or human character upon an emotional base and to help him understand distress for dolphins. In this, questioned are notions of Man's superiority; reflected, sometimes, are stark portrayals of his cruelty and injustice.

Currently, there are testimonies from a variety of people concerning the heightened sense of spiritual awareness and physical well-being that they have felt in the swimming company of dolphins. Some speak of 'closeness' and 'affinity' they have experienced with these mammals of the sea - or of the therapeutic quality for those suffering physical or mental stress. If this leap into 'fancy' seems 'too unlikely', then the following should be contemplated. Learning to adapt to a changing environment is not the unique mark of human intelligence popularly believed. Other creatures show an ability to learn and adapt - some more than others. Is emotion a human experience alone? Who said that telepathy - thinking mind to mind - had to be a startling mind development that could only be a potentiality within human beings? Who argues that an animal has no right to a God and counts little in the scheme of things? Who denies another species the right to know a Messiah - even one of their own?

An interweaving of themes between humans and dolphins in this story is a difficult task and challenging reading. The reader will find that many of his own concepts are compromised. The story is written in the spirit of a necessary consciousness which Man must show in living harmoniously within the 'worldspace' he is close to destroying. The wanton destruction of dolphins must stop. If the need for incarcerating other creatures for entertainment is challenged as an unnecessary and discordant facet of human behaviour, the writer will not be sorry

NOTES ON 'DOLPHINESE'

'Dolphinese' is a label the author conveniently ascribes to modes and interactions through which dolphins communicate. It must be remembered that language used in descriptive passages concerning dolphins, their acts of communication, imagined constructs surrounding telepathic/extra-sensory abilities <u>step into fantasy</u>. Striving to be 'convincing' and stimulating, the story remains 'fiction'.

It is hoped that the reader will be able to adjust to frequent use of compound words. It is requested that they realise the complexity of dolphin communication in terms of sound and song, fin movements and body postures in the real world. Also, it should be realised that such a language has evolved over much greater time than with man. An attempt is made to relate dolphins to their own environment in ways <u>they</u> might see it; to refer to and use their dialogue to reflect a unique and novel standpoint in marine biology. Moreover, an attempt is made to reflect a 'poetry of movement' and heighten the quality of sound in description (by the written devices of alliteration, onomatopoeia, Leonine Rhyme or simple sound repetition) in order to reinforce and reaffirm dolphins in <u>their</u> environment of such apparent joy.

Admittedly, there is absolutely no scientific evidence for telepathic ability in dolphins! Writing a story about dolphins where telepathy is an unremarkable norm has proved immensely challenging. No doubt it will be just as challenging to read. For this reason, the author has found it useful to let punctuation of dialogue and description serve as the obvious marker of 'something unique and unusual occurring'. Although 'a printer's nightmare' to be faced with strings of ... and ... the author believes them necessary.

A reader might ask, 'Why no glossary?' The reply would point out that principal functions of this book are to inform and entertain. Since this is so, the author does not wish to imply an insult to his reader's intelligence. To insult his reader is not a good starting point whilst striving for greater awareness of the plight of dolphins internationally!
The author wishes the reader well in interpreting the differences between 'mindmeet', 'mindmerge' and 'merge' - or what might be meant by 'flukethrash' and 'fluketremble'.

In 'getting there', the reader will be striving to put himself in a dolphin's mind, body and, hopefully, his 'man-made', heavy heart.

NOTES ON 'AGENT ORANGE'

The author is neither a militarist nor an informed chemist. He is aware that PCBs and DDT are being found in increasing levels in carcasses of whales and dolphins.

There is no scientific evidence to support the hypothesis that 'Agent Orange' has infiltrated the food-chains of the Pacific Ocean. There is nothing to support the notion that TCDDs have been dumped at sea by the Military Authorities of the United States of America. Such an implication in this book is purely fictional convenience and fictional licence serving to point to risks involved through the process of dumping chemicals at sea - something for which a commercial world could be more readily indicted.

There may be effects upon life-forms in terms of mutational change as a result of some chemicals but the author is not qualified to write meaningfully upon the matter. He uses TCDD purely as a convenient and probably unjustifiable 'reason for change' in dolphins of this story.

Other possible 'reasons' for remarkable 'developments in mind' in main dolphin characters might have been put forward. The testing of nuclear devices at sea? Visitation by alien intelligences in U.F.O.s? He chose something which was a more 'quasi-reasonable' alternative, knowing that these clear statements would be very necessary.

NOTES ON CETACEANS MENTIONED IN THIS BOOK:

'DOLPHINS'

BOTTLENOSE (Tursiops truncatus)
Largest of the beaked dolphins. Long, robust body. Fins and flukes are relatively small. Short stout beak marked by a crease where it meets the forehead (melon). Colouration is dark grey above, fading on sides to whitish pink belly.
Distribution is worldwide in temperate or tropical seas. Usually seen in coastal waters, but encountered in mid-ocean.
Mature to a maximum length of four metres. Some have been known to live for nearly forty years.

SPINNER (Stenella longirostris)
An agile, fast swimmer. Slender, muscular body with a long, narrow beak. Fins and flukes are long and slender. Dark grey on beak, head and back. Fades to lighter shades on sides. White beneath. Dark patch around the eye extends to the tip of the beak.
Tropical and warm temperate waters. Some live close to shore but others live exclusively in mid-ocean.
Reaches a little over two metres at maturity.
An estimated 15,000 - 16,000 of this species were killed in 1986 through the effects of tuna fishing.

HUMP-BACK (Sousa chinensis)
Superficially similar to BOTTLENOSE but whitish, greyish or spotted. Pectorals brown or pinkish; light pink belly. The dorsal surmounts a hump that is most obvious in those from the Indian Ocean, those from the Pacific having an indistinct or missing hump. Can be distinguished from the BOTTLENOSE by colouration (lighter); shape of dorsal (flatter, low and more triangular), and size at maturity.
Reaches about three metres.
Has been observed hunting with BOTTLENOSES.
Perhaps the story places them too far south and east of normal habitat.

SPOTTED (Stenella attenuata)
Long, slender body with sickle-shaped dorsal. Beak like that of BOTTLENOSE but more slender. Colouration variable but generally steel grey, lighter underneath. Covered with dense grey spots extending to the belly with age.
Coastal waters and mid-ocean in tropical and some subtropical regions.
Length, two and a half metres - males slightly larger.
Often seen in association with yellowfin tuna. Hence, grouping with SPINNERS is not uncommon. Shares same dangers in commercial tuna fishing.

SHORT-SNOUTED WHITEBELLY (Lagenodelphis hosei)
'Fraser's Dolphin'. Bluish grey back. Dark eye patch.
Pale pink or white belly. There is a dark line from the mouth extending almost the full length of body to give distinct banded appearance.
Very shy of boats. Only known from a skeleton found in 1895 until, in 1979, several were caught in tuna nets.
Few reports of regular association with other dolphins.
Indian and Pacific oceans.
Mature length around two and a third metres.

ORCA (Orcinus orca)
'Killer whale'. Largest of the dolphins and probably the best known. Distinctive black and white colouration which is instantly identifiable - if its size isn't sufficient clue!
Females reach eight metres; males nine plus metres.
Dorsal is an elongated triangle; much larger in males.
Tropical, temperate and polar waters. They appear to prefer cooler coastal waters where selected prey is abundant.
Placement of ORCAS in the story is possible but rare.
Preying upon even great white sharks, it co-operates to hunt within groups. Sometimes, ORCAS harry and kill much larger creatures than themselves - even the baleen whales.
Playing with prey, like a cat may do with a mouse, is a common behaviour pattern.

'WHALES'

BELUKHA WHALE (Delphinapterus leucas)
Absolutely no comment! Find out, if you can...

STRAP-TOOTHED (Mesoplodon layardii)
Long, muscular body tapers rapidly behind comparatively small dorsal.
Males have strap-like teeth in the lower jaw which may grow so long that
they touch above the upper jaw. Such may not allow the mouth to open
fully. It is thought that such unfortunates 'suck in' squid prey.
Strandings indicate likely habitat as temperate to cool waters. Known in
waters around Australia and New Zealand, the story might place them a
fraction too far north.
Reach around six metres in length.

MELON-HEADED WHALE (Peponocephala electra)
Dark grey over entire body but with thin white line to lips and some white
marking to upper chest in an almost anchor-shaped pattern. Dorsal large
and sickle-shaped.
Grow to just under three metres.
Distribution in tropical and temperate waters.

'RIVER DOLPHINS'

BOUTO (Inia geoffrensis)
'Amazon River Dolphin'. Largest of the freshwater dolphins. Pink overall or grey on back merging to pink beneath. Indistinct dorsal. Long, powerful beak. Large melon. Well developed pectorals.
Known to swim and navigate through forests when the river floods after torrential rain, returning as water levels drop.
Accounts exist of natives stringing nets across river and waiting for BOUTO to herd fish towards the net-traps. Natives have learned to leave fish gifts for BOUTO to encourage co-operation in the future.
Length, around two and a half metres plus.

BAIJI (Lipotes vexillifer)
'Chinese River Dolphin'. Rare and endangered species.
Bulbous melon. Low triangular dorsal. Stocky body and long beak. Pectoral fins and flukes well-developed.
Lightish grey back to white on belly.
Highly developed echolocation faculty due to silty waters of its habitat.
Mature length of just over two metres.

DALL'S PORPOISE (Phocoenoides dalli)
Talk of astonishing speed in the book is not exaggerated.
Can reach speeds of 27 knots (50 kilometres per hour) and sustain it over considerable distance. Vertebral column has been extensively modified to achieve this.
Body is chunky with small head. Pronounced dorsal ridge behind the dorsal. Distinct keels above and below and just in front of flukes. Colouration is black and white.
Cold waters of North Pacific. Mainly found inshore but sometimes captured by tuna fisherman a thousand kilometres offshore.

N.B. Recommended reading:
'Whales, Dolphins and Porpoises'
Published in Great Britain by Merehurst Press.
ISBN 1-85391-034-1.
This publication has been of immense value to the author in necessary research.

Some descriptions above rely heavily upon contributions by Lawrence G. Barnes and Carson Creagh to this 'Illustrated Encyclopedic Survey'.

Chapter One

GAZE AND MAEVE

The long Nursery period was over. Gaze had surprised the Matrons of the Nursery, jovial Flab and the quieter Doe, with the speed at which he had absorbed their training. Physically average, he had learned quicker than others of his seasons and closed the age difference between himself and his sister, Gape. The recommendation that brother and sister should take first flukingpassage from the Podsherd together had surprised Peen. Such a thing was unusual but she knew of her mate's secret pride. Gale had not interfered with Training but he had heard, as his warmglow in mindmerge confirmed.

Peen fluked easily through waterspace, dorsal slicing surface of wavesurge in airspace above. With slightly less grace, the siblings shadowed her on either flank. One dorsal heeled, only occasionally in wind and wave-pressure, as her son over-compensated in finning. Generally he patterned Peen's easier progress. She knew they would appear as three, white-silver lines in tri-vector from bluer depths. Such was one of the patterns dolphinkind loved to use in communal fluking. Gaze, was coping more intuitively with vagaries of current and wavesurge. He timed his airsnatch to less than a pause, a blinking intersection of the surface. Despite a certain abstraction of mind, he would make her proud in finning with Wanderer's warmstream Podsherd.

Wanderer! Every dolphin female dreamed of flankers to match the life he had lived. He had become legendary. No, more than that, for he had achieved near idolatry. No other had been quite so revered.

He had been a Voyager; one who travelled forcelines through waterspace of reefrise and trough, to the limits of dolphin endurance. Returning, he had set about passing his discoveries to the Storytellers for several lightwaters. His urgency and obvious dedication had proved justified. The other Storytellers, selected custodians of knowledge and tradition through the long span of dolphinhistory, had been astonished at his discoveries. Indeed, they had found it too hard to understand everything in mindmerge! Making the story of his voyage into a saga to be retold to new generations had proved too difficult.

Suddenly, Wanderer had decided something more than the tradition of passing knowledge through sagas to new generations had been needed. Abruptly he had disappeared. It was during the period of his second absence that his most remarkable legacy to dolphinkind had taken form. Wanderer had cavern-dived within the steepsides of deepwater, close to the Podsherd's waterspace and...

Peen pinged warning to a cruising shark which veered away.

Few sharks threatened dolphinkind, lacking agility of mind and body

I

to sustain an attack. Yet she was vigilant with Gape and Gaze at flanks. Although they were already capable of self-sufficiency, it was hard to break the habits of a dam. Both siblings would be distressed to feel she still regarded them as her 'calves'. Sometimes Peen forgot they were near-matures. Soon they would mindmerge in their own right, Gape sooner than Gaze, probably... although...

As a female, Peen had never seen Wanderer's Cave - the legendary cavefloor patterned with signs which the Storytellers tried to interpret. Few gained mastery of everything there for the demands of living - finding food, warmth of water and rearing young in respectable patterns - were great. Also, dolphins shared a zest for life and were fun-seekers in general. Only a few concentrated for long periods.

Wanderer had concentrated - reflected and invented. Every so often in legend, a dolphin was described as having more than ordinary interests and abilities. Wanderer had been one such - a special dolphin endowed with unusual reflective ability and powers of deduction. When asked, he had called the process 'patterning'. From that moment, 'patterning' had tended to replace 'imaging' in scholarly use of Dolphinese.

The Storytellers had admired him and copied him in many ways. He had taught new fishmuster techniques and his suggested changes in the heirarchy of the Storytellers had been adopted. Previously, there had been only Voyagers, Clerics and Historians quartered in the Storytellers' Caves. Now, there were Navigators and Inventors.

What accident of birth had made Wanderer unique, Peen could not guess. All Storytellers gave information in more than sagas now. They could use signs understood in sandfloor and position of stones. Through Wanderer's teachings and sandfloor signs, the Storytellers were changed to leaders and teachers, held in high-esteem and respected for their justice as much as the Master Guardian, Tinu.

The Guardians protected the Podsherd in the face of danger and always led the fishmuster. Even now, three Guardians, Shadowers, were following their flukingvector unobtrusively. Near-matures on first flukingpassages were never told that they were really being accompanied still. There were also Observers and the Butting Pods had their Trainers. Tinu, as Master Guardian, carried much responsibility, great trust being invested in him by all of the Storytellers. Wanderer had fostered respect for the Guardians and made it clear organisation and planning of a lightwater's needs should be left to their good offices. In more weighty matters, the Storytellers made plans and decisions.

The Storytellers scorned those who sought acclaim through individual achievement. Differences in abilities were recognised but the conceited or the power-hungry were only temporarily tolerated. A few males had been banished from the Podsherd over the seasons. She wondered if - and where - their flukingpassages had terminated?

Peen felt the questing lateral-presence of Gaze. He was about to ask another question.

There was marked difference in the siblings' dispositions. Gape was healthy, revelling in approaching maturity; vibrant in movement; liable to fluke a rash passage in pursuit of pleasure. Gaze, not quite her equal in speed and turn, had eyes with an almost phosphorescent gleam - insatiably curious in this his sixth season, learning quicker than Gape despite the three seasons age disparity.

Garni would have been three seasons old now, Peen thought, but closed access to mindmemory rapidly. It was too painful.

Monitoring the more electric movements of Gape, she slowed slightly and waited for the question to come from Gaze.

'The sagas have not spoken of the origins of sharks or our differences. They merely caution all dolphins of the bloodlust that comes upon them. Why do they... seem to image so differently and not attack us as often as once they did, my dam?'

Why did she feel he was asking another question - unexpressed in mindmeet?

'They would have the Butting Pods to answer to. No shark attacks a dolphin without the Butting Pods taking revenge. They hunt an attacker down and damage him to the same degree.

'There have been fewer attacks and the times of killing have not been needed,' Peen answered, carefully adding, 'You will meet your sire's Butting Pod later.'

The last words were added with pride in her mate's physique and courage. Unusually, she had coupled only with him. She did not voice that a certain brashness he possessed - perhaps passed to Gape - had sometimes infuriated her, caused her nameless fears.

'Has my sire killed a shark? They seem so... so cold and... their imaging is different. They...'

Peen wondered if her son had ever tried mindcontact with sharks? She mindsmiled at the stupidity of the notion.

He would have to be a special dolphin to have succeeded with those sea-scavengers! Mindmeeting and mindmerging, dolphin to dolphin was one thing. It was stupidity to try with other creatures of the waterspace.

Really! Sharks were cold, unfeeling scavengers - but the big ones could attack. Dolphins learned to be cautious with sharks - especially near bloodflow or during... fishmuster...

Garni's phantom mindscreamed on the fringe of the fishmuster. Peen had heard it often. The passing seasons muted memory. She could keep control now... but she would never forget. Neither would Gale and his Butting Pod forget the Large White shark.

She did not want to share her imaging of sharks... Peen jerked back to the present.

Gaze was quiet - 'patterning' again. She did not reply, thinking it was fortunate he seemed to have switched to other things in his imaging.

Peen smiled as she tried to follow his imagewaves. They were surprisingly rapid and shifted from question to abstract observation in a series of bewildering connections. Mostly his mindlights blushed far too fast for her - and there was that discomfiting facility he had in shielding his mind from hers with a reefside of images she could not penetrate. He did not do this deliberately for he was always polite and respectful.

Once he had apologised, explaining that he had been 'patterning' and he hadn't meant to be rude.

Patterning! She had not told him that the Storytellers used the technique to make sense and order of the waterspace around - even conjecturing on the airspace above.

Gaze surprised her with a clear imagewave of, 'Yes, I thought they probably did.'

She did not reply, astonished that he was still capable of mindmeet when his reefside - his 'patterning'? - was so intense!

Out of mindmeet with Gaze, she wondered quite how far he was from the ordinary? Uncomfortable, she sought another subject to turn her mind away from a disturbing drift. She grasped at the unanswered question concerning sharks.

'As far as sharks are concerned, we share the waterspace,' Peen said, 'but sharks are... instinctive. They scavenge the seas for the weak and wounded and even turn upon their own. They are a constant threat but they have learned to respect dolphinkind.'

But the Large White Shark had not respected Garni...

Peen mindshivered, paused... found the strength to continue...

'The Butting Pods are there to remind them. Yes, they are cold for they are nearer to fish than to us. Their thoughts are for fishflesh and they scent and sense for the dying and the dead. Treat them with caution, both of you, but be not afraid.'

She found herself adding, 'Your sire and I are your beginning; the shark is likely your end. To know your beginning and end does not stop you enjoying a life of fluking between.'

Both siblings acknowledged in mindmeet. Why did she feel that Gaze had something important he wanted to say rather than ask?

He said nothing - as if it was too difficult? Was he afraid of something? The reefsiding process was very active.

Long moments later, they asked when they would meet their sire - Gape, in the thrall of male-worship already, with mixed images of courage, strength and tenderness; Gaze, with more queries on tactics and deep dives and - half-formed questions endless... behind anxiety?

What was there for Gaze to be anxious about?

They continued to fluke in tri-vector, fixing on forcelines from fathoms below, arrowing towards a distant islandmass and the meeting with the siblings' sire.

It was Gape, less preoccupied with patterning and personality, who sensed a hardside first. She pinged with excitement!

Peen chided herself for her lapse!

Gaze had been blocked laterally with her own flukingshape and water disturbance. She or Gape would have sensed the hardside first - but she should have been more alert!

The hardside was moving on a suitable vector and it would provide an opportunity for further learning. She veered towards the white shape, the flankers in precise newvector. She would warn them of the hardside barnacles and the cutting edges - of hazardous twistingfins and the suction force. There were dangers - but there was also speed, the forewave pressure to fluke upon and, perhaps, a brief glimpse of the Splitflukes who moved upon the airsides of these surface shapes.

Splitflukes were intelligent creatures of such astonishing inventiveness! She did not know all that Wanderer had seen but he had reported wondrous things.

Closing, Peen pinged exploratively. Once, in welcome and expressing willingness to mindmeet out of courtesy; the second time, to assess precisely, what was on vector front. There was no answer in return to the first ping. No other dolphin was fluking the forewave. The echo-returns to both echo-calls indicated the hardside was smaller than she had thought. It had two twistingfins and the mass cut cleanly through the surface. There again, she would not have expected the large hardsides on this vector. They seemed to prefer fixed vectors of passage above deepwater many dolphinspans beyond the horizon.

It was not the kind which trailed fishtraps. Neither was it one of the larger, grey shapes, with the strange pinging noises which could be confusing.

The grey hardsides were fun to forewave fluke upon but they were dangerous at times! If the mindblanking noises became too strong, and a dolphin's useful lateral sensing was reefsided, it was time to make a newvector. Sometimes waterspace erupted into the airspace unexpectedly for many dolphinspans around and pressure was subject to violent changes. Dolphins, many fish - even sharks - had died in consequence of these pressure changes accompanied with inexplicable sounds of incredible magnitude - hundreds of times larger than the crash of surf.

Grey hardsides were unpredictable - as were the Splitflukes, many having white head-tops, who moved upon the airsides of these giants. Some hardsides were larger than blue whales!

Peen slowed, veered to approach from behind on parallel vector. Gaze was still in mindmeet but there was the accustomed degree of reefsiding. His mind seemed in constant motion. He must concen...

She realised, with a start, that he was saying, 'I am concentrating but there is something else as well.'

On the verge of mindlashing him, she could hear Gape saying, 'He's like that all the time. Don't worry, my dam. He is concentrating and so am I. I'll keep checking on him. He just keeps imaging so much it gets irritating.'

'At least I scan before fluking off to butt my head against something!' came a strong imagewave from Gaze.

5

'You spend so much time patterning you don't see the obvious. You're...' came the retaliation - but Peen made them both keep peace.

Near-matures! At least they showed the normal, healthy regard for one another - including the universal banter.

Peen began to categorise the various kinds of hardside with her son following closely. After a short period of time, she had covered the risks and the dangers. In mindmeet, she covered the techniques of forewave fluking and, veering to demonstrate, instructed her siblings to fluke in parallel bi-vector.

The small forewave was sufficient to give her flukes greater impetus and she did not need such forceful flukesweeps in the vertical plane. The instant she thought it was time for the siblings to try, they veered - with Gape racing to be first. Her speeding form made bi-vector - but Gaze missed his joining opportunity and he fell dangerously off the forewave into the turbulence! He managed to remember to fluke for calm water!

Peen and Gape dropped off the hardside - Gape stabbed by sudden guilt. Peen sped to place herself alongside Gaze so that he was vertically above her right forefin. Gape fluked alongside. They tried again in tri-vector.

His guided, second attempt to join the forewave was smoother and better finned. Gape could not resist an opportune sarcasm.

'Sea-snail!'

Gaze said nothing but Peen caught an echo of the half-expressed imagewave, 'I got... distracted...?'

Was that what he meant?

'Hold in mind your responsibility for younger Bottlenoses, my daughter,' was all Peen needed to say.

She acknowledged Gape's deserved apology.

With hardside assistance, it was easier to maintain rhythm and the forcelines below seemed to flick by with regularity. It was just before vertical sunlight when the question she had sensed growing in her son was posed...

'How many Splitflukes can you sense on the hardside?'

Peen laughed inwardly. What kind of question was that? Presumably there were Splitflukes on the mass of the hardside behind but there was little point in trying to guess how many.

'I really don't know Gaze. Is it important?'

'You can't even guess?'

Gaze sounded perplexed and he began to veer off vector, having to correct with rapid forefin adjustments.

'You wobble like a sea-snake!' came the tart remark from Gape - which her dam might have anticipated.

Peen used the opportunity to scan her son's mind.

For a fluke-interval his reefsiding had stopped. He had been hiding things! In bewilderment, she had confusing images of three Splitflukes on the airside above and behind! One of them was looking down at their small familypod. But there was more... Her son was examining their...!

6

The reefside fell like a cliff! Peen covered her confusion with a reprimand to both flankers to concentrate. The images had been so certain... so strong! He was able to count... No, he wasn't using images like that. He could 'quantify' or 'qualify' a presence of Splitflukes nearby! He could mindscan in ways she could not! In strange ways that...!

'Do you mean the sires can't scan like me?' came a sharp imagewave from her son. 'What about the Storytellers? Can they?'

Peen was nonplussed! She did not know how to answer. This was different! It was alien to her experience! But how much different? What should she say?

Gape, unaware of her dam's mindmerge scan of her brother, did sense her confusion. 'Don't worry about him. He's just a bit odd. He likes to think he's different... but he's alright.'

'Not as odd as you,' came the retort from Gaze, but only Peen caught the heavy irony. 'Yes, my dam. Please let me go to a Storyteller. I'd like to talk with one.'

He had anticipated her next remarks. She hadn't even formed the thought consciously. How...?

And then, in horror, she realised that he was in mindmerge with her alone!

Only much older dolphins did that! And only by consent!

Gape was excluded - a physical presence moving in harmony - but unaware of her brother's second remark to his dam.

'Please don't worry, my dam. I've sensed I am unusual in a number of ways. Sometimes it has frightened me. I need to see a Storyteller but I promise, I will not disgrace you.

'I've been wondering how to talk to you - to sort out why I can do things you can't. I've been wondering what my sire can do. I needed to reefside to stop you worrying.

'I do love you and I have so much to learn.'

So that had been his anxiety! Now it was hers! He was puzzled at his... difference? What else could he sense and do?

Peen felt his forefin contact on her fluking form. The touch was calming, gentle - loving. It was only for an instant. Their tri-vector fluking prevented longer contact. It conveyed so much her son did not need to mindimage... It was reassuring... in most part.

'After we have seen your sire, you will see a Storyteller, Gaze. Your sister will fin with the other near-matures.'

She was reefsiding against her knowledge of 'Abominations'... trying desperately not to let him sense her mind.

There was a reprieve. Quite suddenly Peen sensed Gaze withdraw from mindcontact of even a surface kind. He seemed to become totally engrossed in something else.

What? She had thought she had known her son well - but not now... It was impossible to penetrate his reefsiding.

What was Gaze!? Peen dreaded the answer. He was her son!

'Well. Let's cast off and get going,' said Ciaran Pearce, not verbalising the accompanying thought - and for God's sake let's stop snapping at one another over the next three weeks!

Damn Deirdre and her randy, arty-crafty types!

He retained the image of that blonde, bearded American body-painting Deirdre as she leaned against the trunk of a gum, her well-formed rump already camouflaged as a protuberance. He could still see the brush moving down and between her lengthy thighs, the smooth strokes.

Abruptly he closed his mind.

Let the kids continue in the belief that he had been a bastard in not sharing her passion for art.

Rather that than they should know the truth. All that crap about wanting 'freedom to enjoy life's rich experiences; trying to share it with others in painting and sketches'. How she 'felt stifled' and 'the kids were old enough now to fend for themselves'.

Deirdre had been... a good wife? She had been the bedrock of his soul! He was supposed to 'understand the medium of body painting'?

The brush had had mixed motives!

The 'decree nisi' had arrived two weeks ago. It had taken a year of in-fighting, tug-of-war. His final concession that they could have the beach-house, provided he had token custody of Maeve until she reached majority, had brought truce. Donovan was already at University.

What had clinched it was Maeve's sudden assertion that she wanted to stay with him! Why she had changed her mind after being so vehemently assertive of her unwillingness to live with him, he could not understand.

Late one evening, she had banged through the rear porch - it would take the Yank an hour to straighten the flyscreen - tight-lipped and white-faced, flounced to an armchair and looked steadily at him.

'Okay. I agree. I'll live with you until I've finished my education. I'll spend vacations with you but, when I'm through University, I'm on my own,' she'd said.

He'd realised she was a great deal older than the six and a half year toddler he'd taught to swim.

'Well that's great Maeve. I know it'll all work out. You know I love you and...'

He had stopped when he had seen her hard-faced stare. There was no denying she had felt her decision to be a case of practicality. There was an emptiness there. Something had died.

When the divorce had come through, Donovan and Maeve had been at the beach-house. He'd driven home from the Bank with the ingredients for a barbecue. They might just as well have one more beach party before they moved into one of those apartments the Bank let out to employees on reasonable terms.

The barbecue had been efficient, workmanlike but with no spirit. Father and son had been the only two to speak. Maeve had had one foot in the past; Donovan had been trying to live up to his concept of manhood. Ciaran had known stress and fatigue before but it had been quantifiable.

Something had been torn from within the family. Not just a mother's love or the love of a wife - some reason for co-existence was drowned.

Ciaran had found himself making the suggestion that they take two or three weeks away from routine. He was owed twice that in annual leave. There was no risk to the study commitments of son or daughter. Ray had said they could borrow his boat - a twin-engined, sea-going cabin-cruiser moored with friends on Fiji - provided they left it at its normal mooring in Tutuila in American Samoa. His own cruiser was still careened for keel attention. Ray had made it big in investments - perhaps a hint of insider-dealing? Ray was a fanatic for exploring the Melanesian Pacific.

In the mood of that night, whilst not jumping with enthusiasm, they had agreed. Perhaps they had felt he had needed to be humoured and he was doing his best?

Waving goodbye to Ray's friends, grateful for their understanding and hospitality, Ciaran steered the cruiser away from the jetty on Suva. Ray's friends had been quick to turn their backs and walk away. They were probably glad to see the backs of the moody Australian trio! He shuddered at the reports which would be sent back to his fellow departmental manager. As a threesome, they had done all the trendy tourist trips: climbed the major peak to scan the archipelago, tasted the food whilst watching the dancers and talked boats and weather over drinks.

Maeve had been quiet, introverted. So much so that Donovan had been affected and become snappy. Not his normal, affable self, he had turned on Maeve with all kinds of stored resentment - real and imagined - and ended up slapping her!

Ciaran had managed to pull them apart before Donovan lost more than just one handful of hair. All three had stared at one another in breathless ineptitude.

Fiji was probably better off without too many visits from the Pearce family - or what remained of it.

Conversation was minimal as they headed East to round Ngan, to check serviceability and acclimatise to the craft. They had substantial experience. Enough to know that groups did not venture on long trips without checking everything thoroughly - down to the operation of the 'John', and, above all, the radio.

Obtaining the latest weather forecast, which gave good omens in the long term, they headed out to pass Ngan to the South and make for Lakemba Passage. Overnight there, the morning view would allow sight of active reef-building which would form, in the way of the Pacific, other islands in centuries.

By then, Ciaran thought cynically, the walls of the beach-house at Redland would be thick with painted nudes and be crumbling under the weight of paint. He wondered when the Yank would stop painting the trim form of his ex-wife, actually or, in the normal manner, using a canvas surface. Maybe, if he had taken more interest in her sketching and water colours... maybe...?

Donovan was busy with oil can and cloth. The boat had been well-maintained but mechanical things fascinated him. There was the outboard to check. It was a simple enough task to change the chipped prop. He needed time to cool off. He hadn't intended to slap Maeve. Damn it! They'd all been through the mill after the last twelve months... They'd been a great family before. Why couldn't...?

It was at that point that Donovan made an engineer's decision. If something failed, like an engine part - you chucked it away and looked for a replacement. He couldn't find a replacement for his mother - or a compatible part for his father. For himself, he would find a reliable, working partnership eventually. Until then, he'd put the whole can of worms called 'relationships' to one side and get on with other things! His father's recognition of the need for time-out as a family was sensible. He wondered if Maeve would ever laugh like she used to? Trying to knock sense into her wasn't the way...

Sitting at the prow after reef-watch - although there was little danger now - Maeve was still cursing herself for her over reaction the night before. She was struggling to climb from a morass of disillusion and disgust threatening to overwhelm her.

She had walked, one afternoon, the five miles South from Redland to see her mother and Doug in the torment of choice. With which of her parents should she declare willingness to stay?

Doug was fun - light-hearted, artistic, played the guitar and sang well. Rugged in appearance, with blue eyes and a blonde beard without moustache, he swam and surfed well. His family made money in Californian wine. It was good that her mother had an artist to share her interest. But, less dry than her father, was it a 'dad' who had held her so close in dancing? Had there been something more in the movement of his hands, low on her back?

As she had approached the riverside chalet, she had heard her mother's peal of rich laughter - but with an edge of licentiousness, unrecognised and unexpected. Closing quietly to the rear, the window of the bedroom had been open with the curtain nets rippling in the breeze. The nets had snagged on a leaf of uplifted paint on the sill, leaving a gap through which the greater part of the bed could be seen.

Shocked in disbelief, Maeve had seen her mother astride the American. A small 'roo' had been outlined in paint on her back. His hands had come forward to clasp her hips. He had pulled her four or five times downwards - vigorously.

Her mother's head had arched backwards and turned to the window, meeting her daughter's widened eyes...! Maeve had turned and left.

She had been sixty yards away when she had heard the guitar strumming in complete discord with the beating of her heart. She had started running when she had heard her name called in a voice edged with hysteria.

Her father sometimes seemed dry. Stuck in routine, he did try! He didn't deserve...

Maeve had come to a decision in the blood heat of a moment. But the torment was not over. She had felt betrayed. She knew she could never let her father know what had sparked her explosive change of mind...

They began to come together again on that first evening.

Ciaran had pushed hard across the Koro Sea - only the necessary words exchanged. There had been a kind of lull in personal relationships. It was as if they all needed to let the wind sweep them clean. Even meals had been a sombre assembly. Each had been polite, co-operative to a fault, but no-one had spoken what was felt - or needed to be said.

The weight of waiting for closer contact, for distance to be travelled, was unbearable!

Ciaran said, 'Look, we've all had a bashing. I can't stand not really talking. I feel a bit cleaner after today but we've a long way to go. Words aren't easy for any of us. Including me. Maybe it's a pipe-dream but maybe it'll be... We'll find we can...'

Hell! he thought. Find the bloody words! He couldn't afford to muff it. His family hung on this. A family?... Huh!

Neither son nor daughter seemed to be listening. They stared into the corners of the cabin.

'From now on in, I'm going to try and enjoy this trip. Let's look around us. See things again. Go for a swim. Let's talk. Please. We don't have to say everything that's got to us. We don't have to talk about... the past.'

He had paused, seeking the way... the entry...

'This could be the only floating island in the South Seas. And us - three bloody castaways!'

He reached across the table and took the hands of son and daughter.

They looked steadily at him and he thought he had failed.

Deliberately he placed Maeve's hand on Donovan's dirtier mitt.

Son and daughter looked at the hands, looked at him, then...

'You might tell this lummock to wash his hands before he touches me,' Maeve said - and smiled tentatively.

Donovan thumped her lightly on the back.

The first breakthrough was made!

In the absence of any more creative action, Ciaran reached for the charts and sought their route preferences.

It was a start.

Eleven days later, leaving Tiavea behind them on the starboard beam, it was better still. Maeve and Donovan were just as companionable as they had been in the past.

Donovan's relationship with Ciaran was forged in the engine compartment and tempered in the anvil of sunshine on the open sea. He was relishing the opportunity for showing proficiency in taking his duty turns as 'skipper'.

The weather had held good.

Maeve had laughed.

The first peal of laughter had been brought forth with the sudden breaching of five Strap-toothed Whales. They had been far out in deep water on an Easterly course for Western Samoa. Ciaran had heaved to. They had watched, listened. The long sounds of surface panting had been an indication of a previous deep dive. Ciaran had talked of the old whalers' belief that for every minute under water a whale must spout once.

After a considerable period of separate minutes and a period of short, rapid breathing, the school had sounded again with seconds only between the first and last flukes disappearing.

Apparently, Maeve had been thinking intermittently of University over the last few days.

She said, 'I think I'd like to study Marine Zoology as soon as I can. Do you think I could?'

Pushing all preconceived notions for his daughter's future from his head, he had wisely replied, 'I have a feeling you'll make good at anything you set your sights on - and good luck to you. How about setting your sights on a couple of tins of spaghetti?'

She had huffed but smiled with a thoughtful background to her eyes... then touched his forearm and turned for the galley.

They anchored, that evening, in quiet water off Cape Taputapu. They were ahead of schedule. It was Maeve who suggested they take their time and quietly explore the whole Northside, the East Coast and then follow the South Coast to Pago Pago.

'We've got another ten days or so and we've covered a lot of sea miles. Let's slow down. Anyway, both of you look savage. Isn't it about time you both shaved?'

She was right.

They hugged the coast around Cape Matatula with a reef to port. It was when they turned south westerly to head for the open seaward side of Aunu'u that the bottlenose dolphins joined them, an adult with two accompanying near-matures, judging by the relative sizes.

Maeve rushed to the side to watch them. She looked spell-bound. Father and son smiled at each other. Ciaran could tell that tea-break would be delayed this morning and he quietly put a finger to his lips. Donovan nodded in understanding and went below to find the camera.

It looked for all the world as if the largest had decided to test the bow-wave before suggesting that all three of them hitch a ride. Ciaran thought the largest was probably a female. She rode easily before the bow for a minute or two whilst her probable off-spring swam in parallel.

What made the Pearce family keep turning to look at the smallest?

Donovan, now on deck again, took his first picture of the siblings some seven yards away. Then he realised the obvious first shot would have been the mother on the bow.

Maeve was staring in fascination at the pair and not at the athletic grace of the larger mother. So was Ciaran.

Suddenly the pair swooped towards the bow but the smallest appeared to be caught in turbulence.

Maeve gasped loudly. A muted scream would be more accurate. Father and son looked anxiously at her.

'It's alright,' Maeve said. 'They're both coming .... going to help it, I mean.'

Ciaran and Donovan followed her wide-eyed gaze.

The dolphins reformed as a threesome and tried again to plant themselves in front of the bow. They were successful. During the manouevre, for minutes afterwards, Maeve made no sound at all.

Finally, she turned and said the last thing either of them expected to hear.

'Something spoke to me.'

She shook her head, raised her eyes to them, saw the astonishment and added ... 'I think I'd better make a cup of tea.'

Father and son were left alone with the silence - and the bottlenose dolphins enjoying the trip. Neither felt they could explain her comment. It would be wise not to make reference to it. Women had occasional aberrations it was best not to mention...

Half an hour later, Maeve reappeared wearing a swimming costume. Donovan joked about there being no 'hunkies out here'.

She smiled ruefully and asked them to heave to because she just wanted a quick dip over the side. For once, Ciaran made no comments about the risks and shut down the engines. There was little wind and the sea calm.

He watched her drop neatly over the side with face mask and flippers... and then instructed Donovan to get the rifle just in case. The risk of shark attack was minimal but it was better to be safe.

Within a minute of Maeve circling the boat, she had company. First, the larger near-mature. Then came the mother and the intriguing, slightly smaller dolphin. The mother appeared to try to interpose her body between Maeve and the ... but then there was... a sudden change of mind?

The youngest was entirely at ease, completely unruffled by human presence, allowing Maeve to reach out and touch it.

There was a moment of pure magic as a peal of the old laughter rang out.

No-one saw the piece of rope-entangled cork drift against the propellers and snag.

The forewave of the hardside fell into a rippling insignificance. The repetitive propulsive pulse was still. Their tri-vector formation faltered....

'I don't like this. Let's fluke for distant water!' said Gape, a confusion of possible image alternatives carrying a plague of panic.

'No! Wait!' came a command, incongruous considering the source was Gaze.

Peen and Gape felt themselves pulled back from the brink of flukefleeing.

'It's alright. I know what's going to happen. There's no need to worry.'
'What do you mean? Don't be ridiculous. How can...?'
Gape was silent as she heard her dam's imagewave, 'How do you know Ga..?' Black and white mindmeet was converting to mindmerging colour!?

Incredibly, Gape realised her brother and her dam were now locked in mindmerge! She was excluded! Only adults and lovers mindmerged! Her first reaction was to mindscream indignation but... 'Wait, Gape.'...? Who did Gaze think he was!? She felt peace as his forefin touched hers. She floated quietly.

Gaze was odd. She would never understand him.

Peen asked, 'You are sure there's no danger Gaze?' She felt his affirmation. 'How are you so certain?'

'For two reasons. I can hear the mind of one of the Splitflukes - a female. She is troubled by a relationship... or lack of one. She is good and not dangerous.

'Secondly, there are three - you call them Shadowers - just inside your range of scanning and we both know we could call them if they were needed.'

How had he known the Shadowers were there? Or what to call them? Her own mind!?

Mindmerging, Gaze said... 'That is why the Splitflukes are here. They, too, needed some isolation to find themselves and each other... The female Splitfluke will join us shortly. She needs some peace... She needs laughter.'

'That's impossible Gaze! You can't read the future. You can't...'

There was a splash behind them. A Splitfluke had entered the waterspace!

Astonished, Peen felt Gaze's forefin on hers. She knew that he was touching Gape also. She felt calmer... and she hadn't the first notion as to why.

'Let us fin gently towards her. This time you can be first Gape,' said a voice like a gentle current in two minds.

The Splitfluke had grace of movement, in a slow-motion manner. There being no threat posed, Gape gained in confidence and finned closer, to within touching distance. One of the Splitfluke's forefins reached out tentatively.

The touch was warm! Almost tenderly, the 'fin' moved on her back, close to the dorsal. Gape finned aside leaving waterspace for her dam and for Gaze.

Peen knew how curious her son could be - but curiosity could kill. She interposed her flanks between the Splitfluke and Gaze, allowing the gentle wind to nudge against their exposed dorsals and drift them as a pair towards the... 'young woman'? How did those... 'words'... images, come out of her mind? Mind-reflections from Gaze?

'My dam, you are too protective! Let her touch me!'

Peen quashed her maternal instinct, finned semi-circle and allowed the drift to take her son towards the... the 'girl'? The long forefin of the Splitfluke reached out again.

This time there was a wonderful peal of noise, joyful ... delicious; vibrant and warm. It was sunshine on a safe, shelving shore. There was... 'relief'?... expressed by the hardside Splitflukes.

This was Gaze's first contact with Maeve. It was not to be his last. He did not know that immediately but began to feel a joint destiny. What he sensed was a caring mind that he could contact, possibly at great distance. Meetings with Maeve, significant for both, would affect profoundly the lives of many dolphins and Splitflukes.

Divine Mercy held a cloak across events. It was about to lift briefly...

Fate was kind, revealing to Gaze, and those that knew him, only those things he needed to know gradually and fortuitously. Soon he would use a new mindskill - known within but unshown to his dam. It would add to her fear - her doubt.

They finned in association for a period. A second Splitfluke appeared on the hardside top calling to the 'girl'. He used her name... 'Maeve'... and there were more 'words'... Shortly, there was another splash and the second Splitfluke, the one 'Maeve' called 'father', was in the waterspace.

The 'father' was near the twistingfins of the hardside. Something long had become entangled in one of the twistingfins. A sharp, bright shape appeared in a jointed forefin. No, the 'word' was 'hand'... The Splitfluke began 'cutting' the entanglement.

Suddenly the bright shape fell away. The 'father' shouted... An angry soundwave... It was important!

'Gape, please dive and fetch that shape but hold it gently. It cuts if you grab too hard!' urged Gaze to his sister.

The 'father' Splitfluke was holding a wound in his 'hand'. Red blood stained the surface. The cut was deep. Gape dived. The shape had not fallen five dolphinspans before she had it. She did not breach but nosed to the surface and finned gently towards Gaze.

'Not me Gape. Take it to the Splitfluke by the twistingfins,' he said, adding, 'Thank you sister.'

'Not at all, Trainer!' came the sarcastic reply.

They both knew they would have to spend time with a Butting Pod Trainer some time soon.

The 'father' Splitfluke looked disbelievingly at the 'knife' in Gape's mouth. He reached for it with his 'hand' and began to cut at an old fishtrap piece. Why was it so important? Gape wondered.

Peen scent-tasted.

'Blood! That Splitfluke had better be quick. Gape, close in. We must flukeflee from this waterspace,' she mindmet urgently.

She pinged identification - made a summons call to the Shadowers. There was a distant answer but the echo-interval was long. She pinged acknowledgement.

Closer echo-returns below? Two echoes from shallow depth and the intervals were much shorter!

She circumscanned. There! And there!

'Sharks below!' Garni's phantom joined her mindscream. 'Gape! Gaze! We must fluke towards the Shadowers. They have been near us for some time! Are you...? No!'

Two sharp, sharkdorsals surfaced down watermovement from themselves and the hardside. They turned and nosed questingly towards them... They were between their best tri-vector and the Shadowers!

There was a sudden loud noise - like a sharp flukeslap on water. The third Splitfluke on the hardside had made it - was making some shrieking airsounds.

'Gape! Gaze! We must fluke from here! There is blood in the waterspace!' mindscreamed Peen.

'No! Stay here! Don't worry! I think I know...'

The rest was lost from Gaze. Peen felt a surge of mindenergy building in her son. Why?

The sharks were scenting up the bloodflow!

The 'girl' Splitfluke finned rapidly for the hardside and grabbed at something. The 'father' Splitfluke was slower, tugging loose something from the twistingfins. There was still blood around him!

The dorsals were accelerating - beginning to submerge as they sharkfanned far more purposefully.

Peen mindscreamed near hysteria, 'Gape! Gaze! Fluke towards the reef! Quickly! Now!'

Gape fluked in obedience, bi-vector with her dam... but Gaze remained!

Peen sensed the 'father' Splitfluke thrashing away from the twistingfins, striving to reach something on the hardside. The third Splitfluke was reaching downwards.

Miraculously, a Butting Pod appeared between the two sharkfanning striking-vectors and the struggling Splitfluke! There was a great sense of more dolphins beneath! How could the Shadowers have joined them so quickly!? No, there were too many dolphins to be the Shadowers...?

The sharkdorsals veered, slowed... accelerated into distant depths with the Butting Pod in pursuit!

'Marvellous! Great! Did you see that!?' came an excited mindscreech from Gape.

Peen was silent.

She finned to face Gaze.

'There are no echo-returns from the Butting Pod. There are only three calls from the Shadowers, coming as quickly as they can... two echo-returns from the sharks in another scan direction and diminishing.'

There was a pause.

'Gaze, what did you do?'

She had felt exceptionally strong emanations of mindenergy from her son. Not communicating, he had been... What? Things had happened too quickly!

Peen's heart raced rapidly. She knew she had just witnessed a marvel which she could not... 'qualify'. Irritated, she realised she was using one of her son's 'words'. By the White Dolphins, Gaze was not... could not be a Visioner!? Such would make him an Abomination!

Gaze remained silent in mindmerge with her. How could he do that? The reefside came down like a giant cliff. He was co-operative and finned to place himself at her flank.

There were no answers for Peen.

'Let's fluke towards the Shadowers. We will finish the rest of the flukingpassage with company,' said Peen, trying to mask her troubled thoughts, to shield her heart.

Gape asked, 'What are the Shadowers?'

With a shock, Peen realised that she had been in mindmerge with her son all the time. Gape had been excluded unless spoken to - no, 'commanded' was better expression - by Gaze, her younger brother!

'Aren't you going to tell me?' came the question again.

Questions seemed to be a growing habit.

In tri-vector, they circled the hardside. The three Splitflukes seemed too occupied now. They vectored towards the Shadowers, Peen explaining their existence and purpose to Gape, something she had not needed to do with Gaze...

...and Gaze reefsided whilst he maintained a diminishing contact with the mind of 'Maeve', sharing a novel certainty. At the end of the absorbing process he pinged towards... a white dolphin he thought he had seen.?

There was no echo-return.

Lightplay in seashadows beneath the sighing surface...?

He must have been mistaken.

The arrival of Peen and her flankers at the Podsmeet - with the Shadowers as escort - was a moment of sheer joy. She was popular and respected for her dedicated observance of traditions. The Matrons of this warmstream Podsherd - stout Flab and the slimmer Doe - had recognised her potential for the heirarchy of the Nursery Dams.

It had been Flab, cheerfully practical, who had assisted in the birth of Gaze, returning to the Podsherd with the firm instruction that Peen should train her calf well prior to Nursery attendance.

Sire appraisal was approaching now. Flab was determined to keep her promise to be at Peen's finside at this next important stage for Gaze. She did not offer such companionship with every dam for the demands of her task were great. After sire appraisal came selection by the Storytellers and Induction to the Podsherd. Flab would be near on these occasions also. Doe was getting older... Flab would need Peen's help shortly...

As Gaze was male, he would be treated differently to his sister. She could expect a period of fluking free with near-mature females. They teased the males - which was considered healthy and tolerated, to a point. Gaze, however, would be expected to express his regard to his sire and present himself for inspection, his fitness and fluking skills being severely tested. Most males, but not all, took the duty of sire appraisal very seriously. It helped to maintain social bonds in the Podsherd - if not family ties. Those sires who adhered to the new teaching concerning curbing too much freedom in flesh-fervour, were generally the most diligent in ensuring thorough appraisal.

At least, that was Flab's opinion...

Wanderer's patterning concerning flesh-fervour had not been welcomed whole-heartedly by as many dolphins as he had, perhaps, hoped. Flesh-fervour relationships with numerous partners had been the norm of the seasons - even between dolphins of the same podfamily. Cautions concerning the risk of creating Abominations, as a result of incest, had been beakscorned by more than some. Most dolphins, dams as well as sires, seemed promiscuous by nature.

Flab had seen products of loose carnal coupling. She agreed with Wanderer's teaching and, she knew, so did Peen. Such podfamilies as Peen's were always welcomed by this Matron in the hierarchy of the Nursery Dams. There were some foolish dolphins in the Podsherd who seemed to be ruled by biological need - never questioning the quality of love which Wanderer had urged.

Around the fluking group of new arrivals, there were loud pings of identification and greeting: numerous invitations to mindmeet; the joyous surge and spray of breaching and sounding to shallow depths, and the breaths of surprise at her earliness.

It had been the same when Peen had returned with Gaze as a calf, six seasons ago...

Inquisitive, non-coupled females had finned forward to fawn over Gaze. Congratulatory, 'first-time' calvers had cheerfully expressed both their good wishes and concerns over an adequacy of milk...

A cruising male or two, off-duty and holding Gale in high regard, had made complimentary comment...

Now, a courteous Guardian informed Peen that Gale would be returning soon! His Butting Pod were finishing an escort duty near one of the Cleric's caverns. He did not know what the duty had been.

Gale! She had missed his presence.

Fluking together, the waterspace had seemed theirs for eternity. She remembered breaching in the broadside of bi-vector their forefins inseparable... their coupling in calm water, belly to belly, with his forefins constantly mobile. He was vigorous, penetrating in his observations during the quiet moments of rippling seas brushed by a warming, off-shore breeze...

Peen jerked her attention to the siblings.

Something...?

Gape was intent on scanning for friends to greet and gossip with.

Gaze! Gaze was quiet, as unobtrusive as possible. Observing... noting... everything... in open mindmerge to everything...!

'Gaze, have you...?' Peen began the question but the answer came before she finished.

'Your training has been sound. I have respected your privacy. I note your love for my sire, and I am glad.'

Gaze paused then said, 'I would share nothing... nothing without consent, unless there was danger or trouble to your spirit. It was not my fault anyway. You were not reefsiding at all... and what have you to feel embarrassed or ashamed of?'

'Your love for my sire is all I would wish for you. One lightwater, perhaps, I will know a similar joy.'

Who could wish for a more understanding mind in a son? The reason for Peen's embarrassment was not the content of the image she had accessed unwittingly to Gaze. She had shown, through the imaging, depth of emotion and commitment to one male only. Often, dolphins had various coupling partners. Her sole couplings in flesh-fervour with Gale were not wrong. Indeed, some Clerics, in a minority, advocated such pairings. However, most dolphins were gregarious, sensuous, promiscuous. She would not like other females to regard her as odd... peculiar.

In a lightwater of surprises, there was time for more. Peen heard in mindmerge,

'My dam, it is good to know that I was calved out of love into a podfamily of caring regard, warmth and understanding. Splitflukes do not have the same freedoms as dolphins. Their notion of what gives happiness, what is happiness, is not the same as ours. Their pain and disillusion is sometimes great in consequence.'

'Gaze! Do you mean you have been in mindmerge with a Splitfluke!? That is not possible! You could not have...'

Peen did not finish.

She remembered... remembered how he had locked... was locked... in mindmerge... and not declared mature! His prediction that the 'girl' Splitfluke would enter the waterspace... and she did! The insistence of his voice which was like a command! The strange 'words' he had used... and, most troubling of all, the mystery of the Butting Pod which had no echo-return!

Sweet Wanderer, what was her son?

'Gaze, you must say nothing about what happened on the flukingpassage here. Not to your sire, to other dolphins... not even the Storytellers. They would think your head worm-infested... You would make them worry... make them afraid. Afraid because they would think you are...'

Peen had a series of recall images of 'different' calves she had seen. A few of those had been Abominations. The products of couplings which were... They had been awful to see. Worse had been the knowledge that the calves would have to be...

She might have anticipated the next question.

'Do you feel I am an Abomination?'

The images were quietly expressed, almost hesitantly... with a tinge of... Not anxiety for himself...

It had been said out of anxiety for her! Out of love for her! thought Peen.

She knew there was only one answer.

'No, Gaze, I do not think you an Abomination. You are good... You are almost... pure? No... almost too good for others to be able to understand you. They may fear you and you don't want that... although you may need to make dolphins fear you later.

'You must, like the small fish on the reefside, hide what you are in crack and crevice. It will be important for you to reefside constantly in your mind. Do not let others too close yet to what you can do.'

Again Peen fell silent. They were both silent in mindmerge.

Then Peen said, 'Other dolphins may not know the bond of love which outlasts the coupling in a quiet cove. I know there is a longer-lasting love. I have always needed it, always known it was possible.'

Peen paused. Mindmerge had never been closer than this - not even with Gale, his sire. Was it because Gale was his sire? Why was Gaze diff...

She stopped herself.

'It is also my need to love my calf beyond the demands for milk... beyond training and Induction... beyond my next calving... even to the time of the deep-dive and the sharks. Remember always, I love you, Gaze.'

The reply was not in mindmerge but in a touch of a forefin against hers as they drifted within the Podsherd - His touch which was warmth in the eternity of a moment and remembered always. A time when ripples sighed silently past the silvered basking backs of companionship and there was peace.

Donovan helped his father aboard. Ciaran was breathing rapidly, his face tight beneath the tan. Years in steering a pen across a sea of paper were not conducive to rapidity of movement. He had to admit Donovan's shouts, the crack of the rifle, his anxiety for Maeve - and then the realisation that he was likely to feel the first tearing of flesh - had been unnerving.

It had been his splashing; the blood in the water. The transition from tranquil lapping of slopping water around the twin screws aft... and the treasured image of Maeve's lovely face in company with the dolphins; the sound of the old, clear, tinkling pleasure... The change to terror had been like a knife slash across the face of a girl. Nature had smiled and scowled in seconds. Laughter had vanished in apprehension and fear.

'I think it's time you took over the maintenance and keel inspection,' said Ciaran, smiling ruefully at Donovan. 'I'm not quite as fit as I used to be.'

Turning to Maeve, he did not read the apprehension he had expected to see. He didn't need to speak reassuringly. Joy was in her face but mainly... gratitude?

She looked - as if she was thanking someone intimately? Then her features changed in very obvious relief that he was safe... and he read the love that had always been there.

They did not need words. The love was the concrete clasping of flesh to flesh and the tears on Maeve's cheeks. Ciaran's left arm fell away from Maeve a moment and he drew Donovan into a family embrace.

'You're getting blood all over us,' said Maeve, lifting her head to kiss her father... then Donovan. 'We will all need a wash... but I don't think we should have another dip. Let me look at that cut.'

She was practical. The youngest there knew what to do next. Father and son acknowledged with smiles. Smiles grew all around. The sea smiled.

They had found themselves again - found they had not lost each other.

'We were bloody lucky that school of dolphins turned up when it did,' said Donovan. 'They seemed to chase the sharks off. How many did you think there were?'

Maeve kept silent.

They readied themselves to round Aunu'u and make for Pago Pago harbour.

Maeve was quiet and staring astern.

She remained that way for a long time. Ciaran and Donovan left her to it.

Chapter Two

TOWARDS MEETING THE STORYTELLERS

As the sun began the last arc of descent to take the deep sounding - much later to breach in a new lightwater - it was Flab who wallowed towards Peen and Gaze bringing news. Gale's Butting Pod was on the fringe of the Podsherd! They would be the darkwater Guardians.

Would Peen take Gaze for sire appraisal immediately? In mindmerge with Peen - or so she thought - Flab let her knowledge of a reefside secret slip by saying,

'Gale has missed you Peen. He has coupled with no other. I have known such loyalty and abstinence from flesh-fervour in only a few of the sires. Perhaps it is time again for a sheltered cove? I remember how the sires used to be so... One must not give up hope, I suppose.'

They had fintouched. There was nothing else of substance to say. As Flab finned fleshily away, Peen felt a silent whisper in the corner of her mind. She reefsided urgently... and gave up.

'What did you say Gaze?'

'I was only saying that Flab is a good dolphin. Maybe she should not be... so sad so soon,' came the reply.

'What do you mean?'

'Only that there may be one dolphin... one who... is regretting his age... and he... He admires Flab but he... He is afraid? He... No, to uncloak all secrets is wrong...'

'I should think so too!' said Peen, and laughed inwardly, noting a flanker's apparent embarrassment - wondering who and what he meant.

They finned towards the fringe of the Podsherd.

During finningpassage, Gaze said suddenly,

'Yes, I promise. I won't. I shall stay with Gape and Flab.'

Mindpink herself, Peen realised he had answered her unspoken request that he should mind his own business when Gale and Peen needed to... be by themselves... needed to...

'Good. Now be quiet and think about meeting your sire!' she replied.

'That's what we are both doing,' said Gaze.

Peen deafened her mind with a surging crash of surf on a reefside... but... she still heard quiet laughter, completely without malice - totally understanding.

'Remember what I told you and... Well, just be a good, normal flanker!' Peen commanded.

He was following fluently as a flanker as they cleared the Podsherd... and there were the Guardians!

Gale's Butting Pod were steadily patrolling... sounding... surfacing.

Occasionally, one dolphin would breach and roll airside so that waterspace and airspace around were all monitored and watched for anything threatening.

He had seen them, sensed them!

Peen felt the heightened awareness of herself and everything around her. There was a nervous shiver of anticipation that trembled from fluketips to settle excitedly in her belly. Soon he would be near. She would hear his voice, feel his caressing firm touch. They would talk, mindmerge... be together... and touch... Gaze!!

There was nothing from Gaze. Just her ordinary Bottlenose son, finstirring close to her forefin, meek, expectant... compliant and respectful.

She brushed the underside of his chest... tenderly... Gaze was innocence and trustfulness. He finstirred...

'Did you say something, my dam?' said Gaze, in ordinary mindmeet... perfectly ordinary mindmeet, simple and respectful!

'Oh you lovely calf. I do so love you,' said Peen... as the waterspace erupted around them and there was Gale!

Gale exploding from water in the exuberancy of greeting...

Gale breaching alongside and the waves and spray falling like warm rain on her back...

Gale flukeslapping the water in the pride of sirehood...

And quiet Gale, tender Gale, flank by flank Gale... touching her forefin... her lovely mindmerging... her lovemerging master.

And here was an appraising Gale, checking for straightness of line and firmness of fluke...

'His name. You have kept his name the same?' asked Gale in mindmeet, knowing the answer perfectly well but distancing himself in sire appraisal. He knew the risks of over-familiarity; the value of formality.

'He is Gaze, my love. Each half of our flankers' names shall be half of yours. You cannot have forgotten what we...' replied Peen, in slight, mindmeeting disappointment.

'It pleases me that you did not forget, my dear. I could not,' Gale said, in mindmerging privacy - he thought.

Peen fluketrembled again as his flank nudged hers.

'Now, Gaze! Follow me. Join the Butting Pod with me. Let me see you fluking. Let me see your training so far. Are you ready Bottlenose?' said commanding Gale.

'But the Butting Pod are mature dolphins... large Bottlenoses. I am much smaller,' came a quiet reply.

'No son of mine feels small in his mind! Do you understand that, Gaze?' came the voice of stern Gale.

'Yes my sire. I understand,' said a bigger mind than in all dolphinhistory in a small voice. 'I will try not to shame you.'

'Good. Follow me!' ...and Gale was gone, not at top flukespeed, but quick enough.

Gale thought Gaze still on the surface, adjacent to Peen. It would have been a lesson in anticipating orders and responding immediately. He was already framing a mild rebuke reappearing, a few dozen dolphinspans away, looking to where Peen finned in the water with Gaze at her flank.

His offspring was not there!

A bottlebeak broke surface at Gale's rightfin side!

'You do fluke too quickly for me to keep up, my sire,' said a complimentary voice.

How...?

Gale felt a prick to personal pride.

Only two dolphins in ten would have been able to keep up with him, he thought, and they would have been more advanced in training than this maturing shrimp beside him.

'Um... Well done Gale, so far. Keep trying. I will try not to change flukespeed and vector too rapidly without clear warning,' said a thoughtful sire. 'Come... let us go.'

...And Gaze realised in time a grave mistake he was making.

Needing to do well in sire appraisal so that Gale would be proud of him, he could not use mindskills he had discovered within. Sires sought a secret self-satisfaction...

Mindmerging without detection was not the way!

He had sensed the discomfort he might cause to Peen if he maintained too close an association with her mind, her spirit. How offensive that could be. He was on the verge of transgressing in the same way with his sire through mindreading before the action.

...And he learned that his special mindmerging abilities needed to be constrained.

It was not the simple lesson a sire had wanted to teach a son but of far greater significance. Gaze realised, more pointedly than ever, he should not intrude upon integrity. He saw a curse of mindshadowing - that he could disrupt rather than aid.

He would not go that way to satisfy selfish pride. A secret he must guard, he had skills sharper than sharkteeth. He had to keep them hidden - keep a lonely self vigil.

The rest of sire appraisal was exactly as Gale might have expected.

He's a little slow in the turn and his lack of strength is obvious, thought Gale, then... He has the potential for sound navigation... Now that is disturbing... He needs to be more confident in a sounding dive but he can't have had much practice in the Nursery area. Ah, that was better! The calfshrimp enjoys airsiding. That wasn't a bad half-roll in airflight.

'Not bad, Gaze... not bad,' said Gale and touched his flanking son with a fin. 'Now, finline in vector with the Butting Pod. Try to keep close flukingspan.'

'One whole circuit of the Podsherd my pretty Bottlenoses! Keep scanning... Medium flukespeed... Go!' said a growling Gale, with a warm feeling of pride which was unobserved by any of the Pod, even down to the smallest recruit.

24

'I've brought Gape with me,' said Flab, appearing quietly in a slop of water alongside Peen. 'She's had an argument with two near-matures. Nothing serious. 'Apparently they fell out over something trifling and Gape said she would get her brother 'to sort them out'. The others thought that was a stupid image and started teasing her... and, well, Gape butted one of them.'

In mindmerge with Peen she added, 'About time some Bottlenose butted that one - a right little sea cow if you ask me. Anyway, I've come with Gape as agreed and, when sire inspection is over, I'll watch over Gaze as well.

'How's he doing? Gape obviously has some admiration for him.'

'He's doing quite well, 'said Peen. Shifting to mindmeet with Gape, she said, firmly, 'Gape, do behave yourself and don't let your sire down! Try and remember he is a Butting Pod Leader and behave with a bit more control. You stay quiet and be sensible.'

'It wasn't my fault, my dam. Dazzle made a finnose at me and...' started Gape.

'Enough! Now just be still and finstir and do some imaging,' Peen said, with a half-shadow of Gale's authority. It sufficed. Gape kept her bottlebeak shut and began reefsiding a bit sulkily.

Mindmerging, Flab couldn't resist the comment...

'Shouldn't be long, and the pair of you can fluke off. There's a nice cove just around the promontory. I'll keep an eye on the flankers. Maybe we'll look in on Doe and her podlings in the Nursery. You'll be back at darkwater - well, not much later...'

Understanding Flab!

'Mirrored parabolas of perfection,
Breaching the image of spray!
Flukefoaming towards a conception...
Harmonious love-spirits gay!
A fintouching... a flukestirring...
Nothing darker occurring
Spoiling coupling dolphins and play...'

Such was the joy for Gale and Peen. And later... a generation of moments later... there was peace.

Time to listen to a harmony of hearts quietening to a music in the sea...

Time to listen to the surfside whispers of love...

'Seems a good flanker, my love. Bright and alert... even sharper than I'd expected... hoped for.

'Diving skills need improving but he has completed this phase of his training well. Now we must leave things to the Guardians or the Storytellers - whichever it will be.'

The corner of Peen's mind which was duty and pride, fluketrembled with pleasure. She kept another area heavily reefsided... that which held the secret of the extra mindskills Gaze seemed to have. And her uncertainty... but she said,

'My love, I am so pleased. I feel... I cannot say why... that he will be offspring to be proud of... even proud to serve, perhaps... one lightwater...'

Gale placed little importance on the imaging of his coupling partner at the time. Indeed, it was common for the females to witter on about many inconsequential things after the pleasure of...

Yet his heart stored the imaging which a practical mind dismissed.

Karg was disturbed... uneasy. Karg had not had the pleasure of his kind of flesh-fervour. Something... Somewhere... another dolphin?

Well before vertical sunlight, he had completed a gruff training period with some trainees and returned to the Cave of Pleasure unobserved. He had taken two, small fish as usual.

Only Karg and Finwarp had known of the existence of this Cave. The reefside entrance was well-obscured with coral and kelp. From the access cave, it required an airleap to a shallow pool and some careful finning through a flooded passage to find the copy of the entrance to Wanderer's Cave and pleasure beyond... if one knew how!

Finwarp had only known for as long as was useful. Karg chuckled as he recall-imaged Finwarp's 'unfortunate' encounter with the 'Squid'... The diminishing mindscream into the dark depths had been superb! It had echoed in every corner of his observing mind...and the tenor of terror had titillated every nerve end. Karg finshivered... His mindchuckling had been belly tightening.

No other Storyteller ever finned that part of the reef. Why should they? They were too preoccupied with their normal pursuits of training, seeking understanding and finding the White Dolphins...

White Dolphins... huh! Karg regarded such things as a lot of superstitious wastecloud. The lightwater he saw a White Dolphin, he'd chew his own flukes!

What or who were the contacts, the mindenergy he had felt?

He had always been careful to guard the discoveries in himself. As a flanker, he had become aware of the way he had been able to influence his dam's mind... and so nearly control what she imaged...

Later, as a Storyteller Navigator, had come startling revelation that he could make her image events without the suspicion he was doing so! That had come shortly after Wanderer's deep-dive. She had become increasingly mindtwisted. It had been pleasurable to plan, execute, observe in mindmerge and share her torment... Wonderful!

The Podsherd had been convinced her head had been worm-infested.

Karg had felt no pain as she had deep-dived to the sharks before her time. It had been a pity that her mind had so deteriorated that he could not have shared that last exquisite tearing of dam flesh. She had been unreachable in her extremity... just as this new mindpower... this new dolphin was unreachable at the moment. What a dolphin to make suffer... to share the suffering! Just as...

Just as Finwarp had suffered... but it had been too quick.

He had had to rid himself of Finwarp once the Cave of Pleasure had been completed. He could not let Finwarp share the secret. The termination of their contracted promise had been so easy... so totally 'unexpected'!

Karg, gaped and smiled, showing rows of twisted teeth. There was pleasure in the 'unexpected' - when he saw it coming.

An airslab with a chain had been slotted into place, using Finwarp's Inventor knowledge, to act as an escape closure over the inner cave. The two trainee Storytellers, who had assisted in recovery of the airslab from a wreck at Reefbase and manouevred it into position, had expired from existence. They had begun butting and tearing at each other quite 'unexpectedly'. The blood had attracted the sharks and...

Oh, their prolonged mindscreams had been maniacally melodious; mindmergingly musical!

Finwarp's death had been a tingling double experiment, a physical act and a prolonged mindvision, so convincing, Karg had wasted his bowels in excitement!

He had invited Finwarp to join him later near the Cave of Pleasure, to discuss some minor details.

Hidden in a crevice, beakgripping a fishspiking shaft lost by a Splitfluke, he had waited. Karg had wound the cord trailing from the fishspiking shaft around a clump of coral about as large as a dolphin's chest, making sure it would not slip loose. It had been difficult but he had managed it well.

When Finwarp had finned past the crevice, firmly grasping the blunt end in his beak, Karg had fluked in ferocity outwards - faster than the Moray eel.

The fish spikingshaft had plunged - so perfectly - into the target's side below the dorsal!

Finwarp's wild thrashing had dislodged the coral... and then the real fun had started! Karg had projected a mindvision of a giant squid attack into Finwarp's pain-crazed thoughts. The fishspiking shaft in his side and the weight of the coral had been reinforcers. The stricken dolphin had actually felt himself being dragged into the depths! For mindbending moments, Karg had been a squid fifty feet long, dragging his victim towards his beautifully cruel beak. His huge round eyes had seen every weak wriggle. His mind had heard every heart-stopping mindscream. Then Finwarp had drowned... or dropped down deep from contact to the sharks...

Oh, the joy Karg would have in 'unexpectedly' arranging the demise of this new contact... This dolphin nearer his own stature!? Perhaps this new dolphin would be brave enough to struggle against a giant squid... ? Or could he vision something better? The stranger dolphin deserved to suffer after distracting him in his earlier flesh-fervour.

He had been head to flank in coupling with the Pleasure Cave captive... beak-scarring her flank and mindvisioning a shark attack for them to share in copulation when he had been distracted...

Inexplicably, he had had a sudden mindvision of a large Butting Pod wanting to savage him... wanting...! Karg had withdrawn, physically and mentally, to face immediate danger he was convinced... But there had been nothing! No other dolphins had finned in the confines of the cave.

A dolphin had been visioning! Yet he - the first Visioner - had not been able to locate the source!

Karg would find the source.

Gaze had felt fatigue half through the circuit of the Podsherd. He had dared not fall behind for fear of causing embarrassment to Gale. The flukingpassage earlier that lightwater: the excitement of meeting the Splitflukes and 'Maeve'; the constant patterning and the drain of mental energy; the emotional costs, and the present demands, had created an energy debt...

It had been hard - too much.

And Gale had known it.

Gale had known the value of stretching new 'recruits' to the limit and just beyond - but no further.

Suddenly Gale had been there...

'Well done Gaze. Now we will return to your dam.'

'But I haven't finished the...' Gaze had whispered, dreading the censure of his sire.

Gaze had known he had a way to discover his sire's thoughts... silently, unobserved... but he would not use it. That way was selfishness... another's pain.

'You have done enough to satisfy me, son,' had said a factual Gale. 'Many would not have fluked as far in one day as you and they would have been complaining and whining in the mind. You have not done so... and I am content.

'Now, back to your dam. We will go together.

'One day you will fluke with a Butting Pod, perhaps, but we both know you have yet to mature. Then you will circuit the Podsherd... and you will keep circuiting for lives will depend on you. Until then, you will attend to your training, obey your leaders and learn the happiness that comes with knowing you have done your best as far as you can. No dolphin can ask more of you... but only you will really know what your best may be.

'I am pleased with my son thus far. From now on you must learn the independence to fluke the freedom of the waterspace. You must learn to seek your own satisfaction - always having regard for security of the Podsherd. Know your enemies and be constant with your friends. Follow the teachings of Wanderer...' Gale had hesitated, '...and may you find the blessing of the White Dolphins.'

Gale had never been an outwardly religious dolphin.

His faith had come from within, through observing the wonders of the waterspace... and by questioning its purpose. Gaze was too young, he had thought, to understand this... and so Gale had fallen back on the

Clerics' beliefs. Who knew? Perhaps there were White Dolphins?

Gaze had heard and had accepted.

They were drifting in a familypod... He felt, in his one-eyed sleep, the loneliness again - and the despair of the lost spirit. Somewhere... somewhere... perhaps over there... distant, lonely in a dark place was the solitude, disfigured and alone. There was fear... a half-crazed terror... a desperate need for contact...

Gaze finstirred uneasily. In half-somnolence, he scanned for the source...

There, perhaps there... a warped mind, and a wound. A need for... for companionship... for... forgiveness?

And a solitary fin aslant a dark surface... and hiding... afraid... ever-alert, ever-questing and, pulling in the tendrils of existence like a miniscule, nervy sea-creature.

This was the second time Gaze had sensed the presences. Where? Where exactly? The same dolphin who thought of Flab tenderly... and another who...?

Gaze used his skill of mindscanning beyond the drifting podpartners.

Water noise came from the flukingpassage of the darkwater Guardians circuiting, circumscanning the Podsherd. Gale was out there, unresting and unwavering...

It was then that Gaze sensed the squid! A huge squid rising from beneath, questing for...!

Gaze pinged once for confirmation. There was no echo-return - yet the image persisted!

'Be settled Gaze. You are over-excited. You must rest,' Peen said. 'Are you frightened of something?'

Gaze slammed the block of the reefside across his mind. Some other dolphin was looking for him! And this dolphin was powerful! This dolphin was... was malignant... twisted, warped... This dolphin was evil - an opposite of Gale and Peen!

The young Bottlenose made himself quiet; insignificant in silence and out of reach!

Gaze ignored the feeling of a squid's tentacle sliding across his form... made no reaction. He was fluking with his sire and proud... watching the Butting Pod surge and scan, twist in airflight, breach and sound... watching the Butting Pod protecting the Podsherd in the darkwater...

Gaze was not there to see a giant squid's eye looking quizzically at the drifting dolphins.

Absent from nightmare vision, Gaze found the refuge.

If Gaze had mindscreamed, Karg would have found his source... He would have found the new dolphin...

However, that one echo-locating ping from the Podsherd... that one pingquery, solitary in the middle of the sleepers and disassociated from the constant sounds of the Guardians, showed the new dolphin's presence. This new Visioner was close!

Karg would find him. Soon, he would find him.... when it was 'unexpected' - and then there would be pleasure!

There had been no gratification this darkwater for he had been preoccupied; too preoccupied to think of the Pleasure Cave captive. Somewhere close was the potential for higher enjoyment...

Karg finstirred along the reef in his flukingpassage of somnolence, one eye open in the habit of dolphinkind. At each turning sweep, one eye closed and the other opened... and always the wide-eye gazed across the waterspace towards the Podsherd, watching... watching...

The Pleasure Cave captive had reprieve in the dark.

She had long ago ceased her calls for assistance. No amount of pinging could penetrate the entrance closure far... and then there was the coral wall at the end of the shallow pool to block the whispers of her distress.

For one sea-season she had been there. She knew she had changed from a graceful, recently mature female. Now she was scarred, blind in one eye and her finningpassage wavered. She was a creature of faint-light, only safe in solitude. Another dolphin was the signal for suffering.

The reprieves were scarce and to be savoured. On rare occasions, she had been left in peace for a span of two darkwaters. Perhaps this would be another? The hunger pains, were preferable to...

Finwarp and Karg had enticed her to the cave. Finwarp had been ugly with his fin aslant but Karg had been... Karg had been so beautiful! How could she have known of the strength of his Visioning? She had seen him as one of the Butting Pod Guardians; young, firm-fleshed, vigorous and brave. Karg had smiled and his teeth had been even, his gaping expression so warm and friendly. She had fluketrembled with anticipation, tri-vector to the cave, pursuing pleasureable images of intimacy and...

They had both teased her that she was too nervous to take the leap over the coral wall and fin the flooded passage to the cavern. Images of a wonderful place of marvels dappled with light and shadow had filled her mind. She had heard the soft sound of surf whispering against the reef. She had seen herself coupling with Karg as the ripples patterned the surface of an in-reef waterspace and gently whispering of love... and, perhaps, a calf in a secret place of peace and safety from sharks.

In youthful innocence, she had leapt towards the lie... and the truth was now and she wished for the sharks!

Finwarp had not been seen after that finningpassage to the cave. She had entered the faint-light and the entrance closure had sealed her fate with a hollow, booming reverberation.

Karg usually arrived after the blackness of darkwater. He always arrived as the real Karg - larger than the entrance waterspace, with no finningpassage free for her to pass, accompanied by the fearsome squid which lay in the flooded passage blocking all but a glimmer of light. The squid watched from outside through huge, cold eyes - watched everything, every finmovement... each carnal act.

The squid heard every mindscream, the hard beak moving expectantly.

The squid knew each image... felt each... pulse... heart-beat. It strangled her breathing... knotted her bloodflow... seemed to know each pain. The cruel squid-smile in the eyes mirrored everything; knew her suffering.

The squid knew when her flukes had been torn, her eye gashed and each scar on her sides, intimately.

Karg fed her after coupling - and obeyed the squid who ordered the closure of the entrance.

She craved for a deep-dive and sharks - but the squid held terror beyond imagining. The squid would know if she attempted to flood her lungs, smash the entrance closure and savage her with his squidbeak - his tentacles squeezing the sea from her body. She had never dared her own death.

She had forgotten her name.

Many dolphinspans away, out of range of the questing mind of Karg, nearer to another islet and another reef system, dozed another dolphin. Distance was safety. This Bottlenose, too, would take his lonely chances with sharks.

His side below the tilting dorsal was deeply disfigured by a hideous wound, the flesh white and twisted with scar tissue. Another wound on the flanks was evidence of shark attack.

His sleep was troubled. He had finned his way to the hardside wreck as usual, dived to the entrance of the towering tunnel and now finned within the confines where it broke into airspace. It was relatively safe here. He always blocked the entrance after access with some hardside debris.

Today he had seen Flab! Her closeness had been a consolation. She was stouter but still her normal self it seemed. How he missed, needed her light-hearted cheeriness.

But he could never return.

The sun breached into a new lightwater. Peen was excited. Gale's Butting Pod would be off-duty soon!

When the flankers had been attended to, they could be together!

Of course, Gape would have to join the other near-matures for continued training in the Nursery and spend some time with Bottlenoses of her age.

And today, Gaze would go for potentiality testing with the Storytellers. What a wonderful day! Peen could hardly control her excitement!

Chapter Three

CONTINUING EDUCATION?

Maeve had gained entry to University!
They had experienced moments of sheer jubilation with some very unadult clowning in the kitchen. Her entry requirements had been met and her prospects augured well.

Ciaran and Maeve had talked at length. She had seemed dead set on Marine Biology/Zoology. She hadn't quite decided the exact avenue yet for the terms were still a bit vague to her... but there was a steady insistence in wanting 'to study the life of the sea'. What seemed to have tipped the option for her generalised concept of 'studying sea-creatures' were her two encounters with whales and dolphins during the vacation - particularly the latter.

On return from holiday, the transfer of personal goods from the beach-house near Redland - now the property of Deirdre and her 'house-guest' – had been effected rapidly. There had been no real dialogue between mother and daughter. Ciaran had been puzzled why this was so. In the apartment, Maeve had assisted with decorating, tidying and surface home-building but nose-dived into the local library stock on 'Mammals of the Sea' at the first opportunity. She did not appear to give her mother a second's thought. He had decided to let things rest, admiring Maeve's resilience... but he suspected her mother would resurface in Maeve's mind some day, like one of those bloody dolphins she was reading about.

He supposed what really mattered was that they were a unit. They could co-operate and respect freedoms each required... yet come together to face trouble.

Gale breached in his usual shower of salty spray and effervescence and surged around the familypod. One would not have thought he had spent the darkwater on continuous Podsherd patrol! Forefin passing in a long, sweeping caress of Peen, he bored into their centre as a clustered group. Gape was wide-eyed in expectancy and admiration; Peen seeking to control fluketrembling she felt in his presence, and Gaze was observant attentiveness.

'Good lightwater, my love. I hope you rested well. Now, Gaze, it is time for you to fluke with me to the Storytellers' Caves. Gape, you will continue your training with the Nursery Dams and, later, you will accompany this Guardian during fishmuster.'

Gale flukeslapped the surface and another Bottlenose's head appeared a few dolphinspans away. The bottlebeak moved closer to the familypod, finning respectfully forward.

'His name is Beak Spot,'...for the dolphin did indeed have a darker spot on the upper part of his bottlebeak... 'and he will call for you later at the Nursery when he has slept. Mind you behave yourself, Gape, and do exactly as he tells you. Beak Spot is one of the Guardians of my Pod.'

In the manner of most near-matures, Gape finstirred already in provocation with forefin on her side best observed by Beak Spot... and he smiled, acknowledged her! Gape felt late adolescent flukeshivers which seemed to run the length of her spine.

'That is all Beak Spot. Get some rest,' said Gale with authority - the precursor of, in mindmerge, the caution that when Gape was capable of mindmerge, that would be the time for Guardian relaxation - and flesh-fervour - not before!

Gaze listened to both comments without detection for he was curious and excited... and then censured himself for so easily breaking a self-promise not to use such mindskill.

He blanked his mind. He must not do any mindreading at the Storytellers' Caves or they would quickly sense his difference... and he did not want to be classed as... He did not feel an... Abomination. Gaze reefsided and patterned. He needed time to pattern and reflect upon the squid and the feeling that...!

The moment he entertained the mindvision of the squid, there was the mind, malignant, sneering!

Gaze reefsided... reefsided... imaged other things... anything but the sq...! Reefsiding! Reefsiding... and Gape had become beautiful. Just a few more lightwaters and she would probably mindmerge and be mature. Why was he capable before her? The sun is warm today? I wonder what the Storytellers are really like? The starfish has five arms... and sometimes more. An octopus has eight arms and flukes moving backwards. It looks peculiar but not as peculiar as a sq...!

And there, in the middle of the familypod was the malignance - unseen by any Bottlenose save the youngest who could not send a Butting Pod to chase a vision.

'So you are young and your sire flukes with a Butting Pod... and he is... ?' the squid said through a beak shiny and hard.

The malignance must not know the name! He must camouflage...

Gaze was surf-spray on the reef and a growing gale of violent wind bending the landside palms in blasts of air... surging across the waterspace in rolling breakers... Stormwind and water in maelstrom...

'It does not matter,' said the squid with a row of twisted teeth, 'for you will be meeting me soon. You and I are destined to meet in grappling embrace and twine together... you and I... soon... soo... '

'Gaze, give me your attention! Never has an Induction candidate been so inattentive!' mindbarked Gale... and could not understand why his flanker looked at him with such... gratitude?

The malignance had gone.

'I apologise, my sire. There was...' replied a meek flanker. 'I was patterning about...'

'Twaddle! You were lightwater dreaming! Snap to! We are going to the Storytellers' Caves and you need to be alert. Now fluke in bi-vector with me and keep your mind sharp. I will see you later, my love. Perhaps...'

Gaze was not listening to the rest...

Reflecting behind a heavy reefside, he realised that any attempt at mindscanning by him... or any mindvisioning ... allowed the access! He could not mindread or vision the slightest, however secretly, now that this 'other' knew of his difference... his closeness to being... an Abomination? Was this other one such?

He became an ordinary Bottlenose fluking co-operatively towards the Storytellers, to any mindobserver.

Somehow his mind was tuned to another dolphin. Malignant, this Bottlenose enjoyed another's fear and... wanted to cause him harm. But they had never met? If he used mindreading or the other mindskills he had, the other dolphin was immediately aware and discovered more about him. Gaze sensed the threat to himself and his podfamily!

'Know your enemies and be constant with your friends,' Gale had said, but this 'enemy' was unknown and threatening not only Gaze. He did not know how to deal with this. If he told his sire, there would be the risk of rejection... even condemnation as an Abomination. He knew already his dam would be unable to conceive any action or plan. Perhaps he was an Abomination - dreaming delusion...? No! The presence had been too 'real'.

The vast mind in his fluking body quickened...

'Keep vector on me Gaze! Concentrate!' came the rebuke from his sire. 'Remember where you are headed.'

Two quick finsweeps corrected Gaze's drift from vector.

His mind continued the patterning process. There had been no echo-returns from the projected Butting Pod... or the 'thing' which had risen from the depths during the darkwater. Even in the safety of no other mindfunction than reflection, Gaze hesitated to image the 'squid'. Both the Butting Pod and the 'thing' had lacked substance. They were only images projected to instil fear in the observer. They could not actually cause harm. Last darkwater, he had seemed to feel the tentacle slide across his back and had blocked his fear by recall-imaging his sire's appraisal...

The other Bottlenose needed his fear to identify him!

He was safe for now - and, more important, so was his podfamily Peen, Gape... and Gale fluking firmly beside him.

For how long could he contain his fear and dread?

The Storytellers' Caves were not strictly 'caves' in the full sense but, rather, a natural maze on the island side of the rock and coral reef. The roof of each 'cave' was usually the airspace above although occasional falls in the vertical strata of rock - or storm damage to the coral - lent the appearance of 'caves' along some parts of the maze passageways. There was, in fact, only one cave along the reef - Wanderer's Cave - and the entrance was in deep-water on the seaward side of the reef.

A deep-dive into a tunnel entrance brought a dolphin into an enclosed airspace within the reef itself. Wanderer had discovered this many seasons before and his secrets were within the reef - but access to them was only achieved by solving the 'puzzle of the cave'. No dolphin was accepted as a Storyteller trainee if he could not find the secret access.

Prospective trainees came to know of this problem after two lightwaters of potentiality testing. If successful, a trainee would receive general training as a Voyager, Cleric, Navigator, Inventor or Historian. All Storytellers had additional duties besides teaching and taking their turn in recounting the sagas. There was the expectation that a Storyteller would make a real contribution to dolphinkind, just as Wanderer himself had done. The Storytellers decided when it was appropriate for a trainee to join them in the 'caves'... and, later, when an individual contribution to dolphinkind was to be undertaken.

'Do you... er... both of you, Vorg and... er... Glaze, was it? No, Gaze... that's right... Do you both follow so far?' said an elderly Bottlenose.

Obtaining an affirmative from the two near-matures, he continued with his introduction to the programme of the next two lightwaters. He seemed to fumble constantly his images in mindmeet as if he was preoccupied with alternative problems - as, indeed, he was.

Gale's Pod of Guardians had brought some interesting finds from a Splitfluke hardside on the shelf-floor some distance away. Apparently, they had followed Gale's orders to investigate and had gained access, through a hole in one side, into a large waterspace area which had been dark but navigable. A container, larger than a giant clamshell, had been turned on one side, perhaps as a result of the deep-dive the hardside had taken. Some of the objects within had been interesting. After some preliminary beakprodding, Gale had made a selection to take to the Storytellers, believing they might be worth studying.

Gale was very sensible. How he had failed the puzzle of the cave was beyond Ardent, a Historian/Cleric. He had always muddled the distinction.

Perhaps Gale had been a late developer for he had an alert mind... and now, here was his son, Gaze.

'Both of you will need to be on your flukes while you are here... Garg, and... er... Vaze. Work together and concentrate hard,' continued Ardent, pausing and sensing a slip... 'I mean, Gaze and Vorg! Yes, that's right. I do apologise. I'm afraid I keep thinking about the objects your father brought to my cave lightwater last... Gaze. Some are very interesting... like the one which is a hard cross-shape with... a Splitfluke on it? Perhaps Splitflukes have a religion because there is a sense of... a sense of...

'Oh, I'm sorry. Now, shortly you will see a number of Storytellers from the different disciplines who will want to ask you various questions. Don't be uneasy. They will want you to express your views and beliefs... not test your knowledge for you are both young.

'The attitudes you express may affect the decisions the Storytellers make concerning the discipline it is felt you should study - or whether you should become a Guardian.

'Now, welcome once again... and er... you should fin around here until the next Storyteller arrives to see you. I really would like to meet your father, Gaze. He said he would wait for a short span. We will meet again later.'

With that, Ardent finned away, narrowly missing bumping against a coral outcrop.

Vorg and Gaze met in mindmeet for the first time...

'What kind of fluking nightmare was that!? He's either worm-ridden or it's about time someone vectored him to deepwater and he took the deep-dive. His mind is dead already,' said Vorg, adolescent aggression pronounced. 'I'm Vorg. Blue Anemone is my dam. Who are you?'

'My name is Gaze and Peen is my dam,' he said, making the instinctive decision that any relationship with Vorg would be of a surface kind and relatively short-lived...

Blue Anemone was well-known, according to the mindimages he had collated soon after joining the Podsherd last lightwater. From all unsolicited accounts, she was well-associated with a number of the sires. There had been one female Bottlenose he had finned aside from. She had seemed to be assessing him and gauging his maturity. Gaze realised this had probably been Blue Anemone. Her fins had stirred provocatively near all the sires. It had been grotesque exaggeration of Gape's more innocent finstirring when Beak Spot had arrived earlier.

How vastly different Blue Anemone had seemed to the graceful Peen beside him! Gaze could understand that Peen was subject to flesh-fervour... and, presumably, every other Bottlenose was... but Blue Anemone had an... 'appetite'? Yes, that was the 'word' 'Maeve' would have used... which seemed a... 'mania'. Maeve knew other 'words' to describe a Splitfluke equivalent.

Gaze was right to construe that Blue Anemone had more than regular contact with a variety of the sires, including the fact that some Storytellers, normally conservative in their need for flesh-fervour, had been seen in her company. He did not know, yet, that Vorg was the offspring of a Storyteller - or that Blue Anemone had found that particular session of flesh-fervour the most painful of her vast experience. The carnal coupling had seemed to last a very long time for his dam - with accompanying visions she could only put down to poisoned fish.

He could not have known that just then...

'...and how many reef-dives have you done?' Vorg was saying.

Gaze became conscious of Vorg's mindmeet voice beyond his reefsiding.

Quickly he replied, 'None really. I've only just joined the Podsherd from the Nursery Area. I haven't had long here.'

'I've done a number. I had to wait for a Guardian to give me sire inspection for several lightwaters. My real sire died in a Butting Pod assault on some sharks. My dam told me. He was very brave,' Vorg said with pride... but Gaze detected a slight tinge of doubt because... He must not mindmerge!

Suddenly there was a pressure-wave flowing along the maze passageway followed by a mature dorsal. The dolphin bottlebeak was not showing!

For a few moments, both waiting flankers thought a large shark was on striking-vector towards them and they were trapped within the confines of the cave off-shoot. They both felt helplessness - the forerunner of fear... then a head rose above the forewave.

A confused image of a shark's gaping maw was replaced by a mature Bottlenose's head, bottlebeak open, showing two rows of... Gaze had a mental hiccup... two rows of twisted teeth!

That one parallel with a stored image in the mind of Gaze was enough for the young dolphin to thrust all mindactivity behind a heavier reefside block than he had ever used!

Karg attempted mindmerge with the two prospective trainees as they finned uneasily a dolphinspan away. Young near-matures should not be capable of more than mindmeet. He was ever alert to rivalry ...and the stranger Visioner might be even one of these unlikely candidates.

'I am Karg, Navigator, and I have some questions.'

Neither young Bottlenose made any sign of recognising mindmerging association... except, Karg noted a mind... closely symmetrical to his own?

This had not occurred before... Unusual, was it a clue?

'You! What is your name?' demanded Karg.

Both near-matures hesitated, unsure to whom the question was addressed.

'Speak up!' said Karg, giving one of them a butt of moderate proportion. 'What is your name?'

For a fleeting moment, Karg felt a pulse in mindmerge of sheer frustration and the desire to butt back. Was it the beginnings of mindmerging maturity... or did this one already possess those adult skills? Was he the...?

'I am... Vorg!' came the surly reply.

Karg finned a little closer, one eye fixed on Vorg. Perhaps this was the one; the source of the visions he had found disturbing? Aware of similarities of mind, Karg did not know they were based on biochemistry and inheritance - that his kind of evil had a transmissible pattern.

Karg began the 'pursuit of the red herring' which he had often warned his trainees against...

Since Karg's admission as a Storyteller, he had become an unrecorded master of sudden assassination. Karg's personality demanded unrestricted freedom for himself and domination of others. He had been very different from sire or dam as sometimes happened in the world of waterspace. His kind tolerated no restraints but enjoyed constraining others, eliminating competition - ruthlessly, if necessary. Since he enjoyed observing suffering, he had sought greater excitement and closer observation of the effects as his seasons had passed. Visioning power he kept secret...

Finwarp's death and the condition of the Pleasure Cave captive were but the underwater peaks of achievement. Karg would demand higher achievement yet, in proportion to his swelling ego.

Potential competition in his quest for domination gave minor satisfaction in progress, small peaks of perversion. There was no guilt felt in the process. A shark's blood ran in this dolphin's veins.

Karg sensed the prospect of a striking-vector...

Apparently ignoring Vorg, he finned threateningly towards Gaze.

'And you?' came the question. 'What is your name?'

'I am Gaze, son of Gale. My dam is Peen,' answered Gaze, with all mindactivity at a minimum except a reflex action to fluke away at speed if necessary... and fuller concentration on a reefside block hitherto unpractised.

'It is good that sardines know their sires and dams but I only asked your name?' Karg replied.

This one is on the verge of panic, he thought. Another small-minded flanker who would pose no threat... But the other one... ?

'You, Gaze, what kind of a Storyteller would you like to be?'

'I don't know, yet... Could I train for different disciplines and... er... make up my mind later?'

'Typical! No ambitions before coming for potentiality testing. You will receive training in all the disciplines and specialise later... provided you solve the puzzle of Wanderer's Cave.'

Karg snorted, expelling a plume of exhalation from his blow-hole. A fanciful dreamer if ever he'd seen one! He would probably fail two lightwaters from now - no capacity for imaging ahead.

Karg finned around, one eye fixing Vorg and mind-antennae reaching out.

'You, Vorg. What about you?'

'A Voyager. I want to be a Voyager,' came the quick response ...and Karg had anticipated no other.

A Voyager travelled vast flukingspans of waterspace, essentially as an explorer, needing self-reliance, sometimes aggression and faced many risks that other Bottlenoses dared not contemplate. Some Voyagers did not return. If they did, they were greeted as heroes and quizzed for many lightwaters on all they had observed - just as Wanderer had been. Now that had been a Bottlenose Karg would have liked to surprise... Karg chuckled inwardly.

There followed brief questioning of them both. Karg the Navigator questioned Gaze in a perfunctory manner. He paid closer attention to Vorg's answers, analysing each shade of possible meaning. He watched for mindmovement which might betray hidden, mindactivity - or the suggestion of something in reserve, heavily reefsided.

It was always difficult in mindmeet to sense anything but surface reasoning power. A dolphin's personality was revealed but shallowly. He found nothing to substantiate his conviction that Vorg was the new dolphin capable of mindvisioning... but he persisted in his search for proof. His vanity and his unwillingness to admit he might be making a misjudgement, continued to prompt him to examine ever more closely.

Gaze, dismissed in Karg's search, thanked Wanderer for the cursory examination!

Finally, it was over and, without the usual courtesies, Karg fluked abruptly away. Neither candidate showed any sign of hearing the mindimages within Karg - threatening, cursing - or felt the inner rage and thwarted lust for violence. Neither gave any sign - but one of them observed and began to question his future.

An Inventor, another Cleric and a Historian came at intervals to ask simple, direct questions in a much more congenial manner. Each seemed easily satisfied. There followed a tour, led by Ardent, along the various maze passageways and 'cave' off-shots. It was easy enough but Ardent occasionally finstroked the side of his head in a perplexed manner.

Only when their 'line ahead' vector approached his own 'cave' area did Ardent seem to become entirely at ease. The Cleric obviously preferred a cloistered environment for his mood changed. He appeared to become increasingly self-assured...

'Perhaps you would like to see inside a Storyteller's Cave,' he said. 'Would you care to fin inside?'

With that, he finned left through an entrance, pausing reverently to beaknose something in a coral crevice.

Puzzled, both flankers finned behind. Vorg cast a cursory glance at the object in the crevice but was more interested in the 'cave' to dwell long examining anything outside.

It was Gaze who paused longest, lifting on slight rise and fall of water-movement. Light played on the crevice from cracks in the coral reef above, creating constant change of shade and hue. The crevice seemed filled with whitish blue light, playing around an object shaped like... like a dolphin! It was not realistic in form but truer to life in its summary of dolphin qualities.

This small... 'sculpture'?... yes, that was the image in the mind of 'Maeve'... was of a greenish stone. It was beautifully... 'carved'... as if a hidden essence within a dolphin was freed to view. Gaze finned closer to beaknose the carving in the same kind of reverential manner which he had observed in Ardent moments before.

Perhaps it was coincidental that the reef seemed to vibrate with the pressure of a billowing wave... but, at the moment of contact with the carving, Gaze seemed to hear distant dolphin voices. There were kaleidoscopic images of strange, distant coasts... and Splitflukes!

The young Bottlenose's eyes closed as if in sudden giddiness...

There were voices in his mind, calm but assertive - quiet but strong. They ran like currents through every nerve and seemed like pulses in his blood...

But he could not distinguish the ... 'words'!

'Words' and meaning, images and visions seemed to form in his mindeye - or scream in the surf of strange seas.

Gaze sensed he was on the verge of sense or chaos but it was too soon to understand which...

'Gaze, where are you?' Ardent called. 'I would like you to see what your father has brought.'

Opening his eyes, Gaze fought the dizziness and finned through the entrance to Ardent's Cave. It was light and airy. One side - the shallow side - revealed a litter of odd shapes, shell-like containers and debris of different kinds. The impression was a place of comfortable clutter, perhaps a little claustrophobic, but a place for quiet reflection. The deeper pool on the lagoon side of the reef-walls seemed clear but with a light blue tinge at a depth of two dolphinspans. Tiny creatures moved at the bottom of the pool. They seemed oblivious of the three Bottlenoses above.

Then Gaze saw something... a bleached white with two vacant holes staring towards the surface.

He felt a surge of panic!

The skull of some creature, long since stripped of flesh, seemed to stare at the surface and the airspace now beyond reach. Gaze began to attempt to build flesh and skin around the skull in his imaging. Shocked, he realised this was the skull of a Splitfluke!

Ardent noticed the fixed attention of Gaze, but kept his own counsel. Vorg was finning near a variety of metal objects in shallower water, most of which had pointed ends or sharp edges.

An abrupt mindimage came from Vorg...

'What are these? They look like Splitfluke weapons!'

His aggressive spirit was imaging a tearing and slicing of flesh.

'Gale's Butting Pod brought these for inspection by the Storytellers. They support the sagas as evidence of the Splitflukes as a violent species. Their inventiveness is apparent for they build hardsides. They have constructed hardsides for many, many seasons but the sagas tell of constant conflict above the waterspace.

'The Splitflukes are warm-blooded, like us, and they fluke short spans - but not very well. In recent seasons, they have come more often to our waterspace. There are reports that they have gone deeper into the waterspace than any dolphins - but in special underwater hardsides bigger than the largest whale. Some rumours suggest they have taken dives down to total darkness - down to unimaginable depths in strange hardsides attached by vertical umbilicals to the surface.

'We have many things yet to learn. We know only that... Splitflukes are unpredictable. Some pods of Splitflukes fish from the shores or in small hardsides trailing fish traps. These items show their capacity for mass murder not merely for food.'

Ardent paused, the next images too awful to recount. Perhaps Gaze and Vorg were too young?

'Remember that Splitflukes have ways of killing beyond our imaging. They are capable of hideous acts. Yet some... Some may be capable of acts which show they are not all evil... Some may show something of goodness and love...'

He finned to face Gaze.

'You are looking at a Splitfluke skull and you both need to know a story...'

He had the attention of both flankers. For the most part, his hesitations were forgiven; his revelations were gripping.

Long seasons ago, soon after the warmstream pods had arrived in this part of the waterspace, Wanderer had left on his epic voyage. Within the next season, the grey-hardsides were seen in greater numbers. There was a time of great uncertainty in the world of the Splitflukes... and a time of great violence.

It had become obvious that two sorts of Splitflukes had been seeking to kill as many of each kind as they could. The weapons they used were like no others reported before in the sagas. In some of the great Splitfluke warring, the waterspace would seem to boil and erupt with titanic upheavals. Many hardsides took the deep-dive, thousands of fish, sharks, dolphins, Splitflukes and creatures of other species died in these vast concussions. Some Bottlenoses thought the end of the world of waterspace was coming. A number of the Clerics began to say that the time of the White Dolphins was near.

Rarely seen before, the warmstream pods had seen giant hardsides which seemed to carry on their airsides large, noisy airthings thousands of times larger than flying fish. These airthings dived into air from a hardside and defied gravity by climbing higher. They were seen diving at other hardsides seeming to make water burst into airspace around. Only dolphins some distance away had lived to describe such things.

The senseless loss of life had been heartrending...

'It is the saddest part of the sagas in recent history,' said Ardent. 'There are reports of the waterspace stained red with blood - or black with choking substances. Even after these warring periods, there were still tragedies for fish and birds.'

There was a pause...

'My sire spoke of a close friend who died after finning through some strange material which seemed to burn his flesh and choke his breathing. His friend had finned quietly for a few moments in calm water and then said, in a weak voice, that he had not thought the time for the deep-dive would have come as the result of finning through some hardside debris and waste... The pain had been great. His friend had breathed out and deep-dived from sight to the darkness below...'

There was a silence.

Ardent seemed to shake himself then added ...

'Beware of the hardside debris for it can kill in ways we do not yet understand.'

Gaze said, 'But that was not the story of the Splitfluke skull.'

'No, Gaze... I shall continue,' Ardent replied after a fluketremble.

He told them of the two airthings coming down to crash into the waterspace, black clouds streaming from both, within fluking distance of a Butting Pod. Of how the Pod had divided into two podunits to investigate.

The first podunit had stopped flukingvector toward one of the airthings when, incredibly, a thing like an airborne jelly-fish had descended to the waterspace with a Splitfluke beneath! Acting upon their own initiative, later earning praise for having done so, they fluked towards this strange phenomena.

The Splitfluke had been wounded. Half his fluking limbs were bleeding badly and he would have been shark-food quickly. The podunit had carried out Guardian procedure whilst the Splitfluke had done things to keep himself afloat. He had something on his chest and around his neck to keep himself upright on the surface. Whilst he was struggling to stop the bleeding, the first shark had arrived.

Keeping to Guardian procedures, the podunit had pinged warning and kept the shark off striking-vector. The Splitfluke seemed to stop most of the bleeding but it was obvious he would need escort away from the area of blood-flow. After some weak struggling, the Splitfluke had quietened and allowed himself to be dolphinherded away. He had not responded to any attempts at mindmeet... but the podunit had reported that he had seemed astonished... and grateful for assistance. He had placed a forefin limb on a Guardian's dorsal and allowed himself to be towed towards the other distant airthing which still floated... and the other podunit.

Rejoining as a complete Pod of Guardians at the floating airthing, they had expected the two Splitflukes to greet each other but no communication was made. One Splitfluke was still within the airthing. He was conscious but his yellow-skin face was tight with pain. His chest was red with blood. All the Guardians agreed he would never get out. Eventually the airthing would deep-dive and the yellow-skin Splitfluke would go down with it.

One Guardian had towed the white-skin Splitfluke nearer. The Splitflukes had looked at each other. It became obvious they could not speak to each other... and yet they both seemed to know what was going to happen...

The Guardians nudged the white-skin Splifluke above one of the large airside's fins so that... he could reach the yellow-skin Splitfluke. There were few words and the Guardians had not thought any words were necessary.

Ardent paused, then said, 'Perhaps there may be times when Splitflukes are capable of mindmeet. We cannot be certain... but there have been times when... when Splitflukes have seemed to share a mindbond or kinship. Times when mindmerge has almost seemed evident.

'I do not think they use mindmeet as we do but, perhaps, in moments of great crisis for them, they show the beginnings of a kind of mindmeeting and merging.'

Ardent was quiet for a few moments and Gaze was reflecting but remained silent.

'What happened next?' said Vorg, for once not as abruptly as usual.

The Cleric told them of how the yellow-skin had touched the forefin of the white-skin; of how his pain had caused him to airsnatch rapidly and of how his noises had been variable in pitch. Sometimes the yellow-skin had made noises, jerky and soft; some-times louder and gasping. Each had seemed to know the end.

The yellow-skin had removed a white thing from his head with black markings and something green from around his neck. He had passed them to the white-skin. There had been silence... Even the sounds of the waterspace had been muted.

The Guardians had towed the white-skin Splitfluke away and all had watched the airthing slip down for the deep-dive. Nothing else to be done, they had dolphinherded the white-skin Splitfluke away and escorted him to the Storytellers.

It had been Ardent's sire who had brought him to his Story-teller's cave...

'The white-skin Splitfluke is still with us. We tried to bring him food. He was too weak to fluke far.

'On the second lightwater, he endeavoured flukingpassage for the islandmass and the Guardians tried to give assistance but... He was too weak and kept slipping away. The Guardian escort nudged him to the surface until vertical sunlight, keeping sharks off striking-vectors.

'It was useless. All dolphins decided it was time for the deep-dive and the sharks. The yellow-thing around his neck was bitepunctured and torn away to let him sink.'

Ardent, Gaze and even Vorg, observed a respectful silence.

Eventually, Ardent said, 'Sharks made striking-vectors on the Splitfluke two hundred dolphinspans from shore. He did not mindscream when his head breached once...

'He had left the things the yellow-skin had given him here in the cave. My sire had his skull brought here to be with us. That is the skull you can see Gaze... on the cave floor. At least he is with friends here.'

Gaze looked down to staring eye sockets... staring up to the airspace and he felt sad. He felt the need to beaknose in respect. He dived the two dolphinspans down and finned towards the skull of the Splitfluke.

At the first touch, Gaze felt the same dizziness as with the green dolphin 'sculpture' outside - the same kaliedoscopic blur of images and 'words'.

It was then he realised the beginning of another new power but, in respect, he finned aside from the skull's after-imaging.

Gaze could not read the future but he was able to sense the past! This was a new mindskill and awesome... How?...

Investigating other objects within Ardent's cave, he began to stabilize the images and sounds in his head... and felt more equilibrium within. Using the mindsense, he knew not how to name it, he could sense the purpose of an object and the intent of its owner. Occasionally, his mind seemed focused on an image which was like a frozen memory of the past. The longer he beaknosed an object, the more he was able to piece together - to 'quantify' purpose. There was no 'word' in the mind of Maeve to describe this mindsense - only a vague notion that Splitflukes of a different kind in her own 'home' island - no, it was bigger than 'island', 'country'? - had spoken of a few - 'aborigines'? - having the same ability.

A sharp-edged thing, Gaze recognised as 'knife' for 'cutting' or 'stabbing'. It could be used for violence but for many useful things besides.

A longer, sharp-edged 'sword'?, used 'two-handed'... for killing, sometimes 'execution'? Killing in ... 'punishment'...!?

Gaze recoiled in horror as he saw a Splitfluke in white garments swinging the 'sword' downwards against the neck of a... a... 'criminal' or... 'traitor'. The neck of the victim was cut through and the head rolled away. There was much blood.

It was happening on land! Splitflukes had their own kind of sharks!

Chapter Four

THE POWER AND THE WAY

K arg would have his chance two lightwaters from now. Waiting could be enjoyable, drawing out the climax of planned events. It was better if one could sense the growing fear in the victim but Vorg could not be allowed to mature for long. He was potential danger. The climax of unexpected suffering could be prolonged a little longer than Finwarp's had been but no chances could be taken.

Two lightwaters from now, Vorg would have to solve the puzzle of Wanderer's Cave. That would be the time to remove his potential threat and feel him die in the deep-dive with Karg's squid embrace around him. He had a way to make it happen...

Perhaps Vorg was unaware of the latent power of Visioning as yet? There was an undercurrent of aggression and malice which Karg understood well. It would be foolish to wait overlong.

At some considerable length, Ardent talked to Gaze and Vorg, following astutely their interests and curiosities. His seasons in the Storytellers' Caves had led him to believe this to be one of the better ways of assessing potential trainees. Slowly, he began to perceive that Gaze had wider areas of interest. Vorg appeared fascinated by stories of bravery, struggle and death whereas his attention wandered on matters Clerical or Historical. Gaze listened attentively and his mindmeet questions were penetrating, revealing a capacity for analysis which surprised Ardent.

Before long, elderly Storyteller and young near-mature were engaged in dialogue which Ardent would have expected only from a Bottlenose of greater maturity. Gaze had an alert mind...

'Earlier, you were distracted in your imaging by one of the objects my sire brought to your cave. I do not think you have shown it to us yet. Could we see it?' asked Gaze.

'Well Gaze... it has yet to be seen by the other Storytellers. The Inventors and Historians may be mildly interested but I feel the Clerics will be most... er ... intrigued, I think. For once, I will break a rule of our collecting code.'

Ardent beaknosed aside a flattish piece of rock debris revealing a small cavity. He beaksnouted out the object he sought. Thus innocently, indirectly was the first clue for solving the access puzzle to Wanderer's Cave given to both near-matures, if remembered. It had taken Ardent longer than usual to pass the clue. The mindmeet with Gaze had been stimulating.

He placed the cross-shape on the cavefloor and returned to the surface. Airsnatching, he passed on the clue in the traditional mindmeet phrasing...

'Sometimes innocent objects hide secrets.'

Duty as a Storyteller discharged, Ardent watched interestedly as both candidates beaknosed the cross-shape, neither seeming to give the cavity cover further attention as it bobbed, restrained by a chain. Only Ardent appeared to be aware that the cavity cover was buoyant and not stone. One young dolphin stored the knowledge. Gaze carefully shielded his awareness for already he knew his future did not include a period in Storyteller training. There was danger he felt unready to face!

Vorg, disinterested in the cross-shape, returned quickly to more enthralling Splitfluke weaponry.

At his first beaknose, Gaze felt the giddiness he recognised. A whole series of whirling images, stretching from now to infinity and back through swirling seasons of dolphin history, threatened to overwhelm him. There were images of pain and sorrow; Splitflukes in strange garb, and of... 'nails'... through Splitfluke fins; a... 'spear'... in the side...

... Maeve's mind acknowledged the Splitfluke on the cross - knew the story of his life, and his death. She knew of his love even for those who had killed him - but she knew as a flanker; she knew as a 'child'. There was much she did not know; much she did not feel. This Splitfluke was goodness beyond qualifying. He was the opposite of everything malicious. Peace and forgiveness... He was... He...

Gaze rose to airsnatch.

There was much in the world of Splitflukes he had to discover - and it was not in a Storyteller's Cave that he would find any answers. Already he had one reason for leaving as soon as he could. Karg the Navigator wanted his death and soon. There were other reasons.

Gaze knew, in himself, he would have to learn to be a Voyager without the formal training he could receive here. Karg was that which his dam feared - an Abomination, wholly malicious.

Ardent watched Gaze some moments. He sensed a decision in the young Bottlenose's mind, but there was an outstanding reefside he could not penetrate. Were there hidden depths to this young Bottlenose...?

Gaze felt the presence of Ardent's questioning tendrils beyond the reefside... The elderly dolphin was a threat without realising it - a more immediate danger than the malignant Karg! Gaze would have to extinguish the glimmers of doubt... and hope?... on the fringes of Ardent's mind...

He said, in mindmeet, 'Do not ask me how I know. You wonder if the Splitflukes have a religion and the answer is I believe they do. I will not share my knowledge of how I know. In Wanderer's name, you know that not all dolphins are as good as yourself.'

Startled in his imaging, Ardent felt suddenly, forcefully in short-range mindmerge, the mindvoice of Gaze...

'Share your thoughts of the cross-shape with other Storytellers and speak of the Splitfluke upon it. Some will want to believe. Others will scorn the possibility. I believe... I know it is true. Say nothing of Gaze, the son of Gale and Peen for I must fluke at variance with tradition.'

46

Unaccountably, Ardent felt he was hearing a voice of authority far sterner than his deep-dived sire, stronger than a trained Guardian in fishmustering, and delivered intensely in short-range mindcontact.

'Lock such knowledge in your heart and reefside against any dolphin's knowledge of me for I am young. Yet I have an enemy already with powers beyond your imaging and an evil beyond your simple faith in the goodness of others.

'I command you to silence and the inner peace of forgetfulness.'

It pained Gaze to do this but it was necessary.

He knew Ardent's potential as a friend but there was too much danger to face. He could allow a minor revelation and sow a seed for the future... but that was all. He had to use the voice of command. Ardent could not be allowed to crystallise half-formed imaging in his mindlight's clustering...

Ardent's reply was slow in formulation as if gathering his absent-minded reveries to focus on the present...

'Yes, the cross-shape is interesting. I shall speak of it later to other Storytellers...

'By Wanderer,' he continued, 'you must be hungry. Come both of you, let us join the Storyteller fishing pods. We are late for fishmuster!'

Ardent was troubled with a sense of forgetting... something else... but, try as he may, the something eluded him. Never mind, it would wait until later...

Finning in tri-vector, the Cleric/Historian and two candidates vectored towards the pods forming the larger fishmuster.

There was the usual bustling excitement in the Podsherd. Three wings of the fishmuster were already discernible, Guardians present with each. Pinging calls of greeting were a music merging with the screaming of gulls overhead.

Each lightwater, the gulls seemed to know when to swoop towards the dolphins mustering. They had eyes to see beyond the near horizon and would appear magically on cue, arcing and swinging across airspace in a gyrating, graceful expectancy.

Gulls were part of the pattern, aiding the fishing dolphins by spreading panic and confusion to a herded shoal. There had never been a declared partnership but the individual acts of the diving gulls provided fishmind diversion. They were always there at the end to clear the injured and concussed, squawking their disgusting fussy screeches of gratitude.

The three elements of fishmuster would fluke parallel vectors several hundred dolphinspans apart, the central muster lagging three hundred dolphinspans behind the leading wings. Guardians would locate a large shoal by pinging ahead... and the signal would come for the central muster to finstir and wait. The leading wings would vector forward but at tangents to the shoal. When the three elements were equispaced around the unsuspecting fish, the signal would come for line-ahead vector in rotation around the shoal. The circle of the three muster-elements would contract, tightening to encompass the prey.

Some of the Guardians would deep-dive below the shoal pinging ever louder to disorient the fish. These Guardians would reduce the depth at each flukingpassage beneath, denying escape. Their task was the hardest for they were playing a deadly kind of mindgame, always pretending their numbers were greater than they were.

With the fishshoal drawn tightly into crowded waterspace, the Guardians would signal flukingassaults. Not every dolphin at once, but a third of each element would make striking-vectors. They would converge into the milling fish, already under gull attack. When a dolphin breached, he would flukeslap the surface violently, concussing some of the victims and creating further fishpanic.

At a signal, the feeding group would withdraw and a second third of each element would fluke rapidly to replace them - until, eventually, all were sustained.

The litter of injured and concussed victims on the surface provided more food for those Bottlenoses with larger appetites... and, of course, the gulls.

Gaze saw his sister with Beak Spot in one wing element, his sire and dam in the other.

In apprehension, he noted Karg was in his sister's part of the fishmuster... but she was safe. Such was an occasion of co-operative pleasure. Each Bottlenose shared in the task for the good of all. Even those absent were provided for, some fish always beakcarried to the Podsherd waterspace. Although each dolphin could fluke independently to feed himself, it was far easier this way and there were stories to recount, in a state of contented repletion.

Gaze smiled inwardly as the wing elements fluked away. Gape was fluking very closely to Beak Spot, their flanks seeming to be inseparable. It was just as well their sire and dam were on the other wing. Teasing the Guardian was an obvious pleasure to her and Gaze almost mindmerged to pass caustic comment... but Karg was too close, too imminent as a danger...

The pinging command came for the central element to begin flukingvector keeping equidistance from both wings. The Guardians kept commands to a minimum as the Podsherd moved with practised precision. Excitement began to build.

Around, Gaze could see dorsals surging forward. An occasional careless fluke would slap out of a wave. There were some explosive airsnatches but, for the most part, there was quietness. Only the gulls squealed above. Some drifting clouds cast shadows on the surface.

The wings began to vector outwards in vast sweeping turns. The command came to finstir and wait. Some Guardians separated to join in deep-diving beneath the shoal which few could see visually but all sensed was there by the echo-returns. Fish appeared, striving to flickerfan the airspace and escape.

The gulls began their stooping dives, plummeting in vertical vectors to disappear beneath wavesurge and, feather-wet, reappeared with struggling victims of gasping silver. Panic beneath the waves became increasingly obvious by the shattered echo-returns which seemed a chaotic sing-song of signals.

Obeying the Guardian command, the central element of the fishmuster fluked right forefin following a spiralling vector which bunched the fish. The wings proceeded with the same pattern. All around dolphins breached, sending spray spattering down like rainsqualls across the sea. Nearing the shoal, the fishmuster was a circle and the trap closed. The Guardians began flukeslapping the surface with loud reverberations.

Gaze saw two fish turn bellies upward from beneath a flukeslap but they disappeared quickly in dolphinjaws.

'First thirds of muster, shoal centre vector... Go! Good fishing!' came the order.

Finstirring, diving and pinging to confuse the fish, Gaze remained on circle station. He opened his mindmerging, determined to listen behind a reefside. He could no longer sustain the rigid discipline he had avowed - not in this excitement!

There was Vorg, also on circle station, mindscreaming with impatience for the kill. He was flukeslapping like a Guardian, watching for surface prey.

A flanker was excited... yet nervous he would not play his part. A multitude of minds whirled in and out of contact.

There was Gape, moving in symmetry with Beak Spot in the first shoal assault, closing a fish and snapping shut her jaws. A thin jet of blood stained the waterspace about her head for a fleeting moment and disappeared in eddies of disturbance. She was elated! She had taken the fish Beak Spot had strike-vectored upon... but there were so many darting silver forms... He soon had another.

His sire was rising from beneath! He had two fish in his beak. Gaze knew the intention before the event. Gale burst into airspace beside Peen. Gaze knew the words...

'There my love! You need to keep your strength for this darkwater! I love y..!' came the clear mindmerging images. The last part was lost in his exuberant re-entry to foam and spray.

There! There was... was a dolphin with a squid's beak questing the fishmuster!

Gaze became ordinary behind a reefside of anxiety!

Would he do well? Would he let his sire down? Would Ardent think well of him? It was noise and pounding blood within, fish wastecloud and torn flesh without!

The menace faded... was gone.

'Second thirds of muster, shoal centre vector... Go!' came the order.

Vorg was fast away, fluking with lusty purpose, strike-vectoring on a cluster of a dozen fish. He had one before any other Bottlenose in his assault wave and his shout of victory was loud in mindmeet. It was followed by a second mindscream of pain!

Another Bottlenose had beaksnapped Vorg's flukes as sometimes happened in the confusing life and death struggle shoal centre.

No dolphin seemed to know who was responsible.

Vorg retired from fishmuster mouthing public mindmeet threats vituperatively but no Bottlenose fluked forward to apologise. Only two dolphins knew the culprit and neither would speak just then. A Guardian fluked immediately to bi-vector with Vorg. His wound was painful but not disabling. Nevertheless, he would need escort when the sharks vectored to this place of carnage. It should have been the Bottlenose responsible for the accident to take escort duty upon himself.

'Surely one dolphin must know of an error in confusion,' mindimaged many.

Gaze kept his knowledge to himself, wondering at how Bottlenose could injure Bottlenose... yet feel no disgrace. And for what purpose?

Karg derived minor pleasure in bitemarking his prey. His fish tasted particularly good.

'Final thirds of muster, shoal centre... Go!' came the command.

Bi-vector with Ardent, Gaze fluked forward. They were soon separated in the twisting turns chasing silvered panic. Gaze's reefside slipped. He had his fill... but became aware of the tiny mindscreams flitting in and out of his consciousness in a spiralling nightmare. The short, sharp mindimages were cold and white until a beaksnap changed them red then black.

Fish were cold and their minds lacked creativity.

There were instinctive calls; urgent demands to keep together. Unspoken was the realisation that it was time to give the predatorial toll and all in cold emotion.

Startled, mooncycles before that fishminds were accessible, Gaze felt that he might even be able to... No! Now was the wrong place. There was another...!

The reefside block slammed down.

The dolphins regrouped and the Podsherd was one.

Sharkdorsals were strike-vectoring upon fish, injured and concussed. Still the surface seethed. The Podsherd witnessed a gull and shark closing the same prey. The gull arrived a squawking moment before the gaping maw... disappeared with the fish in a twist of red. After that, the surface was crazed with fishfins, sharkfans, with the gulls at distance.

Dark, dazzling death held sway for moments more until the surface-spray settled to peace.

Closing darkwater, Gaze rejoined the familypod.

He had attended an Inventor on his return to the Storytellers' Caves. The imaging in mindmeet had been of using echo-return calls to sense density of objects and hidden hollowness; of camouflage techniques and choice of material appropriate to mask objects in a vicinity, and of various kinds of dolphin harness, ties and knots.

Gaze knew a second clue to the puzzle of the cave had been given:

'He who senses hollowness may find waterspace or air.'

The image had been repeated twice by Sinu, a practical Bottlenose whose cave had been compartmentalised tidiness... apart from a variety of cork-shapes and floating spheres which bobbed in a hollow space below the cave roof. There had been clamshells of a number of strange objects; piles of loose tie-material sorted in sizes, and odd fishtrap pieces in an off-shoot area. Specially prized had been some interlocking chain and a coil of bendable material lost by a Splitfluke.

Vorg had been largely disinterested - more concerned with a sense of injustice concerning the beakbite on his flukes. The pattern was punctured and torn, irregularly, in one flukefin, fitting the fact known by Gaze. When Vorg finned and fluked, there was a wavering vector which served to exaggerate his injury... his subconscious appeal for sympathy? Gaze knew it hurt a little but not in proportion to the visible signs. He also sensed that Vorg had missed both clues that lightwater.

Gape was bubbling with excitement over the fishmuster. Her teasing of Blue Spot had been delightful satisfaction... and she had begun to sense his mind touching hers, not only in terms of Guardian duty...

Mindmeet had begun to magnify into a different kind of awareness... She realised the verge of mindmerging maturity! It was a pity that her own buoyancy of spirit had made merging with Beak Spot's mind impossible - but she could begin to see the way! If she could mindmerge, that would be the occasion for...!

She fluketrembled anticipating... remembering their flanks touching... his fintouching restraint on her back when she was too rash...

Gape was lost in the future.

Gaze patterned concerning his own self-discoveries. Whatever had given rise to mindgrowth beyond the normal experience of the Podsherd, the pace of development was increasing. It was awesome - almost frightening... And Karg?

Karg was also a threat he needed to face!

And somewhere, there were dolphins suffering... Where? Why?

Flab breached alongside, her portly flesh never quite leaving water support. She reported her readiness to take Gape to the Nursery for a short period of suckling training.

Gale spoke to his son, 'It is time you were with other maturing males. Join in the games and remember, you most certainly need some deep-dive practice. Be off with you and join Bottlenoses of your season. Your dam and I will return before darkwater and both Gape and yourself will join us here.'

'We will see you later,' added Peen, seeking to contain her urgency to be alone with Gale.

Gape and Flab fluked towards the Nursery podlings.

Gaze finned obediently towards the male near-matures further along the reef. It was then he felt - almost heard - the pathetic mindscreams of a female dolphin dwindling in helplessness - beyond hope, beyond sanity. They were the sounds of a sorrowing spirit in solitude and terror... but where?

No other dolphin seemed aware...

Once more there was... a cry? Gaze slipped sufficient of his reefside block to reach out tentatively. He allowed the longest, thinnest tendril of consciousness to circumscan. He brushed across the Podsherd, largely content in congenial commune; the pods of young females, giggling, fanciful in suggestive tales; the Nursery Dams and the podlings, most of whom were at rest, and groups like the Guardians, vigorously moving a cork float in a passing game...

Nowhere was there any sign of that desolate, pain-wracked cry in the planes of present...

Unless... There! A mindscream further down the reef... Further... Within the reef!?

Despite his immaturity; contrary to training, Gaze vector-changed towards the possible source.

The Guardian, Gannet, meant to deter out-reef fluking without permission was spectator to a game and did not challenge Gaze as he dived through the lagoon entrance. It was an extremely rare lapse for which he would be reprimanded later by a furious Gale - or so it would appear.

Gaze kept his mindscan, a weaving tendril, locked to the reef where it angled from range, following a curve in the shelf.

Suddenly there was the blurred image of a squid!

Instinctively he withdrew his questing but then realised the squid was not watching him. The squid's full attention was on something else. With some trepidation, Gaze scanned an outranger thinner than the tip of the hermit crab's antenna...

A cry came again and a mindchuckle, harsh, gloating... The large squideye mirrored the carnal coupling of... Karg! The female was...

Gaze's heart was gripped by a force which attempted to tear it in two!

Fintwitching, four hundred dolphinspans away, his eyes widened and he flukethrashed the surface in agony... but...? It could not be happening... It was a Vision!

It was not... real! Gaze controlled his mind... Nerve cell by nerve cell, he assumed self-authority...

He fought to calm himself... heart beat was normal... but he still felt the shock of that chilling seizure which had all but overwhelmed him.

Stored in recall was an image - abhorrent, disgusting, sadistic... and the image of the squid! In the squid's eye, Gaze had seen everything... the reflection of perpetrated evil... the helpless suffering of a broken spirit. Karg had been unaware of an observer, so intent on inflicting pain, feeling the result.

Karg - the squid - had reached within the female to wrap two tentacles around the heart and strain to twist and tear it open. The nameless female had tried to flukethresh but the squid had her by the flanks and the bottlebeak, stretching her... holding her taut with compelling power.

It was the strength of the projected mindvision which had wracked Gaze. Absent from the event, he had shared the suffering...

And the suffering was now!

Karg was an Abomination!

Karg was more than malice... and no other Bottlenose would believe him. Gaze could say nothing without branding himself as different - sharing the same potential for good or evil.

The cry of the unknown female echoed through the spaces of empathy in his mind.

Sympathy was not enough! Something had to be done...

By all that was good in the world of waterspace, it could not continue! She... she wanted the freedom to deep-dive and die...

A quiet flanker, finstirring and wallowing on the open seaside of the reef, subjugated self and began to think of another...

Gaze sounded close to the reef. No dolphin witnessed his vectoring at depth through the expanse of waterspace...

No Bottlenose witnessed his airsnatch many dolphinspans at sea - or the other sounding and the strange metamorphosis further out - further out, beyond the range of Karg's awareness...

What was about to happen had not happened before.

Out of necessity, a new young force in warmstream waterspace was seeking allies... seeking assistance far larger than himself...

Gaze checked and mindscanned; first the tendrils of contact... slowly magnifying to blasts of mindscanning location. He felt the heat of anger within but he was cold, calculating. He would not have dared before... There were the minds he sought!

He made a pinging call, lower and more penetrating in tone.

The return-call seemed puzzled.

Adjusting tone and pitch, Gaze flowed along the mindcontact to fix his reference. He moved within the distant mind...

Here were mindimages he needed! Here, the strange ally...

He explored the distant mind and found it hungry; found it to be more instinctive, rigid in patterning... needfully ferocious!

He registered calls and responses; codes of behaviour, and the conditioning of tactics...

Gaze summoned assistance - signalled the promise of prey...

In apprehension, he waited...

He waited.

The next pinging call came at substantially closer range. Gaze shuddered at what he was about to do...

Four orca-dorsals appeared above distant wave billows. Four echoes returned to his identification call, loud, low noises from four large shapes.

The killer-whales were closing!

Visioning, Gaze made his own sail-like dorsal stand proud marker. He appeared to flukeslap the water with a loud report, mindvision directional to the orcas alone. Karg... must not see...

The real form of Gaze was surrounded by an adult orca! A large bulk distinctively marked with white blotching and the tall dorsal a magnification of his own.

Gaze was a male, killer whale - if he could sustain the mindvision and control his own fear!

The orcas were nearly there... and, Karg had not yet left the hidden cave containing the female dolphin...

Another shocking squid-image served only to fuel the cold rage the young flanker was feeling. There had to be an end for Karg and the... the female, but it had to be an accident.

Gaze would have to join the pod of orcas, maintaining a short-range vision of a form larger than himself and more aggressive. Rapidly, he would have to learn the networking of conduct in the alien pod... How to behave in assuming control...

Karg was delighted. This lightwater he had marked his prey for the morrow, beaksnapped Vorg's flukes and briefly sensed the bewilderment and outrage. The pleasure had been short-lived but he could wait for the finale.

He had not returned to the Podsherd waterspace but had sounded to follow the reef towards the Pleasure Cave. He needed a minor climax to make his waiting more tolerable... Anticipating a peak of enjoyment was not enough in itself.

She was there as usual when the airslab lifted, finstirring weakly at the furthest corner of the waterspace. Karg compared this female with what she had been... He felt no shame for her denigration of spirit - only distaste for what she was. It was time she disappeared for sharkfood.

The near-mature female, flirting in the company of a Guardian during the fishmuster, had had far more spirit. What pleasure to restrain that youthful vigour? Perhaps he...!

For the first time, Karg experimented with an additional image to that of the projected squid in the tunnel behind. The cowering, finstirring shadow of femininity was to be transformed into the near-mature he had seen with the Guardian who had a spot on his beak. Karg concentrated. He was trying an extension to visioning power. Not once did the squid shimmer or blur... but he realised he would need to sacrifice some mindpower to change... to change...

It was done!

Just as the captive once had, an image of Gape was at the far end of the inreef pool, finstirring provocatively, smiling encouragingly. The image shimmered, altered... Karg concentrated, projected with more intensity... and hypnotised himself.

He closed with the image which was Gape... and so did the tentacles of the squid behind...

It was delightful! It was a new peak in his power. Each spasm of the coupling was magnificent - accentuated by the youthfulness of the image. He felt her squirming, involuntarily twitching at each insertion of mindlimb.

At the moment of climax, he had voided his own bowels, sharing the terror of the image while he twisted its heart. In the heat of desire, Karg wanted more. The image held hard, tangible... real.

The image was too weak to take the two fish he offered... but she still smiled, provoking his lust, demanding more.

They coupled again and Karg took his time...

The five orcas were vectoring at an oblique angle of approach to the reef! The Guardians were directing the whole Podsherd into the lagoon, as prearranged, towards extensive shallows.

Gale and Peen hastened to rejoin. Peen could detect Flab's urgent mindmeet calls. Gape was with her. Would Peen come to assist with the podlings?

No, she did not know where Gaze was. She thought he was with the males of his season. Please hurry...

'Go Peen. Forget other things. Flab needs your assistance. I must go to the Storytellers' Caves. Gaze will be alright. Some Guardians are escorting the Podsherd. I will make enquiries,' said Gale, finslapping her tenderly on the flank and turning at speed to a newvector.

Peen swallowed her anxiety and fluked for Flab. At times of stress, all Bottlenosess knew their duties. Gaze had been told what was expected.

Gale arrived at Guardianmuster, checked his Pod of Guardians. They were present except for the three allocated for escort duties.

He reported readiness in mindmeet to Tinu, Master Guardian, receiving gruff acknowledgement. Orders to send his Pod to guard a lagoon entrance followed quickly and the specific request that he send three Guardians as out-reefers to watch for the pod of orcas.

He sounds very worried, thought Gale.

On Guardstation, Gale despatched Beak Spot, Esu and Mimic seaside of the reef with orders to watch and report the first sign of the killer-whales' presences. They were not to attempt any engagement but 'report back immediately to this lagoon entrance'.

Beak Spot and his two companions nodded gravely - were gone, through the lagoon entrance and into an anxious, fretful swell. The seaspace seemed apprehensive...

Beak Spot fluked out-reef a hundred dolphinspans; Esu and Mimic swung left and right reefedge the same distance. All three finstirred, wallowing backs awash in wavesurge. Each Guardian ranged for the first whispers of approach. An outsea Observer Guardian, Crest Spray, had brought the urgent news of five orca sails and 'about the same number of large echo-returns' vectoring towards the reef! The alarm had spread, mindmerge to mindmerge at speed... followed by mindmeet orders that the whole Podsherd fluke for shallow water of less than half a dolphinspan.

Gale was not the only Guardian puzzled by Crest Spray's inexactitude of 'about the same number of large echo-returns.' Tinu was equally disturbed. No Observer Guardian would make an unclear report unless he was doubtful or in panic... and Crest Spray was a reliable Observer, respected as being clear, cool and accurate.

Tinu joined Gale's Pod accompanied by Crest Spray...

'This lagoon entrance is likely to be the nearest available if the orcas wish to gain access to the lagoon. Sharks are one thing Gale; orcas are... The last incursion of our waterspace was many seasons ago. It was a bloody affair. They are unpredictable if the bloodlust comes upon them.

'I am puzzled. I need to know the exact number of their pod. There is something you should know - an anomaly in Crest Spray's report. He is a good Observer. I trust his judgement and the accuracy of his observations.'

Tinu paused. Gale was astonished at what he heard next.

'Before fluking to the Podsherd, Crest Spray noted four large echo-returns equating to orcas. Slightly in front, and calling loudly, was a fifth, smaller echo-return... about the size appropriate to a maturing dolphin. The mindmeet calls were not dolphin but in the lower-pitch of orcan. From a wavesurge, he did catch the briefest glimpse of five killer-whale dorsals. He cannot explain the contradiction in his report to me... yet, I have no reason to doubt him.

'Whatever pod is closing our waterspace, the number is uncertain. We must be prepared for some strange phenomena. Keep this to yourself but I want a Pod of Guardians here with the sharpest scanning skills in dolphinhistory.'

The mindmerge message ended. Tinu was gone to the Podsherd. Crest Spray remained by Gale's side. They mindmerged:

'My mindwaves cracked his reef tonight, Gale. I know what I scanned and saw,' came Crest Spray's mindvoice.

He sounded almost apologetic but Gale knew him well.

If Crest Spray reported something, it was as he said. He did not embroider fact; he had clear opinions and his integrity was doubted by only the foolish. Doubters had paid for unwillingness to trust him before now.

'Beak Spot is out there. Fin bi-vector with him. This Pod trusts your scanning and your eyes,' Gale said.

They fintouched and separated.

Gape, with the podlings in shallow waterspace, had tried to assist a burdened Flab. Peen was with the more elderly Doe who lacked the stamina to keep up with the lively bustle of youth in the excitement of the unusual. Peen had fast realised that watching two podlings was Doe's limit. Her mindmeet commands needed firmer expression than creaking mindvoice and withering frame could muster in authority.

Peen had no time for anything other than striving to maintain order, calm a podling here and stem the cries of a calf there. All the females were stretched. There had to be quietness. There had to be nothing but a whispering sea on the shore. Again she warned those around that noise travelled far.

She was forced to press a female calf below water against the shelving slope until the giggling stopped and she could let her up. She flukeslapped another twice.

There was silence.

And Gape kept silent about two horrible visions that had crept insidiously into her mind. Being with a male could not be like that! She was being foolish...

The large male orca surged closer to the reef ahead.

A sharp command came to wait. He sounded. They waited, for the first time questing for the promised food source but the reef blocked most echo-returns...

The orca beneath was also echo-sounding but... the sound was different... higher-pitched, not orcan... more like a dolphin? The sea shuffled restlessly around their sails, slapped impatiently against their sides and shivered before their jaws.

Gaze pinged and listened to the echo-return, the words of an Inventor in his mind...

'He who senses hollowness may find waterspace or air.'

There! An entrance to the reef! Not as deep as he had thought. Part obscured by coral and kelp was the entrance he sought! Gaze had little time. He needed to hurry whilst striving to be as heavy-fluked as he could.

He needed a distraction. One large male would be more than sufficient...

Three of the killer-whales heard echo-returns from a shoal of squid, deeper and behind them, out to sea. They swung away to sound and circle the promised food source, sure the remaining two would close the trap.

Two orcas dived. Drifting weed tentacles were brushed aside as they entered the reef through coral and kelp...

Karg heard the whisper of a pinging call. A stranger dolphin was searching for the reef entrance!

He had been trying to force a fish, held in a squid tentacle, into the mouth of the captive... Who?

Only one dolphin would wish to seek him out...

Vorg! Vorg was looking for him!

It took only moments for Karg to decide. The captive was too weak to leap the coral wall to the pool beyond. Watching the entrance would not matter. She could stay for now. The squid would meet Vorg! Yes...

What a day of pleasure!

It was earlier than he had intended but the present was so opportune. Karg gaped. Water dripped from twisted teeth. Soon it would be blood.

He chuckled hoarse sounds in mind and throat...

It took him moments to fin through the tunnel. He wasted a few moments in diving to retrieve the fishspiking shaft he had acquired from the cave of the old fool, Ardent. He was ready.

He sent the image of the squid questing outwards beyond the coral wall, the deep pool, through the kelp curtain and coral screen. He knew Vorg was out there...

'Vorg! Vorg, beware of the squid. I'm here! Through the kelp, quickly!' he mindscreamed.

Moments passed. Karg repeated his call to hurry, his mindvoice urgent, insisting...

'By Wanderer... I've never managed anything so big,' came the mindvoice of Vorg. 'Where are you, Karg?'

Then strange questions...

'Did you lose control of your own mindvision? Were you not strong enough? It was slightly unnerving Karg, but I fluked straight through your squid. Did you imagine I would really be so terrified I would lose control of my own mind?'

This was not quite the plan Karg had wished to spring. A tentacle... two tentacles pierced the kelp curtain questing for Vorg. The mind of Karg reached beyond the coral wall... touched the mind of Vorg...

Ah! There was trepidation... There was the birth of terror! Karg wanted that terror! He would gorge himself on the fear of Vorg!

The tentacles sought the flukes he had bitten earlier. There! He visioned grasping the flukes, then sliding the other tentacle around Vorg's head and towing the flanker in position beneath the coral wall where he would enter waterspace, downward in his dive. Vorg was paralysed with fear... motionless, stretched rigid.

The foolish young Bottlenose was reefsiding in his mind as if to block out the image of the squid...

He could not! Karg gripped the fishspiking shaft in his beak. He could see the exact spot in his visioning... The exact spot; the same place Finwarp had been spiked.

He fluked forward and leapt, arcing over the coral wall. The spiking shaft was a gleam of solid light before his mind... This was joy!

His visioning shimmered as he cleared the wall... changed!

Vorg was not there...! Or the squid...!

Incredibly, in slow-motion, he was falling towards the gaping maw of a killer-whale! A young Bottlenose - not Vorg? Gaze! - was by the orca's side!

Instinctively, Karg flukethreshed in the air.

He twisted in airflight, trying to change direction, already screaming in body and mind...

In so doing, he lost his only chance of survival.

The fishspiking shaft would have entered the mouth, the throat of the gaping orca... but it was loose in his beak, off striking-vector... useless.

Karg's flanks collided with the open jaws, the force of the impact pushing them below the surface. Water boiled at collision point. Already beginning to fluke on entry, he was almost clear... A second orca blocked escape!

The vision shimmered, changed into Gaze... just as real orcan jaws closed around him!

Through the pain was the voice. A quick voice as penetrating as the teeth which were clamped in his flesh...

'Your vision could not kill me any more than mine could kill you! Visions are not enough, only mindthreats. It is time to feel
a suffering of self, Karg!'

Karg still heard the voice as he was thrown... as he impacted against the sharpness of coral... as he wallowed side-upwards on the surface... as his blood stained the water.

It was impossible... but the agony was real.

'Your mind has some power, Karg... but you never quantified mine. Now you must give pleasure to others.'

He was seized again! Dazed, he was powerless... could not resist as he was hauled through the curtain of kelp, scraped against rock and coral. Gaze... the killer-whale... made strange low-pitched singing noises out towards three other sail-like, orca dorsals!

They vectored rapidly towards them. Mindvoices, harsh in rapid orcan exchanges, were ringing in Karg's head. They changed into a cacophony of hungry, screeching.

He knew he was dead...

'But my friends must first play a game, Karg. Hunters must enjoy the sport. It cannot be too easy. Orcas frolic before the feast. Take pleasure in the game!'

...Still the image of Gaze shimmered within the centre of the large male who seemed to control all events.

The three orcas had not found the shoal of squid. The sounds had disappeared but the summoning call to prey was still strong, insistent.

The prey was a mature dolphin!

Hunger fluked through the sea-swell with gaping maws.

Karg relived his dive towards death more than twenty times... Progressive weariness overtook him... Each time he smashed against a sea, which was hard with flukes and teeth, there was pain... more pain... the voice of Gaze... and finally a rending of flesh... the tearing of his heart from within by unimaginable forces...

At last the crimson surface of the sea settled. Four orca dorsals vectored to the open waterspace away from the reef. A fifth orca sounded to be seen no more.

On Guardian station, off-reef at three hundred dolphinspans, Crest Spray was the first to pick up the weak echo-return of three orcas heading out-reef beyond the reefangle to the right of the lagoon entrance. Beak Spot's actions were immediate - earning him later commendation from Tinu himself - for he directed Esu closer to the lagoon entrance, moved Crest Spray to replace Mimic right of lagoon entrance and finned cautiously along the reefedge to the distant angle, bi-vector with Mimic.

If there had been a flaw in his plan, it was that Crest Spray would have been able to make clearer distinctions in that which Beak Spot and Mimic would soon observe. However, Crest Spray was on good station to give early warning to Gale's Guardians at lagoon entrance and Esu was able to scan other directions unimpeded by blocking effects, remaining as unexposed as possible.

Within the lagoon, the Podsherd was silent with the nervousness of uncertainty. Each roll of wavesurge into the shallow waterspace might bring death. The Guardians of the escort were the only moving dorsals. They were finstirring gently and quietly scanning the short range. Pulses of quiet clicks and pings were unnerving. The podlings of the Nursery were very still...

Peen's authority had been stamped on many more than one or two. The Nursery Matrons knew Doe's replacement before very long...

Gale finned quietly, checking Pod positions. Tinu, appeared at his side.

'There is a Pod of Guardians at the second entrance - with two out-reefers and an Observer in position.

'The remaining Guardians are across the lagoon as reserve. If you have an incursion of the waterspace, let them through before you engage. Half of the reserve will engage from the island side if your Pod begin striking-vectors. I dare not commit the whole Guardian force at once,' mindmerged the Master Guardian.

There was a pause. The silence needed filling with action or other imaging.

Tinu said, 'No individual acts by any Bottlenose, Gale. Pairs commitment only... By Wanderer, of course you've ordered that! My apologies.'

'Yes, Tinu.' There was nothing else Gale could say.

'Nothing from your out-reefers?'

'Beak Spot and Mimic are investigating possible echo-returns moving out-reef beyond the reefangle - only three of them,' replied Gale.

There was silence again.

'Very well, Gale. I will return to the reserves,' said Tinu and was quietly gone, making minimal disturbance to the water surface.

Nearing the reefangle, Beak Spot and Mimic slowed further. They dared not ping in echo-location at the closer range. Three sail-like dorsals could be seen... but on squid-herding stations? The huge dorsals wavered a while.

Beak Spot sensed a growing impatience and puzzlement.

Suddenly the dorsals were in motion... heading across their waterfront. Two other sails were moving, more slowly, converging!

Beak Spot was wondering whether or not to return and raise the alarm when Mimic said, in urgent mindmerge,

'One of the orcas has a dolphin!'

In horror, they both watched as the orcas, with one exception, tossed the unfortunate victim into airspace!

Many times the victim slammed down into the water... only to be seized by another orca and tossed again.

Initially, there were incredibly strong mindscreams of the dolphin's distress but they were blocked out by an even stronger stress-image of teeth and blood... savage tearing!

The rending of flesh ceased.

It was finished.

Four sail-like dorsals vectored for open waterspace; one orca sounded.

In alarm, Beak Spot pinged in echo-location. The echo-return, close to reefedge - was smaller than expected?

Where was the orca!? He pinged again.

There was no equiponderate return to that of an orca... but the smaller echo-return equated with... another dolphin of maturing stature?

Mimic pinged and confirmed.

Beak Spot had no alternative course of action. He despatched Mimic to report the danger seemed over but to strangely request further assistance. Mimic could not fluke away fast enough.

Beak Spot caught his half mindimaging of, 'May the White Dolphins protect us! My head must have a worm in it! I am...' and Mimic was gone.

Finning cautiously, pinging as he went, Beak Spot progressed towards the disappearance of the smaller echo-return he thought he had heard.

Gaze passed through the kelp curtain again. He had little hesitation in taking the leap over the coral wall for he was aware of many things which the young are generally shielded from or slow to learn. The contact with Karg's mind had been distressful... shocking... but there had been revelations. That sordid, sadistic entity had held many secrets...

Karg's visioning of Gape had been the beginning of access for Gaze, through to other passages of knowledge. There had been a cold logic in the insanity; many sea-shadows behind the reefside which had crumbled. Karg's mind had revealed much before a curtain of red had drawn down and his imaging had dwindled to greyness and darkness.

Gaze knew of the death of Karg's dam - the name of a murdered Storyteller - the route to the Pleasure Cave - even the solution to the puzzle of Wanderer's Cave. More, he knew the interior of both Caves. He even knew her name...

Finning through the passage, down past the airslab entrance seal and up again to the cave, Gaze could think of no other way to present himself to her... other than to be as himself...

She heard him finning through the passage!

If only she had the strength or the will to have finned, to fin outside... Dimly she perceived 'outside'... The points of light at darkwater and the fintouching presence of others who did not bring pain... A rain shower on an exposed back feeling like a gentle prickling. Rain droplets entering the waterspace... The dawn of the lightwater with the sun breaching slowly and majestically... How she used to wonder where the sun had deep-dived to?... The wind swaying the Podsherd of dorsals...

He was finning into the pool!

Finstirring weakly, she turned to face the horror of the pale squidorbs... Perhaps, this time she could die...?

There was no squid!

Karg was not there - another! A near-mature in the growth spurt towards maturity... Where was Karg? Where..?

It was another illusion! Karg had once been beautiful but he had lied. Karg could not be trusted. She saw things that were not there for he could change what she saw. She knew not if what she saw was real. Only Karg was real... and the squid... and the suffering!

'It' would change to Karg and she could not resist. She waited for the horror and the pain to come...

Images of 'outside' kept filling her mind!

Gentle images... soothing. Only slowly did she begin to hear the voice, soaking through the dryness of her mind.

'I am Gaze. You are Cyrene... Do not be afraid... Now is the time to leave.'...?

'He' was being just as cruel. She was too weak. The power of youth had deserted her. She did not know the way to... to the end of the passage... to the end... end of...

Oh, the cruellest of voices!

'He' was finning closer! If only 'he' was real, as gentle as 'his' voice... 'His'... voice...

'He' had stopped. Finstirring, 'he' was watching.

Always watching with eyes cold and lusting for her. Cold, squid eyes that filled her head. She would not look at 'his' eyes... would not... 'His' eyes...

'His' eyes were different! This was not Karg!

'I am Gaze; you are Cyrene. Please, may I touch you?'

Karg would never ask to touch her. Karg grasped her; grated her against the gravel of his mind, the hardness of his limbs... She watched him, whoever he was...

Gaze finned slowly to her side. Their fins touched; their flanks were close together.

The touch was gentle, soothing!

The touch was warmth of the sun arcing down to darkwater. There was the sense of Podsherd protection...?

There was peace...

Unable to resist, her flank drifted apart but her forefin remained in contact with his... Her head drifted sideways to touch his. If this young dolphin wanted her, she would not... could not resist...

'Cyrene, I have come to take you outside. You are free to find the peace you need. You know it is time to fin the passage. No, the squid is no more.'

He did not want her for flesh-fervour... He was really trying to help her! He was assuring her it was over. Three times he had used her name...

I am Cyrene, she thought. I used to be so proud of my name. My friends used to call me by name... but now they would not know me. I am changed...

She did not think it strange when Gaze mindmerged; only wondered at his gentleness and the soothing quality of his imaging. She allowed herself to be led through the entrance and down along the passage... to resurface in a shallow pool; to airsnatch below the coral wall...

Cyrene was prematurely old. The ravages of Karg, inadequacy of diet and the shadow world in which she had survived had made her pale ghost of former self. Gaze doubted she could make the leap across the coral wall. Not so difficult from this side... but he needed assistance...

It was then he heard a Bottlenose's echo-locating ping from beyond the kelp curtain.

'Trust me Cyrene. Wait here, away from the coral wall. I am fetching help.'

His voice was command with the added weight of total empathy. She finned mutely to obey.

Leaping the coral and entering the waterspace screened by the kelp - the place of Karg's confrontation with death and unforeseen power - Gaze pinged identification and passed through the curtain. He knew Beak Spot's call at once... and more, that he was a dolphin he could trust.

The sudden mindmerging with Gaze astonished Beak Spot, but only for moments. He would never remember what happened next.

Beak Spot would never remember how he finned with Gaze beneath a helpless female. How they surged as a trio towards a coral wall and leapt over to waterspace beneath. How they parted the kelp to assist her to open waterspace. Or keeping station at the reefangle, waiting for the young Bottlenose to return...

Several hundreds of dolphinspans beyond the shelf, above deepwater which fell below to darkness, Gaze finned flank to flank with Cyrene. He was careful to fin on her blindside so that she could see as much as possible of the real waterspace she had craved.

She could see the distant greyness of the islandmass; the whiteline of the seasurge and reef at very late light-water.

Recall imaging her dam... her sire, the fire of feelings she once had known was clearer, more certain.

Cyrene knew he was helping her. A light rainsquall swept over their wallowing backs... the drops tingling dully. Once the rain had felt sharp, fresh... exciting. Her feelings... her sensitivity was sluggish now...

There was still the sound she enjoyed... Psst, psst, pssst... and the sudden seething in the squall fading to... kerlop, klop, plop...

And more music in the sea... the sounds of the distant Podsherd...

of relief and happiness, joy and peace. She could hear the pings of identification... dams and calves.

Cyrene wished she had had a calf...

There were other calls even happier below... So welcoming... Such a promise of security...!

Separating from Gaze, she found a strength in curiosity to dive and ping identification below...

Inwardly, she laughed; the ping-pattern was her name!

There was no echo-return to an echo-locating ping but she heard the acknowledgement of her name! The other dolphins were deep but rising!

Several white dolphins seemed to appear.

It took several finstrokes to realise she had seen them with both eyes!

In joy, she rose to airsnatch!

Gaze was still there... Gaze, beautiful and patient...

Beyond him, one of the white dolphins breached!

She finned to Gaze but could express no imaging... could only stroke his side with her forefin. Cyrene felt his touch in body and mind; felt him reach out his love in mindmerge.

There were more white dolphins!

She had to dive to join them! They were so welcoming; so joyful!

Cyrene took several short, shallow airsnatches - not filling her lungs - in the manner of dolphinkind preparing for a deep-dive... a deep-dive... the deep-dive...

She knew it was now and was grateful.

Gaze watched her sound; knew her next airsnatch would be deep-down... that she would not rise. The sharks would find her...

Over visual left, Gaze saw a white shape sounding. This time he did not ping identification or seek an echo-return...

It was not his time.

Chapter Five

BEYOND THE PODSHERD

Bveak Spot felt no sense of anything unusual as the near-mature finned along reefedge and joined him.

He understood the need to shelter within the reef when the orcas had been detected. They finned in bi-vector to join Crest Spray, who was feeling discomfited as they approached.

Was it possible that this young dolphin was the source of the strange fifth echo-return he had sensed? Why had the orcas not attacked him? Where had the fifth orca sail gone? Crest Spray dealt with facts. The fact that he had seen a fifth dorsal and heard no echo-return from the expected mass beneath - only that proportionate to a maturing dolphin - bothered him. Not until he was a season older would Crest Spray begin to guess the truth. For now, he would report that the threat of killer-whale incursion of their waterspace had diminished.

The Podsherd had seen strange phenomena before... Two seasons ago, a hardside had dropped some waste in deepwater far out-reef and four Guardians had died... poisoned? Yet they had eaten nothing unusual nor been in contact with any strange objects. Spotted cousins had brought the news of their deaths having seen two Guardians take the deep-dives. For several light-waters afterwards, some of the newsbearers had been sick themselves but had recovered. A dolphin had to accept that one did not, could not understand everything.

Young Gaze, son of Gale, seemed innocent and his account plausible enough. The next lightwater, Crest Spray would seek the curtain of kelp and the cave he described... but discreet observation of Gaze would be prudent. Gale was the likely candidate for Master Guardian before long. Tinu was getting older...

Gaze read his mind but remained silent. He would not tamper with recall too much. He realised the need to be careful with this wise Observer - also, that here was a Bottlenose who could be trusted implicitly.

The three dolphins finned towards the lagoon entrance.

Both Guardians made their reports to Gale, finstirred respectfully and awaited the storm to break over Gaze.

Before the mindlashing began, Gale ordered, 'Guardians off-watch! Grey Band, duty-watch on this lagoon entrance. This darkwater Podsherd patrol report to Tinu. The rest of you join the Podsherd... and tell them to stop worrying.

'Take your rest Guardians... and thank you.'

Not one Guardian made any remark. Gale, was too respected; held too much in awe to risk smart mindmeet asides.

No Guardian wished to share in the predicament of Gaze. The law of the Podsherd was that no Bottlenose finned the out-reef waterspace alone, unless a Storyteller. Only a Voyager fluked long dolphinspans in isolation.

Gale's mind coloured a darkline of storm on a windswept sea. The billows of ragesurge were magnifying. Only the astute observer of dolphin-personality would have seen the benevolence of sunshine behind such a lowering horizon... or a mindreader...

The mindstorm broke.

Gale was half-through mindgnawing any self-respect Gaze might have had with an oppression of images and gusts of gale-force emotion when he realised, in grudging admiration, that his son was unflinching. Puzzled, he asked that which he should have asked at the onset...

'Why were you fluking out-reef, against training, Gaze?'

Three bottlebeaks were pointed towards the flanker as Gale, Beak Spot and the watchful Crest Spray, awaited the reply. His answer would be measured, qualified. This was an appraisal more severe than any assessment by a sire.

The pause was only slight. Not enough for a Bottlenose to be seeking prevarication but enough to equate with the difficulty of finding the imaging. The answer tallied with Beak Spot's report of an unknown dolphin having died out-reef in a terrible way, events unseen and undetected by Crest Spray...

'I was following a Storyteller. His flukingpassage was odd. I was curious - then the orcas came. He died out there. He was torn to pieces. The orcas must have been very hungry.

'I know I was in the wrong waterspace. I apologise, my sire. My dam is right for curiosity can kill.'

Gale was dumbstruck but his sense of leadership rescued him.

'Beak Spot, give my respects to Ardent. Ask him to muster the Storytellers. We need to know if any Storyteller is... missing. I want you back here as quickly as possible.

'Crest Spray, fetch Tinu.'

Both Guardians were gone. Crest Spray still had a nagging uncertainty but the pieces of the coral appeared to be assembling.

Gale finturned to his son.

'Not every dolphin witnesses death in savagery whilst so young, Gaze. How do you feel?'

'I felt cold my sire. I feel cold now... but I am glad I am here. I am sorry to have caused you anxiety - even moreso that my dam may be beside herself. I try not to let you down.'

'You sheltered in the reef? You will show me this place. Not now, in the lightwater. Beyond the reefangle? Hidden by kelp? It will be useful to the Guardians to know of such a place.

'Ah, here are Tinu and Crest Spray.'

Within moments, Gale appraised Tinu of his son's story.

The Master Guardian was closely attentive.

It was agreed that, the following lightwater, a Guardian pair would accompany Gale and Gaze to investigate. Crest Spray volunteered, thinking still of the fifth orca, visualising a hidden, waiting menace.

Beak Spot arrived. A Storyteller was missing! Karg had not answered the muster-roll.

There were moments of grave silence...

Gaze learned how to use an economy of truth.

Blue Anemone had lain with her son in the shallows and watched the passing of the crisis. She had done little to assist the other females beyond volunteering to keep station with the near-mature males.

The comings and goings of Guardians and the flurries of movement at the major lagoon entrance had been interesting - but only so far as events figured the magnetic presence of Gale. He was a Bottlenose with whom she had not coupled. She coveted him from a distance, sought always to intersect his flukingvector... but his eyes were hypnotised by that seacow, Peen. The Guardians were generally good in flesh-fervour, certainly better than most Storytellers. There was one Storyteller she would never couple with again!

Flesh-fervour drive, strong in some Bottlenoses, was marked in this female. Despite the fear in the shallows, she still finned in currents of passion and need. Her faith in the capacities of the Guardians was unshakeable.

Blue Anemone was conscious of the flanks of Vorg beside her. His flesh was firm and warm. Unseen in the crowded waterspace, she began to finstroke his belly... It was not uncommon for dam to offer to couple with son, as in the old way before Wanderer... before the new teachings of Clerics in which she placed no credence...

Vorg saw Gape in the shallows, the sister of Gaze...

He had not paid much attention to Gaze in the Nursery training. Too intent on maintaining high-status with the larger, more aggressive of the podlings, his pursuit of pleasure and proof that he could dominate, impose his will, had led him through differing flukingpassages with more likely competition. Gaze was not large for his age, just 'average' in the hierarchy of youthful assessment.

His sister, though... Now there was a female worth cultivating! Just on the brink of mindmerging maturity, Vorg was conscious of many males assessing the time to make an approach. He had begun the foreplay of flesh-fervour with a few near-mature females, responding to their giggling suggestiveness, but not really following through. In the manner of dolphinkind, there had been other ways of self-gratification in mindplaying with images of future couplings in his head. Gape had often been one of those images...

He felt himself aroused now, watching from a distance. It was then he became conscious of his dam finstirring, finstroking his belly... nearing the red place of urgency that was a growing demand!

Only semi-conscious of the decision, Blue Anemone radiated the mindmerging image that she and Vorg should find a quiet cove when the alarm was over. With questing fin-touching, it was pleasing to feel the firmness of her flanker's coupling member in his pouch as a promise of pleasure... She realised he was too young for mind-merging... unless?... He was trying to reply!

She was obviously the first to mindmerge with him!

His images were shimmering slightly with the ardency of the initiate... but they were remarkably strong ... and then faded as he lost the delicacy of mindcontrol he needed to maintain. She waited. It was important a young male found the way himself...

A strong flash of mindlight swept her. Too strong, it was a pulse of desire and need. She picked out excitement and joy; numerous images of lustful fancy. He was maturing and his mindmerging was a beam of hotness and expectancy!

Blue Anemone was titilated. Coupling with the young males in the first throes of mindmerging facility, excited, challenged her. Images rushed through joined minds too quickly to savour. In the past, it had been like trying to flukeslap the lightning which scythed the sea... too quick, too electric. But young male energy constrained was almost inexhaustible, prolific, dynamic! There was great, great pleasure after containing the storm, to goad it to frenzy again... and again...

She finstirred, fintouched beneath his chest, waiting.

Recognising a sustaining image of a female dolphin... Gape, daughter of Gale... she beaksmiled. So, it seemed her son found the daughter of that Guardian interesting and was enchanted. Well, she would train him in her practised ways of flesh-fervour... and, perhaps, play a delightful imaging game for herself, that he was... he...

A voice in her mind was saying, 'You brought me to the waterspace, a place of fun and beauty. You are beautiful still. Are you going to give me more pleasure? At last I can mindmerge! Now I need to learn more. There is much to learn in myself and of other... other things.'

He had found the way! Later, he would discover so much more. Vorg felt her flanks tremble against him as he, in turn, finswept her beneath the surface from chest to that secret place...

The alarm was over for now. The Guardians had prohibited all out-reef flukingpassages until an inspection at next lightwater. The Podsherd regrouped into family and friendship pods, lagoon centre. The darkwater Guardians were already established in patrol routine.

Gaze was with Peen and Gape, who was idly finstirring and imaging of Beak Spot. It had been an eventful light-water; they were not always as exciting. Peen had made her feelings known to Gaze in unequivocal terms. He had regretted his behaviour, apologised profoundly for fluking out-reef unaccompanied and appeared so admonished that Peen had finally relented. Gale would have been hard-pressed to withstand the mindgnawing to which Gaze was subjected without some form of retaliation, she thought. Gaze submitted meekly.

Eventually, finstroking his side gently, Peen was surprised to find him asleep. Well, she thought, events were bound to catch up on him...

In a cove on the flank of the island, away from the slumbering Podsherd, Vorg was satisfying a hunger. His dam had expected the boiling breakers, the demanding surge and ebb in the rapid pursuit of pleasure.

Fingrasping the sidewalls of his chest, she had kept her movements tightly controlled as he had used the pressure of water beneath his back and flukes to give impulsion in his urgency. She knew she could harness the storm... but not this first time... not... this... first... He climaxed.

She was swept by a mindmerge image of great intensity. Blue Anemone recognised the female Gape... but was flattered rather than disturbed. Her son surfaced and airsnatched.

'That was good! I enjoyed that,' came his excited voice.

Typical, thought Blue Anemone. Young Bottlenoses were so self-centred when it came to the first time! So caught up in the need to prove their maturity that the female was nothing more than a receptacle - not a willing partner with equal expectation of reward.

'Vorg, you were too quick, too insistent. You spent so much time enjoying the physical experience, you forgot to elaborate it with pleasing mindmerging images. You can heighten the experience by opening your mind. Physically you prove everything works for you... but you were missing out... and so was I.

'You have a strength in your imaging which you suppressed just now. You lost sight of other ways of pleasure because your blood was racing hot. It is often that way the first time. Now you will listen and be taught. You have a good teacher if you will hear and become a breeze and not a storm.'

His silence was not sullenness... although she knew he was smarting with the realisation that he had not totally satisfied her. A dam had to be so careful in what she said to the young male, son.

He was reefsiding now... probably running through every image in mindmerge. His mind was electric and deep.

She reached out to finsweep his chest, belly...

'Let us go to a slightly different place, Vorg. Come with me,' she said, her voice in his mind husky, seductive ... a rich, warm mellow...

The smooth rock-cleft was admirable. Her back fitted neatly into the support. The wavesurge was a steady rise and fall in the cleft. Vorg, head and beak clear of the surface, was watching...

'You are of the waterspace, Vorg. It is a place of freedom and pleasure. Waterspace provides all your needs if you know how to use it. Come closer. Your lesson begins now,' said Blue Anemone.

Beak to beak, they fintouched to arousal. He was less urgent, more controlled. The reefside in his mind was impenetrable but she knew he was learning.

'Do not labour so hard, Vorg. Use the rise and fall of wavesurge... aahhh... and try to use your im... aahh... imaging. Do not try to force...

the... aaahh. That is much better,' she said, slowly image-building the beak and face of Gale on the surface of her mind.

No dolphin in Vorg's short experience had ever made him doubt himself. His dam had not insulted him deliberately. In her selfish way, she was trying to help him... but an insult had registered. Vorg would play, for now, but unexpected images were building behind his reefside. His dam would know the power he was discovering within himself. Whatever rogue gene had been within his sire was about to reassert as far darker than the evil that had been Karg...

Vorg concentrated. He was the force of maturity; he was the force of flesh in Gale. It was Gale that rose to wavelift thrusting within his dam. It was Gale who part withdrew. Gale who transfixed her, rubbed his bottlebeak against hers and nipped her faceflesh with teasing snips... Her idol pinned her forefins against her sides...

Blue Anemone was in the seawrack of surfside passion. With the strength of the imaging radiating from Vo... Ah, Gale... she climaxed once, but it was not over!

The billows stretched for hundreds of dolphinspans, rising and falling... rising and falling for an age of waterspace. In weariness, joy built again. Only dimly did she perceive this was abnormal; that her peaks of enjoyment were becoming exhausting. The pressure of her son seemed crushing; the cleft, a giant clam-shell.

She began to cry out, clicking beaksnapping distress. Vorg was tiring her! He was untiring...

Her mindscream was what he wanted! It came... and only then did the rock-cleft seem to release its hold.

The lightwater was not as bright as usual, the sun seeming to climb tiredly through a cloudline on the horizon. Freshening winds were causing the spray to spatter across the reef and fracture the lagoon surface. A storm neared. Gale knew the signs.

Generally, storm duration was not long but fishmuster would be in waterspace sheltered by the islandmass. He was organising a few Guardians for shoal-location reports when Tinu swept alongside. Gale anticipated the context of his mindmerge.

'I want your son's story checked before we muster for fishing, Gale. I trust shoal-location Guardians are fluking in pairs?'

Gale knew that Tinu was not doubting his leadership; knew there was more to follow. Beaknodding, he waited...

'Gale, our sagas speak of a dolphin 'who shall know before he is taught'... 'know wisdom before he is mature'. That has always been doubted by many... regarded as just a part of the sagas which has been recounted poorly and many have finpointed at the Story-tellers as being inadequate in some way.'

What else was in Tinu's mind?

'Wanderer left a message in trust which those privy have never divulged. I have not spoken of it for it has seemed too improbable. Perhaps I should...'

Tinu finturned to face Gale. Their bottlebeaks were motionless. The strength of Tinu's mindmerging was strong with a faith and love that was unswerving.

'We all know of the maze passage to Wanderer's Cave. Fewer of us know how to solve the puzzle of the entrance. 'One dolphin will come, at a time of danger, to find another entrance to Wanderer's Cave.' That was Wanderer's message - something I have kept reefsided in my mind all these seasons.'

There was a pause, then Gale heard, 'Watch your son closely. Allow him the freedom he requests... should he do so. I know of no other way to Wanderer's Cave but, perhaps ... Perhaps I am having an old dolphin's fancy.'

There was silence. Ripples of finstirring faded. A gust of wind flurried the surface.

Crest Spray arrived with Beak Spot. The moment had come for them to accompany Gale and his son to locate an in-reef waterspace shielded by a curtain of kelp... to check for the fifth orca.

'Thank you Tinu. I have heard you,' Gale said, in mindmerge. In open mindmeet, he said, 'Guardian detail, wait here. I will fetch my son. Shall I escort you to the Podsherd, Tinu?'

'No, off you go, Gale. I will check the other lagoon en-trance.'

Not fully comprehending, Gale watched Tinu's unwavering flukingpassage for some moments.

The growling sea had removed any trace of the struggle in the pool shielded by the kelp curtain, save for the fishspiking shaft on the bottom. Gale made mental note of the find. Ardent would be pleased of an addition to his stock of Splitfluke artifacts and his sire was pleased Gaze had indicated it. Did it look familiar?

There seemed little else of interest. Gaze could have sheltered here. All four dolphins had finned through the kelp - three of them with some trepidation. No orca had been within. The mystery of the 'fifth orca' was insoluble. Crest Spray could be forgiven any error. Events had been confusing.

For no apparent reason, Gaze pinged in echo-location.

'There is hollowness beyond the coral wall,' his son said, in mindmeet, 'Please may I investigate?'

Gale pinged to confirm. There was hollowness! How large was not easy to discern... Tinu's imaging echoed in Gale's mind. He would give his son a minor freedom...

'Go ahead, my son. Be a small voyager if you must,' he said. There was little danger from any shark, he thought.

Crest Spray volunteered, in mindmerge, to fin bi-vector with Gaze... but Gale said, 'This will be good experience. Let him have his dolphinhead. There are times a Bottlenose must fin his own passage.'

Crest Spray acknowledged, content for now.

Three pairs of dolphineyes followed the arcing leap of young Gaze over the coral wall... and finstirred to wait beneath. They would wait for longer than they expected.

Gaze cleared the wall and retraced his finningpassage to the Pleasure Cave. The only thing out of place would be the airslab entrance seal. From Karg's mind, he knew how to unfasten the Splitfluke connector from around a coral stump and let the airslab float to the surface. It was easy to drop the airslab on a rock shelf... less easy to make sure the chainlink was hidden from sight. Several sideways flukeflaps were required before the connector, larger than the links, slipped from immediate view.

Beaknosing rockchips and debris was the only camouflage required to break up the outline of the rectangular entrance of the sump shaft which led to the Pleasure Cave itself. Everything returned to the natural; no outline of a fateful entrance seal could be seen. Perhaps he should inspect the cave just once more to make sure no sign of Karg's evil remained?

Bendfinning through the sump, Gaze entered the cave for the second time. Cyrene would not have had the strength to lift the entrance seal in the confines of the sump with the added weight of the coral clump Karg had always nudged across.

There was nothing in the cave to cause suspicion of the awful secret it had harboured. The only creatures in the gloom were pale, shrimplike - small and fast-moving. Their thoughts were too fast to follow; a kind of high-pitched singing. Gaze recognised some creatures as unreachable in mindcontact. He watched as a pair disappeared through a crack in the cavefloor. They did not reappear...? He finturned to examine the crack; beaknosed aside rockchips and pieces of broken coral. Why was coral in this gloomy place?

He finned with greater purpose. Four larger pieces of rock would take some hard flukenudging to move aside... almost too much. A part of cavefloor rose upwards as he removed two weights and an 'air-filled seal' rose higher! Hardside debris? Removing two other pieces of rock allowed the slab to floattremble freely revealing another rock held in some fishtrap netting beneath it! If he could release the knots, the enmeshed rock would fall and the slabseal would rise...

Almost in disbelief, Gaze conjectured that here had been a possible way-out for Cyrene that she would have never expected to find... Karg! Had Karg known of this odd slabseal? He finned to the slab and beaknosed it, his mind open to receive anything of its history... any trace of Karg.

It was hardside debris made with Splitfluke hands... but he detected nothing significant of Karg. There were images of evil around the top surface but nothing of Karg beneath. Karg had not discovered a possible escape route! He had not looked beyond the sadistic pleasure of the moment. Gaze would be the first to fin through into new waterspace since an unknown dolphin had sealed and camouflaged the entrance. The shrimplike creatures had passed through to some other waterspace. Gaze would also try.

It was a narrow sump which re-emerged in... It had to be... Wanderer's Cave! Light was coming from cracks in the island side of the reef. Water dripped occasionally from the caveroof but, for the most part, the water was clear and still. He finned slowly across poolsurface looking at the cavefloor which seemed to be divided into sections. One section was recognisable!

Rocks of different shapes and sizes, coral pieces and sand - were the diagrammatic representation of the warmstream waterspace! He could detect the line of the reef, the Storytellers' Caves and even the out-reef entrance towards Wanderer's Cave which all dolphins knew. There was no indication of another entrance ... except... a piece of old seaweed was trapped by a pebble where the curtain of kelp could be found beyond the angle of the reef. Nothing else gave any clue to a second entrance.

That small piece of seaweed had probably caused Karg to investigate... One small clue on one of seven diagrams...

It would take a Bottlenose many visits to comprehend all the signs on the cavefloor. Gaze would return but others were waiting. He had to hurry.

He finned through the sump to the Pleasure Cave - realising he must not use that name - through the second sump and along the passage to the pool before the coral wall. He clicked his presence and made the leap over the wall.

What he had to say to three waiting Guardians was greeted with stunned silence.

Gale recalled Tinu's timely imaging. He would check his son's find. They would report to the Master Guardian... and Tinu would have more to say perhaps...

Something had changed... A storm was nearing. He could tell by the heavier waveslap against the hardside tunnel which rose vertically above the surface... but it was not only the magnifying billows. There were only one or two whispers of echo-sounds from the distant Podsherd.

Last early darkwater, he had heard orcan echo-calls and distant alarm pinging from the Guardians. A Bottlenose had died in the early moonglow. Just before peace had returned, strong visions in a waterspace of huge teeth and a surface slapped by giant flukes had terrified him. He had thanked the White Dolphins for a safe refuge.

Only one Bottlenose could be responsible for visions of that intensity. Karg had come close - too close! He would not return to the Podsherd whilst Karg was there... and Karg was younger.

Finwarp was not dead. There had been occasions he wished he was. Yet he feared death. On the rare lightwater that he saw a few Bottlenoses in flukingpassage - when he overcame his dread of detection by Karg and finstirred near the bulk of the sunken hardside - he fought the desire to return to the Podsherd. The terror of the murder attempt by Karg had been too awful...

In his darkwater dreams, he relived the terror. The fishspiking shaft penetrating his flesh had been a shock of pain, a white heat of agony. But the squid vectoring to grasp him with tentacles had made him mindscream in a wail of high-pitched intensity. As he had been dragged to the depths, Finwarp had been conscious only of the curved squidbeak to which he had been pulled inexorably. Struggling, the end had been unavoidable...

Then the squid had faded... had gone! He had been sinking with the weight of a coral clump tied to the spiking shaft. He had struggled further but it had been hopeless. Gathering quickly, sharks had made their striking-vectors...

For Finwarp it had been the end... but then the miracle!

The first shark had caused an instinctive, hopeless twist to avoid the gaping maw. The jaws had snapped closed - not on Finwarp but on the spiking shaft. The shark had twisted... and torn the spiking shaft free! The agony had been an explosion of white heat in body and mind. He had not observed how it had happened, but a second shark on striking-vector had jabbed itself upon the spiking shaft still held by the first. The wound had been shallow but had torn a blood vessel. Confusion had reigned. More sharks had strike-vectored through the blood-scented gloom.

Lungs bursting for airsnatch, bleeding himself, Finwarp had spiralled dizzily to the surface to emerge near the sunken hardside, resting on a shoaling reef. He had acted quickly, seeking refuge. He had not been quick enough to avoid a shark's teeth tearing at his flanks but had blocked the hole in the vertical tunnel by pushing over hardside debris and floated up to airspace he had hoped was above.

For several lightwaters he had stayed there. The bleeding had stopped. Eventually he had ventured out. During that period, he had realised several things. The attack had been made by Karg. There had been no squid! But the experience had been stronger than imagination...Karg had been the squid! He had mindvisioned the squid until he, Finwarp, had fallen from range! Finwarp was extremely lucky to still be airsnatching...

Karg was not like other dolphins! The 'Pleasure Cave Captive' had a deeper, sadistic purpose than flesh-fervour fun! Finwarp knew remorse. She would suffer but Karg was too strong for him... and he was afraid, more fearful of any Bottlenose than he had ever been.

These realisations, a combination of horror, fear and guilt, had kept Finwarp at distance from a normal dolphin's needs of pleasure, companionship and the love he did not feel worthy of... The lightwaters of seasons had passed.

But now... now something was different? Something...

At times, the vertical hardside tunnel seemed to amplify the seasounds of dolphins. Finwarp detected the echo-location pinging of Guardians for shoal-seeking. They would be fishing near the hardside wreck this lightwater!

With finning care, he would see Flab! The changing weather had brought fishmuster to a different waterspace!

He might see Flab - but he could not fin by her side. Guilt and fear, in this unwilling accomplice to the evil of Karg, hung as heavy as a coral clump upon his heart...

'Crest Spray, find Ardent. Tell him I want him here as a matter of urgency. If he starts to make excuses about lectures or something of interest at the moment, just tell him I think, 'Through Wanderer, he is here'. Ardent will come faster than for fishmuster. For once, forget all formalities... Go straight to him,' said Tinu, his beak not once pointing away from Gaze, as if locked in one direction.

'Gale, stay here. Fishmuster will be a little delayed. The rest of you, join the Podsherd.'

Gale could not credit the sudden departure from routine. Tinu was of the old school of dedication to discipline and order. Something was afluke which was unusual. To his knowledge, Tinu did not normally confer in his decision-making with the absent-minded, old Cleric, Ardent. Was this an indication of another Master Guardian secret?

'Gale, fetch Peen and be back here as quickly as you can. Your questions I will answer later. I wish to talk to your son,' came an order Gale did not expect... but he finturned and fluked in obedience.

Tinu directed even fuller attention to the near-mature finstirring before him. How should he begin? 'He will know your imaging behind your reefsiding, no matter how you seek to shield it.' Thus had Wanderer spoken...

'He will have extraordinary mindskills, abilities you have dreamed of but never possessed... but so might an Abomination.' How could Tinu distinguish between the Bottlenose whom Wanderer had prophesied and one whom nature should abhor? What should he say? 'He will know your thoughts...'!

Gaze was silent, respectful. He was total innocence.

'Gaze, are you a good, obedient dolphin?' Tinu asked, to break the silence.

'It depends who is judging me in dolphinkind,' came the reply. 'I try to be a Bottlenose my sire would be proud of. My conscience troubles me sometimes... but not recently.'

'Can you mindmerge already?' Tinu asked in mindmerge, prepared for anything...

There was a pause...

'Yes,' came a clear mindmerge answer.. and the mind of Gaze was gone! It had been too quick for anything to register in Tinu's mind except the knowledge that Gaze had been reefsiding heavily. What was Gaze hiding?

Tinu did not expect the next mindmerge imaging... 'But you are reefsiding too.' The young Bottlenose's voice was there and gone again but he had read his mind! He had done it without Tinu being aware!

To his credit, Tinu sent a clear mindmerge image that he would say nothing else until Ardent was here. He could not escape the instinctive response of keeping two clear dolphinspans between himself and whatever

Gaze was. His Guardian mind kept track of a clear flukingvector, if he needed it.

Master Guardian and young Bottlenose finstirred a waiting circle. The former would have been astonished to know his mind had already given up a wealth of experience and a hoard of secrets. If Gaze could have touched him, no shadow of the past would have been unidentified, unqualified.

Crest Spray arrived first in a welter of spray, forgetting his normal manners. He need not have been anxious.

Tinu derived comfort from his arrival. He laughed inwardly, ironically. How could this near-mature pose a threat to a Guardian pair?

Ardent was fluking a less energetic passage towards them. The beak of Gaze was following his vector... and turned first to pick out the vectors of Gale and Peen. Many bottlebeaks were following the vectors but they were too respectful to close with the gathering of influential Bottlenoses. Some wondered why a near-mature was there...?

Ardent radiated expectancy. His finstirring strokes were quick and nervous... trembling.

Tinu spoke immediately in open mindmeet, 'I did not know how to proceed. He is capable of mindmerge and I... Perhaps you should find out for yourselves.'

Gale could not believe the mindvoices. Peen was speaking in mindmerge... 'I think you are about to be greatly surprised, my love. I can only tell you Gaze is a very special dolphin. I am his dam and I know he is... he ... is good.'

Her statements did nothing but add further confusion in Gale's mind. She was trying to reassure him... but sounded worried at the same time?

Ardent recognised the near-mature as Gaze from the last lightwater's meeting.

'You will be seeking to solve the puzzle of Wanderer's Cave, Gaze. I wish you luck. Now, Tinu, your message was one which I had thought, at times, I would never hear. I am growing old. You would not toy with an old dolphin,' he said in mindmeet.

'Ardent, I cannot explain... but this young dolphin has found already another entrance to Wanderer's Cave. It is as Wanderer prophesied... but I had expected a Bottlenose of greater maturity. How should I proceed?'

Ardent paused and answered, in mindmerge, 'There was something out of the ordinary about Gaze when I saw him in the Storytellers' Caves... but what, particularly, I found most interesting I cannot quite remember. I... My mind is blank.'

He wallowed in uncertainty and then... 'I believe we must both allow mindmerge with this Gaze, withdraw our reefsiding piece by piece... and... er... let us just see what happens. I can think of nothing else.'

Startled, Tinu and Ardent both heard the voice of Gaze!

'If I agree to such a thing?'

There was an uncomfortable pause of five finsweeps.   G a z e continued, 'I have one condition. I wish to fintouch both of you before I agree. It is important to me.'

'You have a condition! Of all the dolphinnerve. You show some respect for your...' began Tinu... but Ardent was laughing a joyful mindmusic.

'I think we should do as he asks, Tinu. What do two old dolphins have to lose?'

First, Ardent finned alongside Gaze.

Gruffly, Tinu mindassented and finned to the other flank, moving along to fintouch the young dolphin's forefin.

Bewildered, Gale, Peen and Crest Spray watched. There were many bottlebeaks in the lagoon pointing towards the influential pod, puzzled; sensing a moment of significance but not comprehending clearly.

Nothing did happen which any other Bottlenose observed. The trio, ageing dolphins around a central youthful pivot, seemed oblivious of everything... for long spans of billowing rise and fall.

Reefsides crumbled and mindspace opened. There were no secrets, only truthfulness. Three minds merged as one; self was sacrificed in a sanctity of meeting...

'Wanderer's message across the seasons...

Abomination killed - and the reasons...

Recognised - in sagas predicted...

Mindskills unknown, now heralded...'

First Tinu, then Ardent finned away. Both seemed moved by the contact.

It was Gale who first spoke.

'Tinu, has my son offended you? Is there anything I should do?'

Tinu finturned towards him, his eyes misty as he said, 'No Gale, be at peace. Your son will tell you in his own way. I serve your son.'

He said nothing else!

Ardent finned to Gale's side.

Fintouching both Gale and Peen, he said, 'It is as the sagas tell us. The rest is unclear. Know only this, that your son is very special. We have known he would come. Wanderer told us. Do not look to us for advice. It is time to listen to your son.

'Come Tinu, we must think of the fishmuster before the storm. We have other duties, don't we old friend?'

In near disbelief, Gale watched them fin away!

Gape could no longer hold her curiosity back. One of the bottlebeaks questing the strange group near the lagoon entrance had been hers. She passed Tinu and Ardent, finning away in bi-vector, and joined her familypod.

They appeared to be concerned about young Gaze - or he was concerned about them. From a distance, it was not easy for curious Bottlenoses to determine.

The familypod formed... touched...

Gale withdrew from deeper mindmerge than he had ever known,

deeper than with his own dam... or with Peen.

In humility, he finturned to face his son...

'I have been foolish in some ways... but I could not have known. Perhaps I would have been afraid... aggressive, if I had. You are my son... and I am proud.

'It appears, Peen, you knew more than me. What did you say? 'I would be proud to serve him!' Wanderer save us from dam intuition!'

Peen was close to his flanks. She did not need mindmerge.

Gape was looking in astonishment at her brother, her beak hanging open and her even teeth gleaming. There were no words ... no silly insults... just wide-eyed wonder.

Gale broke the spell.

'Well, Gaze, is it fishmuster or something else?'

'Perhaps Gape would look to my needs and Peen to yours, my sire. We will also need fish for a third and fourth. Would you ask two Guardians to fish for two others? Could Peen ask Flab to join us?'

Peen smiled. Always the questions... but always something else behind them.

Keeping carefully close to the hardside tunnel so that any echo-locating ping would not reveal his presence, Finwarp watched the fishmuster closing in circle around the shoal. There was no sign of Karg... or the other fleshy shape he sought. He dared not ping until assault-vectors began. Perhaps he would detect her then...

The fishmuster circle closed. It was so much easier working a team plan. How many times had he missed a fish he had strike-vectored upon as an individual? It did not help that he was slower now. His injuries and his age were weighing increasingly heavy.

The first assault-vectors were away! A cacophony of identification calls and echo-locating pings sang in his head. Oh, to be with the Podsherd now!

'You could be if you trusted me.'

The mindmerge voice was strong and close! Its effect was immediate, instinctive. Finwarp dived for the hole in the hardside tunnel! Frantically he wedged debris across the entrance and floated to the airspace above.

He surfaced alongside another bottlebeak and head which was... beaksmiling!?

No dolphin has ever been so astounded, fearful and puzzled as Finwarp at that moment!

'There is no need for fear. Karg is dead. You are Finwarp and I am called Gaze.'

The mindmerge message was given twice. It was needful for Finwarp was a swerving shoal of emotion... fear, guilt, hope, need, anxiety, doubt. All these swirled within and before two minds.

He was young. Karg could appear as anything he wished!

'If I was Karg, I would have attacked before now... unexpectedly, without warning too openly given. That too is true... and you know it Finwarp.'

Finwarp did know... wished he could forget. But how could this young dolphin mindmerge so early? How did he know his thoughts? How had he arrived so... unexpectedly!? There were too many uncertainties. Finwarp would not trust him yet.

'When you are ready Finwarp, you must touch me. Only when you trust another will you find what you need. Is your need stronger than your fear... and your guilt?'

Was this Gaze reading his mind? Or was he anticipating his thoughts?

For the first time, Finwarp spoke in mindmeet. He did not trust sufficiently to open his mind further... 'You say Karg is dead. How do you know?'

'You know yourself. You saw it happen early darkwater last. He met his death in orca jaws. They were hungry. It was a needful death.'

Finwarp remembered his mindvision; his darkwater dreaming. Had it been a dream? How could this...?

'When you are ready Finwarp, you must touch me. Assure yourself I am real and not a vision... that I am what I seem to be.'

A season of loneliness flashed across his mind... and a desperate need.

Finstirring, he edged closer to the vision or the reality. If it was time to die, to know the truth beyond the deep-dive...

Finwarp touched the flank of Gaze. It was a fleeting brush of a forefin... Gaze was real! The young Bottlenose was tangible - and still no threat.

'Touch me and stay in fincontact!'

It was a command; Gaze would not be disobeyed.

Finwarp moved his forefin to rest on that of... a Guardian?

There was peace - no danger... just tranquility!

'Good. Now take the next finstroke. Open your mind for mindmerge and be not afraid.'

Finwarp complied ... to know truth.

The third assault-wave by the fishmuster had finished before Finwarp released his forefin touch of Gaze in the hardside tunnel. The mature, scarred dolphin opened his eyes. They seemed brighter, more hopeful.

'The captive dived to the White Dolphins? Gaze, I am so glad you told me. And Karg really is no more!'

Gaze beaknodded in simple affirmation.

'I may return to the Storytellers... but I have not been worthy.'

'You were misguided, Finwarp. There is an end to suffering. The Podsherd exists to help us all find the peace and security we need. Before you return you must also know that there is another you may help. I know you would wish to if you could... and now you can. It is time to fin from this place. Let us go.'

Puzzled, but with some delight, he dived with young Gaze, removed the obstructions from across the tunnel base and rose to airsnatch... alongside Flab!

She was concern; she was fussy care.

Gaze retired to the open seaside of the hardside tunnel to fin with Gale and wait.

'We shall not be long, my sire. Perhaps I can be an escort Guardian, with you on the flukingpassage back?'

'I have a feeling you are the only escort they need, Gaze,' said a wondering sire.

Chapter Six

SEEDS OF REFORM AND RIVALRY

The return of the four dolphins to the Podsherd passed unremarked until the disfigured Bottlenose was recognised as Finwarp! Many then were the pings and clicks of greeting in acknowledgement. Bottlenose curiosity was obvious. Absence of a Storyteller was expected now and then, when predetermined as part of a Storyteller task, but only a Voyager would have been absent for over a season. Finwarp was an Inventor. Hence, why had he been missing for so long? Politeness and respect forbade too direct an enquiry.

It was Gale who fed the explanation to those he knew would spread the news quickest and furthest. A Guardian learned the facility of how to spread messages in the social network of the Podsherd. Sire and son remembered Guardian training well...

'Mind to mind, news travels far
Like growth within a Basket Star.
To the outer edges of the herd,
A message will be roundly heard
If dolphin beaks are chosen well,
Faster fluking than you can tell!'

'Finwarp had had terrible wounds due to shark attack. It had taken courage to survive as a solitary dolphin for so long. His recovery had been slow and it had taken many lightwaters to regain strength. His memory had been affected and his lateral sensing. Gaze had heard echo-identification pinging last darkwater. They had found Finwarp during fishmuster. He had nearly returned entirely on his own.'

Before long, bottlebeaks had pronounced Finwarp a special dolphin and his disfigurement as a mark of his courage. The warmth of his welcome increased a hundredfold.

Gale acknowledged a son's wisdom in mindmerge and forgave the minor transgression of being prompted after subconscious imaging had been read.

His only gruff comment was, 'I would like to keep my imaging to myself and Peen... later. Is that understood, Gaze?'

Sire and son touched forefins. Gale had his answer.

Vorg failed to solve the puzzle of Wanderer's Cave.

Three times he deep-dived to the entrance, ascended the flooded shaft to airspace above and spent useless finning circles examining rockwalls looking for something to push or tug. Not once did it occur to him to ping for hollowness in the descent.

If he had, he would have detected a hollow ring from a rock shelf a third of the way down. Here there was an airslab weighted down with a rock. Nudging the rock aside would have given access to another shaft which led directly to the cave he sought. He would have seen nothing for it was too dark to find the entrance. Pinging up the shaft was useless. Pinging down the shaft was very misleading. Some candidates missed important clues or failed to use their minds fully!

Vorg did not yet have the capacity of his sire, Karg.

Ardent insisted that, for the sake of appearances, Gaze also sought the solution...

'Do not hurry, Gaze. You will find the Splitfluke cross-shape inside Wanderer's Cave. Bring it back to me. I believe you wanted to see more of Wanderer's Signs anyway. We have restored the second entrance. Perhaps you should know we are already calling it 'The Entrance of Gaze'... That is, Tinu and myself. We shall speak afterwards,' he had said.

Only later did it occur to him that Gaze probably knew already... and he beaksmiled, recognising the politeness of silence.

In the cave, Gaze finned slowly above the seven sections. For the first time, he dived to gently beaknose the cavefloor...! He rose to airsnatch. What he had sensed was startling!

There was no voice. There was no sense of Wanderer as an entity alive... but Gaze was seeing different images and mindpictures of distant places! Below him was a... a place the mind of Maeve recognised!

It had a name and Maeve knew it; Gaze knew it for Maeve was part of him!

Somehow the intensity of Wanderer's imaging lived in the mindpictures he had created... recorded...

Gaze dived again. When he resurfaced to airsnatch, he knew there were limits to what Wanderer had seen... and what Maeve had known. Now, however, Gaze knew more definitely that his immediate future was not with the Podsherd. He would spend some lightwaters examining the... 'maps'? Yes, that was the 'word'... His own destiny required that he find the 'girl' Splitfluke, Maeve.

He grasped the Splitfluke cross-shape in his bottlebeak and finned to leave.

Ardent was waiting, with Tinu, when Gaze returned to the Cleric's cave. Without a word, he dived to the bottom of the incave pool, and placed the cross-shape exactly as it had been the lightwater before. He rose to airsnatch.

Force of habit made Tinu remark, 'Well done young Gaze...' but then he realised just how foolish that sounded. 'I mean, you were just a little longer than we thought you... You know what I mean.'

'Thank you, Tinu but there is a problem. What do you expect me to do now?'

Ardent's reply was full of faith.

'I rather expect you will tell us something like... You wish to be a

Storyteller but really you will be guiding us... That you want us to consult you over major decisions. You want our advice and require us to be your public voice?'

'You would feel a little awkward, both of you. There is only one solution. I need to tell you of something in Wanderer's Cave. Not everything, but enough for you to understand why I must leave the Podsherd. Will you both touch me again?'

Thus did two Bottlenose elders learn more quickly than either had learned anything before of the Splitfluke world in the mind of Maeve. Of Splitflukes - their intelligence, their achievements and of their mixed strengths and frailties.

Images of dolphins in captivity, held some horror!

Worse came with images of Splitfluke conflict and senseless destruction... Worse still of Splitfluke killing Splitfluke with unbelievable weapons.

The most horrifying was the hunting of other toothed or untoothed whales!

It was hard to credit religious conviction or a genuine love of life to creatures capable of such carnage.

There was a pause of long, long moments when Ardent and Tinu broke forefin contact with Gaze. Hunting... killing for food, a dolphin could understand... but this...?

'I must learn more of the Splitflukes. Dolphinkind must endeavour to understand more of their personality and beliefs. It is for these reasons that I must leave... and, because not all Bottlenoses are as understanding or have the respect for others which you both possess.'

Neither of the elderly Bottlenoses could disagree.

Ardent said, 'Have you nothing to say to us? Nothing you would wish us to do?'

They were such simple questions. Ardent and Tinu had waited until the approach of old age for the special dolphin Wanderer had said would come. The waiting had conjured different images of what dolphin he would be. They expected the weight of leadership to be lifted from their flukes... but he was so young. And now he was leaving!

'Would Wanderer have expected you to leave aside your responsibility for the Podsherd?' asked Gaze in turn.

Two bottlebeaks nodded a negative and waited.

'It would be impudent to give orders but I believe there should be some reorganisation. Are you prepared to pass the role of Master Guardian to another, Tinu? Would you join the Storytellers, work with your friend here who needs your decisiveness? Could you bring better discipline and routine to the Storytellers themselves... and, above all, watch for another Abomination such as Karg?' said Gaze, knowing the answer but observing the need for a formal reply from a Guardian mind.

There was a short silence.

Tinu said, 'It is about time some Bottlenose took the Storytellers to task. There has been slackness of late. I have heard you, Gaze... and I would enjoy shaking this old fool into the present. He was never tidy enough in mind or habit for my taste anyway. There again, some of his 'things' I would like to know more of... and, in that sense, we need each other. We shall do our best to ensure there is no other Karg.'

Ardent and Tinu fintouched. The trust of many seasons was a deeper friendship than was comprehended by most Bottlenoses of the Podsherd.

Gaze was already beaksmiling before the next imaging...

'As for my replacement as Master Guardian, that is a Guardian matter to be settled in... You know already!'

Tinu laughed at himself. It was hard to break the habit of Guardian discipline. 'Beak Spot to replace your sire as Butting Pod Leader. Gale to be Master Guardian...'

Gaze said, 'And Crest Spray to form a Pod of Watcher Guardians with access to the Storytellers' Caves. Your own son, Esu, to be one of those Watcher Guardians.'

'How did you know Esu is my son? I... ' Tinu beak-nodded. 'My own mind perhaps but I felt I had reefsided that information even from you!' He sounded disappointed - did not mention Sinu...

'Then let us just say that it was the last sound of his name. Did you know my sire has the same tradition with a name... but not the last sound, the first?' beaksmiled Gaze.

'Perhaps it is a Master Guardian tradition,' said Tinu, beakgaping. 'I agree to your ideas... and I feel Ardent will not object.'

'Only in so far as I have to share my cave with... er... a pompous prawn who will be sleeping with both eyes open the darkwater long! 'Silly old fool', my flukes!' said Ardent.

The cave rang with joyful laughclicking.

The largest addition to the Nursery was beginning to become a hindrance. Twice, Flab had flukestumbled in trying to separate squabbling male podlings as she flukeflapped to veer past him. Twice, he had apologised with a beaksmile.

His eyes had followed her every finningpassage. The only time he had been of any real use was in repairing a cork float for a game. She had almost wished it had taken him longer. Flab might have felt flattered some seasons ago...

Flattered! She was getting flustered! She would have some sharp imaging to pass on when the podlings joined their familypods soon. She hadn't felt so fussed... so...

Flab caught sight of Finwarp's wounds again. For the tenth time, she knew the pain they must have brought.

Her own caring nature would soften any sharpness of imaging, recognising the needs the poor Inventor must have... his loneliness, his need to be with other dolphins, his need for fun... his need for...

Flab slammed a reefside across any more images of that kind! It couldn't be much longer before the podlings were gone. What a lightwater of hectic surprises! Oh, great seasnakes! There he was again!

84

'Finwarp! Now will you be a good, sick Bottlenose and give me some flukingroom? Really, you are a bit big for the Nursery. Can't you find something else to repair? It's always busy before the podlings leave...'

He was beaksmiling again. Such a warm smile. Gaze had said Finwarp had talked of looking for her over several moon cycles. That was silly! She was too old...' and too fat?

The dams were gathering to collect the podlings at last!

Flab wondered if she could keep her promise to herself to halve the number of fish she ate as she finned bi-vector with Finwarp towards his Storyteller Cave.

The love-bond between Gale and Peen was strong... expressive. Gape accepted the need to fin with her brother for a while. The sun was well-past vertical sunlight, beginning to arc at a steepening angle downwards. It was not only to keep up appearances that she finned with Gaze. She wanted to talk... to mindmerge with him if she could.

With sire and dam absent, Gape fintouched her brother.

'Gaze, show me how to mindmerge as you did earlier. I wish so much to be mature. I know you showed me some terrible things... but you showed our sire and dam, and the others, more than me. Was that fair?'

'You heard all that you needed. You were troubled by visions you sensed rather than saw last darkwater. If such could distress you... If you sensed another dolphin causing pain to an image of yourself, then the reality of knowing all would have been too harmful. Cruelty and death are things I would shield you from for I am your brother.'

Gape remembered the sense of huge eyes and pain in a coupling embrace which had troubled her in the shallows during the alarm of the darkwater last. It had been more than a shadow of apprehension females knew before the first experience of flesh-fervour.

Gaze was saying... 'You are mature Gape. Already the capacity of mindmerge is growing in your mind. I know you nearly mindmerged with Beak Spot this lightwater... and so do you. What you really want from me is not to show you how to mindmerge. You want me to tell you of Beak Spot before you... before you willingly surrender to him. Isn't that so?'

She missed a flukesweep. There was nothing she could say.

'Would that not take away some of the pleasure of discovery - some of the excitement you crave, Gape? Beak Spot is a good Bottlenose. If you want an affirmation of his perfection, I could not give it. I am your brother - not a White Dolphin.'

'Does he think of me? Does he... like me?'

'Do you think it would be proper for me to tell you, sister? You really would prefer to find these things out on your own, wouldn't you? I must learn not to betray other dolphins' trust... whether they have placed it in me willingly or not.

'Who has the harder task, Gape? A sister I love who is impatient for knowledge she will surely have in a few lightwaters... or the brother who knows many things he dare not share... cannot share... or will not share? Are you, sister, being fair?'

There was a long pause while Gape thought about those questions. Sometimes she wished her brother would say exactly what he thought or knew instead of asking questions! Slowly, the questions made her think... begin to see things from a different vectoring-angle...

He was right! He was always right, dam authority right. Why did she have to be blessed with a brother like him, the little... ?

His voice came... in mindmerge, 'I might have objected if I had known who my sister would be.'

She retaliated, in mindmerge, 'Don't be so cheeky you shrimpcalf. You should show...'

She was imaging in mindmerge! It was a lightning flash across her consciousness! How did it...? Gaze had said...!

Gape finturned to face her brother...

'Gaze, you don't know how much I love you. No, that's silly. How did you do it?'

There was another pause and then a huge, unfeminine beakgrin. 'Alright, stay quiet. It doesn't matter.'

She beaknosed him with affection.

'I think I will fin to see Ardent. See you later, Gape. Take care.'

Vorg was too late to intercept Gape with Gaze in bi-vector. He noticed that, on separating, she vectored at an angle to intercept Gale and Beak Spot who had been finning together for some time. He did not think she was going merely to talk to her sire...

The Podsherd rumour was that Gale was to be Master Guardian very soon. It would be necessary for Vorg to temper his actions; satisfy an intriguing appetite with other females for a while rather than negotiate need with Gale's athletic daughter. There were plenty of willing coupling partners now he could mindmerge. Perhaps it would be as well not to make it apparent just yet that he was mindmerging unexpectedly early. He would be able to satisfy his base desires with a dam for a while longer.

He mindchuckled. His mother had been near exhausted!

Only one other Bottlenose had ever done that before but it had not been a pleasant experience. She would not tell him who that dolphin had been... only that he was dead now.

A heavy reefside had been over part of her mind. Blue Anemone had acknowledged he had a gift which, used wisely, would make him welcome as a coupling partner with a very large number of the females - that it took a very special dolphin to tire her! He would see her early this darkwater. She had agreed - provided she could stop when she asked.

Vorg vectored to intercept Gaze. He had solved the puzzle of Wanderer's Cave! Perhaps the shrimpcalf could be pumped. After all, Vorg would have a mindmerging advantage. This would be fun!

His flukingpassage converged on Gaze.

'Well done, Gaze. So you're going to be a Storyteller. I'm glad one

86

of us solved the puzzle. The Butting Pod Trainer for me for a number of lightwaters,' said Vorg in mindmeet, not observing the normal courtesy of pinging identification and expressing an invitation.

Only Bottlenoses of superior or similar status spoke in mindmeet without the formal courtesies being expressed... or close friends... or dolphins of a familypod. There was an unspoken implication that he regarded himself as an intimate acquaintance. Also, that he was not recognising any difference in their status as yet. It would not have been worth any over-reaction but served only as a signal to put Gaze on his guard... if he had not been already.

'My sire says that Butting Pod Training is tough and demanding. You are a strong dolphin. You should enjoy it. I wish you good fortune,' said Gaze. 'Perhaps I will meet you later when the Storyteller trainees have to attend. I expect you will know a lot more about discipline and procedure before I see you again.'

'If we do, I'll try to give you some tips,' said Vorg.

There was silence for a few flukestrokes.

'I spent ages looking for the way to activate the entrance seal in the airspace above the shaft,' said Vorg. 'I could flukeslap my beak for missing the clue. I tried echo-location. I looked for signs of camouflage... but there was nothing.'

He was quiet, waiting for Gaze to elaborate. There was no answer.

In the silence, Vorg exercised his new mindskill and began to probe the adjacent mind. The shrimpcalf was thinking about seeing Ardent. He did not have the least idea Vorg was a mindpresence! Gaze needed to be prompted to think of Wanderer's Cave again...

'Did you find the entrance easily?' Vorg said in mindmeet... but with mindmerging antennae waiting for the images of the entrance to materialise...

Something was forming in Gaze's mind... The darkness and gloom of the ascending shaft... Vorg could see, in recall, the airspace above the shaft. The walls were grey in mindvision. Every crack and crevice was revolving as Gaze had fincircled. The eyes of Gaze had centred on one niche and he had finned closer... He had beaksnouted in the crack. Part of the cavewall had suddenly swung inwards!

Vorg had it! No storyteller or trainee was ever to divulge the entrance to Wanderer's Cave... but Vorg knew! He was elated! He had a secret he would be able to use at some future time. It would be wise to check the entrance. Was there time before he was to see Blue Anemone?

Gaze was saying, 'You know I cannot tell you anything Vorg. It was not easy but that is all our tradition and law allows me to say.'

'Yes, of course. My pride was a bit hurt, I suppose,' said Vorg. 'Keep the secret, Gaze. May your flukingvectors be straight and true.'

Storyteller trainee and the son of Karg separated.

The Guardian, at the lagoon entrance, denied access to open seaspace reminding Vorg he could not fluke out-reef unaccompanied. He would find a way.

Ardent was reflecting and patterning. The contact with the mind of Gaze had confirmed his suspicions about a number of the Splitfluke objects. Others remained obscure in terms of intentional use. Gaze would be invaluable in answering a great deal of his questions through his learning from the mind of Maeve...

He was doing it again! Ardent had realised he could not use Gaze to answer all his questions. He knew it was more important that Gaze became the youngest Voyager the Podsherd had ever known. Small mysteries would have to stay subservient to those which Gaze wished to unravel... and the precautions he wanted to take against another Abomination perpetrating the evils of Karg!

How any rational dolphin could do such things had been a shock to Ardent and Tinu. If ever a dolphin had deserved the death he had experienced, it had been Karg! And Cyrene's sire and dam must never know...

He finstirred.

Here he was, wondering about Splitfluke artifacts when the younger Gaze was dealing with life and death, security and suffering!

'Small mysteries may make giant discoveries when they are solved,' came the mindmerge voice of Gaze from without the cave.

He wasn't in the maze passageway! It was several long moments before he finned into view. Ardent could not mindmerge at that distance!

'I think it is getting further as I mature,' Gaze said... and Ardent realised he had read his mind, anticipating the question concerning the range of his mindmerging and mindreading!

'It seems to be a matter of avoiding contact with a number of minds in order to be able to hear the mind one wants,' said Gaze.

'There are times I must not look beyond myself but draw in my mindreaching for I need to seek solitude and rest. Sometimes I retreat from contact for it is an offence to witness some imaging. Dolphins are varied in their needs... different in their desires. Good or evil, selfishness or sadness surround us... me... I must learn to protect my sanity for in reaching many minds lies madness...

'I know I will have to leave in two or three moon cycles...'

'And in the period before you leave?' asked Ardent.

There was silence.

The old Bottlenose finned towards Gaze. The Cleric sensed anxiety...

'You taught Tinu and me much in short moments when we fintouched. This time, I ask to fintouch. I am a Cleric as well as Historian, Gaze. I do not have your mindskills but I can tell you are... you are troubled in spirit. Show me your anxiety and let us stop fintangling in the weed.'

Gaze met him half-way across the cave where the only witness was the skull of a Splitfluke watching from the cave floor. They were in contact a long time.

.... In another Storyteller Cave, two dolphins, well-past middle age, reverted to adolescence for a while... Finwarp continued to sport a very warm beaksmile. Flab began to rediscover the warmth in male flesh. Both spirits were consoled in the process of tidying his cave... and of seeing to his needs...

Considering the close proximity, neither felt the need to thank a Storyteller trainee for observing propriety...

.... Gape, in finning communion with Beak Spot around the perimeter of the Podsherd, was learning much of a Bottlenose she desired.

He had relaxed a little after the surprise of mind-merging with her... but he did not lose beakhold upon the new responsibility with which Gale had invested him.

'Responsibility increases the weight of the body a dolphin nudges upward to airsnatch.' It was an old saying but Beak Spot knew its truth. If he was to discharge his responsibility as a Butting Pod Leader, he could not act with the females in quite the same way as in the past... and Gape was the daughter of the new Master Guardian...

Yet she was beautiful with a lively zestfulness. He enjoyed her company and he told her!

Gape was delighted and took a large flukethrust into maturity by quashing a growing urgency for greater intimacy. She recognised Beak Spot's need, at present, was not for flesh-fervour. There was warmth enough for the moment in the pressure of his flanks against hers... and the delight of a fintouch, significant of more than temporary pleasure. Let Dazzle and her kind flukejerk and tremble with the new matures; Gape desired a loving relationship like her dam and her sire.

.... Peen said, 'He is so young. To fluke the distances he contemplates, he will be isolated from the security of companionship. It will mean solitude in the darkwater without full Guardian training. We cannot permit him to leave for many moon cycles.'

Gale finstroked her side.

'No Guardian training taught him the mindskills he has... or how to confront evil... or how to kill. He needs no escort to survive. The companionship he must seek is beyond the Podsherd, for the good of the Podsherd. Did you not say I would be proud to serve him? Did he not say, 'My dam, you are too protective'? Whose son was it that protected his dam and sister on the out-Nursery flukingpassage?'

Peen said, 'But he is so young. 'Mindvisions do not hurt in themselves' Gaze told us... and that will be his only defence! Can he control the wavesurge? Can he still the wind? Can he fish for himself? He is too young, Gale!'

Gale beaknosed her cheek.

He said, 'Do you think I could stop him? A sire knows the limits of control sometimes earlier than the dam. He has faith in us... respect for us... love for us. He has not sought to manipulate us and yet he had the mindpower. Are you being fair, seeking to constrain him? Hold to his imaging and know his strength of spirit, Peen.'

.... Ardent felt and heard these minds... and many dolphin minds and others... widening to expand to infinity...!

.... Ardent withdrew from fincontact... retracted from mindmerge with shock!

'You hear all those minds? See all those images?'

The Cleric began to understand. Gaze needed to avoid the bewildering mindscreaming confusion of open mindmerge.   The ebb and flow of mindenergy was a force of suction which could so easily become a whirlpool of self-destruction.   Ardent began to marvel at how a young dolphin had learned mindselectivity... to concentrate on one mind or problem at a given moment. So easily could he become a finless dolphin unable to change vector in a mindstorm of incredible magnitude!

Gaze said, quietly, 'I dread any other mindpower. I can project a vision, read minds undetected, sense the past in an object, alter memory... command others to my will. I can do this with minds of other creatures to an extent. I have the power to be the Abomination I fear. I am life or death to others... the truth or the lie. It is so terribly hard to rest... to find peace in tormented waterspace.

'Even fishing, I sense the pain. There is so much suffering... and I am not a White Dolphin... or the 'God' in the mind of Maeve.'

The Cleric was thoughtful... and so was the mind within and with him.

For a long time, Ardent did not speak...

Finally, he said, 'Yet you have abused no dolphin without cause... or used mindpower seeking more power... Your suffering and solitude is the burden you finsteer through existence. Such you share with every other dolphin, every other creature of the waterspace or the airspace above. If you continue to fluke for the good of creature-kind, there will be consolation for your spirit. I believe you will, for you abhor evil. I can do nothing for you except seek to cede your spirit to the White Dolphins and hope that may bring you peace.'

Ardent turned again to fintouch Gaze but this time with a fin to his forehead...

'One who shows love shall find the peace he needs.'

The blessing was given in the privacy and humility of his muddled cave but it gave consolation to a troubled spirit when it was most needed. It was never forgotten.

Tinu took station near the Storyteller's Caves. Ardent had arranged a complicated transfer to ensure Tinu was quartered close to the main entrance passageway with a good position to scan the lagoon and watch the movements of the Guardians with a professional eye. He was watching now as Gale checked the darkwater patrol muster. Everything appeared in order.

'Did you really expect anything else? Gale was trained by an excellent Guardian. He knows how to discharge his duties,' came a mindmerge voice he was learning to recognise...

It was still a shock to know his mind was open to Gaze at all times. Tinu felt as disconcerted as a Guardian recruit facing a needful rebuke.

'You know your privacy will be respected. It is just that I need your help, Tinu.'

'Well that makes a change, young Gaze. How may I help?'

Why did speaking in mindmerge when he couldn't see the other dolphin seem so difficult? thought Tinu.

'I would prefer to be with you but that would not be appropriate. A Storyteller trainee would not be in your constant company,' said Gaze.

This Tinu understood.

'I have spoken to Ardent who understands some of my problems. He will tell you in his own way. There is one thing I could not tell him.'

There was a pause.

'Karg had a son, Tinu. He will be returning to the Podsherd shortly. He has been with his dam for some time. He is not like Karg but he is developing some visioning power... and he enjoys dominating dolphins. If you must watch the Guardians, then watch Karg's son carefully. His name is Vorg. His mindskills have not fully developed, but he is a potential danger to others... including my sister... even to me.

'You know I will not always be with the Podsherd and my familypod are in no danger yet.'

Tinu said, 'What are the extent of his mindskills?

'You are wondering if he could be an Abomination... even if I am. Let me say that his desire for power is stronger than mine and he is prepared to hurt the innocent.

'I cannot assess the limits of his mindpower for he is maturing. Neither can I anticipate how he will use them. I ask only that you watch him closely... especially when I am gone. You will know the time to confer with my sire if it is necessary.'

'Why are you asking me?'

'You are closer to understanding Bottlenoses who are tough and aggressive. You have lived and fluked with them. Vorg may be a useful Guardian. It depends how he matures... what he desires and how ruthless he becomes. I know of no better dolphin eyes to watch in my absence than your own.'

Tinu understood, in part, for he was used to moulding aggression for the common good with insistence upon discipline. Constantly measuring Bottlenoses for the tasks in Guardian duties to which they seemed suited was habit entrenched in seasons of service. The Butting Pod Trainer would test new Guardian trainees thoroughly, even such as Vorg. Tinu was proud of Guardian training procedures. Few dolphins hid much of character and potential.

Gaze was not convinced.

Vorg was kept extremely busy over the next moon cycle. His competitive nature and his desire to appear superior to others in his quest for dominance were to lead to his eventual downfall. Frolic, the senior

Butting Pod Trainer, was the first Bottlenose to suspect Vorg's possession of mindpowers which were out of the ordinary. Alerted by his old friend, Tinu, to keep close watch of Vorg without being told the reasons, Frolic maintained high demands in a tight training schedule for the new Guardian recruits.

During this period of time, it became obvious that Vorg was a splendid physical specimen. He was robust and strong; most of the other trainees appeared to tire before him. His rugged zestfulness and his caustic comments about observed shortcomings in others, earned him a grudging respect from the near-mature males who sought temporary freedom from any censure of themselves by appearing admiring accomplices.

In Frolic's experience, good, future leaders of Guardians rarely courted the acclaim of their peers and, despite Vorg's high performance and apparent dominance of his peer group, the trainer began to suspect some flaws in character.

With some surprise, Frolic noted a complete change in the pattern of Vorg's behaviour after his thoughts. He could not have known Vorg had read his mind. Vorg was polite and co-operative, suggesting rather than insisting in training exercises, appearing to anticipate other dolphins' needs and anxieties before they were outwardly apparent to Frolic himself. Impeccable results were being achieved in the training schedules, forcing a reassessment.

Why, then, had Tinu asked for such close appraisal of Vorg?

Chapter Seven

DECEPTION AND CONSTRAINT

Gaze used every spare moment absorbing information in his meetings with other Storytellers and sharing their experience... or he finstirred, patterning above the 'maps' in Wanderer's Cave, beaktouching features on the cavefloor many times. The Storytellers agreed that Gaze appeared to learn rapidly and asked extremely pertinent questions. Indeed, some found the questions Gaze asked, stimulating and that their own thoughts took a more promising direction in approaching perplexing problems. Of course, no Storyteller confessed this new direction of investigation in the patterning process was attributable to Gaze. All would have been astonished, if it had been known, beyond a tight circle of confidentiality, that Gaze had rapidly surpassed the limits of knowledge in the Podsherd through his previous contact with Maeve... and his unique mindskills.

At times, Gaze became conscious that certain Storytellers possessed unrealised potential in their own patterning processes which needed only minor inputs from another's thoughts to make positive bounds towards new discoveries. On three occasions, he meekly suggested that a meeting with another named Bottlenose might prove beneficial to a Storyteller on the verge of expanding known horizons - geographical or mental.

Ardent began to perceive the manifestation of exactly the kind of co-operation between Storytellers - or other Bottlenoses - which Wanderer had envisaged but which had degenerated to petty parochialism. Within a mooncycle, there was new energy appearing in the joint investigation of all manner of things. It was not uncommon for a Historian to consult a Navigator, or a Cleric to be patterning with an Inventor.

Curiosity arose with energy. Gaze suggested that Ardent take an odd, stretchable, closed tube-thing to Flab, knowing already its purpose, but unable to resist flukepulling the old Cleric... The young Bottlenose had not quite lost a sense of mischief...

Flab, party to some of the unusual qualities in Gaze - held in the strictest confidence - enjoyed giving Ardent a factual account of how male Splitflukes used such a thing to prevent unwanted flankers from being conceived in flesh-fervour, as primed by Gaze in mindlink!

After some temporary discomfiture, Ardent was pleased to realise that Gaze was also making him aware of two other dolphins, Finwarp and Flab, in whom he could have absolute trust. These three dolphins would continue in companionable co-existence for the remainder of Ardent's time in the waterspace... Tinu would remain his closest friend.

Yes, Gaze had a sense of fun, largely innocent and never malicious. He endeavoured to have a faith in the basic goodness of others. Aware of Vorg as a potential problem, he never saw the full extent of the evil to come.

And then Vorg made mistakes.

During a recreation period, of which there had been very few, Vorg was in flukeflashing pursuit of a cork float in a possession game. Frolic recognised the type - a larger than average, physical player revelling in competition and capable of instilling fear and apprehension in others. Vorg, brawny, vigorous, high-spirited and enthusiastic, would need a few knocks to his self-esteem before he would see the need for team co-operation, essential in Guardian service.

Distancing himself from the game, and placing himself out of range of Vorg's mindreading capacity unwittingly, Frolic had a few, quiet mindmerge words with some Guardians off-duty. He suggested a game challenge which would start the process of grinding down the self-esteem of all the trainees, including Vorg. Later training would afford ample opportunities for rebuilding confidence whilst emphasising the need for responsibly functioning as part of a team.

Frolic brought the trainees' game to an end. They click-clustered around him cheerfully. The challenge of a possession game against a team of Guardians was extended and accepted willingly. Explaining that the Guardians would seek to dolphinherd the cork float to waterspace above a distant rockrise, the trainees were instructed to attempt to deprive the Guardians of possession, if they could, and take it to a designated capture area.

The Guardians were already at start location with the cork float. Frolic watched the trainees disperse into an approximation of dolphincordon, across the anticipated Guardian vector towards the target area, and finned well-aside to observe.

The three Guardian pairs began finning towards the cordon, nudging the float before them steadily.

Exactly as Frolic anticipated, several trainees began making uncoordinated rushes towards the Guardians. Four of the latter began breaching and diving in patrol patterns, successfully confusing the initial moves. The surface Guardian pair continued edging relentlessly forward.

The first rushes terminated, the Guardian pairs reformed and the trainees relined as a cordon considerably further back.

After several long moments, the first signs of co-operation emerged in the trainees. Two of them maintained station on a direct vector between the opposition and the target area. The remainder began making underwater finning-vectors to intercept. The response was as immediate as mindmerge thought facilitated. Four Guardians dived and filled the waterspace with reverberating echo-sounding calls whilst finning erratic underwater passages, always seeming to shield progress above. When any trainee appeared to be nearing, at least one Guardian would make a series of violent surface flukeslaps to cause further disorientation.

At one stage, the float seemed to disappear entirely, trapped between the mirrored finning bodies of two Guardians making further progress underwater. Manoeuvre and counter continued with the trainees achieving nothing but increased frustration.

Game rules forbade physical contact between opposing dolphins other than the unavoidable or the non-deliberate but some trainees were nearing the point where they were sorely tempted. Common sense prevailed; taking-on an experienced and physically fit Guardian would have been an ill-advised, if not daunting, prospect. Guardian approach to the target area was steady and faultless.

This would be a lesson the young dolphins would not forget, thought Frolic.

Then, just as the Guardians neared victory, the forward progression floundered... A second float appeared on the surface!

In the confusion, Vorg made off with one of the floats towards the safe area. He was twenty dolphinspans ahead of pursuit before any Bottlenose realised an intercept play had been successfully achieved. The second float appeared to sink from sight!

There were moments of heated clicking discussion amongst the Guardians and several echo-locating pings beneath in disbelief. The trainees were off after Vorg and there were several impudent air-rolls performed together with one or two cheeky flukeflips of water in the direction of the finstirring, defeated Guardians.

Frolic was thoughtful. There was need to confer with his old friend, Tinu... and to keep at distance from Vorg until he had.

'Tinu, Frolic is in flukingpassage to see you. He is disturbed about something he has just witnessed. Please listen to his account. I wish to join you shortly. I have been lucky to have part seen something myself,' came the mindmerge voice he recognised. 'May I visit you in your quarters?'

No observer would have seen the least sign of surprise in Tinu's demeanour as he finned away from his vantage point which over-saw events in the lagoon. He was growing used to that voice from a distance, readily accepting the wisdom and awareness that underlined the contacts. Perhaps the time would come when this subterfuge was not necessary...?

'Not yet, Tinu. There would be many, more apprehensive and suspicious than yourself. Wanderer gave no message to them to be stored in good faith through the seasons. I will join you shortly.'

Later, Gaze would wish that he had monitored Vorg's mind much closer, instead of relying on the imaging of others... Perhaps he had respected Vorg's rights as a Bottlenose too much - or he had feared him even then. These matters he would reflect upon much later... Too late for another he had called a friend.

'As you wish, Gaze,' Tinu replied... knowing the effort of mindmerging was not needful.

'... After that, there was no alternative but to give them a free recreation period. The Guardians I co-opted in the exercise are as puzzled and suspicious as myself. They feel duped; that they have been made to look fools. Yet they performed exactly in accordance with trained Guardian procedures,' finished Frolic, finstirring pensively close alongside Tinu.

'You saw the second float?' asked Tinu.

'Fleetingly, two floats did seem to be on the surface. When one of them sank, I was just as astonished as everyone else.'

'Vorg... your thoughts about him?'

'His reaction time was far quicker than anyone else... almost as if he was aware of what was happening. Oh, he's basking in the warmth of admiration and his popularity has breached to new heights... but I suspect his real satisfaction comes out of some kind of superiority contest he is waging against all other Bottlenoses.'

Frolic paused.

'In the first ten or so lightwaters of the training programme, I had begun to think I recognised his type. Thriving on competition, he was not slow to point out any weaknesses in the other trainees. You know, it was almost as if he had read my mind. Since then, he has been courteous, helpful, supportive, open to suggestions... a model trainee. But there may be more to young Vorg... There is, possibly, something different...'

Frolic finturned to face his old Master Guardian. Eye to eye came the mindmerge question... 'Why did you ask me to watch him closely, Tinu?'

There was no immediate answer... only the explosive airsnatching intervals of two elderly Bottlenoses whose friendship was a bond across seasons of dangers in the waterspace.

The reply was not in the least that which Frolic had thought he would hear...

'He will come and answer your questions, old friend. Nerve yourself for some shocks and surprises. Trust me and trust him, in Wanderer's name. Wait just a little longer,' Tinu said, reaching out one forefin and gaping a warmer beaksmile than Frolic had ever seen. 'Try to remember that he is trusting you as far as myself. He will be here soon.'

Frolic, astute Bottlenose that he was, had already made the leap to the astonishing fact that Tinu had been in mindmerge with another at considerable distance! Who this other adult Bottlenose could be he had no idea. Maybe a Storyteller? Or one of the new Watcher Guardians?

Then young Gaze, son of Gale, finned politely into Tinu's cave... but that was only a tiny surprise in relation to what he discovered next!

'If Vorg is capable of this mindvisioning as you say, Gaze, and of mindmerging without detection at close range, why did he fail the puzzle of Wanderer's Cave?' asked Frolic. 'Surely he could have used his mindskills to find the answers he needed?'

'He did not discover the facility in himself until too late and was more concerned with using his mindvisioning skill for self-gratification in other ways. If he were asked to solve the puzzle again by a Storyteller, he would not fail. He thinks, even now, that he has the solution and plans to enter Wanderer's Cave unobserved. He sought to read my mind to gain the information he needed but I misled him deliberately. Vorg is balanced between potentialities for good or evil. Maybe he has no further mindskills yet to develop. I cannot tell.'

Gaze finstirred awkwardly, in mindmerge with Frolic and Tinu, seeking to convey his feelings... Touching Frolic had been necessary but he had not shown him everything... He had not shared all of the suffering or the guilt...

The mindpattern within Frolic was so similar to that of Cyrene. He had not reminded Cyrene of her sire's name or that of her dam for there had been enough suffering. The sire could not be shown the whole truth; best that he continued in the belief Cyrene had deep-dived a season before in consequence of sudden misfortune. Neither could the dam, Dapple, be expected to face the truth having only recently accepted the fact of her daughter's demise.

Finwarp knew Cyrene's name... It was time that his memory of her name was impeded for he, too, needed to forget. Ardent could be trusted to keep the secret.

Never was practised a more sympathetic censorship than in the mindimages and visions shared with Frolic then - covering the deaths of two trainees and the attempt upon Finwarp's life with all the horrifying truth, barring the past existence of a 'Pleasure Cave' captive. Finwarp would substantiate this economy of truth later...

'Karg deserved such an end,' said Frolic, with complete, cold conviction, 'but why have you shared this with me?' Realisation breached... 'Vorg is Karg's son!?'

'With something of Karg's powers... but how much I do not know.'

Reeling in the dizziness of revelations, Frolic could only ask quietly what should be done.

'It is time to allow Vorg access to a vision himself,' said Gaze, 'but this will be an answer only for a short while. How strong Vorg will become I cannot tell - but he needs to recognise he has limitations - and not yet know whom he has to fear. Fear is the only check upon his need to dominate others... but for how long..? Perhaps he can fluke for the good of dolphinkind... perhaps...'

At last, Vorg would have an opportunity to seek the entrance to Wanderer's Cave.

Fishmuster was over. The sun was a clear illumination of the waterspace. The surface was unruffled by the breeze and the still waters of the lagoon almost uncomfortably warm. The Guardians had declared free out-reef fluking for all except the podlings of the Nursery who would bide close to the major lagoon entrance with the Nursery Dams and a few assistants on a rotating basis.

Some four hundred dolphinspans seaside of the reef was the Guardiancordon... with four podpairs of Observers maintaining the ever vigilant monitoring of waterspace and seascape further out.

Stretched, the Guardians had stood down lagoon entrance sentinels. There was little risk of danger in such balmy periods when all creatures seemed to live at peace. Even the voracious, quick-striking cuttlefish seemed stilled from the quest of shrimp-seeking. Cold-blooded clouds of reef-sheltering fish drifted in lazy eddies above unmoving banks of kelp, unafraid and tranquil. Two sharks fanflicked half-heartedly within bodylength of a shoal, appearing to pass unnoticed, unremarked...

Still Vorg waited for somnolence to settle like an invisible mist across the seascape; for the dorsals of drifting dolphins to seem stationary signs of sleep...

Then he shallow-sounded and finned silently towards the point where he would deep-dive for Wanderer's Cave.

He surfaced only once to airsnatch, causing no more than a gentle ripple. Convinced he was unobserved, he disappeared beneath.

Three dolphin dorsals, from different parts of the Podsherd, converged and followed Vorg's underwater finningvector but did not deep-dive.

Close to the reef, directly above the entrance to Wanderer's Cave, they fintouched in close communion...

Ascending the flooded tunnel was easy. Vorg breached into airspace above and began to finturn, examining crack and coral crevice seeking that which was identical with the stored image from the mind of Gaze.

There! He had beaksnouted there, feeling for what...? All he needed was the correct thing to push or pull...

There was a larger space beyond the narrow opening! He could not feel the sides of the crack beyond the length of a third of a bottlebeak. How did Gaze make the coral wall swing open?

Something touched his bottlebeak! In panic, Vorg backfinned away from the crack in the niche! It had felt like... No, it couldn't be. He was allowing his excitement to over-rule his common-sense. No giant squid would be within the reef. He had felt some weed drift across his snout from within the cave the other side of the coral wall. It had been unnerving but there was no real danger. After all, Gaze had been unafraid and he was considerably smaller, certainly not an imposing dolphin. Gaze would not have made a Guardian; he was lucky to have made Storyteller trainee!

Vorg finstirred some thoughtful moments but finturned towards the niche in the crack again. With direct, positive beaksnouting, quelling uncertainty, he explored again, ignoring the brush of weed from within the cave the other side of the crevice...

His bottlebeak was seized by a force beyond anything he could have expected! He glimpsed a huge eye through the crack and a large squidbeak!

There was no escape! He was jammed headfirst in the niche and sensed the coral beginning to break apart. He would be cruelly torn by the coral as he was pulled into the cave towards the waiting squidbeak!

Vorg mindscreamed! Flukethrashing, backfinning he tried to resist... It was useless!

The enormous tugging force diminished... but still the squideye stared malevolently through the crack. There was a pause... and then a high-pitched singing sound in his head. Light was ascending the shaft from below!

He heard a strong voice filling his mind and the closed airspace... a voice of command. His bottlebeak was released and he backfinned rapidly. Dazed, it was moments before he could finstir to face the speaker.

The light was coming from a Bottlenose, apparently illuminated from bottlebeak to fluketips with a pale, spectral glow! How? Who? Vorg wanted to touch him, had to touch him. Was he real?

Tentatively, he extended a fin to touch the dolphin's glowing side. Vorg recoiled with the sense of intense cold! No living dolphin could be that cold... but he was tangible.

He was compelled to mindmerge! He could not resist...

'Vorg, there is much in the waterspace and airspace above which is real and beyond your visioning, beyond your experience,' said a strong, mature voice emanating from this strange, powerful dolphin.

Bewildering, swelling visions of alien creatures, utterly unlike the known inhabitants of the warmstream waterspace, emerged from the crack in the niche, growing out of the cave behind. They growled and padded across the in-reef pool, soared and swung across the enclosed airspace or paddled and wallowed by his side. Vorg recognised them as mindvisions - but they were sharply defined, convincing.

Superimposed on rock and coral walls were images of Splitfluke inventiveness - of towering structures and unnatural shapes with Splitflukes inside. The airspace whistled and bleeped... or hummed and howled with sound.

No dolphin could have seen all this, know all this... unless this dolphin was...

Astounded, apprehensive, Vorg asked,'Who are you?'

There was silence.

The glowing dolphin finturned to stare with one fixed eye which seemed to magnify... Huge, a malevolent squideye was fixed upon Vorg! Coldly, the eye appraised him. Vorg heard the voice again, paternal but edged with absolute authority... like the sire he had not known but half-feared.

'I am part of your beginning; I can also be your end.

'I am your potential and your constraint. Any gift you have is magnified in me. Seek power, Vorg, and I shall be there to tear your flesh. I know your mind but not your heart. Fear me but fluke free for now.

'Outside are the Watcher Guardians - and I watch you through them. I give you warning... Use your gifts for dolphinkind for my eyes see your ambition.

'Live as a Guardian or live not at all.'

As the last words were uttered, the glowing Bottlenose sounded.

It took many long moments for Vorg's eyes and mind to clear. He did not finturn towards the niche again but deep-dived himself, thankful to seek the sunlit waterspace.

As Vorg breached out-reef on the open seaside, Frolic was waiting for him!

Bewildered, Vorg heard him saying, 'You know, now, that not many things escape the Watcher Guardians, Vorg. You do have some developing mindskills which will be useful. Remember that no dolphin can know everything or have all the skills he needs to fluke for the good of dolphinkind.

'We know you for what you are. You are one of many... and not as experienced as most.'

How had the Trainer known where he was? Who were 'we'?

He had read Frolic's mind once without detection. Vorg reached out in mindscan...

... and retracted immediately! A squideye was there!

'And so will you be watched, Vorg,' said Frolic. 'The disappearing float was a good ploy... but you played outside the rules for your own needs.'

How had Frolic known!? Was there more to some Guardians than he had thought?

The conceit of Vorg questioned itself for the first time. He was not as unique as he had thought... and he did not have the full measure of his superiors!

Tinu, Esu, Crest Spray and the other Watcher Guardians surfaced in a tight circle around them. Vorg and Frolic were surrounded by serious, snouting bottlebeaks.

The whole finning group were finstirring within a shimmering squideye on the surface of an eerie sea! Vorg was on the edge of mindscreaming in flukeflailing panic...

Tinu was saying, 'You have the potential to be an excellent Guardian, Vorg. Fluke to that potential... or practise the deep-dive, for it is the alternative you will surely face. Your training continues. You will have no other warning. Look at the Watcher Guardians!'

Vorg finstirred within the circle and, horrified, realised each bottlebeak seemed to be holding a small squideye which was staring at him unblinkingly!

At a clicked command from Tinu, they dived and finned in the direction of the Storytellers' Caves.

Before he, too, dived, Frolic said, 'Fin no more the access to Wanderer's Cave, Vorg. That is not your flukingpassage. Is that understood?'

Vorg could only nod his bottlebeak dumbly and watch as Frolic finned a solitary passage to join the Podsherd. Like a wounded pilot fish following a basking shark and too weak to ride the forepressure, he wavered a vector meekly behind.

He did not see Gaze emerge from the shadows near the reefangle and sound on a vector towards his familypod drifting in the Podsherd. Neither did he hear the mindmerge laughclicking of Frolic, Tinu and Gaze in joyful unison.

Crest Spray, Esu and the other Watcher Guardians saw no point in their summons by Tinu to fluke towards Frolic and that upstart trainee, Vorg.. and do nothing. Still, their's was not the reason why...

'He has the potential to challenge you successfully, my sire. Perhaps he can be contained for a while and the evil of a sire will not manifest itself... He has limited mindreading and a small visioning power. What other skill may develop is uncertain. No decision maker should be alone with Vorg for long. Let us hope his ambition can be answered within acclaim afforded to a successful Guardian... Perhaps there is no need for my anxiety...

'The squideye each of you has in the reefsides of your minds will deter him only as long as he fears and doubts within himself. I am anxious for the Podsherd but you know I must seek the mind of Maeve. There is much to learn for the good of us all.'

Gale finned around the perimeter of the Podsherd in bi-vector with his son and listened thoughtfully. His son had planned and thought ahead but he could not anticipate all the risks. He was warning of potential danger and was like an Observer beyond the Guardiancordon... except he would not make his reports in mindmerge, bottlebeak to bottlebeak... Inescapably, he would be out of mindcontact. His flukingpassage would cover vast dolphinspans of the seascape...

Gaze interrupted his sire's patterning...

'I can establish mindmerge at increasingly greater distance but I do not know my limit. I have to avoid other minds in seeking an individual mindcontact. It is easier if I can visualise the Bottlenose with whom I wish to mindmerge as being in a fixed place at a fixed time. I have to make an arrangement with Ardent. That is why I shall meet you in his cave, when you have finished your Guardian inspection.'

'Very well, my son, I shall be there,' said a serious sire, adding, 'Your dam would welcome occasional contact.'

Gaze beaksmiled. It was puzzling but his dam's mind seemed to anticipate his need for contact even before he felt the need himself. Dam intuition he supposed...

Saying Gale had no need for anxiety on that account, son separated from sire - Gale to complete his inspection and Gaze vectoring towards the Storytellers' Caves...

Ardent was expecting him and watched Gaze beaksnout the green dolphin carving respectfully. He realised the carving had some kind of special significance for the young flanker.

'It is of great significance, Ardent. I hope it will provide a focus for our mindcontact across greater distance than we have ever achieved. I have watched your habits.

'Whenever you enter your cave, you always beaksnout this crevice and beaktouch the carving. Have you ever heard voices?'

Ardent was not surprised. He knew Gaze would know his thoughts - all of them.

'You know the answer, Gaze. I hear a confusion of sounds: half, voices - half, a wild music of sea and wind. Sometimes it soothes me; sometimes I feel dizzy for moments afterwards. It interested me when you beaktouched it the first time. Something happened to you... and it made me wonder about your potential. The same thing happened with the Splitfluke skull in the cave pool, didn't it?'

Gaze watched the old Cleric. It was promising.

'Beaktouch it now, Ardent.'

Co-operatively, the elder dolphin finned to the crevice at the cave entrance, beaktouched the carving... There were the sounds and images but nothing he could focus upon, nothing that was... Something was new!

There was a new image... or perhaps it had always been there and he had not brought it into focus. A Splitfluke head was looking at him from within his own mind. The yellow-skinned Splitfluke that his sire had known! The Splitfluke who had deep-dived to death in the airthing so many seasons ago! But this head was speaking! Speaking in the mindmerge voice of Gaze!

'This is one of the images stored in the carving, Ardent, and you know it well for you told me the story of this Splitfluke and this carving. That story is treasured in the deepest part of your mind... the most sensitive. That is the part of your mind with which I shall seek mindmerge from across the seascape.

'I shall speak to his head in the carving... and he shall speak to you. You will talk to the yellow-skinned Splitfluke... and he shall speak to me.' There was a slight hesitation. 'Macabre it may be but let him live a while yet,'...Ardent detected sympathy... 'for as waterspace covers his corpse with anonymity, so shall he mask my identity. When I am gone, you will not forget this face.'

Gale finned through the cave entrance and stopped politely by Ardent's side, waiting...

The secret was shared with his sire only... possible contact declared - but not the manner...

*****

During that last nightwater, when Gaze was still with them, his familypod drew closer together than ever. Envious dolphineyes noted the family drifting within the Podsherd in quiet contentment. So obviously locked heart to heart and mind in mind were they, that it seemed the Master Guardian and his dam, Peen, with their near-mature off-spring were the living example of Wanderer's Teachings.

There was more of fulfilment in procreation if flesh-fervour was based, perhaps, in love. They seemed complete and self-sufficient, honouring responsibility to the Podsherd and earning honour within it.

A number of Bottlenose dorsals hesitated below the moonglow and starshine and quested afresh for another to love beyond the heat of temporary passion. Some beaksnouted for a sire or dam not mindmet for too many lightwaters and gossiped the inconsequential - or remembered the need to speak emotional significance. The lonely sought hope in love observed from a distance.

No dolphin would have believed one familypod was the visible and focal point for a mindmerge network encompassing all of those in whom Gaze trusted. No hint of plan or caution, advice or the devotion with which his words were heeded was visible. His parting from each was accepted as necessary but sorely felt... in a dam's anxiety, a sire's pride, a sister's gratitude and by those who loved him, in thankfulness.

Before the breaching of the sun in a new lightwater, Gaze had gone, out-reef from beneath the Podsherd and fluking a vector towards open seaspace. His sire, unaccountably, lost his son's echo-return as he passed beneath and beyond the darkwater Guardian patrol! No Observer reported the passage of a dolphin - or his breaching, at a distance in the seascape of the sun's deep-diving...

Gale could only beaksmile as he heard his son's mindmerge comment, 'No sire, the Observers and Guardians were fully alert. A good watch is being maintained. What would have been the point in reporting some drifting weed to you? Farewell, for now.'

Gale finturned towards his Peen. He fintouched her gently, not wishing to disturb her sleep.

She surprised him.

'I know, my love. He has gone, hasn't he? Gone... but for how long?'

Peen's bottlebeak was following something sensed a long way off... and she knew the distance was increasing.

Gaze would be absent for several mooncycles. His disappearance was put down to fluking out-reef ill advisedly and without permission. He was deemed to have met his fate in unpredictable waterspace.

Gale's familypod grieved... but appeared to take their loss stoically.

Gaze should have listened to his sire when he was reprimanded the first time he fluked out-reef alone, thought all Bottlenoses but a few.

Chapter Eight

THE SOLITUDE

In the vastness of the seascape was the solitude in variance from others - and severance from the familiar.

Pings and echoes from the Podsherd had faded lightwaters ago to whispers and tailed into silence. He was quiet, not responding in registering other signals from toothed or untoothed whales - wanting a period of observation and reflection... and he needed to prove his self-sufficiency unto himself, alone...

There were minds but they were alien, engaged in pursuit and escape, or questing for sustenance. Here was subterfuge and cunning; a place where the unwary and weak lived but briefly. Existence, sparked in a multitude of minds surrounding the fluking form of Gaze... a veritable galaxy of creation in which identity could be lost in the infinitude. Here and there, mindlights would flare in stark awareness and panic and wink into darkness; others would dim through progressive shades of grey to black, ebbing and stilling - too tired to turn from mouth or sting.

Sympathy for the vanquished was wasteful emotion. In such indulgence, he teetered from mind-equilibrium. Most death was mercifully swift - the weakest succumbing first. Gaze, himself, strike-vectored upon the slower moving, the aged or inexperienced, for he did not have a fishmuster to aid him... although he seemed accompanied.

Two dolphins fluked in tri-vector with Gaze, reflecting his movements. This pod followed the forcelines he had memorised from Wanderer's 'maps'- and from the after-images which that hero of the sagas had left imprinted, through experience and memory, in the act of creativity. His two companions did not mindmeet with Gaze - neither did they click in conversation. As mindvision extensions of himself - an act which he was making a reflex - they shimmered, ceased to exist when he knew it was safe to sleep in shelter of reef...

When Gaze slept, part of his mind was alert for an unusual vibration, a change in behavioural sea-patterns or a difference in the rhythms of the waterspace. As with the universal sleeper, he woke to alarm signals registered unconsciously. In truce periods he slept best - those periods when all creatures ceased the struggles of the food cycle but during which the fallen remains were consumed by claws, plants and collective functions of digestion and decay. Such claimed the cadavers or fragments of 'others' upon seafloor and in deepwater. He was of the surface creatures, illumined by the lightwater. Dependent upon air, he participated briefly in the ceaseless carnage beneath... witnessing swirling motion of survival and death.

Predators of dolphinkind were few but the habit of vigilance was necessary and hard to break. Gaze was unresting in sleep in the open seaspace. Conditioned to the security of the Guardian patrol, he was afraid to relax. His respect for the Voyagers - and all they had encompassed - increased tenfold. Could he make a reflex vision in sleep to camouflage his exposure as a Bottlenose alone? He would fluke greater passages if not forced to seek security of shelter when physical and mental fatigue threatened to overwhelm him...

...He had made of himself an orca... but this had been a fearful thing he would wish to forget. Perhaps there was another way he could camouflage himself near the surface...?

...A way in which he would be unchallenged, avoided and yet not be so threatening...?

The youthful observer had his solution at the next breach of sun...

Awaking, in a calm sea, Gaze scanned - not in echo-location - but in his unique way of seeking mindlights. He was finding this more reliable in seeking friend or foe ... or, indeed, noting life-forms which lacked any interest in such distinctions, like the shoal which was surface floating before the breeze, twenty dolphinspans away...!

He finned away from the shoal. Nursery training had warned him of these ghostly jelly-fish. Maeve's mind recognised them, too, but with the odd name of 'men o' war' and she feared the stinging tentacles which trailed beneath. They drifted with the current and before the wind, using a poisonous touch to paralyse their prey. Only some small fish, associating immunely with this wandering death, accompanied these lonely drifters... and the partnership was productive.

He watched as a larger fish chased a smaller, immune shape into the tangle of drifting tentacles - which looked no more than weed. He felt the sear of stinging pain as a shock across his mind's awareness... and then the grasp of the lift towards extinction in the gastrozooids. The smaller fish emerged unscathed and would share choice morsels in the symbiotic exchange.

These 'men o' war' were avoided. The armoured turtles made striking-vectors upon them but not without risk and discomfort to the eyes. Pain and death was cradled in the trailing tentacles... which looked no more than weed...

He had 'looked no more than weed' as he had cloaked his departure from the Guardian patrol, invisible in the ordinary... Gaze knew what he must do to find his rest in the open waterspace!

Choosing his position on the fringe of the jelly-fish shoal, he dissolved his current camouflage of the dolphin podpartners. He projected a balloon-like sail around his dorsal. With mindtendrils, he made a trailing, downward extension of weed-like tentacles... and waited.

After long moments of patience, a small fish fanflicked agilely to investigate the unaccompanied 'man o' war' at the perimeter of the shoal. Gaze detected puzzlement and disappointment at finding no morsels of food, but the vision was convincing. He had greater proof when he noted a few larger fish sheer away from his drifting course.

He tried to read the minds within the spectral shoal but found them cold, too fluid and distant. They were reflexive, instinctive... a network of nerve energy reacting to waterspace within compass of the tentacle spans, and little else. There was no real sense of living in co-operation or needing companionship. They were utterly dissimilar from his experience and his concept of living. It mattered not if they were loosely joined in an extended shoal... or if an individual drifted in isolation.

Gaze knew the manner of his darkwater hiding from now on. It was a projection of a nerve network he could easily achieve. Shimmering and pulsating under the moonglow, would not matter but merely add to the spectral quality, deterring further investigation.

He gained strange comfort in recalling his lightwater fluking partners and found himself clicking greeting to his own imagevisions. Inwardly, he mindchuckled. He should not leave it too long before he sought the companionship of his own kind!

He checked the forcelines, sensed the lightwater objective and, in tri-vector, continued flukingpassage...

After vertical sunlight, he heard dolphin echo-locating pinging. For a moment he hesitated... but vectored towards his own kind. This would be the first time he had joined in a fishmuster of the deep waterspace. Ranging ahead and mindprobing, he read the pattern of the fishmuster plan.

It was a different technique. These dolphins were the long-snouted Spinners who enjoyed such gyrations in air or waterspace. They were a light-hearted assembly of loosely co-operating pods and, amongst themselves, volatile in mood and temperament. These were the sometime predators of the flying fish which finglided above the waves in the airspace, seeking frantic escape from dolphinteeth beneath.

The main body of the fishmuster would soon be setting off to fluke in an extended 'U' to herd a shoal of tuna before them. Gaze detected, beyond the tuna shoal, an outlying dolphincordon, mainly mature males. These were to serve the two functions of barring escape and causing underwater confusion for the fish. Unlike Bottlenoses of Wanderer's warmstream waterspace, the Spinners relied on a series of surface rushes and allowed more independence of action underwater. The system would work but he could not help feeling that the Guardians would have organised things to the better advantage of the weaker, less mobile dolphins he detected here and there.

Dissolving his camouflage of podpartners, Gaze pinged identification, expressing willingness to mindmeet and join the fishmuster.

He received acknowledgement from several Spinners, lightly inviting him to take what he could.

He noted, with half-bottlegrimace, one adult female's mindmerge observation of, 'A young bottlebeast! Little smartnose wants to join the fun, eh. Might catch a shrimp or two, I suppose.'

'And a fish or two for you, my cousin,' Gaze said, in open mindmerge... and mindchuckled at her obvious surprise in his apparent maturity, despite his size.

The snoutclicking laughter at her discomfiture was rewarding... and then Gaze detected alien minds and the hardside, beyond the shoal, on a wide, circling vector...

There were Splitflukes nearby!

Before he could have time to mindjoin with another Splitfluke, the fishing formation of the 'U' began to close in leaving open only a narrow, escape-vector for the fish. Some did escape before the outlying dolphincordon closed the gap. Almost leisurely, some Spinners fluked beneath the shoal, beginning to echo-call from below to disorientate the fish; others began the flukeslapping routine to stun and further confuse. Inevitably, gulls and gannets made their appearances...

There were not the disciplined striking-vectors of thirds of the fishmuster to which he was used. Instead, a series of uncoordinated rushes began. Acting individually, Spinners began a free-for-all of surface striking-vectors and underwater, through the glittering, swerving mist of the bunched shoal. Sweeping in a tight circle, a dolphin would trap some fish against the wall of its body, and pick off a target with ease. Another would use speed and agility to chase down prey. Many fish were taken, but far greater numbers escaped - many more than would have been declared acceptable by the Guardians of the Podsherd, thought Gaze. However, all dolphins fed.

Gaze could not resist taking one more fish for the impolite female, as he had promised... and noticed that the escapees had not fishfanned very far. Seeming to be hemmed in by something unseen, they were bunching in the depths...

They were panicking below!

Whatever was causing that thickening crush of fishfans, fins and struggling sides, it was no dolphin!

Gaze breached and mindscanned. He released his fishgift which bellied to the surface and was seized in a gannetbeak.

Beneath, the turmoil - a crushing, a gilltearing... Fishtrap! That was the panic... and death in the wriggling weave! There was terror in the cold minds to which he was attuned...

Gaze shared the fear. He was in the centre of a closing fishtrap!

He had not taken the precious moments he had needed to mindscan the Splitflukes he had seen. Suddenly the horror of Spinner mindscreams, sharp, incisive! Three... no, five Spinners were trapped in the weave of the fishtrap!

Helpless, these Spinners would drown! Their last moments would be a tiring struggle to tear themselves free in the desperate need to airsnatch...

Two of the Spinners, flukethrashing wildly, tore themselves free from a final embrace with Splitefluke inventiveness. Three others were tiring. Nothing seemed to come of their frantic efforts. Gaze could sense a red haze of overwhelming hopelessness - sensed the gripping tightness of lungs deprived of airsnatch...

One of the trapped Spinners was the female who had ridiculed him! Enmeshed a mere dolphinspan beneath the airspace she needed urgently, the weave of the fishtrap was tangled around her beaksnout and a fin. Gaze dived, only dimly aware of another strange sound.

She was surrendering to the inevitable, gathering herself to release the last residue of air to the sea and flood her lungs. Gaze finstirred at her side, his mindvoice commanding...

She was still, relaxed...

He beaknosed the tangle. It could be done! Slipping the mesh from her fin, he grasped her flukes in his bottlebeak and fluked to release her snout, dragging her backwards... She was free!

Too weak to rise, she needed his support to the airspace above and wallowed long moments in the wash and surge...

Gaze mindscanned... A Splitfluke was in the waterspace!

Some dolphinspans away was a small, flat hardside with a tiny twistingfin which sliced a passage in buzzing interference of any echo-scanning. Another Splitfluke was riding the hardside, rising and falling to effects of seasurge, just beyond a line of floats he perceived were supporting the fishtrap walls.

The Splitfluke, within the perimeter of the fishtrap floats, was finning closer! Gaze had to read his intended purpose!

He carried no weapons except for the 'knife' in a 'sheath' on his belt. Killing was not on his mind. He wanted to... assist? He wished to assist trapped dolphins to clear the barrier of fishtrap floats! It was not out of gratitude. It was... It was to avoid damage to the 'nets'. Also... also, because...

...'Every assistance shall be given to dolphins caught inadvertently whilst fishing for tuna using purse-seine nets. Such nets shall employ a Medina panel, sited on the far side from the vessel thus affording greater opportunity for dolphins captured incidentally to see it and escape over its rim, aided where necessary by divers.'...

This Splitfluke predator was under orders to help the dolphins caught in the fishtrap of the nearby hardside to escape!

Understanding the reason for his presence, Gaze finned by the side of the exhausted female Spinner whilst the Splitfluke steered her to the floating perimeter. Gaze read the Splitfluke mind further... He was a white-skinned Splitfluke. His 'father' was the 'skipper' of the 'fishing vessel'. He was recently mature and he was 'Australian'! He was from Maeve's landspace or 'country'!

This 'Graham' heaved, helping the female over the fishtrap perimeter. Gaze leapt free himself. On sheer impulse, he finturned close to Graham who was airsnatching in short bursts...

Knowing he was recognised as a different species, Gaze mindmerged fleetingly with the nearby Splitfluke mind, separated by the wall of the net and a gulf of evolution...

'Thank you, Graham,' the beak of a dolphin seemed to say! Graham shook his head in near disbelief and watched the bottlenose dolphin swim towards the weaker spinner he had assisted over the net. It could not have happened...

The fragmented fishmuster was regathering. Elated at escape from the fishtrap, numbers were breaching, spinning in the airspace above. Others were gathering wits and shallow-snatching air nervously, gratefully. Very few suspected that two Spinners had flooded their lungs a few dolphinspans beneath the surface. The frolic terminated abruptly as...

The hardside was hauling in the fishtrap. Long-snouts and one bottlebeak watched as two Spinners appeared above the seasurge, already limp, unmoving. Water dripped from flukes and dribbled from clickless, open mouths. One near-mature and a middle-aged dam had died. Only Gaze heard the voice from the dimming mindlight of the elder...

'Oh, my son... I saw you catch... your... fisshh.h...'

The fishmuster was silent.

Through wet eyes, Gaze thought he saw a white dolphin hanging in the swaying weave, just below both dead Spinners, appearing to struggle to touch them with a fin. But his eyes cleared...

A pod of mature females began a circuit of the hardside and the echo-lament of the deep-dive. The calls rang louder and further than Gaze had hitherto heard, returning as plaintive echoes from the abyss.

There were also the ping patterns of two names... but he could not be certain if they were acknowledged...

Gaze was conscious of dolpinteeth lightly grasping his flukes and a quiet, mindmerging voice...

'Thank you, young bottlebeast. You saved me from that. I forgive you for the marks you have left... as if I was your property. Am I your property now?'

Gaze finturned to face her...

'My name is Gaze, not 'bottlebeast'. You are called 'Starshine'. I am glad I could help you... and I do not seek the reward you are half-contemplating.'

Startled, Starshine finstirred awkwardly and chose to ask the least disturbing question.

'How do you know my name?'

'That matters not, Starshine. For we must join your podsherd. Think of the present. Can you not sense the sharks?'

She did not reply but fluked in bi-vector with him to the regrouping Spinners, compliant and grateful of escort.

The fishmuster separated into small pods, once removed upcurrent of bloodflow. Sharks fanflicked downcurrent and close to the drifting hardside which seemed to be swallowing vast quantities of tuna, emptied from the 'net'. Only one dolphin observed the final fate of a dam and near-mature, through his human mindeye.

Gaze maintained his mindcontact with Graham. It was not as close as with Maeve, lacking a certain solidity of empathy which had been evident in her.

Graham was a 'fisherman' and sufficiently practical - and hardened - in his youthfulness, not to dwell too long upon the unfortunate ends of two dolphins. The catch of tuna had been good; the loss of two dolphin allies, however unfortunate, was one of the tolls to be paid in the turn of events.

Graham stared at the prostrate forms of the two, sleek, - but warmly dead - dolphins on the deck. In horror, Gaze realised that other 'fishermen' caught dolphinkind as food. Dolphinflesh was favoured by some kinds of yellow-skin Splitflukes! An intelligent creature himself, Graham did not recognise the potentiality of intelligence in dolphins. They seemed more akin to fish and simply alien!

Graham liked dolphins... There was even a hint of guilt if he failed to rescue them when they were ensnared in the 'mesh' of the 'net'. However, he was too practical to waste time in moping over the misfortune of the 'unlucky'.

Heads banging and scraping against the roughness of the deck, the dead Spinners were dragged to the side. Conscientiously, Graham chose the side furthest from the 'school' of dolphins so that their re-entry to the sea would be unobserved... The sharks were waiting, as they always waited for offal and scraps...

He watched the twisting turn and tear, which left the circular wounds in unfeeling flesh, entirely alone. His mindeye partner could not look.

Gaze finned in association with the Spinners during the darkwater, not needing his 'man o' war' camouflage. It was rest and companionship he welcomed.

A debt of gratitude kept Starshine by his side. Although she would have permitted - even welcomed - greater intimacy than the brush of companionable contact, she respected the wish of the young Bottlenose for nothing further. He needed respite from solitude... to sleep in security after a joining of minds.

Slowly, as Gaze retracted the reefside from those parts of himself he was prepared to share, she began to sense that he was a special dolphin. He appeared warm and considerate.

He was knowledgeable but very young to be one of the Story-teller trainees. She had heard of the Voyagers from Wanderer's warmstream Podsherd but she had never met one. Some of the elder Spinners spoke of them passing in flukingpassage, over the seasons, on their Storyteller tasks.

The Spinners' sagas spoke of Wanderer as a dolphin of courage and vision who had intended to voyage further than any dolphin had ever been. He had not bided long. They had wondered at his determination and puzzled at how he would rest in the open seaspace with no other dolphineyes to watch in the darkwater.

Wanderer had said that, 'His faith in the White Dolphins was his protection' and that, 'Some season hence, would come a Bottlenose larger than himself. He would travel further for all dolphinkind but only a few would know him, save in their hearts'.

This small Bottlenose, barely mature, she could not associate in the least with the ramblings of elder Spinners. If a large 'bottlebeast' ever came, he would be remarkable indeed if this one was anything to go by! It was relaxing to fintouch and finstir by his side - such a sense of peace seeming to radiate from him.

She would never insult him again... but would remember him always as her 'bottlebeast'. Perhaps the lightwater would come when she could repay her debt... or, when he was less tired...

'There is no need to show gratitude. It is enough to know we are friends.'

He had read her mind! Yet they had not been in mindmerge! There was no threat... Nothing but a sense of closeness...

'Who can tell how we may need to help each other in the waterspace, Starshine? It is good to know there are others to finturn towards when we need comfort. I shall remember you, 'longnose', as you remember me. I am glad to know you but, in the darkwater, we should sleep. It is time to sleep.'

Starshine felt drowsy. She was tired - too tired to argue over silly names. She snoutsmiled. 'Longnose' was deserved she supposed. He really was a ... wonderful... 'bottlebeast'... She did need to... sleep...

Gaze did not surrender to darkwater rest for a shortwhile longer. He had a message to leave with someone else beyond the present...

Starshine did not know she finstirred restlessly during her descent into the dreamworld of watershadows which deeply reflected the moonglow and her sparkling name-sisters of the airspace.

Mindwaves rode the seasurge and echoed through the valleys of the forcelines... bent to converge upon a distant reef system... curved to negotiate a narrow reefmaze, passed watchful Guardian sentinels unnoticed... and centred, concentrated within a tiny jade carving of a dolphin resting in a niche. Within the carving, an image began to whisper through Splitfluke teeth set in a grimace of pain etched on the yellow-skinned face.

Ardent had beaknosed his carving thrice sun-around, unobserved. There had been nothing. The yellow-skinned Splitfluke had stared through brown eyes into his own, the black pupils swollen, but the lips of the mouth drawn tight, thin and bloodless. Several lightwaters had passed. Out in the sea-circumference, beyond compassing, the young flanker he sought to serve - and loved already - was silent in the immensity. Still Ardent kept to the agreed ritual.

The faith he had demonstrated in keeping the promise he had made to Wanderer, many seasons ago, was unswerving. In moments of doubt, the eyes of the Splitfluke head were steady and Ardent knew they would continue to gaze at him - as long as the young Bottlenose who had given them sight was strong in himself.

Last lightwater, he had consulted Gale and Peen. Gale could offer no explanation of the silence.

It was Peen who had said, 'He is safe. I would know if it were different. There are many things to do in finding one's way in the waterspace... and we could not teach him so many things... but I know we will hear of him soon.'

In the face of such simple certainty, despite anxiety,

Cleric/Historian and Master Guardian had learned the need for patience anew.

Finning from his cave-entrance, at the breach of the new sun, he had finturned to the niche, prepared to be disappointed...

Ardent had not looked within to the eyes - but to the mouth of the Splitfluke head. The lips were moving!

The Splitfluke was talking but Ardent could not hear the tongue! Ardent stared inwardly at the image of the head. The moment his mindeye focused upon the eyes in the head, he heard the voice of Gaze!

Ardent was late for his first training session. Gaze had spoken at length. It was with great relief that Ardent spread the content through the mindmerge network of the dolphins who had been waiting. They learned of his flukingpassage; of his lightwater camouflage and that of the darkwater in isolation; of his meeting with the Spinners, and of his encounter with the white-skinned, Splitfluke 'fishermen'.

Gaze had two requests... He wanted Ardent to consult with Sinu, the Inventor, to learn as much as he could of the different kinds of Splitfluke fishtraps and their fish-hunting methods in dolphin-knowledge. He was then to offer open mindmerge to the Splitfluke head in the carving. The young Bottlenose had realised the need to learn some things fast. Ardent could not have guessed that Gaze was planning to assimilate dolphin-knowledge with information yet to be obtained from a certain young, Australian fisherman.

The second request concerned the possible despatch of a podunit of four Guardians to advise on safe fishmustering to a podsherd of Spinners with whom he had associated for a short period. He gave the name of a contact, the waterspace towards which the podunit should vector and gave the strongest recommendation as to the Guardian who should be given the temporary status of Pod Leader.

'Crest Spray, Mimic and two other dolphins, at the descretion of the Master Guardian, to comprise the outfluking podunit... Starshine, a Spinner dolphin, to be the contact and the means of introduction to certain influential elders.'

There was need for a conference... and much to do.

Ardent was suddenly busier than he had been for long seasons - but dived into everything with infectious enthusiasm.

Starshine ascended from the depths of the dreamworld, eyes adjusting to the half-haze of new lightwater. She knew her 'bottlebeast' had gone before breach of sun. Her lateral-sensing confirmed it.

She echo-scanned the seascaping circumference.

From far dolphinspans came a whisper of the echo-return she was seeking, two forefin spans left of sundive. In that secret, sad corner of her mind, near the quickening rhythm of her heart, she mindmerged her farewell. She wished events might have been different...

'You will meet other 'bottlebeasts' soon, Starshine. They will seek your friendship and they will know your name. These Bottlenose friends will seek to help you further,' said a mindmerge voice that thrilled her!

But the voice seemed so close - as if from a dolphin finstirring by her side...!?

What trick of light focused her eyes in the dark shades of the horizon and the distant breaching of... a dolphin of indeterminate size?

In those moments of communion between mind and heart - perhaps, she realised, during the darkwater as well - Starshine knew of the propensity for good in Gaze... She would do as he desired.

She finned towards friends, curbed her caustic tongue - for which some Spinners were grateful - and showed more of her true self in sympathy and care. In the lightwaters ahead, she was surprised at how her popularity seemed to increase when she no longer courted it. Soon, there were other Spinners' eyes looking, echo-locating towards the seaspace of the sun's new breaching and watching for the friends of Gaze whom Starshine said, emphatically, would eventually come...

Gaze rode the forewave pressure of the hardside which was returning to 'New Caledonia'. Gaze knew this from the mind of Graham who stood at the 'bow', staring thoughtfully at the bottlenose dolphin moving so effortlessly ahead. The 'Hunter Island Ridge' beneath, was recognised by the young Bottlenose from Wanderer's 'maps' and from the 'seamanship' knowledge stored in the mind of his spectator. No dialogue in any open sense took place between the mammal of the airspace and the mammal of the seaspace, but the latter learned... of Splitfluke practicality and of Graham, a Splitfluke, as much as this simple son of the sea had known.

It was in the crossing of the 'New Hebrides Trench' that Gaze began to recognise the magnitude of divergence between the two evolutions of Splitfluke existence and dolphinkind...

Graham was the product of a species which sought to profit from utilising landscape and waterspace, paying little heed to the weft and weave of interdependence which most creaturekind acknowledged.

Splitflukes changed the natural order for short-term gains, harvesting and killing more than was necessary... poisoning land, air and water and killing further in blind consequence. Graham was discomfited by many things which he knew were happening but failed to recognise the full extent. He knew of water pollution and health risks... but not of the harm to the bases of the many food chains... of the genocide of species and the pauperism of life thus caused.

Some Splitflukes took too great a share of an abundance - ignoring the suffering and the impoverishment for others. Greed and a need for domination carried the seeds of life's destruction in all the worldspace!

Gaze sensed the existence of Abominations in the world of Splitflukes... Abominations like Karg - yet worse in the scales of utter indifference to anything more than their own exaggerated ambitions. The lifespace could be altered irrevocably before such creatures stopped the abuse.

The young dolphin was the product of contrary evolution - one which sought to live in tune with the lifespace. The laws of balance in harmonious co-existence - flouted by the tool-users - could not be disregarded in perpetuity.

Yet, the Splitflukes had great intelligence... Could they learn from mistakes? Could they demonstrate the capacity to image ahead, view the consequences and avoid a projected disaster - for themselves and all creaturekind?

Perhaps, some like Maeve - the youthful, intelligent Splitflukes who possessed conscience and empathy - could avert the chaos and destruction which Gaze was beginning to visualise? To do nothing, knowing the inevitable, was madness - a worm in the head of life.

It took Maeve four weeks to realise the apartment was like a shelf on a cage wall in the City Zoo. The weeks of decorating and furnishing had not yet created the feeling of home. Too clinical, the Coral Sea seemed far away.

Her father was throwing himself against a logjam of paperwork and arrived home tired each evening. His tie was always loosened and his hair dishevelled when he came through the door. Despite his attempts at cheerfulness, his relaunch into the financial world had not been a smooth re-entry. Within an hour of homecoming, he was dozing in an armchair. Dutifully, Maeve tended to the superficial ceremonies of housekeeping but the three of them were concerned only with a semblance of lived-in tidiness.

Donovan's room typified the disorder of the student on vacation. His head hit the pillow at infrequent intervals as he whirled between social entertainment, sporting fixture, a secretive date or a fleeting, fit-of-conscience confrontation with his vacation assignment which seemed to be taking an extraordinary length of time in planning - let alone actually writing.

One sweaty night had changed into grey daybreak before the young-blood had kissed his pillow goodnight in a state of contented exhaustion. Maeve had not asked the reason for his mid-day emergence from tumbled bedding. She supposed the young male was predatorial with regard to her own sex and there was ample prey for an intelligent and resourceful banker's son. Her brother had his good points but his willingness to leave everything associated with domestic matters to his sister was irksome... even to cleaning lipstick from his shirt collar.

Progressively, the isolation and claustrophobia of apartment walls impelled Maeve to seek air and freedom. Then came the conscious decision to seek contact with dolphins in a more tangible form than the books she was reading.

The apartment and the immediate locality, fostered a growing sense of isolation and gave her too much time to brood about... the past.

She began a campaign for the personal freedom to visit the Dolphinarium near Brisbane. No, she wanted to go alone. She could travel into Brisbane with her father, Ciaran, and return in the evening. She avowed that Donovan could look after himself.

She dropped dark hints to her brother that he might welcome the apartment being empty to get on with 'things he needed to do'...

He thought it best to concur, knowing it was not in his 'interests' to be obstructive.

Ciaran suspected nothing but welcomed the co-operation between brother and sister, remembering the confrontation of Fiji. Yes, Maeve deserved the opportunity to follow her latest 'fad' further. Maeve had outstripped his knowledge of cetaceans... and it was time she looked for social contacts. Such might follow a trip or two into Brisbane... Donovan could do with some days alone to finish his study assignment... How could Ciaran have known that his son had one or two other short-term objectives?

That evening, Donovan began to tidy his room and assisted Maeve in the circumnavigation of all rooms with the vacuum cleaner. Father watched their task-sharing, mind fogged in financial reviews, and completely missed the quiet, disparaging undertones from his daughter.

The following morning, Maeve accompanied Ciaran to Brisbane. Donovan certainly looked as though he was going to throw himself into study, carefully preparing pens and reference books... but his sister knew better.

The girl, just approaching the full bud of womanhood, had sat adjacent to the 'lagoon', outside the latticed perimeter fencing, for over an hour and a half now. She smiled easily, eyes fixed on the circumnavigating 'stars' - the bottlenose dolphins. Her hands were conducting unheard music responding to jump and dive or the underwater ballet of the sleek forms. Slowly, it became clear to Rick Dortmann that she was not one of the hangers-on who came to ogle the two bronzed, male assistants with their sun-bleached, blonde hair - his 'boys'.

Phil and Rod were hardened to the sirens who screeched in discord, simpered enthusiastically and stretched lengthy brown legs inconveniently close to their honest endeavours whilst fetching and carrying for the 'stars'. Rick had made it abundantly clear that the prime responsibility of this family was to conduct the affairs of the Dolphinarium efficiently. The pursuits of the beach and any amorous undercurrents in swimming and surfing had to be governed by the demands of the 'Show' and 'the welfare of the stars', as he put it. Earlier working experience with their father had taught them who held the purse strings and what a constraint that could be. Both had learned to bide their time in dealing with romantic associations - and that these were best encouraged on the beach rather than at work.

Rick gave her another half hour before he sat down, a yard or so away, splicing a new rope end and sucking on his short-stubbed pipe. He noted, with surreptitious glances, a well-thumbed library book on cetaceans - and some rapid outline sketches on a pad...

The lines were not heavily accurate, nor was much care given to a photographic representation, but there was an astonishing quality of zestfulness and mobility... the sense of living water in spray and foam - of effervescence. She was capturing far more than the vacuous crowds observed in the afternoon 'Shows'. He watched her rise and move to purchase her second drink. If only more casual watchers of the morning shared such genuine interest...

He was tired of the lager tins lobbed over the fence and the few who paid the morning admission bent on pushing 'unfortunates' into the pools. This one was a different and genuine brand.

He watched her walk back to the seat, her brown, page-boy hair stirring in the sea-breeze. She was still watching the dolphin female swimming with less energy than her pool-partners. Those brown eyes were puzzled. She sat, leaning forward, elbows resting mid-thighs and her fingers stretched over her mouth.

The rarity of the occasion lost on his two sons, busy at distance away, Rick spoke across the fence to the girl who was simply dressed in white tennis shirt and red Bermuda shorts.

'You've been there a long time. I've watched you. I'm the Manager and I think you'd like to get closer still. Am I right?'

Sunshine broke through the girl's eyes. She walked towards the locked gate which he indicated and waited for it to be opened.

'Thank you. My name is Maeve. I promise I won't interfere.'

'I know you won't. Let me show you around - after you answer two questions.'

He paused as those brown eyes looked openly and honestly into his own.

'May I have one of your drawings? Secondly, why were you watching one dolphin in particular just now?'

'Take your pick of the sketches. They're not that good.'

She was quiet... Then came a comment he was half-expecting for she could have the empathy he suspected was there...

'The dolphin with the white tip to the dorsal seems sad. Why is she sad?'

Straight to the problem, thought Rick. No wasted time on silly questions about what dolphins ate or how high they could jump - straight to his headache. So he told her...

Further up the East Coast, in a straggling coastal community, a shop-owner had hit upon a gimmick to attract the passing trade. On the pretext of having rescued two dolphins needing treatment after incidental capture in drift nets, he had installed them, a male and near-mature female, in the swimming pool at the rear of the premises. Their actual origins had proved impossible to ascertain.

Passers-by were invited to take a dip with the dolphins and a number of children did enjoy the experience. Numerous holiday snaps were taken and light refreshments provided in an outhouse, began to make the weekly turn-over look quite healthy. An arrangement with a local trawler skipper, for some cheap fish, saw to the needs of the dolphins - or so the conscience of this would-be entrepreneur affirmed in later dialogue with a newspaper reporter.

The resultant article invoked a backlash in expressed opinion - such that the anticipated wider publicity was very largely negative - not the useful free advertisement the shop-keeper had desired.

Uncomfortable comments were made about 'cleanliness of water for bathers' and the 'inadequacy of insurance cover'. The readership became incensed over the risks to which children were being exposed.

Ludicrous statements were made concerning the possible dangers of dolphin attack and the need for emergency medical treatment to be readily available for bites and cuts.

Sensible, informed comment decried dolphin attack but could do nothing to assuage doubts concerning health risks for children.

Very few letters to the Editor of the small-time newspaper pointed out the sad plight of the incarcerated dolphins... but, when the point was made, the crusade for closure of the venture gathered momentum. The universal Mother was worried more over 'children and dirty water' and 'the danger' than the two, large, 'fishy' things... but it helped the cause to suggest that the dolphins were 'being mistreated'.

'The shop-owner contacted this Dolphinarium a couple of months ago, asking for advice on 'a cheap way to keep the water clean'. I was furious. The fool had no notion of 'salination' or 'filtration'!

'I went to see him. The whole thing was pathetic. He had an area of the pool fenced off, with a mixture of garden fencing panels and two old bedframes, supposed to serve as a pen overnight. A large net-scoop was used to clear the pool of leaves and waste material but he left a number of coins, tossed in for luck, on the bottom. He said he always left a fifth of the 'take' to encourage others who wanted their share of 'dolphin-luck'.

'Christ knows how I stopped myself thumping him when he said he did his best to keep the water clean and that he had doubled the 'dose' of chemicals added! The idiot had to be stopped.'

Maeve was fully attentive...

'She was one of the dolphins from that place? How did you stop him? What happened to the other one?'

Rick studied her. There was no need to talk of the half-threats involving Legislation - or the markedly less 'legal' comment he and the 'boys' had made on a follow-up visit with the pick-up. The shop-keeper had wanted to sell the dolphins to the Dolphinarium but Phil had had a rush of blood to the head. Phil had let the avaricious sod get up - when it was 'agreed' the dolphins could go to Brisbane free-of-charge... and Rod had put down the hammer which was about to set about the tea-room shack. His 'boys' had needed some firm talking to. The shop-keeper had agreed that he didn't want any more adverse publicity.

Maeve was waiting...

'Yes, she's moved home. The shop-owner agreed with our point of view. She's sad because her young mate died soon after arrival - if you believe dolphins have emotions...'

He watched the brown eyes mist. He had known they would. He waited... Then...

'You've met dolphins before, haven't you?'

Maeve said, quietly, 'I've been close to three. I touched the youngest... or he touched me. They let you know how they feel, don't they? And they can... speak...'

Rick was convinced. Maeve had empathy with dolphins. He guessed she hadn't told him everything... but it could wait. The next comment the girl had obviously not expected....

'Got a swimming costume?' Rick asked. 'If you haven't, you can borrow a wet-suit. Rod's grown out of his old one.'

White Tip finned the lonely circuit. She knew Bloom was... How could she expect these other Bottlenose podpartners to share her grief? They had told both of them there was no possibility of escape to free waterspace; that it was better to resign themselves to the inevitable and make the best of opportunities. 'Casualties had to be accepted in the waterspace,' had said one of the 'trick-learners' who had been in Splitfluke captivity for three seasons.

Both young dolphins had been advised to forget the real waterspace and seek to please the Splitfluke captors.

Assurances were given that it was possible to enjoy pleasant relationships with the three Splitflukes who had brought them both to this cleaner waterspace.

A land travelthing had journeyed a great distance whilst they lay on the airside exposed to the sun. One of the younger Splitflukes had kept their bodies moist and their eyes - but could not alleviate the discomfort of bodyweight against the jolting solidity beneath.

On arrival, they had been lifted into the airspace in some kind of support. A fourth Splitfluke - the one who had seen Bloom later when he had been sickening - had looked at them closely before they were returned to needful coolness of water.

They had been fed better. There was the company of the podpartners - if they had wanted it. For a while, she had thought Bloom might improve but he had never recovered full health. Something had made him sick in the old waterspace. The onset of pain had been sudden and intense.

He had mindmerged with her on few occasions - partly because she had only just matured; partly because there had been that awful sense of sadness flowing across the rippled sandbanks of his mind which she had found hard to bear.

Bloom's longing for the open seascape, in its strength of feeling, had been a song of the sea in images alone, calling to him across the distant surf which they had both sensed and heard. In that last series of internal agonies, he had mindmerged for the last time... tried to make images of affection and expressed hope for her future. They had fintouched as he shallow gasped prior to the deepest dive he could manage... before flooding his lungs.

White Tip grieved.

She did not know the ping-patterns of the echo-lament and had not asked the podpartners to grieve with her... but she had vowed complete silence for one mooncycle. Perhaps the White Dolphins would accept this mark of sorrow for Bloom's passing.

When the Splitflukes had taken him from the pool, she had not watched. Instead, she had joined the ripples running across the dip and peak of sandfloor in a lifeless, shallow sea... that only sustaining contact with the life of a young mate...

In her relentless finning and circling, dimly she became aware of the Splitfluke in the waterspace, shadowing her finningpassage, falling behind, intercepting at a tangential vector, flukeflipping a dolphinspan apart... No attempt was made to move closer.

Still the Splitfluke moved like a shadow. Each airsnatch, this new, extra shadow was near. On the landside was the elder Splitfluke she recognised, watching.

There was no threat; neither was the new Splitfluke uncertain or apprehensive.

Despite her inner turmoil, White Tip felt herself slowing the rate of each circular evolution. She had kept her mooncycle of silence but the habit of separation was hard to break. Growing like the living coral, minutely from tentative beginnings to firm substance, curiosity broke the 'lagoon's' surface...

Helpless, her fincorrecting angled her sleek, thinner form closer to this patient watcher of the waterspace. At each finningpassage, she felt herself allowing forefins to spoil the flow along her sides... and then she was... finstirring, waiting, lifting her head to look...

Maeve lowered herself into the net restricted area of the 'lagoon'. The wet-suit was a little loose but was sufficient to cover near nudity beneath - and the slightly smelly, rugby shorts she had borrowed. All other dolphins were being encouraged into the flooded dry-dock, by Phil and Rod - who were busy examining their condition. She had not heard Rick's firm instruction to his sons to keep a very low profile... but she felt their eyes from time to time.

Rick, standing on the bank of the artificial 'lagoon', smiled encouragingly but said nothing. He didn't even know why he was allowing himself to play the hunch he had. The girl wanted to be with dolphins. If nothing came of this - if the girl could not penetrate the wall of indifferent isolation - it would all have been for nothing. A period of disorientation was one thing but... He'd let her swim with the others later, before the two o'clock 'Show'.

She swam well, in a graceful, elegant way which lacked the aggressive assertiveness of his sons. Nevertheless, her fluidity of movement was economic. She would be able to keep that rhythm going for a long time. He watched the tighter circle of her swimming pattern closing, shadowing and merging with the finning circles of the female dolphin who seemed locked in mechanical, repetitive evolutions of the water. He had not told her what to do, not felt it was necessary. Hell, he didn't know what to do himself!

Almost imperceptibly, the circling rate of the dolphin was slowing. At first, he wasn't sure. He began to watch the second hand of his watch, timing the passing torpedo shape. Second by second, the interval was growing longer!

He switched attention to Maeve. There were no rushing movements; everything carefully calm. Those brown eyes were fixed, studying her swimming partner. The face was full of concern, her lips slightly open and making slow movements as if... as if she was whispering. He could hear no words? Perhaps she was mouthing her encouragement, her lips following the pattern of her thoughts. But she was a young lady who was too controlled to show a child's unconscious ramblings. She was trying something else... but what?

Then he saw the change from circle to elipse in the shape of the dolphin's passing. The white tip of the dorsal was inclining slightly towards Maeve as if she was the pivot of each arc. The fins were more positively persuading a change of course.

Several circuits betrayed an awareness of Maeve and more than a hint of curiosity. Two tight turns confirmed the intention of stopping...

It seemed as if the mainspring of a clock was running down...

The dorsal was stationary!

Rick's face broke out into the broadest smile he had worn for many years. He bit back any comment. He noticed Phil beckoning to Rod. In moments, the pair of them were watching through the mesh above the net floats.

Rick did not need to gesture silence. Two equally inane grins told him they recognised something special was happening.

Only the sounds of the traffic bustle - some shrill shrieks and shrewish maternal invocations outside - spoiled the peace. One or two of the 'stars', not yet in the dry-dock, seemed to be beak clicking. Did they sense something?

Maeve's face did not change. Still her soundless lips were moving. In astonishment, a father and two sons watched the dolphin swimming partner raise its head and beak gape at the young woman who remained motionless except for the flipper-flicking treading of water. The female finned closer... allowed Maeve to gently stroke her back, her sides and her head...

And now there was a change in Maeve's face!

From metres away, three observers watched her face crease and saw the tears coursing down her cheeks.

They were not of joy!

Rick signalled his sons to stillness. They could not go to her yet.

He waited a full two minutes and indicated, with a wave of his hand across the front of his body, that they should move but kept a straight finger to his mouth.

Both sons nodded and took their time. They paused four yards from Maeve, who seemed to become aware of them... to see them from somewhere very far off. Phil asked, with his eyes and the slight tilt of his head, if she was alright.

A sad smile and a nod was his answer.

Phil tugged Rod's arm.

They swam to the nearest steep side and levered themselves out.

'I think we're a bit superfluous, pop,' were the only words Phil said to his father.

'I think you're probably right, son. Make some coffee. We'll have a chat with Maeve - when she's ready.'

At that moment, the three of them saw Maeve being towed gently around... but she wasn't watching them.

Half an hour later, Rick was handing her a coffee as she stood, dripping by his side, saying, 'Will you stay awhile, Maeve? You wouldn't be interested in a job?'

He was not surprised to hear, 'I've got to come back. She needs me for some time yet - but I'm not sure I can give her all the help she needs.'

'We'd better have a chat. Come and meet the boys... and welcome aboard.'

He was walking towards the old, three-master, seemingly moored alongside the jetty, but his words meant more than that.

Maeve had a most unusual period of work experience. Her father had not taken as much convincing as she had anticipated. She had decided it would have been foolish to try to explain the commitment she was feeling to a female of an entirely different species. It would not have been an argument to cut any ice, or so she believed. Donovan had been overtly supportive... most definitely enthusiastic about the opportunity for his sister to earn some ready cash before commencing study at University. He certainly didn't mind cooking for himself - and he could get on with his study assignment in complete peace during the day. Ciaran concurred with the scheme, recognising the need to give wider freedoms to son and daughter.

Any notion that her brother was being wholly altruistic vanished from Maeve's mind - when she found a green, plastic ear-ring in Donovan's bedroom, whilst vacuum cleaning, the next evening. She handed it to him quietly and told him he had better see to things in his room himself.

Donovan knew he was rumbled and could only be grateful it had been his sister and not his father. His romantic associations were maintained at distance from the apartment and he did make genuine progress with his essay. In such strange ways, the family continued to build a mutuality of trust and understanding, continuing a process begun in the Coral Sea.

Maeve agreed to assist the Dortmann family in the Brisbane Dolphinarium until mid-September. Five days a week for five weeks, with a request 'that she helped where she saw the need', was what Rick had suggested - and that 'she continued to bring back the female dolphin from the 'dark place''.

It was an unusual phrase for him to have used... almost as if his constant attendance upon his 'stars' was a service of 'light and joy'. She could not have known he had seen such an essence in her sketches. He was spellbound in the delight of the ballet in air and water, which he sought to share with the crowd, despite the artificiality of the pools and the old dry-dock.

Rick was convinced it had not been mere curiosity which had made a dolphin fin towards his new employee, lift a head from the water and share an immense solitude in the tears on her cheeks. He felt the girl had done something else. There had been occasions when some dolphins had almost appeared to be trying to speak with him. How many times had a beak-clicking head appeared to be trying to use human words? They had never managed to train a beak clicker to make approximations of 'Hello' or 'Yes' or 'No' as in some of the dolphinariums of the U.S.A. But he had not discounted the possibility of speech entirely...

Neither had he shaken off the possibility that dolphins communicated by other means than clicks and echo-calls. There was something about the harmony of movement and rapid response that suggested a joining of thought. He didn't regard himself as a freak - would never admit his thoughts openly - but maybe the 'stars' spoke mind to mind.

Was Maeve tuned to the dolphin mind?

However she had made contact, she had done something in the 'lagoon' the boys and himself could not. It was going to be interesting watching her. Rick chuckled. Maybe it would prove profitable too...

During the first full day, Rick noticed that his 'boys' were also watching Maeve, with increasing awareness and respect. She was intelligent, honest and direct. She worked hard and with enthusiasm. When she laughed, both boys' heads turned towards the melody. Dressed practically, she was not immodest but, thought three Dortmanns, she had a natural grace that was silk and velvet compared to the 'bikini bouncers' set like traps to trip two of them up. Her pleasure in working with the dolphins was like contagion in a schoolroom, shared with the family.

The 'Brisbane Dolphinarium' was a high-sounding name for the establishment outside the modern harbour facilities. It had grown out of an original concept, from an idealist working with the authorities, to maximise the potential for an old, dry-dock many years obsolescent. As part of the process of rationalising harbour provisions, building more dwellings closer to the city centre, providing better recreational facilities and cleaning up the appearance of sprawling development and sea defences - the Dolphinarium had been born.

It was sandwiched between Australia's past and present; between the harbour of cranes and diesel-driven lorries... and a maturing park plus pretentious golf course, bordering a beach upon which indigenes had once collected shellfish. Sand, regimented by marshalling groynes, had been brought to augment the cosmetic shore - burying the beach of the past but satisfying the new house owners' needs to believe that Paradise was reachable.

Rick Dortmann, as Manager, lived on the three-master - a relic of trading under sail - 'moored' near the lock gates which created a false 'lagoon' between a grassed bank on the docks' side and the park area on the other. To be strictly accurate, 'moored' was the wrong word. The old vessel was largely encased in concrete with only the top two or three feet of the hull above the water surface on one side. It had been someone's idea of adding the 'nautical touch'.

He and his sons took responsibility for all matters pertaining to the dolphin 'stars', their welfare and their training. Refreshments, ticket sales, books and pamphlets were overseen by the authorities who tended to sub-contract as much as possible. An Arts and Recreation Committee was responsible for other displays of shells, coral, art sales etc. The organisation was really a cartel of co-operating interests even the Golf Club in a more narrow-minded fashion.

Lockable gates provided access to the dry-dock, flooded to the same level as the 'lagoon', and also the three other pools de-scribed as 'Jump Pool', 'Aquarium' and 'Rest Pool'. The Dortmanns, not overly concerned with the Sea Aquarium, were asked, occasionally, to seek new or replacement exhibits. Both the latter pool and the 'Jump Pool' had facilities for underwater viewing through strong, plate-glass panels.

The public were not encouraged in the desire to swim with the dolphins. There was a very good swimming pool close to the Golf Clubhouse and the open-air bar, 'The Red Bottlenose'.

In Rick's five years of managing the Dolphinarium, Maeve had been the one exception as far as Rick was concerned... although there had been an occasion when the 'boys' had once been smitten by an irresistible advance. When Rick had returned in the pick-up and discovered the misdemeanour, the Manager had 'fined' his two 'boys' very substantially. They had not tried it again.

Maeve picked up things fast. At the end of the first day, she was capable of standing in for the 'boys' in a number of ways. The 'stars' responded to her more quickly than the Dortmanns might have reasonably anticipated, such that it was proving easier to ask Maeve to do the 'sheep-dogging' as they called the summoning of dolphins to the dry-dock main display area.

She had swum through the gates in the centre of a jostling group with an elegant arm looped around a dorsal, her laughter the only oral direction. One of the 'boys', Phil, had been there to help her from the water.

A dolphin seemed to jump higher as Maeve held out the fish and sustained beak clicking gratitude for longer intervals of time.

Slowly, energy was restoring to the 'orphan' - as Maeve described the rescued female. A few simple tricks were being 'learned' - but only if Maeve was in attendance.

On the third day, Maeve passed some comments which Rick pondered for hours...

'Don't think she's over it. She needs another kind of help... and he's... it's coming soon. White Tip is like the others. She's hungry for freedom to live and she's living a half-life here.

'Rick, could I possibly stay here during the week and go back to the apartment... to home... at the weekends?'

Ciaran and Rick met the following day and found, despite differences of background, a certain commonality of outlook. Her father heard his daughter's laughter as an echo from the Coral Sea and gave his agreement.

Rick wondered why Maeve had named the 'orphan' bottlenose 'White Tip'. It was, perhaps, an obvious choice but he had the feeling the dolphin had been named with... certitude? Also, was the 'help' she spoke of more than fanciful femininity or some kind of intuitive foreknowledge?

Friday saw her dropped off at the Dolphinarium, by Ciaran, with a small suitcase. The request to stay the weekend had also been made and gratefully received. White Tip seemed to be developing a kind of dependence on Maeve.

When she was not around, the dolphin seemed to sense the absence and would fall back into a morose, finning solitude. It was obvious that this behaviour was more than the pining of a domesticated creature. One had only to be near the Rest Pool to sense a feeling of gloom and despair which permeated water and air for yards around. It had been uncanny to watch the beak-clicking of other dolphins whittle to silence in the vicinity... as if they, too, were sensing a kind of double grief. White Tip could only be allowed the company of other dolphins if Maeve was close, such seemed the effect upon their natural exuberance and their responses in the demands of the 'Show'.

Rick had watched Maeve closely. She tried to remain close to the Rest Pool or accompanied White Tip in swimming with the others. Any further improvement in the dolphin's demeanour was not materialising. It was as if clouds parted infrequently to give a glimpse of radiance but closed to shield the light with the turning of Maeve's back.

Rick knew White Tip would have to be released to the sea shortly if she continued to be counter-productive or a mal-influence upon the others. He had not admitted failure before - but this sickness of spirit was harrowing. There was also the uncertainty of the dolphin's survival after reintroduction to the sea. She had been young when captured -

too young? Each evening, Rick had noticed Maeve hovered close to the Rest Pool for half an hour, spending half the time speaking and singing quietly near White Tip... and fifteen minutes staring out beyond the distant harbour entrance. None of the Dortmanns had sought to join her, instinctively respecting this period of companionship for White Tip and the need of quietness for Maeve. It was puzzling why it was always the same time - almost a ritual in looking out to sea. In the end, Rick moved to be at her side.

He waited, watching until his presence was noted. She turned as he struck the third match to light his pipe. Her eyes were bright with expectancy. His wife had looked that way when she knew... a secret she was going to share? When Fiona had known about Rod as a reality in the womb, there had been the same swelling of the dark centres to her eyes...

Fiona had not known... nobody had known that she would not see the second child she had wanted... Rick had not allowed himself to remember Fiona's eyes for many weeks, lately. The memory led to lonely discourse with a whiskey bottle even these many years since...

'Rick, it's about White Tip. You're thinking about returning her to... putting her back out there, aren't you?'

Maeve had spoken his business thoughts aloud! He felt his stomach muscles tighten and forced them to relax their grip at the bottom of his heart. Fiona had shared that disconcerting habit as well...

He tried valiantly, discreetly to swallow the shadow of the past in the unseen gulp of his throat.

There was no course but the same directness.

Quietly, Rick said, 'We can't afford to have the other 'stars' upset, Maeve - and she is upsetting them. You can hear their talking fall away to nothing when she's around. She's suffered... and she's suffering now. She hasn't got the strength to shake off the weight on her spirit; lacks the resilience to survive.

'She's got the 'sea-sadness', lass... and I think she's lost to us.'

He paused, then...

'You go home tomorrow, Maeve. Phil and I will take her where she wants to be. Nature demands she'll have to take her chances out there...'

Maeve's expression was unreadable as she turned to look again across distance in the sea. There was a sad smile on her face as she turned to face him.

'He needs me to touch you, Rick. Please hold my hand,' Maeve whispered.

Chapter Nine

WORDS FROM MIND AND HEART

Long before the forewave pressure of the 'bow' subsided and faltered to insignificance, Gaze detected the larger hardside ahead. The sea was dirtier. When he airsnatched, the air was different - heavy with the scent and taste of dead fish and fumes. He finned several times around the 'trawler', tuning once more to Graham's mind...

So this was the 'factory ship' where the 'catch' would be transferred before Graham and the 'crew' vectored for 'Noumea' on 'New Caledonia'. This was the 'ship' which would voyage to 'Australia' with 'trawler catches' from the sea, 'frozen' or already packed in 'tins', for the unseen - and countless - Splitflukes to consume. Some of the tuna would also feed a few of the creatures he had visioned for Vorg - creatures remembered from Maeve's mind.

Gaze could not understand how some 'animals' were fed, loved and cherished by Splitflukes whilst others were hunted mercilessly or used in base slavery which had nothing of the symbiosis he had seen between 'men o war' and their fish. Splitfluke emotions and their motives for doing things did not follow a consistency in patterning.

All this he had deduced and conjectured. He needed to know if he could fluke the forewave of the 'factory ship' when the voyage began. Death seemed magnified upon its airside. Would Splitflukes, on this 'ship', treat him with the same mixtures of amusement and indifference thus far shown? Graham continued to think of him as amusing and with professional detachment. There was nothing to suppose he would be treated in any other way.

Gaze could not fin towards the 'factory ship' hardside yet. There were too many sharks - some of them Large White Sharks and the Mako Sharks - feeding upon a stream of waste and offal. He would wait for the 'ship' to clear this seaspace and join the forewave further away. He finturned aside from Graham's hardside - reconstituting his pair of podpartners. Half-beaksmiling, he noted Graham's surprise at how quickly he had been joined by other dolphins.

And then he read the knowledge that the 'factory ship' would not begin its voyage to 'Australia' until the next lightwater. Another 'trawler' had to bring its 'catch'. Gaze learned of 'fish-freezing' to arrest the rotting processes... and of many of the fish being 'cooked' and 'canned' before arrival at 'port'. Gaze dared not look too far below the surface of Graham's mind... or those other Splitfluke minds in the near distance.

He would vector towards this 'New Caledonia' - spend the darkwater in reefside security, with other dolphins he sensed would be there. Keeping the seafloor trough, behind the 'Loyalty Ridge', on his right forefin would bring him to reefshelter on the coolwater spur of 'New Caledonia' - and the forcelines were easy to follow.

Despite himself, Graham waved in farewell to three dolphins, one of which had seemed to show a kind of persistent affinity with his father's trawler...

Gaze had vague terms, now, to describe his entry into the 'Baie du Prony' from the 'South East'. In time he would make further sense of 'Compass Cardinal Points'. He still felt more comfortable thinking of direction in terms of the forcelines and the suncycle. In his own terms, he was entering the bay from mid-point of sunbreach and vertical sunlight... but he sensed the greater accuracy of the system which Graham was learning to master.

Graham made use of the forcelines - not through any lateral sensing but through a 'compass' which sensed 'magnetism'. Gaze realised that the Splitflukes, as tool-users, might have dulled their own receptivity to natural phenomena, becoming too reliant upon their own inventiveness.

Had they been fooled by their faith in the on-going discovery of better systems - as a constant progression - into regarding the natural way of doing things as being archaic nonsense? Had they lost that essential rapport with the water, air and landspaces around them? Were they able, still, to survive in solitude, falling back on the old skills in self-reliance?

From the nearest reefedge came an exploratory pinging. Another dolphin had sensed his presence before he had searched for mindlights around the bay! Such was a lapse and Gaze chided himself. The podpartners dissolved as he finturned towards the reef some hundred dolphinspans away. He pinged an identification call... and ranged in mindsearch rapidly.

The acknowledgement was cautious, doubtful. There were suspicions that Gaze was not alone.

In mindmeet came the questions, 'How many Bottlenoses are with you? Why did you not ping your approach earlier?'

'My name is Gaze of Wanderer's warmstream waterspace. I seek reefshelter and rest amongst my cousins during the darkwater. Forgive my lapse. May I enter your waterspace?'

'Where are the others of your pod?'

The questioning was persistent, the mind apprehensive. He was of middle-age and one of a ninepod. Speckled Hump-backs!

Nursery training told stories of their sad depletion. Generally they did not fluke this waterspace. They were podseeking a new herdhome!

With a show of aggression - trying to mask uncertainty in his mind - the Hump-back said, 'There were two or three other dorsals. Where are they? There is only one echo-return... from yourself. Speak!'

'Your eyesight is not as good as it once was cousin,' said Gaze, adding in total honesty, 'I fluke alone. You are challenging illusory companions. Assuredly, I am no threat to you or your pod. May I fin towards you? I am willing to offer mindmerge.'

Beyond a reefcorner were two other Hump-back males, three females and two near matures. On watch station, further along reefedge, was another female. She was beginning to fin towards them carefully. The mindlights were attentive, listening but they were making no sound to betray their presence. Gaze reefsided against knowledge of them and opened his mind for mindmerge as the Hump-back finbeckoned him closer. Thankful that he was not being confronted by an Observer of the same astuteness as Crest Spray, Gaze finned forward.

They fintouched in greeting... and any anxiety in the Hump-back dissipated. This recently mature Bottlenose was innocent of any mal-intent.

Gaze knew their names and their story - all of it.

He listened politely as this Blotch told him as much as he was prepared, not knowing the parts he reefsided were known anyway.

They were from a landmass in the other part of the warmstream which divided either side of the 'Fijian Islands'. Graham's mind recognised the landfeatures as the chain of islands in the 'Solomon Sea'.

Gaze finfaltered before a series of horrible images!

The Splitflukes of these islands hunted dolphins!

The sagas were full of stories of their kind being hunted and, in consequence, being forced to migrate to new waterspace. Images of slaughter, in Blotch's mind, were profoundly shocking; of his shore-driven podsherd spiked and sliced in the blood-red shallows... or waiting, gasping for an end of suffering under the weight of the sky, beach-pressure hard against blood-spattered flanks.

Blotch had seen his mate hacked to death by Splitfluke sharpened 'steel', each mindscream urging a speedier despatch. He had flukethrashed with a few to escape when her mindscreams had ceased, aware of nothing but blood, blind panic, noise and grief.

Splitflukes had laughed at their reddened hands; raised the spiking shafts and weapons above their heads in jubilant celebration. Blotch had fluked towards the small hardsides and slapping water disturbance, fleeing the murderous shore, risking other threats closing the seavectors. A sharpness from a small hardside had splitgashed his flesh several times... but there had been a gap to the seaspace!

He had high-rolled airside above some fishtrap floats, seeing another victim drowned beneath him. Bleeding, he had finswerved and fluked to a pitifully small pod of survivors. The sharks were busy, tearing at some floating corpses some fifty dolphinspans away.

This podsherd remnant had vectored for distant reefshelter in heartpounding flight... only ...only eleven of the lightwater's fifty-seven!

After two more lightwaters, they had vectored away from the pain of memories too sharply focused in the island group.

Gaze knew they had voyaged above the 'Santa Cruz Basin', 'South' across the 'New Hebrides Basin' where Mako Sharks had taken one of the young males soon after he had flukefaltered with fatigue. He had lost the sight of one eye from a Splitfluke club, trying to stay with his sire who had mindscreamed already to silence...

Blotch reefside-stored the image of the son's deep-dive and, Gaze realised, the young dolphin had been glad 'to join his sire'. The dam was presumed to have deep-dived, two mooncycles earlier, after some kind of poisoning...

The second fatality had occured soon after entering the reefs to the 'North East' of 'New Caledonia'. Once more, Splitflukes were the cause.

Blotch thought they had been near-matures by their loudness and boisterous behaviour. A small hardside had raced from behind, bump-bouncing on seaswell. Their tenpod had scattered before such wave-shattering progress and heard the airshrieks of the Splitflukes. With a steep, banking turn, the hardside had returned on an intercept vector - reducing speed as it had neared. Sharp noises had reverberated across airspace, followed by the piercing mindscream of Collet, a large male. The water had boiled in flukethrashing red!

From a distance, they had observed Collet's unresisting body pulled onto the hardside... and heard the shrieks of wild delight. They did not think the young Splitflukes had killed for food - but for the pleasure of a sickening sadism in themselves.

Gaze mindmerged the one image that would ensure shelter in the darkwater with this pod of migrant Hump-backs.

'I sorrow for your Hump-backs recently deep-dived. May the White Dolphins bring them peace and joy.'

'Our pod must find security from these Splitfluke sharks,' whispered Blotch, 'for they treat all creatures and the worldspace as their own. I wonder if there is any place of safety for dolphinkind...

'Let us fin to my pod, young Gaze. You are welcome to bide with us a while... although we are heavier in spirit than once we were. We fear the Splitflukes may return and all of us avoid the hardsides now.'

Gaze wondered if it was unwise to seek the distant Maeve... and if Splitflukes were as unpredictable and cold-blooded as the sharks...

He finned, bi-vector with Blotch, towards the grey-minded Hump-backs finstirring behind a reefangle.

Blotch, Gaze realised, not of the calibre of a Tinu or a Crest Spray - lacking much of the quality of a Guardian - was doing his best to lead the surviving Speckled Hump-backs to new, safer waterspace. The co-leader was not another male... but a middle-aged female, Twizzle, who had not mated for several seasons.

Twizzle was a very practical female who appraised potential mates severely and had wavered on the brink of decision between heart and mind lightwaters too long, deterring any ardency of approach by a suitor. Blotch was unaware of any assessment she was making of him for he was embroiled with his own grief - and the need to grapple with decisions for the good of the surviving podpartners.

Undetected, the guest Bottlenose read hearts and minds in all his darkwater companions... and the potential of dreaming liaisons. He knew that time and healing, and the co-operation in facing danger, was likely to bring the leaders very much closer together - if they survived this exodus.

He had helped them... was helping them now...

The pod of Hump-backs had fishmustered - before the return of the fast hardside and the young Splitflukes they had learned to fear...

Blotch and Twizzle had acted as escape-vector closure whilst the other Hump-backs had bunched the fishshoal in the U formation. Only Gaze had finned beneath the shoal - but there had been a sense of many more dolphins than merely one, echo-calling and confusing the panicked fish!

When the Hump-backs had made striking-vectors, the fish had stayed bunched much longer than was usual, as if hemmed in by some unseen fishtrap. Fishmuster had been extremely successful; every Hump-back had fed to repletion.

Gaze had been satisfied with the learning from experience he had derived - and obtained from the minds of Graham and a distant Ardent, the latter having whispered the images of Sinu through a Splitfluke skull.

The pod of Hump-backs had been finning towards reefshelter, with a heavy slowness of contentment, when the young Splitflukes had returned to bring spraying, shrieking confusion! Events had happened too quickly for Blotch or Twizzle to do more than mindscream the urgency for all to fluke for the reefedge!

Only Gaze had seemed to react slower than the rest.   Blotch had flukefaltered; urged the need for flukeflight! Twizzle had been white fear at his side.

Both had seen... a miracle?

The fast hardside had settled nosedown into the sea, speed falling away. Between the fleeing dolphins and the potential hunters had appeared three large sharkdorsals, the sharkfanning bodies, huge and leaden white!

Large White sharks, aggressive and fast, were rumoured to attack small hardsides! The sharkdorsals had turned in response to fincorrecting and had submerged to make striking-vectors!

Blotch, with Twizzle, had watched events unfold, flank to flank... Gaze had been between them and the spectacle.

There had been shrieks of Splitfluke excitement and a series of loud reports making puffs of cloud from strange longthings they had used. A hundred times greater than the sound of rainsplashes, numerous small objects had penetrated the waterspace about the sharks on striking-vectors... but the sharks had seemed to ignore them, intent upon attack! The airsounds of the Splitflukes had changed in pitch and urgency!

Both observers had recognised fear. A whining noise had been made by the hardside and it had puffed several black clouds... During another frenzy of reports and splashes, the awful vision of three, huge sharkmaws, razor teeth glistening, had leapt out of the waterspace!

The hardside had rocked wildly and two Splitflukes had been thrown into the water! A long-haired Splitfluke had wailed a drawn-out, high-pitched sound and fingrasped its head. A fourth short-haired Splitfluke had thrown a rope...

Gaze had fluked towards the hardside! Blotch had mindmerged the caution to keep away - only to be ignored!

As Gaze had neared, two sharkdorsals had broken off striking-vectors and submerged.

The third sharkdorsal had closed a thrashing Splitfluke... The fluking form of Gaze had dived and the shark had appeared to jerk violently! The dorsal had shuddered from an unseen impact. Sharkfan lifting from the surface, the would-be predator had slipped downwards just two dolphinspans away from the intended victim.

Gaze had butted the gills of a Large White! Or so it appeared...

In speechless silence, six spectators had watched a bottlebeak break surface and appear to beakclick a caution. Still in soundless observation, all had seen a Bottlenose dolphin offer support to a Splitfluke... and tow him towards the safety of the hardside!

There had been joyful noises, nervous laughter from the Splitflukes as a bottlebeak had clicked some more - before finning away. Slowly, the hardside had moved towards the islandmass...

Gaze had said that he did not think these particular Splitflukes would harm dolphins in the future... but both Hump-back leaders had seen nothing to countersay their previous fears, although they marvelled at the courage of Gaze. Despite their questions, he had not amplified upon events and could not explain why the Large Whites had sharkfanned so rapidly seawards from the scene - or why there were no echo-returns when Blotch had pinged to confirm their departure...?

Beneath moongaze and starshine, he was helping them still. The ninepod of Hump-backs were dorsal-drifting in darkwater dreaming. Replete, they needed mistfins of sleep to soothe restless spirits - and regeneration of hope.

Twizzle had tried to keep watch with Gaze but had felt the weight of fatigue dragging her into the murmurs of the surf - the memory... of the podsherd... podsecurity... before... before the... shore... But Twizzle was sleeping now.

And Gaze slept with the comfort of the wallowing forms of his cousins - close to the shoal of 'men o' war' whose trailing tendrils coccooned their company.

He slept whilst two Bottlenose Guardians patrolled the fringe of sleeping friendship, unresting in their vigilance... for he had remembered his sire saying 'that lives would depend upon it'...

Gaze had not stayed long at next lightwater.

Twizzle had awoken guiltily, finstirring at Blotch's flanks! She had fluked to her watchstation just before sunbreach. Gaze had been finning a solitary passage. She had apologised for her neglect but he had offered only his understanding of her fatigue... and the hope that she had rested well.

Then he had said something that her mind had not understood as well as her heart...

'In the darkwater, we drift with our heart's desires - and this more freely than with lightwater consciousness. Cousin, where did you awake in the tideflow of your heart and your mind?'

He had not wanted an answer but she realised he had led her to a decision. This season, she would... that is, if Blotch wanted... Young Gaze was very astute!

Later, when he had fluked out of the bay, they had all been sorry to see him go. He had mindmerged his farewells from many dolphinspans distant - too far for them to reply!

He had also promised to watch for a place of security 'for his cousins'.

Blotch had heard the tenor of tenderness in the mindvoice of Twizzle replying 'goodbyes'... and found himself admiring her femininity. He had not done this for a long time...

Graham's 'trawler' was not there. The 'factory ship' was 'loading' from another hardside... the last 'trawler' before 'making way'. There would be other 'fishing vessels' to be met during voyage to 'Brisbane' in 'Australia'. The voyage would be longer than Gaze had thought...

The Splitfluke mindlights were preoccupied in 'work', ignoring much of the seaspace around. Gaze sought a Navigator... and found one mind more learned than the superficiality of Graham.

From upflow of fishwaste and sharkfan, he mindfixed with an unsuspecting tutor... reading the knowledge of reefs and 'courses', comparing all with Wanderer's 'maps'. The process was absorbing, the patterning complex. A remarkably stationary 'man o' war' took up position across the likely course towards an 'Australian port' - but no creature or Splitfluke noticed any change...

Mark Summers, third officer and navigator of the 'Tin Can Tuna', as his ship was affectionately known, turned his attention from the green, circling sweep of the radar and moved out to the bridge-wing repeater.

The lone dolphin had joined the bow just after noon departure. Mark could not escape the feeling that the bottlenose dolphin was hitching a lift. There had been that one, short interval when the dolphin had fluked aside from the bow-wave and let the bulk of the factory ship lumber past... but, within ten minutes or so, it had been back on station.

Mark had sensed a kind of demand for more speed on the return. Dolphins looked playful on the bow, engaging in a kind of tag with the ship. This one looked more purposeful, more urgently intent. Without any possibility of verifying the hunch, he guessed this one intended to ride the forewave all the way to Brisbane, despite the stops for the 'little ships' - as he called them. That was unusual. Mark had not known that these small sea mammals would travel so far as individuals. Whales were one thing, following the cloud-fogs of krill; dolphins did not normally swim alone. If only one had a way of tapping the cetacean mind, what a wealth of secrets might be found...

Automatically, his eyes scanned the radar repeater screen and he would check controls, walking through the bridge. Once, he turned, feeling the presence of someone else... but it was only a gust of wind through some loose wire rigging - or the distant movements of a crew member through the passages in this robotic, sea-going brain of the tuna fishing fleet.

Chuckling at the analogy, he fell into an indolent reverie of peaceful contemplation. Sea-miles flowed past the bridge-wing, as he watched the swoop and swerve of the cetacean pilot.

Soon the rest period would be over and the next work-shift would sweat in the freezing of fish, can the cat food and package protein for supermarket shelves after the next pick-up point. An over-indulgent glutton, the ship would spew out excess and fart in the face of the sea. It was a good job the lone dolphin was at their sharp end! He laughed at the images...

Gaze joined the forewave easily, noting the huge hardside increasing speed. The forewave pressure was broad and firm; his fluking movements needed far less exertion. He sensed that the great bulk of the 'factory ship' would need much seaspace to bring itself stationary for the next 'taking-on' of a tuna 'catch'.

Mark's mind was practical and viewed him with amused detachment. His imaging comprised slight cynicism... elemental self-satisfaction... but it was a mind from which knowledge could be gained.

He made use of many 'tools' - no, 'instruments' was the 'word' - much 'equipment'. The sweeping green of a 'screen' was 'radar'... Echo-location was known by the Splitflukes! 'Radar' and 'Sonar' were ways of detecting other creatures and things far away! A 'Radio' was used to speak mind to mind across the airspace for many 'miles'. They could detect and contact other hardsides on the seaspace, airthings of the airspace and shoals of fish beneath the waves... although not read the minds of the latter. With 'Sonar', the peak and dip of the seafloor, and the rising reefs, could be clearly delineated. Mark could not do this without such 'special equipment' and interpreting the information was much slower than in Gaze himself... but the scanning range was very far in the air-space. Scanning beneath the wavesurge was not as effective as a Guardian's capability in terms of accuracy and precision... but...

Gaze continued to pattern and question. If the Splitflukes were capable of relearning the old harmonies and the interactions of movements in the worldspace, could they reabsorb the need for all creatures to remain in balance with each other? Or would need for a 'surplus', to make a 'profit'... to take more than fair subsistence... continue to bring discord? Would the food-chains be...!

The contact with Maeve's mind was sudden, powerful - overwhelming!

Gaze flukestumbled - fell off the forewave. Aware of the bulk behind, bruising weight, barnacles and the awesome twistingfins, he fincorrected and allowed the giant shape of the hardside to pass him by.

He knew where Maeve was! A series of mixed images raced across his consciousness, dizzying in their confusion and strength of feeling: Maeve in a waterspace but different from memory... 'clothed' oddly; Maeve crying in a grey-mind of grief - shared with another... but not a Splitfluke; a seafloor of rippled sand in a sea of solitude... but not the same waterspace, and a dolphin... a female... sick in spirit and intense with sorrow. There were salt tears in her eyes, a burden on a heart...

Not yet knowing all, Gaze strove to... allowed as much expenditure of mindenergy as manageable to build, amplify, magnify... and released a response...

Faster than the cuttlefish strike - quicker than the seasplitting, seaspitting lightning flash - mindenergy raced to the distant horizon and beyond...

For finstirring moments of movement to seasurge and the wash of the hardside's passage, Gaze wallowed in a redness which blanked his physical vision...

He nerved himself for the acknowledgement, apprehensive of another mindjolt. How had Maeve developed such strength of mindenergy?

The reply was less intense... as if Maeve had realised his awareness... but, also, as if she was seeking to soothe and soften someone simultaneously... as if a dam with a sick flanker...

Mindimaging clarified, the red veil began to lift.

Maeve was with another dolphin... a Bottlenose... like himself! He knew the vicinity: slightly right forefin of Mark's final vector - no, 'course change'. It was difficult to stay in mindcontact... There were other Splitflukes!

They were all watching Maeve and the female dolphin! They were... They were going to...!

Unsummoned, the images of the Speckled Hump-backs shore-driven to the shallows and slaughtered on the sands in a surfwash of liquid redness assailed his mindeye!

Not Maeve! Maeve would not... could not...

The other Splitflukes were leaving! Gaze read the sad smile on Maeve's face from far away. The heaving of his heart subsided. She needed his help but not to stop... She wanted help with the female Bottlenose to end the... to care for and calm...

Already, he was separated from the hardside by long flukingspans. He needed the forewave! He mindlanced the distance to signal his coming and fluked in pursuit.

Rejoining the forewave, he began the patterning of sensemaking. How had Maeve mindmerged!?

It was not until he became conscious of Mark examining the green glow of the 'bridge-wing radar repeater' that he began to be able to understand...

His dam knew intuitively, by strength of feeling, if something was wrong. He felt she would know of his danger before he told her. This other female Bottlenose was locked in the strong emotion of grief. Maeve, sharing an empathy for dolphinkind, had touched dolphinflesh and shared a whirlpool of mindpower. In the dizziness of the suction, fixed within the towering waterwalls of empathies, she had mindscreamed for assistance! And she was tuned to his mind... But more... Sharing the danger of 'mind-drowning', she also shared this female's capacity to mindmerge... Co-joined in crisis, each had approached 'Merge'! A mindcondition only achieved by... by fatepartners in love, danger or death... or, as some Clerics taught, in meeting the White Dolphins!

He knew Cyrene had responded to powerful ping patterns of harmony before her deep-dive and that he had seen the White Dolphins several times. He had felt a power greater than himself... But no, not a White Dolphin... not now...

The 'radar repeater', blinking green across the mindeye of Mark led to the final clue in understanding! In Mark's mind was the image of 'radio antennae' above the 'bridge' - and some knowledge of how the Splitflukes spoke so strongly through the air-space... The mindenergy of Maeve had been the 'generated signal' and the forsaken female had added her mindpower, to give 'directional gain' in mindmerge - like a 'beam antenna using reflectors and directors'! Gaze could not understand everything except to begin to conceive what had happened. Such an analogy explained the magnification of mindmeet to strong mindmerge in Maeve...

This female dolphin felt very deeply... like his dam... and had far greater mindstrength than she realised...

During the darkwater, drifting beyond the circles of false moonshine which the Splitflukes were using on and within the three hardsides at the 'pick-up point', Gaze adopted his 'man o' war' camouflage. The 'factory ship' was 'anchored' on sunbreach side of the 'Lord Howe Rise'. Mark had been disappointed that they had not 'sailed' far before two more 'trawlers' had requested 'off-loading' by 'radio'.

'Sailed' had been a confusing 'word' for Gaze to comprehend. He knew small hardsides used 'sails' to trap the seabreeze and use the force for motion... but the 'factory ship' had no 'sails'. There was no need with the powerful twistingfins - the 'propellers' - to slice through the sea. Why didn't Mark say, 'they had not propelled far'? The Splitfluke 'seamen' sometimes called themselves 'sailors' but only a few had used 'sails'. Why did they use the old 'words' for these 'modern' hardsides? Perhaps it was a matter of wanting to be like the 'sailor Splitflukes' of their sea-sagas?

Whispering at distance, across the darkened dip and swell of water, came a tendril of contact... Through fractured lightdroplets of falling raintears, each winking in reflected moonshine, came the mindvoice he needed! It was quiet and tired, too far to hold in conscious contact for long...

Gaze ceased patterning, finturning to face the seaspace of sundive. The spectral shape of the 'man o' war' shimmered ... dissolved... He felt he needed all mindenergy to listen ... to hear... and then reply...

Maeve was trying very hard to reach him with her imaging and, without the reflection of mindenergy in the unknown female dolphin, she was achieving a wonder!

In their first contact, he had felt her empathy... that she would be approachable, sensitive and aware. He had guessed he could meet her mind to mind at great distance - and here was the proof... Emotion gave her power.

Tracing the tendril of mindenergy back across the seaspace, he felt it thicken, slowly expand, as if he was tracing a capillary through to larger passages of mindflow. Occasionally, he was distracted by 'beings' outside, perceived as ghostly shapes in the surrounding darkness. It required strength of will to ignore such images, to repress the desire to meet 'other' kinds of consciousness.

Sometimes the pathway deceived - leading through a maze of near identical accesses to 'other' minds. Once, he was lost - but before some 'other' felt the intrusion, he turned to feel again the flow. Slowly, all awareness of himself as a physical entity was ebbing away!

He sped backwards in retreat... back along the narrowing tunnels of connection... He could not risk exposure as a dolphin alone! Some small part of his mind must monitor the seaspace around his living reality! He could not drop all self-defence; could not blank out an instinct for survival. Reconstituting, in reflex, the darkwater camouflage, Gaze tried again...

Maeve was in a darkened place. Strange sounds were in her air-space... Subdued sounds; harmonious - 'music'...?

Quietly, softly - fearing the intensity of her imaging; the stormforce of her first mindmerge - he let his mind lap like the water of a lagoon before a zephyr of greeting...

He felt her eyes open! Heart-beat increased!

Before she became a tidal-wave in urgency - crushed their joining of minds on the shoreline of consciousness, he visioned a rock crushing a turtle-egg, redness sink-oozing into yellow sand... and said,

'Merging could damage both of us, Maeve. Find the way to control mindforce. Softer than your 'music' - slower than your heart. Be the off-shore breeze - gullglide an airspace. I felt it could happen and I told you, nearing 'Pago Pago'. Nearly happening then; 'happening' now.'

Her eyes remained open. He felt her 'hands' unclose. She was trying to relax... The high-tension minimised... in and across mindcontact... Yet, her mindimages, racing expectancy still, were... strong emotion?

Her eyes were wet. 'Crying'? How had he hurt her?

'Oh, Gaze. Gaze...' she said... and was shaking her head...?

'Don't dolphins cry?'

Out of their mindmerge came request and plea but no decision...

Gaze could not be with her for some 'days' - the 'word' sounding stranger than 'lightwaters' - although Maeve had not agreed. She did agree to be near 'White Tip' at the 'sun's deep-dive' or 'sundive' - preferring 'sunset'.

In the darkwater, the 'man o' war' camouflage shimmered greatly under clearing clouds - up-bloodflow of the 'Tin Can Tuna' - as Gaze patterned his problems. Only of minor concern were the differences in 'words' - for the meaning of her imaging was far clearer...

Later, more mindenergy arced across the Coral Sea to seaspace of an unseen reef-system. Gaze had need to confer with a Cleric in the matter of 'captive dolphins'. He wanted to explore some associated imaging and patterning...

The Splitfluke skull continued to whisper encouragingly concerning a trainee Guardian ...

Also, the Master Guardian's daughter was finning in bi-vector with a Butting Pod Leader regularly of late. The sire and dam of a young Voyager were in good health and awaited his contacts eagerly.

Gaze beaksmiled at Ardent's unnecessary politeness of naming no names... and began to surrender to darkwater rest. The Cleric's needful responses in the 'patterning' would have to await next 'sunset'. He mindchuckled but his beak soon clenched in troubled sleep - for he was haunted by phantom dolphins enclosed in shallow waterspace above lifeless sandripples on a shelving shore. Some-times the waterspace was stained red - as red as Splitfluke 'hands'...

At daybreak, Mark was in a foul mood. Damn that new Pommy bastard - that apology of an Engineer! Ex-Royal Navy Artificer, my arse! he thought. They should can him and send him back 'for Her Majesty's pleasure'! Why the hell hadn't he seen any signs of the breakdown coming? Had he been contemplating another 'tot' on his navel?

Over thirty hours delay before making way! Needing special parts to be flown out by 'chopper'! Oh yes, there was enough power to 'juice the plant' but severe problems with the main bearings of both shafts! It would be folly to put them under any kind of stress! What about the stress on the rest of us?

Could he fob Dawn off with another excuse? Yet still keep her little flesh-pot on the boil?

Gaze did not share Mark's disappointment in the images of Splitfluke 'flesh-fervour' hugely denied - but did share the sense of frustration. He finned towards the nearest reefrise.

It would be better, perhaps quicker in the end, to trust Splitfluke 'navigation' in finding the necessary flukingpassage towards Maeve...

As events unfolded, it was not a wasted period for Gaze as there was the fascination of the 'helicopter' to qualify; much still to absorb from an alien experience... and he had a great deal of 'patterning' to complete.

Rick studied her face as he clasped her left hand.

Her hand was cool; the sad smile was in and around her eyes.

She did not say anything - as if she was waiting for emptiness of silence between them to be filled... with another voice? Her free hand gestured him to the bench nearby. In movement to the bench, her grasp asserted an authority.

When they were seated, she spoke...

'He wants you to look out to sea, Rick. He is trying to find the best way to meet you and he asks you to keep holding my hand.'

In the short period Rick had known her, she had been practical and calmly efficient. He did not know quite how to respond. Here he was, holding her hand as if they were like... and he was old enough to be her father! Who was 'he'? Was Maeve alright?

'Yes Rick, I'm fine. Please look out to the sea.'

She was reading his mind again, just like...

His grip tightened involuntarily! Maeve flinched, could do nothing but wait...

Superimposed across the distant horizon was Fiona's face, smiling, radiant!

He blinked but the vision stayed fixed. Her lips began to move in the voice pattern he recognised!

'Fiona!'

The name burst from Rick's mouth. His stomach muscles tightened! What was Maeve doing!? How could she do this? Not... Fiona!

'...No, Maeve, not 'Fiona'...' said a voice about the heads of middle-aged man and young woman but neither had spoken.

Rick's eyes closed to crush the image so precious in recall. Slowly, his grip on Maeve's hand loosened.

He became conscious of her other hand on his arm...

'I'm sorry Rick... so sorry. That was my fault. I thought that... Please, Rick, open your eyes and look again. He says there is another way...'

The shock of a shiver ran through Rick's shoulders.

He filled his lungs; his breath seemed to shiver itself in expulsion...

Maeve sensed the apprehension as he opened his eyes to look first at her, as if to confirm the present and not a nightmare from the past. She tried hard to smile, despite the tears in her own eyes, and turned towards the darkline of horizon.

Fearfully, his eyes swept the sea, checking... centring upon a bright, swelling aura... of light? The horizon was fading in an expanding glow of starshine... to moonshine and ... to dayglow? Why was he thinking these strange words? There was rhythmical music in the sound of gentle surf...?

A new horizon existed in the dayglow, the swell of the billows unblemished by fanning windruffle. Seaspace magnified in the newsea and there were sleek, finning forms he recognised...

This was an image to hold! Here was light above; joy beneath...

He fixed on the image.

Dolphins were breaching! Six of them, air-rolling and leaping, higher and freer than he had ever seen. Spinning in airflight, their flukes swept the surface in sideways splashes on re-entry... Suddenly the line of a dolphin-chorus beakclicking in harmony, a sense of 'words' in song.

They were like... were like... It was like he wanted the 'Show' to be... like the images he wanted to share... the dolphins in Maeve's sketches... but alive and real!

Rick smiled. A pain and a fear submerged.

One dolphin was left although there remained a sense of others finning beneath. Rick's mind and eyes focused on the lone dolphin... on the bottlebeak that seemed ready to... speak?

The image was startling but he did not question the vision. His attention was gripped by a... 'Bottlenose'?

'...because you are hurting a bit. You only have to be in light contact,' Maeve was saying quietly.

Rick realised he was gripping her hand too tightly.

The vision shimmered slightly but settled to clarity. He found he could speak. The lone 'Bottlenose' dolphin was closer and sharply defined...

'Are you doing this, Maeve?'

'No, Rick. He is called 'Gaze'. Listen.'

Within his own head was a sound! Not a voice... not a thought... but... There was a pulse beating at different tempo to his surging heart, something growing from near silence to a click whispered... 'ping-pattern'?

At first, it seemed a trick of the breeze in an ear, but the repetition was definitely stronger. He heard a... a noise like the sound of light bells heard through water, echoing, reverberating and swelling.

The identification call of a toothed whale!

Rick had heard recordings made by researchers. He was hearing the call of a dolphin underwater! How?

Unconsciously, then consciously, Rick's spare hand was feeling the bench as if he might find a...

In getting up to look for a cable, a speaker or a visual clue as to the source of the sound, he relinquished the light touch upon Maeve's hand. Immediately there was silence; a blankness of mind.

Nothing spoiled the line of Maeve's clothing; there were no bulky pockets. Her smile was simply reassuring.

Bewildered, looking straight into her brown eyes and not out to sea, Rick reached out to touch her hand...

Maeve winked... said, 'Gaze is having to take a great deal of care with you, Rick. He says you have empathy but you are also suspicious about many things.'

Incredulous, he saw, in his mind's eye, a bottlenose dolphin gaping in a grin, head slightly sidewise and an eye gazing at him!

Something was changing with the eye... The colour was changing to a brown he recognised...

Unbelievably, the 'eye' closed in a wink! At its reopening and restoration of shade and hue, Rick heard,

'I am pleased to mindmeet w...'

Rick's hand broke contact with Maeve as if she had just slapped his face!

If it had not been for the reality of the image - like a colour photograph - this was pure Walt Dis...

It was impossible!

Maeve's smiling eyes were watching him. The right eye closed in a wink. The eyebrows raised quizzically and Maeve extended her hand...

'It is happening, Rick. Gaze thought humour was the only way to soften the shock.'

It was a full twelve seconds before he touched her hand again. Three more minutes passed before the next step of mindmerge and the slowing of Rick's pulse.

Mark smiled ruefully as the 'Tin Can Tuna', Moreton Island to port, filtered into the shipping channel across Moreton Bay. Maybe the Engineer had advised correctly. These things happened. They were overdue but there had been no other unfortunate event.

His mood was buoyant; Dawn had sent a message with the 'chopper'. Of all things, the 'chopper jockey' was a relation! Second cousin, or something like that. She'd missed him. She couldn't wait for him to get into dock. She needed a partner for a shindig over at Moorooka. It wouldn't end until late. If he wanted, they could stay over in a friend's place...

He grinned. Life was looking up a bit. The 'chopper jockey' spent a lot of time going up and down and so did he on the sea. Just maybe there was the chance he'd be going up and down with Dawn...

In this work, you missed out on lots of opportunities. He watched the cluster of hands at the bow, staring at the slow magnification of Brisbane's sprawl across the bay. They were reducing speed already.

Now that was another thing he'd missed out on. He'd felt that dolphin was going to ride the bow all the way to Brisbane. Most of the crew had come on deck to watch the persistence of 'their little pilot'. The bow had been a peaceful place this trip - a place of good humour. He should have opened a book on how long the bottlenose dolphin would stay on the bow in terms of sea miles covered! He could have made a killing.

Surely, it wasn't going to ride the bow all the way into the dock?

A few minutes later, when he moved again to the bridge-wing, the dolphin was gone. Mark's eyes swept the bay. He could see nothing of... There! He had the briefest glimpse of the stream-lined shape he sought, abreast a small in-shore vessel heading towards some distant lock-gates to the right of the main dock area. He reached for the binoculars...

Sandwiched between the outer sprawl of the docks and a pretentious-looking, newish-housing area with a cosmetic beach and the flickering flags of a golf-course, was a large sign. It boldly read... 'Brisbane Dolphinarium'!

Mark laughed aloud. Who said dolphins couldn't read?

The laugh changed to astonishment...

Close to the lock-gates were two human figures holding a sign on something flapping. He focused more precisely, fingers not as deft as usual.

The man was forty to fifty. The girl - young woman - was...

Not bad! Mark read the sign.

The binoculars were lowered. That didn't make sense. That was totally ridiculous. He laughed again. It would make good pillow-talk with Dawn, though. Just one of life's coincidences that you had to laugh at.

The sign had said, 'Bottlenose needed'.

He raised the glasses again. The sign was gone but the man and girl were capering about in obvious excitement.

Was that a dolphin-head, beak gaping open, below them?

The man was moving to open the lock-gates for the small vessel to enter. It was obviously some kind of delivery.

He couldn't see the dolphin anymore. Headed-out across the bay, probably.

A ship's bell brought back Mark's mind to his part in the practicalities of docking the 'Tin Can Tuna'.

The sooner it was done, the sooner he could get excited...

The 'boys' were seeing to the unloading of the 'stars' rations'. Rick looked at the new arrival in the 'lagoon'... and watched Maeve drop neatly into the water. Before she had re-surfaced, the newcomer - a young, bottlenose dolphin - was there.

Two evenings ago, she had told him she sensed a dolphin would be coming. They had been sitting near the Rest Pool. She had appeared to describe everything in graphic detail - but he was foggy in recall now. When he had awoken the following morning, he'd been hitting the whiskey again.

His throbbing head had told him and he guessed the reason... Damn it! Twice, in a few days, was not good...

Phil and Rod had said nothing. Their sympathy was harder to bear than any criticism they might have made.

Maeve had been subdued. Moving quietly through the floating home, she had conveyed a kind of guilt - almost as if she felt she was part responsible for his hangover.

Today he was feeling stronger in some way - more prepared for the future; more secure with his past. Perhaps he had slept better...?

He remembered Maeve's eyes had been almost hypnotic; seeming to know the manner of this dolphin's coming. Going along with her utter conviction had seemed the sensible thing to do. He hadn't believed everything she had said - or the kind of dream-images she could conjure in his mind - but he had promised to let this bottlenose dolphin into the 'lagoon' if he showed. Remembering the way she had clasped his hand so earnestly, looking so directly at him two evenings ago, reminded him of someone... but he couldn't quite recall who. It had been someone -

known intimately - but it wasn't Fiona.

He realised he was thinking of Fiona without pain now!

Rick was grateful. Sadness weighed too heavily on a spirit drowning in solace of whiskey. It was time to break the avoidance pattern of sixteen years.

Thinking Maeve might have brought - even might bring - White Tip back from the 'dark place', she had somehow ferried him! If he had been a generation younger...

His face creased in a grin. His time of closeness with tenderness was over.

They shared an understanding of dolphins and were kin of that kind. Maeve was the natural with the 'stars' he had anticipated. She was tuned to a finer pitch than the boys or himself.

But her latest suggestion was unworkable - sheer folly. It would be interesting watching her try to meet the targets he had set before he would open any gates to the sea and allow his conditioned 'stars' to...

Maeve's laughter was pealing across the water. She was shaking her head, her hair showering a mist spray across the dorsal of the drifting dolphin she had insisted was called 'Gaze'. Had she used that name before they had seen the finning shadow alongside the small drifter delivering fish?

Chuckling, he remembered how the family had watched her use a large felt-tip on some card that morning. 'Bottlenose needed'! He had joined his sons in studying the cabin roof, cheeks sucked in to avoid betrayal in scornful grins.

Standing with Maeve near the lock-gates, it had taken only three minutes for them both to see the dip and surge of the dolphin dorsal heading straight for them...! That had been uncanny! Going along with her like a good-natured fool, he had been wondering how the hell he would cope with the non-arrival of any dolphin without appearing to ridicule her... And, damn it, a dolphin had been closing nearer!

Rick had joined her wild excitement over what could only have been the sheerest coincidence.

She had reminded him of his promise to let the 'Bottlenose' through the lock-gates into the Dolphinarium.

The bottlenose dolphin looked young and fit. Certainly it seemed playful enough...

Attracted by her laughter, his sons were at his side. The Dortmanns watched. No-one knew quite what to say.

'Enjoy the sight and sound, boys. Someone else used to be like this when she was doing something cranky,' voiced Rick, his arms falling around the shoulders of his sons.

'That woman, too, knew how to laugh. Sometimes it was over me, when I got too serious.'

Phil and Rod would never forget the next image of their father turning to face Maeve, palms of hands downwards and fingers spread wide on the low wall. His shoulders were square and his chin set as he said,

'Mark me well. Concern yourself not too much with the shape of woman but listen for her laughter. Choose a rich, round melody and not the false, hand-over-mouth tittering that is an apology for zest. A woman should make music with her mouth.'

The other 'stars' were gathering around Maeve and the newcomer, beak-gaping and clicking. Another peal of mirth drifted on the sea-breeze...

Phil said, 'You are speaking about Mum.'

He paused, then looked frankly at his father. 'I'll take away the whiskey bottle then.'

The eyes of both 'boys' were concern.

'Oh no you don't, son. That's good Irish Whiskey. We'll drink some tonight... together. We'll remember your ancestry... and your mother. Rod's old enough now.

'Don't worry, Phil. Your father's a grand-son of an Irishman who drinks only with family and friends from now on. Do you think our little 'colleen' will take a tickle? Your mother did... now and then.'

The trio's male laughter were the base tones backing the higher-pitched peals from Maeve on that first day of Gaze's coming.

Maeve seemed happy... and relieved. She was calling for Rick, but they all went to her.

She wanted permission to take the newcomer, Gaze, into the Rest Pool. Could she have the gate unlocked? It was quite remarkable how the newcomer seemed to be wallowing and finstirring, waiting for Maeve to take the lead.

'I don't think we've any choice, boys. Get the key, Rod. Off you go, Phil. You've the drifter to let out. Apologise to Tom. Say I'll settle the account after the 'Show'. I'll drive over to his house.'

This was going to be interesting, Rick thought. With some surprise, he heard a beak-clicking from the Rest Pool.

Did White Tip sense something in the 'lagoon'? Was that a witter of anticipation?

He stared across the barrier and noted the dorsal of the female. It was stationary, lined up to the entrance!

He would ask Rod to leave the key with Maeve.

The echo-sounds were confusing in the waterspace. She could hear beakclicking greeting from the podpartners in the false lagoon. There was laughter from the female Splitfluke she recognised. But was there something or someone new?

White Tip had been trying to avoid her mindimages of a shallow sea above rippled sand - to break her sweeping finningpatterns of grief. The female Splitfluke had begun to help her. White Tip looked for her in the waterspace or tried to feel her mindsense which seemed more compatible than any other Splitfluke she had known.

Why did she feel such a sense of promise?

For several lightwaters this Splitfluke's mindsense had seemed to convey certainty that the pain of isolation and loss was nearly over.

At their first encounter, there had been the relief of an outpouring... Something had flowed from herself to the Splitfluke and the pressure had eased in bloodflow, in mind and on her heart. From behind mindclouds she used to fog her horizons of suffering, she had sensed a warmth of sunbreach; heard a new mindvoice, distant but reassuring... This Splitfluke could be trusted. Feeling calmer fluking bi-vector with her, why did White Tip feel a third presence behind a mindghost imaging in Bloom?

Again there was pleasing mouth-melody from the female Splitfluke. She was just beyond the entrance closure!

But was she alone?

Was there another mindpresence?

'She is called Maeve. I am Gaze. Do not be afaid but wait for the entrance closure to open,' said the new mindpresence from beyond the confines of the waterspace!

It was a young mindvoice, controlled, vibrant. How could that be!? They were not close enough for mindmerge!

White Tip waited. The young mindvoice had authority. She realised there had been command behind information.

Finstirring, watchfully close to the entrance closure, she became conscious of the elder Splitfluke also observing her but unthreatening. He had never sought domination; never threatened...

After some sharp, clicksounds and a sliding thump, the woodslab entrance was opening! The female Splitfluke was there...

'Maeve will not fin bi-vector with you for a while, White Tip. May I enter your waterspace?'

A young Bottlenose was at the entrance! She heard the ping-pattern of his name and his Podsherd origin! He was from waterspace beyond her cognisance!

Still he was waiting.

'Bottlenoses of my Podsherd do not fluke new waterspace without recognising rights of other creaturekind, White Tip. I am no threat to you and wish only to help. May I enter your waterspace?'

Utterly curious, she beakclicked permission, her own voice-sounds but faintly recognised through lack of use.

'Will you not ping-pattern your name?' he was saying in mindmerge, his concern half-registering...

Her name... The ping-pattern of her name was...

Bloom had been the last to ping-pattern her name. In remembering his deep-dive, there was the mindvision of the rippled sand in the shallow seaspace - monotonous and unchanging, stretching to infinity...

She was silent, watching her shadow passing the featureless seafloor... Watching her shadow give sandridges a falseness of movement...

She was alone and the seaspace was silent.

The mindvision was hypnotic, unchanging. It was safe to be with her shadow. Consistently faithful, it identified her. It was a podpartner, unvarying and unchangeable...

Another dolphin finned beneath her, never needing to airsnatch. Or Bloom finned bi-vector, a living partnership of her past...

But the shadow of her finningpassage was changing!

Twice it veered away forefin right! Inexplicably, her shadow rolled in an arcing turn!

She could not keep pace with her phantom podpartner! Wilfully perverse, it refused to follow her conscious movement!

Maeve was towelling herself by the side of Rick. He watched her shake her hair. The breeze was cooler now. Already her flesh was goosepimpling.

He knew she would not leave the Rest Pool but she needed something warm.

'I'll fetch your track-suit. Won't be a minute.'

Maeve smiled but those brown eyes soon turned to the two dolphins finning a circular pattern despite access to the 'lagoon' being readily available.

He returned quickly, handed her the track-suit and lit his pipe. As Maeve pulled on needful warmth, he studied the dolphins swimming anti-clockwise evolutions of the pool.

'Seems she's back in the old groove, Maeve.'

She shivered. Why did he think it was not just with cold?

'You are not looking as closely as you should, Rick. Watch. Can't you see something changing?'

The rate of circling was slower. The new bottlenose was finning beneath the female. At first, it seemed as if the young male was deliberately mirroring everything the female did, apeing her movement as if one mind controlled both bodies. Then Rick saw the decreasing distance between the two dolphins and the 'lagoon' entrance at each pass.

'He's trying to get her into the 'lagoon'? She's not gone out unless you were there, love. She won't go out.'

He heard a beak clicking behind him and turned. The 'stars' were gathering close to the Rest Pool... Did they know something he didn't?

He turned back in time to see the first of two deliberate moves by the new dolphin to swim through the entrance. After the second indication of intent, he watched the female. She appeared uncertain or unwilling... and then the new bottlenose was alongside and there was sustained fincontact.

Maeve's face was a peculiar mixture of emotions. She was smiling and crying at the same time. He didn't know what to do or say - was surprised that she spoke first.

'It's alright Rick. They're going out. We can lock the Rest Pool. It won't be needed now.'

First, the new bottlenose finned through the open gate. Following meekly came the female. All of the 'stars' were gathered. For all the world, it seemed like a reception committee! Beaks were clicking all around.

It reminded him of the life-boat bringing in survivors when the pleasure boat had gone down in the South Passage off Reeders' Point. The welcome of those few, brave fortunates had been one of the rare confirmations of genuine humanity he had witnessed.

'Now you have a survivor, Rick. Now White Tip will take her place in the Podsherd... I mean, with the 'stars',' Maeve said.

Rick was getting used to the coincidences where she appeared to read his mind but where the hell had the word 'Podsherd' come from?

Well, that was one small objective she had achieved. But there was no way she could teach the 'stars' to appear to read - let alone the other targets he had set before he would dream of opening any gates to the sea.

Chapter Ten

READING AND INTELLIGENCE

White Tip was not alone. For several lightwaters she had been close to Gaze, sharing her grief and loss; showing Gaze her only safe waterspace to fin in half-life. He perceived the shadows behind her distress - the way she falsified present with reincarnated memory. Slowly her oppression was lifting; new imaging forcing passage through awareness to lightglow again.

Now she recognised the shadow of Gaze accompanying her own across the sandfloor; felt his presence through lateral sensing, blanked and unused for so long.

Blackness and sharp delineation in her imaging was softening. Other creatures, other lives accessed her present. There was Maeve - alien but accepted in a strange kinship. There were the other Splitflukes who finned in such squandered effort. They remained unthreatening - simply pleased for rewards of food.

Fish did not fanflick this waterspace - yet she could hear the distant surf which no Bottlenose seemed able to reach. Hearing anew the song of the sea which had tormented Bloom before he had deep-dived - she was stronger, now, to withstand the pains of both memories... Stronger to face again, separation from a dam and a podsherd of flanker memory... To face truth her podfamily had probably drowned in the fishtrap weave. But she could not for long... Such privacy of sorrow she sought to reefside heavily - even from self. It was her deeper pain, magnified in her loss of Bloom.

Dorsal-drifting with Gaze in the darkwater was her greatest time of healing. There was solace in his gently grazing flank; water melodies heard whispered within weaving weed fronds above the rippled sandfloor. She began to remove her reefside barriers in mindmerge with him. He was both 'sire' and 'brother' in her rediscovery of self.

The sympathetic podpartners exhibited controlled tactfulness which seemed almost orchestrated... Belatedly, White Tip realised that, even in this, Gaze appeared to read her mind and mood for he was master of movement and meeting...

One lightwater, from sunbreach to vertical sunlight, she studied, consciously, the pattern of his intersecting vectors towards other Bottlenoses; saw them as carefully contrived, and finned to face him...

Before she could begin, gently his voice was a soothing caress within her temples of concern and doubt...

'Trust me, White Tip. You are almost well. Malaise of heart and spirit is the hardest to cure - the most contagious. Your spirit has been too close to a deep-dive, your mind seeking in despair a precarious equilibrium. It has taken all my care to creature your shadowseas of grief without creating larger fear. If you are ready to question what I am, then I will show you - if you are unafraid.'

No other Bottlenose was closer than fifty dolphinspans. It was almost as if White Tip and Gaze were invisible to dolphineyes.

The Splitflukes seemed oblivious to them except... except for Maeve who was flipperflicking in proximity.

How had she known White Tip needed the reassurance of her presence? There was a third presence she briefly perceived...

Five dolphinspans behind Gaze was a shimmer - a whiteness. In a windflurry eddying of ripples was a glimpse of a white bottlebeak and a flukeflip - reminding her of Bloom? - as a dolphin dived from view. Neither Gaze nor Maeve appeared to notice...

Gaze said, 'White Tip, can you remember the ping-pattern of your name?'

She looked directly at him and then away. A silence settled over them as the sun was masked by bubbling cloud. Her dam had named her... taught her the pattern... called her from confusing seashadows...

Hesitantly, she made a music from memory in the making of her name. Seemingly a whisper in a dark sea-cavern, her pinging was distorted... The second time was better... like a distant dolphin rounding reefedge, just before sunbreach lightened the darkwater. And then she remembered!

Her name echoed roundly through the false lagoon - precise, clear and with vitality...

She heard the echo-returns confirming the pattern and was surprised at its strength... Surprised again by the acknowledgements which rang from all sides and the joy of the podpartners - who still kept their distance.

Maeve finned to her side... and Gaze.

The podpartners obeyed the request for a surrounding dolphincordon. No dolphin challenged the rights of Gaze as a special dolphin, already accepting his ability to fulfill his promise of freedom. His mindvoice carried certainty. No other dolphin could image so clearly in mindmerge with so many at once.

Rick and the 'boys' found themselves grouped at the edge of the 'lagoon' - each unconscious of a summons; each a spectator of strange events. As cumulus shadow brushed the surface with clear, new light, each of the Dortmanns had a flash of inspirational imaging...

Rod, whose hands were never far from tools and mechanical things, felt his fingers fumble the spanner he had been using on the outboard motor. If he had dropped it in the lagoon, suiting-up and searching the sandfloor would be wasted 'time'. He wondered if a 'star' was trainable to fetch and retrieve... and laughed inwardly at his image of a dolphin apprenticed to a tool-using diver.

Rick saw the dolphin-line appear to divide into two teams and commence a possession game for a cork float. If this was possible then what about 'water polo' with a ball? That would be a real crowd-puller!

She was beaten by logistics - the Dolphinarium could not sustain the number of dolphins required. It was merely a fancy which would require miraculous and continuing visits by a team of trained dolphins from outside - from the larger 'seaspace'. Why did he use that word?... What would he have to do? Stand near the lock gates with a piece of card saying 'Polo Team required'? Reading was a skill utterly alien to dolphin intelligence!

Dolphins couldn't read and they had a life and death struggle on their hands anyway. Rick laughed aloud and was grateful his 'boys' did not appear to notice. Rod was obviously wrapped up in fitting a new ring to the piston of an outboard; Phil seemed entranced by Maeve, finning quietly by the side of White Tip with Gaze, the newcomer.

And Phil came to some decisions.

He could not help himself. He had to respond to the melody that was Maeve. Not since the engagement broken off with Susan at University had he really allowed himself to get involved with another girl. He had ducked out after the exams at the end of this second year - despite reasonable results. He had been unable to tolerate the torment of sharing the same campus and watch the flourishing romance between Susan and Jonathan. Jonathan had been a good mate. He did not wish him ill - but it hurt.

Phil had used the excuse that his father needed his help at the Dolphinarium. He knew that his personal tutor hadn't really believed him but it had been agreed that he would reapply to the Admissions' Office a year later to continue his study programme - unless he changed his mind over the vacation.

His tutor had said, 'This world needs the Marine Sciences more than ever. Man is the dirtiest animal in history. People like you, Phil, have to clean up the mess of toxins - cope with industrial and nuclear waste. PCBs, for example, are being found in higher levels in dead whales worldwide. Man pollutes and poisons so much. You are a valuable commodity and I know you are capable. Take time to find a new stability for your family and yourself if you must... Be sure you come back.'

Not saying more, he hadn't needed to. His words had gnawed at the bones of conscience underlying the frailty of Phil's flesh.

None of this had he discussed with Maeve. Rather, he had licked his emotional wounds in the privacy of 'responsible commitment to his family'. To allow free response to the magnetic Maeve seemed perverse betrayal of a love he had thought existed with Susan. But the pull of the present was too strong...

Maeve's grace was treading water near two bottlenose dolphins in the sunshine... Phil watched, admired...

His mind was huge! White Tip was lost in an immensity larger than seaspace to the horizon! She finfaltered above an abyss. Mindechoes whispered in whirling convolutions. How did he keep a sense of 'now'? How did he sustain contact with mindlights in a chaos of personality and need. She felt herself slip, swept in vortices - emotional interchanges of past, present. Was Gaze unsteady momentarily?

Briefly, she identified some minds as familiar... untuned images from Splitfluke mindpresences; a stronger empathy that was Maeve, and dolphinminds seeming to school around something central - something of warmth and authority which she felt could be trusted. She sought that warmth; held mindmerge vector upon it, needing the reference to keep from confusion.

She joined the jostle about a comforting and larger mindlight that was Gaze and waited for him to move closer. But he was not of one mind!

Dazzled, she saw Gaze's mindlight as fractured interconnections. He was sunshine or starshine glimpsed through spray - or the moon seen whole as a rainsquall on seasurge disassembled it in sprayripples.

In strange calm, she mindfinned patiently awaiting some part of his mindlight to illuminate her and expand to share as much as he dared. She recognised she was helpless; felt herself thrilling in something much more than admiration.

He was harsher than his youth bespoke; more wise than his seasons ought to evoke...

And part of Gaze was separating - expanding towards her. Near hypnotised, verging on flight, she awaited his first brush of contact in a new kind of mindmerge - so different from mindcontact she had known.

Gently she was turning... Increasing images coupled with hugely reefsided emotions - of uncertainty and anxiety? - reeled within her. Amazed by such openness when he could hide anything, she learned...

From the beginning, he showed her the truth of himself.

But she felt an impenetrable reefside shielding some things... out of concern for her?... Or was it a dread from within?

She tried, once, to focus beyond events not as strongly reefsided - to no avail, and received a mild rebuke...

'Secrets need the moment for revelation, White Tip,' his firm voice was saying...

She had the feeling that Gaze had been unguarded, momentarily... that he had been surprised by some strength in herself? White Tip tried no more; remained puzzled at the fleeting images she had glimpsed of a pod of Speckled Hump-backs and found herself lost in a yearning to know more of this... special dolphin?

White Tip had joined the 'stars'! She seemed to know everything required in performing for Maeve. Not quite at the peak of fitness, she could not perform some of the higher leaps but, whenever Rick had turned to quest the lagoon for her, there was her bottlebeak agape following every move. It was uncanny.

Once, the dome of her head had nodded downwards in his direction as if acknowledging his interest in her and his pleasure. On another occasion she was the first to flap fins together in mimicry of applause when 'Samson' - Maeve insisted he should really be called 'Blowhard' - achieved the highest leap he had ever seen through the jump-ring.

Why did Rick feel that she was using the real name? That same tang of certainty in her voice at the time when the 'orphan' was named 'White Tip'? Samson's explosive taking of air was an identifiable characteristic.

Another week should see White Tip taking a fuller part in the 'shows'. Almost unbelieveable!

Rick sat near the lock gates looking out to sea, pipe glowing at each sucking intake of breath. Phil had asked Maeve to go with him to a small place he knew 'for a meal she would not have to cook for herself'! He had insisted that she needed a 'break' and he had studiously avoided noting a stupid grin on Rod's face - or the momentarily raised eyebrows and open-eyed glance from his father.

Maeve had taken some convincing - expressing some concern over the welfare of White Tip... the need to be close to Gaze as a 'newcomer'... some washing she had to do... But there had been a staccato clicking from somewhere in the lagoon and Rick had recognised the glimpse of a recognised fluke pattern. The 'newcomer' had dived quietly some twenty yards away.

Maeve had given in with a slightly odd comment...

'If the break will do you some good as well, Phil - I'll go. If you intend to go to a disco or something - I haven't been to many.'

The sudden sideways flukeflip of water across the low side of the three-master had made them all laugh.

Rod had said, 'That 'newcomer' you've advertised for has got a lot to answer for. Excuse me while I change my shirt.'

The smart comment he had been about to make had been forgotten.

Rick had agreed to keep an eye on White Tip and gone to Maeve's usual observation place near the Rest Pool. The appearance of two dolphin beaks seemed to click reassurance as the new 'Gaze' and White Tip had looked directly at him and finned away together.

There were those freak moments when dolphins appeared almost human and capable of reading your mind, Rick had thought. Moving towards the lock gates, just after the pick-up's lights had disappeared from view, had he heard a peal of Maeve's laughter?

Well, that would do Phil some good.

On their return, just after midnight, Phil was first in to make some cocoa.

Rick paused, then, 'Where's Maeve, son?'

Phil grinned - pointed upwards.

'It's alright, dad. She's on deck. We're having some cocoa up there. Want some?'

His eyes were more lively, his face slightly flushed with pleasure, not embarrassment.

'No thanks son. I'll take something else up to drink. I think tonight needs just one tot. You alright yourself?'

Phil half-turned, a wry twist to his grin. 'Let's just say I heard someone make music with her mouth.' Completing his turn, he finished with, 'I might be fifteen minutes on deck. You've got five. Okay, Dad?'

Rick emerged just in time to see Maeve, thumb to nose with waggling fingers, looking across the darkness of the lagoon. She did not appear to notice their presence. Both heard an unusual exhalation of air from a surfacing dolphin closely akin to a 'rhubarbing' noise.

Helpless, they both laughed.

'Right, that does it. Samson is renamed 'Blowhard' from this moment!' said Rick, when the tightness of his smoker's lungs had eased.

Still smiling, Maeve replied, 'Good but that noise wasn't from Blowhard.' She didn't amplify but appeared to be looking gratefully across the darkened surface.

Phil came up with her cocoa. In the interchange of their glances, Rick recognised something of an excitement he once had known. He'd give it three minutes, not five and be off to his bunk.

Later, in the darkwater, White Tip could feel Gaze's flank brushing against her in the light windswell of water. She was beginning to enjoy his touch as much as the contact of his mind...!

She reefsided as heavily as possible! Astonished, she recognised the signs of an unexpected appetite...

He was physically close, gentle... but his mindmerging differed from anticipation...

'You have a strong mind, White Tip. Do you realise how strong?'

Suddenly she was sharing an image of Gaze fluking the forewave of a hardside... and then the unexpected jolt of mindenergy washing his mind in a wave of greyness. She felt his dizziness close to pain and feared the crushing weight behind - the barnacles and the twistingfins!

Stored images of herself and Maeve, with wetness upon cheeks, appeared - and then the awesome truth of mindmerge across the horizon!

How was this possible?

With careful selection, a series of rapid images flooded in mindmerge and his mindvoice was explaining...

In shock, she realised he could read Splitfluke minds!

There were more revelations! They were joined by two stranger Bottlenoses she did not recognise. Gaze separated from her. He was finning with the new podpartners - enjoying fluidity in the waterdance of celebration. The three Bottlenose males were tied as a tight trio in tri-vector, perfectly synchronistic.

His mindmerge voice was strong - 'Use your awakening senses, sister. How many dancers are we? How many celebrants are seen?'

Obediently, she pinged in echo-location - not fully trusting her lateral sensing which seemed to blur three dolphins into one. There was only one echo-return in the short range! How could that be?

Gaze was by her side. Together, they watched a duo dance - the remaining Bottlenoses in bi-vector now.

His forefin touching hers, she felt a pulse of mindenergy behind a giant reefside in the vastness of his mind...

There were four dolphin dancers! Then eight! The spray falling in a squall; wavelets from the flukingpassages splattered their jostled sides.

She felt excited - wanted to join the racing shapes and leap into the moonsky.

But one by one the stranger dolphins were diving to disappear...

She pinged again. Out of bewilderment, suspicion was born...

She watched a lonely dancer pause and finturn towards them; saw him seem to shimmer slightly as if uncertain of himself, and then watched him fin towards Gaze. The closer the finningpassage, the more the shimmering vagueness seemed to overwhelm...

Not 'him' - 'it'! She was watching an image! The dancing dolphins had been visions from...?

She tried to break off mindmerge - but could not do so until she had seen the outline of the last dancer dwindle in phosphorescence and disappear in the dome of Gaze's head!

He was a Visioner! He could make dreams live beyond the confines of co-joined minds!

His mindvoice was quiet and calm, easily penetrating the kaleidoscopic spinning of reefsides she threw out in a panic of fear.

'I shall not speak or touch you until you are ready. More than sister or cousin of my species, perhaps you could become dear to me. Already I know you better in yourself than you know yourself. I trust you with a secret shared only with my closest friends.

'Are curiosity and courage, Master Guardians of your fears? I believe they are for you are stronger than you know, White Tip.'

Beneath the moonglow, the false lagoon seemed even more unreal. She had an escape-vector towards the drifting dorsals of the sleeping podpartners if she needed flight.

Gaze had to be aware of such a possibility. She watched him fin to widen her escape-vector option. Still he was silently waiting... Unmoving and waiting as he had said he would.

Cloudcover blackwashed the surface! Lateral sensing confirmed he was unmoving... but could she trust her own senses? Poised in panic; uncertain above the abyss of the unknown, she did nothing but wallow with the pounding of her heart.

Slowly, the winking of the stars in unshielded sectors of the sky and safe watersounds of the sleepful podpartners began to quieten her racing bloodsurge. Gaze remained quiet and unthreatening.

He was showing her he would keep his word. She had to make the first move. Was he reading her mind?

There was no sign of his mindpresence. Gaze was out of mindmerge! Her mindscape was unoccupied by anything alien...

He would 'not speak or touch her until she was ready'.

He was trusting her with his secret - only shared with his 'closest friends'.

'You could become dear to me'!

She remembered the soothing quality of his touch...

White Tip felt her forefins finstir an alignment upon Gaze before a conscious decision. She was caught in mysterious currents of waterflow towards him. Her own fins, extensions of her need to touch him again, seemed traitors in the tug of his tenderness...

Alongside, a forefin brushed his as waterfilm cleared from her eyes. He looked from a gleaming eye-centre, into her own. His eye remained steady and open as, with slight uncertainty, his left forefin moved to sweep her side.

He reminds me of a shy brother near an elder sister, she thought... and then came his invitation to mindmerge, expressed quaintly in the formality of mindmeet...

'I am willing to mindmerge again, my sister of this waterspace. Is my mindcontact acceptable? Are you curious yet unafraid?'

His forefin, motionless in contact, was lightness upon her own. A sigh of inshore breeze lap-ruffled the false lagoon and watershivers slop-washed their dorsals.

She heard the ripples fade to insignificance before breaking mindsilence.

'You can be trusted - but what are you Gaze? A dolphin learns to trust instinct. My instinct is to be afraid of you but you threaten nothing.' She struggled for images... 'I do not fear you but I touch you... in awe.'

He beaksmiled as the quiver in his flukes began to shake off the last remnants of adolesence. Deep within himself, there was a fresh confidence.

Amazed in his new self-certainty - trying to pattern concerning himself - Gaze failed to note half-formed images of a seaspace pairing in White Tip's imaging.

She recognised a potential future had fluked nearer...

Why was he preoccupied - not sensing her excitement? This place was safer for the present. The exodus would continue soon but the coral and rock reefs would suffice until sky signs and waveswell signalled a storm. The pod of surviving Hump-backs needed the lee of landmass shelter from a tumult of wind and wave when the elements growled in discontent. Coral reef and rock shallows could become as sharp... as Splitfluke steel...

Blotch mindshivered before the stored image but felt comforted in the pressure of Twizzle's sleeping flank against his own. One had to repress old, painful images...

Blotch and Twizzle had guided their pod from the place of Collet's demise - and Gaze's confrontation with the Large White Shark - loosely vectoring upon the waterspace of the sun's deep-dive.

Somehow, he believed - as did Twizzle - that their vectors were destined to converge once more with the young Bottlenose who had tried to lighten their burden of leadership. These two, middle-aged dolphins continued sharing a vigil of watching for danger in the darkwater. Such companionship had brought them closer...

Blotch remembered how Twizzle had sought to station herself at his flank late in the lightwater of Gaze's departure. He recall-imaged how startled he had been by her in mindmeet...

'We grow older, Blotch. The lightwater's fluking seems many dolphinspans longer. We learn to regret the indolence of youth that should have prepared us better to cope with our ageing.'

He had felt that she hadn't finished.

There had been a pause as he had scanned the seaspace beyond their pod's reefshelter in the reflex watchfulness of the sentinel. Then he had become conscious of the warmth of her dolphinflank against his own!

Calmly, in mindmerge, not observing the normal courtesy of an invitation, Twizzle had said:

'Yes, Blotch, we grow older and our seasons of painful memories stretch behind us. The seaspace teaches caution as needful and to fear the unexpected. We erect our reefsides of coral and rock above the steepsides of our anxieties to bar any incursion of ill-intent. But we also make barriers for friendship and good which should flow between us.

'Thus we grow older in isolation.'

Her flank had separated from his but her mindmerge contact had remained. She had finned forward slightly so that her eye had seemed to appraise him closely...

'We have both suffered the loss of loved ones. Our Podsherd is decimated and we are flotsam in an alien sea.

'Yet we have accepted responsibility to find a new security beyond the next horizon. We share that responsibility but we have never risked sharing our whole minds. In my mind, many reefsides exist - as they do in yours. It is time to show our weaknesses and strengths, our wishes and dreams - for the good of our podpartners - possibly for ourselves.

'Perhaps, Gaze has taught me the need to have courage in a sensible taking of risk. In seeking safer waterspace, we take risks now. I will dare another risk.

'Know me - as I am, Blotch. Please join me in mindmerge as mature Hump-backs may, unafraid and unashamed. Let each... show the other our... mindscapes as far as we dare... the risks...'

Intuitively, momentarily, Blotch had been in another time - a younger time - with a certain shy female in a quiet lagoon, remembering her trepidation and uncertainty...

Twizzle's strong imaging had faltered towards the end. He knew that she had a reputation for the sternest kind of appraisal of ardent males. Some had remarked, in callous disillusion, that Twizzle functioned in flesh-fervour for a flanker rather than for joy. In consequence, she had had far fewer matings than most females of her seasons.

Her faltering this time had spoken of shyness more than dissuading objectivity. Blotch had realised she had been facing down herself when she had finturned to look upon him. He had warmed to her courage in allowing him access to her own uncertainties.

Agreeing, with a kind of solemnity to join her in mindmerge, the very first images she showed were those of her awakening after the shared darkwater station with Gaze. He recalled his examination of Twizzle, herself, as a potential mate - when Gaze had left.

They had continued in mindmerge for a very long time and a strength of companionship was newly born when her flanks had moved once more to warm-nudge his own whilst she doze-drifted needfully.

They had not coupled yet - neither the opportunity nor the heat of urgency having arisen. Underlying contentment in a certain eventuality and a deepening friendship had... A flash of mindenergy startled Blotch in its intensity!

It was as if a moonshaft had pierced his mindeye to shatter his imaging into confusing whirls of half-colours. Briefly, he registered the ping-patterns of two names... Somewhere, a dolphin was calling his name - and that of Twizzle!

He felt Twizzle finstir uneasily, fitfully.

There was mindsilence. Nothing seemed at variance in waterspace... and yet the very forcelines had seemed to tremble.

Twizzle was awake. Familiarly slipping into mindmerge, he sought to reassure her but could not answer her question.

'I was dream-drifting. Who called our names?'

Both Hump-backs found themselves finstirring and scanning the open seaspace. No unusual echo-returns... nothing which appeared to threaten their dorsal-drifting security... Only recognised patterns of a truce period in a darkened waterspace...

And then the mindwhispered pinging growing to name-patterning they both recognised! But more, as mindcontact broadened...! Never, in the sagas of Hump-backs, had dolphins mindmerged from beyond the darkline of horizon!

Yet it was happening now!

Gaze was speaking... showing them the possibility of security - and, at the same time, asking for their help? How could he...?

He was not alone... he was with another Bottlenose, a female...

He was describing flukingvectors to a far waterspace and a promise of peace...

The mindcontact seemed to tire but not before both amazed Hump-backs knew their Bottlenose friend - no, 'friends' - would speak again in the darkwater next...

The pod of Speckled Hump-backs left Wreck Reefs the next sunbreach without ever knowing the Splitfluke name.

Unerringly, they followed forcelines, with deepening water to their right forefin sides - away from vertical sunrise towards the unknown island-mass which Gaze had named Cato Island... and assured shelter in the darkwater.

The Hump-back survivors redoubled the respect they accorded to Blotch and Twizzle for both leaders seemed to radiate directness. Their flukingpassage was accomplished with an ease which brought the reward of more time for relaxation.

Later, Hump-back sagas would record Cato Island as a place of healing for troubled dolphinspirits. They would not record the coupling of two, mature Hump-back leaders in slackwater to the lee of the islandmass.

Flesh-fervour is an unremarkable and accepted norm for dolphinkind. Sometimes it is the expression of great sensitivity and love, as Blotch rediscovered... and Twizzle learned in joy...

'You needed me to reach them... but why are you asking Hump-backs to come here?' came the mindvoice of White Tip.

She had been too close to the mindenergy of Gaze to understand more than the core meaning of the images which they had seemed to share. That and the fact that he had used her own mind, magnifying a message to unseen recipients beyond the horizon. Her own mind had, for moments, brushed in contact through myriads of mindmurmers and vastnesses she could not conceive. It had been too quick.

She had been conscious of recognition - a pulsation of bloodflow through Gaze. His fintouch upon her own had seemed heavier... firmer...

There had been nothing of malignance in the heave of images that had seemed to swell in the melon of her head and leap beyond the darkline of horizon. Neither had there been a sense of being used or invaded. His fintouch had remained reassuring and calming.

The mindwhispers of reply from unknown dolphins somewhere in the seascape had also grown to closeness of near proximity and she had been in different waterspace... close to a reefedge with two 'others'...

And she had shared their experience of loneliness, gratitude and a will to survive despite...!

Suddenly, she had wanted to fin from Gaze's side, feeling - seeing horrors starker than before!

Gaze's mindvoice had briefly washed everything away...

'Trust me, White Tip. You are safe here. These are mindechoes of other dolphins' tragedies. Be strong - as strong as you can - for I need your strength as recently you have needed mine.'

Momentarily, she had flukethrashed in desire to fluke an escape-vector but his need of her had kept her at his flank. She had found more mindstrength; maintained a sense of detachment. She had begun to see further into his intent and beyond the immediacy of his imaging...

'The Hump-backs and our present podpartners need each other to find a greater freedom in larger waterspace, safe from captivity - safe from Splitfluke steel, White Tip,' said Gaze. 'Perhaps we can help to form a new, mixed Podsherd for the good of all dolphinkind. With your help, perhaps a dream in many minds can be realised here.

'Come closer in my mind.'

Another mindlimb seemed to grow from the cluster of mindlight which was Gaze, stretching towards her but waiting for her to mindfin closer.

'It is the moment for another revelation. You are tired my... my... You are tired but we will share my dream of a new Podsherd,' mindwhispered Gaze.

If he thought that White Tip had not noticed his stumbling search for endearment stronger than 'my cousin', he was wrong.

There are parts of the female heart which are inviolable and indiscernible - sometimes hearing the unspoken clearer in the lifenoise than the male.

White Tip welcomed the communion of heart and mind as they dorsal-drifted beneath the moonglow. She was not surprised, now, that Gaze seemed to segment his attention, not regarding it as rude. He had a great deal on and in his mind. Secretly, she was thrilled to note that she appeared to be closer to the centre of his fragmented mindself than she had been before.

There was a clatter of fast footwork on the deck above. Rod had these lapses into adolescent exuberance but it had been some months since he had heralded his presence in this manner. Something fell with a metallic clunk and a word, which Rick had not known was in his son's vocabulary, rang roundly through the three-master.

'Rod! Watch your tongue and mind your feet! That's another sheet of paper I've wasted! I'm trying to work down here!'

Rod appeared, rubbing his elbow. His face was flushed with excitement.

'Sorry, Dad. You'll understand in a minute. You've got to come and see this. Maeve and Phil have been... No, it's better you see yourself.'

'Dad, you've got to come! It's more important than paperwork.'

Rick knew that Maeve and Phil had been together in the outboard, on the lagoon, for the last two hours. Maeve had selected some large pieces of card and reached for some felt-tipped pens. He'd assumed she was going to do some sketches and had been looking forward to seeing the results. Phil had been only too willing to accompany her.

Leaving them to it, Rick had cloistered himself with the chore of paperwork and tried to imitate the 'patient scribe' at the dawn of literacy. Monks, too, had been ravaged by their present - but they had avoided distractions within a family by vowing celibacy.

Well, he thought, I took no such vow... and, on the whole, I'm glad I didn't. Fiona smiled across memories... and that was good...

'This better be important, son,' he said.

'Oh, it is, Dad, it is,' said Rod, with a flashing grin and the infuriating expression of a secret-keeper.

Dismissing the possibility that he was being summoned to witness Phil's loving embrace around the sweetness of Maeve as they drifted in the outboard, Rick negotiated the wooden steps to the deck. Eleven in the morning, yards from a casual paternal glance, would not have been wise in his day. What the hell was going on?

Emerging on deck, it took but a moment to sense that something unusual was happening.

The 'stars' were, without exception, spy hopping in the vertical position. They appeared to be drawn up in a line, facing Maeve and Phil, seated in the outboard. The line was far from random - too controlled, too disciplined. All dolphin beaks seemed oriented towards Maeve and Phil, the latter wearing confusion in excitement and disbelief.

Some words were exchanged and Phil stood up, the boat swayed slightly. He gave the two hand signals for a dive and a jump but no indication as to which 'star' he expected to respond.

With choreographic precision, a ripple seemed to run along the dolphin-line as each submerged at metronomic intervals. In line astern, beneath the clear surface, the 'stars' circled the outboard. Each leapt into the air with the same time interval, returning to their stations of moments before!

It was a perfect extension to the individual training each 'star' had received but Rick had never seen all the dolphins perform the trick with such synchrony.

'Bloody good, Phil! How did you manage that?' Rick called across the water.

'Errm... I didn't. You'd better keep watching. I'm sitting down again. I think I need to,' came his son's reply.

Maeve stood up.

Immediately, the air was filled with beak-clicking and each 'star' mimicked applause. She smiled and raised one finger to her lips. There was silence.

That's new, thought Rick. When had she found time to teach that gesture and response? How could she get such an instantaneous group response anyway?

Maeve, sitting down again, leaned forward to lift a card above her head.

The dolphin-line broke up and, in moments, a sense of normality returned to the lagoon. All the usual groupings and pods were established - with a 'sameness' of noises and swimming patterns.

Rick blinked. Neither Maeve nor Phil had signalled. The 'word' in red on the card had said 'RELAX'!

'I'm coming over, Pop!' said Phil.

Rick watched him fall backwards into the water. He swam in a fast crawl-stroke towards the three-master. Rod dropped the scrambling net over the side. Helping his son over the gunwale, Rick gathered himself.

'Seems to me the pair of you have put in some slick training this morning.'

'You haven't seen everything yet, Pop. I think we'd better get some chairs,' said Phil, smiling. 'You are definitely going to need one.'

In two minutes, Phil and Rod were seated slightly in front of their father's chair.

'Move where you like, Dad,' said Rod. 'We won't move a muscle. Watch Maeve. Watch. I think she's...'

'Let him make up his own mind, Rod,' said Phil, cutting him short... and then...

'Maeve! We're ready!'

Maeve smiled in their direction, reached forward and held up another card. In large, neat letters was a name Rick chuckled over - 'BLOWHARD'.

Within ten seconds, a dolphin breached close to the outboard, causing a sudden wash which slapped against the side. There was an explosive expulsion of air and Blowhard was spy hopping and beak gaping in front of Maeve. Her peal of laughter was real and pleasureable but Rick could not believe what he had just seen!

'Phil, you're not expecting me to believe Samson - damn it, I mean Blowhard - read his own name?' Rick asked.

'I didn't think you'd believe it,' said his elder son. 'Neither did Maeve... Keep watching.'

Maeve held up another card. Rick had barely time to rub his right eye with the base of his right palm before Gaze was spy hopping near the outboard in response to his name display.

'Hold it, Maeve!' Rick shouted with such unexpected volume, it made both sons jump. 'You could have the cards in a fixed order. You don't expect me to believe the 'stars' are reading their names?'

There was a pause and then her laughter again. Rick detected a challenging undertone. He was right.

Her clear voice came across the gap.

'Okay, Rick. The cards are in this boat. Let's swop places. And, incidentally, I'm willing to stay out of sight while you try for yourself.'

She was at it again. How did she know he suspected she was making some signal he had not observed?

'Right. Bring that bloody boat here. I'm too old and lazy to go swimming when it's not necessary.' He added, in an undertone to his sons, 'If this is some kind of joke, I'll have you two.'

Both of the 'boys' were grinning but their faces were open and honest. They weren't up to anything. Nearly half his lifetime had been spent in reading their faces. He was sure... but this other 'reading' had him flummoxed!

Ten minutes later, Rick was moored to a marker buoy some thirty yards from the three-master. He had looked all around the outboard and found nothing suspicious - no way of making any kind of underwater signal. Some felt-tips and a pile of cards bearing the names of the 'stars', in several different colours, were the only additions to normal...

Colour! It took two minutes to rewrite some names in different colours. These would be the cards he would use.

If colour had been the stimulus, that's fixed you my smart, little brown eyes, he thought.

He stared at the 'boys' and Maeve. They were innocently seated and watching him. He would continue to watch them like a hawk.

Rick said nothing; gave no indication that he was ready. His fingers fumbled with the cards. He drew one from the smaller stack. He looked at it before holding it aloft. As luck would have it, it read 'BLOWHARD'. He rejected it. Of course! Quickly searching he found the card he wanted... 'DELILAH'.

Maeve was probably in the process of renaming her but had used the 'star' name, he thought. All the better.

Rick held the card aloft not taking his eye off the three young adults on the three-master. Maeve had turned her back. He watched her for the slightest movement.

There was none. A light breeze lifted her brown hair slightly and fluttered her loose shirt.

A few dolphin beaks seemed to raise from the surface and look in his direction. Nothing else seemed to happen.

Just as he was on the point of shouting to Maeve he was startled to hear a loud beak clicking behind him. The boat rocked as a dolphin beak nudged it from behind him.

Delilah's head was tilted almost quizzically. In a woman, the nearest interpretation of that head angle could only mean, 'Well, what do you want?'

It had taken just under half a minute for Delilah to swim to the boat. Perhaps it had been less, Rick realised. He did not know how long the dolphin had been behind him, waiting.

Maeve's voice came across the water.

'Well tell her to do something. You can't keep her hanging about. Women have busy lives!'

'What do I tell her to do!?' he shouted back, feeling the absurdity of the moment.

He might have guessed the reply would have been exactly in Fiona's vein. Maeve had many similarities.

'If you don't want her to do a trick - at least tell her she can relax. Hold up the card.'

He held up the RELAX card, dumb, mute and watchful.

A very unfeminine snort came from Delilah. Her bottle-beak and dolphin head shook whilst looking at him... and then she sub-merged. He could almost hear Fiona's voice saying, 'Men!'

He heard Maeve laugh and the 'boys' laughing too. There was nothing malicious in the sound but it was like an irritation.

He grabbed three cards and held them aloft, not looking at the names. A puff of breeze took one of them and dropped it into the lagoon. He could not reach it.

Two dolphin heads emerged in front of him. Looking at the cards in his hands, he knew already they would match the identities. DAVID and RUTH had responded.

He was not prepared for what happened next.

A dolphin breached next to the card in the water and submerged. Rick thought he recognised the fluke pattern of the newcomer, Gaze, but it might have been another.

A second dolphin surfaced and airsnatched. It was Delilah, again. She grasped the card in her beak and finned towards the boat. Spy hopping, she was offering the bedraggled card to him!

Rick leaned to take it. The felt-tipped letters he had drawn were still legible and spelled Delilah's name!

He did not understand how Maeve had done it but the 'stars' did appear to be responding to their names. The possibilities were enormous. A loud whoop escaped him!

Three dolphins mimicked applause in front of him!

It took Rick the rest of the day to begin to formulate other notions concerning alternative explanations. These seemed too outrageous to entertain for long. Maeve had, apparently, begun to 'teach' rather than 'train' the 'stars'!

His promise of free access to the sea for the 'stars', which he had made to Maeve, stirred uncomfortably in his conscience. She appeared to be on her way to solving some problems in training which his greater experience had found too difficult. Dolphins could not be taught to read. True, it was a smart trick to condition a response to a given stimulus for a reward.

Rick paused in raising a match to his pipe. The flame sputtered out.

What reward had Maeve offered to illicit the required behaviour? How was she working it?

Eyeing the huge gates, the thought crossed his mind that they would need some attention soon. When was the last time they had been serviced and exposed metalwork greased?

Who could tell? If Maeve was successful in achieving the impossible conditions he had outlined, he might have to open them for the 'stars' to come and go as 'they' please!

Rick chuckled. The lock might see some frequent use!

Two loud noises made him stare into the water close to the gates. Three dolphins had risen, two of them making loud exhalations. The noises had sounded uncannily like two words... 'Yooo', 'Bhhet'!

He might have known that one of them was Blowhard but the other noisemaker could have been either Gaze or White Tip. It was ridiculous to think that they had actually tried to speak...

Rick lit his pipe. As his eyes accustomed to the gloom of twilight, he could have sworn he saw a dolphin head nodding an emphatic 'yes' in his direction...

Unaccountably, he had overslept!

A light-sleeper, the habit of early rising was ingrained in his sub-conscious. Surrender of freewill to the mastery of deep-sleep, he strongly resisted. His fiercely independent spirit was reluctant to be swept in a dream-tide for long. Perhaps he had learned to fear the undertow beneath the washing waves of sleep and the threat of drowning - being torn by torment of memory. Too many nights had seen him wake and seek the companionship of Fiona's warmth. Or her voice had called from another place, beyond the present.

He felt relaxed. It had been years since Rick had slept thus - unless he had sought to lose himself in the headiness of a glass.

There had been no fitful turning. Head sinking into the pillow, he had descended to dream without any anxiety of meeting Fiona's phantom in the underworld of sleep... and meet her he had.

They had been swimming in the joyful sea of their honeymoon. Winning the race to the beach, he had watched her emerge, breasts heaving in exertion of breathing, water a stream on the length of her legs. She had shaken a mist from her hair and smiled at his wondering stare.

Both had paused in the rare moment of open admiration and mutual need, for breathing to steady... and then she had moved towards him...

'I am yours, Rick. I promised 'to have and to hold'. I am not a picture to admire on a wall.'

Fiona had kissed him and he had felt the welding of their skin in contact.

Their mouths parting, she had said quietly, as if praying, 'Please God, I will never be far from your mind. I want to remember the way you just looked at me for years - and, when I get old, I promise I will try to remember what you looked like, before you became fat, bald and grumpy.'

She had gone before all her words had registered, her laughter a trailing challenge of invitation to follow.

Rick had dreamed of her laughter, not of her pain; felt her again as warmth in the night, and had not shivered beneath cold star-stains of destiny.

He awakened slowly, rising from remembrance to the dance of dappled light on the cabin wall as sunshine was reflected from the lagoon's surface through the open port. Watching the interplay of patterns, the noises outside registered.

There was something additional to water lap and gull screech. Something which reminded him of too many years ago, before Fiona - before loving - even before the dreaming of love.

Somewhere from the deep past was the sound which was similar... something the same?

It was Maeve's voice. That was the similarity - well, not the same but the 'way' she was speaking. Her quiet, gentle tones stirred the loose net half-covering the port, joined the light-dance on the cabin wall... and the memory returned...

Miss McClinty had used the same repetitive quality; the same penetrating quietness. There were the same gaps as Miss McClinty had waited for the word of answer from the class.

What on earth was Maeve reciting multiplication tables for?

Throughout pauses in Maeve's voice, there were dolphins beak-clicking...!

Rick was out of his bunk!

Four dolphins were spy hopping near the outboard moored to the marker buoy. Without doubt, they were responding to the chanting rhythm of the 'times two table'! She could not know she was observed. Maeve was teaching another trick. It would be well to watch...

'Two times four is.....,' she said, showing four fingers on each hand.

'Click, Click, Click,....... Click.'

Eight very definite beak-clicks in synchrony....!

Four pairs of dolphin fins mimicked applause....!

Maeve placed a finger to her lips. Silence - water ripples the only movement about four dolphin heads above the lagoon surface.

'Now again. Two times four is......'

'Click, Click, Click,....... Click.'

Maeve's finger at her lips......

'Now what is that?' in a quiet, carrying voice....

A mixture of strange noises emanating from dolphin beaks in a disordered cacophony....

'Ttt..Aay..Iii..Ttt..Iii..Aay..'

Maeve's finger at her lips and silence - her open hand indicating a dolphin head in turn.

'Aay...Iii...Ttt...Aay..Iii..Ttt..'

'Ay..ii..tt..; Ay-ii-tt; A-i-t, Ait!'

Ait! Eight! Maeve was teaching three dolphins to make sounds in sequence to give an appearance of 'words'. Rick smiled. Another good trick but not good enough, my girl.

He watched Maeve indicate the fourth dolphin...

Clearly came the word and the word was from Gaze...

'Ait. Ait.' There was the slightest of pauses and the same high, hollow-sounding voice came from his dolphin beak.

'Ttootighmitz foorritzz ayittt, Mayvvett.'

Rick's hands clenched. He was conscious of nothing else except the dolphin beak which seemed magnified across the yards of distance. His head craned forward.

Maeve's finger to her lips....

The open handed gesture towards Gaze....

'Ttooo tighmitz foorr itz ayitt, Mayvve.'

Rick was half out of the cabin before realising his nudity! He fumbled for clothing.

There had been more than conditioned response in what he had just seen! Maeve had not had the time to train the newcomer so quickly.

Suddenly the card, 'Bottlenose needed', held above her head on the day of Gaze's arrival, had greater significance than random luck and a quirk of femininity! Gaze had swum towards the lock gates with real purpose. Rick had read it in his passage across the bay. Had it been in response to the card in Maeve's hands?

How had the dolphin seen the card - even 'read it' at great distance, if it had been read? Was a dolphin's eyesight as developed as a human in the long range?

An untrained dolphin did not perform the tricks he and the 'boys' had patiently planned and shaped from natural behaviour. Yet, Gaze had required no training! How much training had White Tip really received?

Rick realised he had much still to learn of dolphins...

'Enough Maeve. He is coming. Take care to arouse his interest but not his fear. We must leave you for now,' said his mindvoice, a whisper in awareness.

'We will fin to join the podpartners for there are things we must plan in readiness. Please, will you hold up the RELAX card before Rick calls for you. He will ask to see you, with myself, in the Rest Pool later. I will be ready.'

Maeve smiled and complied. All she had to do was think the words 'Good luck' and knew that Gaze had heard them when his flukes slapped the surface as he left. She knew, too, that she hadn't really needed to think the words. He would have heard her anyway.

That part of her mind close to the centre of his mindlight cluster continued to know a sense of purpose and peace. There was no sense of fearful surrender to an alien malignance. Too many 'others' were close in mind for her to feel loneliness or exposure to any danger. There was joy in such closeness - the contact as tender as Phil's first kiss of last night...

'Uh huh! So he did kiss you! You can't reefside as well as you think, Maeve. But you're getting better,' said the voice of Gaze, his mindsmile a radiance.

'Rhubarb to you!' she said, a flush of pink across mindcontact.

She laughed at the image of pursed lips making a smacking noise which seemed to blot out everything else.

'Go away and play water-polo!' she mindscreamed at him, but she was careful to look happy and unflurried as Rick appeared at the top of the companionway leading down to the cabins.

Rick hurried to the side.

'Maeve! Is school out already? I heard your lesson - wanted to watch. Where is... where are the 'stars'?' he called across the lagoon.

'You've been spying on me! They're relaxing. You've been asleep a long time. How about coffee for the training staff around here?' She couldn't help herself... 'Where's Phil? There's a note in an envelope near the clock marked 'Dad'. Where's he gone?'

Phil? A note? Rick hadn't a clue. At times, his elder son had a closed mind even to his father.

'I don't know. I'll look at it - and make the coffee.' He added,

'Get back over here. I think we'd better have another talk about the 'stars' and that new 'Gaze'. You might have some explaining to do... and I've got some questions...

'Maeve, get over here before the top of my bloody head blows off!'

'Yes sir, I'm coming,' she replied, laughter growing behind her words to reverberate around the dry-dock and across the lagoon.

Several dolphin heads appeared above the expectant surface but submerged.

Rick had an uncanny sense of 'deja vu'. Had there been the time he had used the same phrases with Fiona? Had her laughter been the same response?

Maeve led him towards the Rest Pool, her features open, alive and excited. Her hand was cool but the pressure, firm and confident. Without embarrassment, she had reached for his hand like a daughter... or like a mother to a child?

Rick realised there was kinship of a kind. Many tangible links with the life of his past and the thoughts of his present merged to confirm an affection. He chuckled inwardly. Maeve had the uncanny knack of neutralising his uncertainties at one moment and giving rise to others of greater magnitude the next... but he could not deny the kinship he was feeling.

The bottle-beak of Gaze, too fresh as an image in his mind, could not be as readily accepted in the same light of kinship. He had not yet qualified a sense of dread he had felt when the bottle-beak had appeared to speak.

Dimly he perceived hypocrisy in his senses of decency and superiority. Worse, an accusation loomed concerning the assumed rights of man in the natural world. Too many bloodstains of cetaceans within the oceans precluded an easy conscience. How could a man in a world of men, rest, realising that other creatures of high intelligence were murdered daily?

The voice sounds from the bottle-beak of Gaze had whispered distress in the land caves of Man's conceit, where he hoarded his spoils ravaged from the seas.

Aware of Man's treatment of his own kind - the horrors of genocide, slavery and repression - how should he regard himself? Was the concept of 'Freedom' only applicable to 'Homo Sapiens'? Was he a terrorist in a one-sided battle for the seas in which history would record no victor but only mourn the senselessness in desolation?

For the first time in years, Rick found himself questioning his function as the Manager of a Dolphinarium.

Was he instrumental in bringing greater awareness to the crowds of the cetacean character which swam uniquely between the worlds of air and water through the seas of history? Did the water ballet of the 'stars' create a growing sympathy for the plight of whales and dolphins internationally? Were he and the 'stars' ambassadors for greater understanding to assist in arresting wholesale slaughter?

Uncomfortable in himself, he realised that the chores of paperwork and the attention to detail for programming 'shows', training and liaising with others had created an artificiality which had made him more of a zookeeper. Worse, had the years made him also a gaoler who believes belatedly a prisoner's plea of innocence?

'You are very quiet, Rick. We're here.'

Maeve's whisper filtered through his thoughts.

She was smiling but her eyes troubled him. Her eyes reminded him of a mother or teacher who guesses the nature of a child's concern. Just who was the elder around here?

The gate to the Rest Pool was already open. When had Maeve...?

She was handing him the key...

'I'm sorry Rick. I took the key earlier. I had the feeling it might be needed. Gaze is already inside. Do you want to lock the gate? The 'stars' won't bother us,' she said, almost as if everything was... preplanned?

He could not put all his questions into words - followed sheepishly to the pool's edge.

The finning shape of Gaze changed direction the moment Maeve was in sight. She knelt, reached out a hand to touch his side. Rick felt a lump in his throat. Her expression was much more than practical detachment. In all his experience, no would-be 'trainer' had ever looked thus - friendship had never worn a more lovely... loving?... face.

'Hello, Gaze,' she said, slowly - distinctly.

'Hettello, Mayvvet,' Gaze's bottle-beak replied!

Frozen to immobility, Rick could only watch. There had been no hand signals. It was simply a greeting!

Maeve turned her head.

'Come closer, Rick. You look as though you've seen a ghost. Touch him. He is real you know. Come and meet my friend.'

A smile of reassurance played around and in her brown eyes. She was magnetic. Her voice drawing him to the poolside, he knelt beside her.

In the silence of water-lap, Gaze exhaled and drew breath, his blowhole moving in the fashion of his kind - a perfectly ordinary bottlenose dolphin. The dome of his head lifted from the surface, tilted and an eye, far less dull than he expected, looked directly upon him.

'He wants you to touch him and say 'hello',' whispered Maeve. 'Where's your manners, Rick?'

Her giggle was rich and warm...

Rick's hand moved independently of his mind's command, the palm seeking confirmation of a wetness upon a dolphin's side. The flesh was substance and familiar... and strangely comforting. He could feel his pulse slowing.

He was reminded of the occasion he had touched a captive shark as a boy for a dare. With quickened heart, he had complied and found the flesh cold, alien. With a thrash, the shark had fanned away at speed, its nervous, reactive energy impelling escape. This dolphin's flesh seemed to hold a warmth, something more than instinct.

Was there more in the tingle touch of his fingers? It was hard to distinguish the difference between the sensation of Maeve's hand on his other forearm and the tactile messages from this hand. It was as if there was no difference.

'Well say something, Rick. Aren't you going to say 'hello'?' came Maeve's voice as a quiet reminder, even an insistence.

She stood up, waiting.

He coughed nervously, clearing his throat...

'Hello, Gaze.'

His words hung above the surface. He waited, watching Maeve closely.

He heard an exhalation and intake of air, water sound as Gaze spy hopped. Rick had to take his eyes from Maeve, sensing the moment was now.

'Hettello Rickt. Ittm pleastted ttoo mitt yoott.'

Gaze's beak was open, grinning; head tilted slightly, politely. His head nodded.

Rick was motionless, staring at the dolphin head less than two metres distant. Maeve had moved close to his left side. He wanted to push her behind him away from... No, he wanted to watch Maeve!

He held her in front of him, turning her to face him. He grasped her hands.

'What's the trick, Maeve? Damn it! It can't be real!'

Looking into her face, her eyes, there was nothing but innocent pleasure - no trace of subterfuge.

'Watch Gaze, Rick. The secret you want an answer to is going to shake hands with you.'

Lifting his eyes to look across her shoulder, he could see Gaze progressing across the short distance to the pool's edge in the vertical position. It was a straight copy of the 'star' trick of 'walking in water'.

Slowly, the dolphin partially descended into the pool on an invisible water platform so that tilted head and fins were visible. Close to the side, one forefin extended towards Rick, gesture and invitation unmistakeable.

A smile, crossed Rick's face. He released Maeve and shook hands with her 'friend'.

Maeve's laughter was loud and pleasant but served to spark another doubt.

'Alright, you made no signals to Gaze. How did you know he was going to 'shake hands'? And don't say he must have heard us talking.'

Maeve's reply took several moments to sink in.

'He told me he was going to.'

Rick's whirling thoughts settled upon and examined her answer.

There were only two startling possibilities. Either Maeve was able to talk a kind of dolphin language or... He had not heard Maeve making any peculiar noises at any time since he had known her. Which left...!

Maeve was speaking...

'Yes, Rick. It has taken a great deal of care to arrive at this moment. Cetaceans have a history which is longer than mankind's. They've been around for a very long time. They are not tool-users like us but they have a larger brain and one which is just as complex. They have senses and ways of communicating in a water environment which have taken evolutionary twists you would not have thought possible. Perhaps, in some ways, they are more advanced than ourselves. At least they have learned to live in harmony with their world. It is man who brings discord.'

She was voicing his unspoken thoughts, as if she had some secret access to his mind.

Her mind-reading! The times she had seemed to know what...

'And that is your answer, Rick. Mind contact. But it wasn't me behind it all,' she said, quietly - without prompting. 'Now I think you should sit down.'

He wanted to! He scanned the surface of the pool but Gaze had gone.

He was quiet for long moments. Maeve had appeared to know his thoughts just as Fiona had... but was it merely coincidence?

Dolphins that appeared to read his mind... as when Gaze and White Tip had seemed to reassure him that he had no need to be anxious on their part the night Phil had driven Maeve to a first date in the pick-up...

Dolphins appearing to read? Dolphins appearing to... speak!

He had a vivid flashback to the day of his first meeting with Maeve...

'I touched the youngest... or he touched me. They let you know how they feel, don't they? They can... speak...'!

Intuitively, Rick knew who the youngest dolphin had been.

He turned to face Maeve. He knew already the answer to his question.

'Gaze left to wait for you to call him back, didn't he? Alright Maeve, let's see the demonstration.'

He watched her. She was immobile. She didn't even close her eyes.

There was an exhalation and intake of air behind him.

He did not need to look.

'Ask him what I am thinking, Maeve, and you tell me the answer.'

There was a pause but not a long delay...

'He says you are thinking many things. He says you are troubled and hopeful all at once. He says the one thing you want him to say affects both of us and he's not sure he should say it,' said Maeve, looking confused.

She was quiet, looking at Gaze. Rick watched the blush grow in her cheeks and then the smile, as if something else was being said...

Appearing to make up her mind, she turned back to him. A faint blush still persisted but her voice was steady.

'That wasn't quite cricket, was it Rick? Phil's note has told you he is returning to University after the summer vacation. He has gone to leave a note with the Admissions' Office and that's why the pick-up is not here.'

The slightest of pauses, commensurate with her acting as a relaying medium...

'You are pleased that he appears to be over some heartache due to someone... called Susan. You know he...'

Maeve's eyes fell to her feet.

'Go on,' Rick said, convinced but sensing this was important for Maeve, herself.

She studied him - looked towards Gaze and back.

'You know Phil likes me... and you have some hopes for the future. You... are glad we will be at the same place! I didn't know that!'

Maeve made a very unladylike face across the pool but the only noise was the slap of flukes upon the surface which seemed as loud as a starting pistol.

A very clear voice spoke in two human minds...

'It wasn't my fault you felt embarrassed Maeve. Rick, I think you are prepared for me to declare myself within your mind. Am I right?'

Rick's eyes widened in a stare of wondering fear!

The mindvoice was different to his own and within, it seemed, the secret centre of himself! He felt a dizziness of panic as if fearing a fall from a high place!

In that moment there were revelations - his God existed and Lucifer was real!

He collapsed to his knees at the edge of the pool, a supplicant...

Gaze achieved mind-access he needed... but it was unwise...

Rick's realisation of dread did not manifest for long. Shortly, it was as if he was guided as a blind man along the precipitous edge of his fears, never seeing the fall.

Only Maeve witnessed the changes within, as an ally of aid. She saw an alteration of memory and did not complain; perception of herself blur into other imaging...

This man, like a second father - and certainly a cousin in spirit - would view things afresh.

There was no violation of heart or mind... but, Gaze insisted, the variation of truth was necessary. Rick's dread and sense of guilt were just too immense to be able to accept...

They would have to find another way.

Chapter Eleven

EXODUS AND AID

As Gaze had said, he had moved beyond the range of his mindmerge contact. Three times each lightwater, Ardent beaknosed the carving in the niche but the image of the yellow-skin's head had merely looked at him dully, the lips closed and immobile. There had been no message from his young friend and master since he had moved beyond the seaspace of the Spinners' Podsherd. The huge gulf in flukingspans was too great for young Gaze to mindleap.

Ardent had done everything requested of him.

Crest Spray and Mimic had been directed towards the Spinners. It had not taken Gale long to decide who the accompanying Bottlenoses should be.

'I will deplete Beak Spot's Pod of Guardians no further. With Mimic gone, Beak Spot has already lost his second-in-command. Gannet goes, from the lagoon-entrance sentinels, for it's about time he had to fluke for his fish instead of gorging himself at the end of fishmuster.'

Ardent had beaksmiled. Gannet was well-known for his habit of feeding upon stunned fish amidst the swooping gulls and timing his exit from the sharkfanning mania perfectly. He was a popular dolphin with a huge appetite for fish and fun. Yes, the exercise was necessary and his good humour would be beneficial to the podunit of four.

'But the fourth?' Ardent had prompted.

'Vorg,' had come Gale's quick reply. 'He is a Guardian trainee and ambitious. Let us see how he responds.

'Crest Spray has the deterrent of the squid-eye which my son has placed within his reefsiding and Vorg is still afraid. There is no risk to the Podsherd if he is absent and Crest Spray is a very competent Observer. I shall tell him to observe Vorg closely. I shall tell Vorg that he is being assessed for early attachment to a Guardian Pod. Let Vorg's ambition work for us - too many Bottlenoses need a rest from watching him closely.'

Ardent had hesitated, said quietly, 'But will there be risk to other dolphins?'

'Gaze himself is unable to assess the potential for good or evil in Vorg. For the moment, we shall treat Vorg in just the same way as any other Guardian trainee of promise. No Bottlenose can control everything in the waterspace. Let this be simply a time of testing for Vorg - a period of normality for ourselves. Do you not think Gaze would agree?'

Ardent had said nothing - could think of nothing to countersay the Master Guardian. Respecting the teachings of Wanderer, realising that decisions in Guardian matters were Guardian affairs, he had assented. In any case, Gale possessed the towering personality he did not - and Gaze was too far away.

He had beaksmiled and nodded before finning to leave a message in mindmerge in a place only three Bottlenoses knew - the green carving of a dolphin which Gaze said was made of 'jade'.

Gale's Guardian mind was content but, like his son, he could not read the future...

Thus, time-shadows assembled the sharks for the death of a Spinner dolphin in a distant seaspace.

Through Gale's mindmerge, White Dolphins finned nearer Gaze, his son, and began to image-form the ping-patterning of his name...

Vorg was excited but he became conscious of too many unanswered questions.

Fluking as two Guardian-pairs, following the forcelines from far below, the podunit had passed beyond the known waterspace boundaries of Crest Spray - out across the white-flecked blue, towards the mysterious horizon's darkline.

Vorg began to wonder how the Master Guardian could have been so explicit concerning flukingvectors.

Had Gale sent the podunit as the result of a discovery, made by Finwarp in his long absence, in this other Podsherd comprising of Spinner dolphins? If so, why hadn't Finwarp accompanied them? Was the Inventor so befuddled by the fat Flab that he had refused to give more than precise vectoring instructions?

Did, perhaps, the absent-minded Cleric/Historian, Ardent, believe there was the possibility of learning more of the life of Wanderer from their distant cousins? It was the sort of worm-ridden notion he might have had...

Why had there been such an insistence that the podunit consult so closely with the fishmuster Guardians? Spinners were dolphins who would have mastered their own techniques. Vorg would not take too much heed of any smartnose trying to tell him how to fish. Why should Spinners feel differently?

Why had Sinu, another Inventor, spent so much time explaining so tediously as much as was known concerning Splitfluke fishtraps? And where in the waterspace had he ever heard of Splitflukes assisting dolphins to escape from 'incidental capture'?

During the lightwaters of flukingpassage, there had been much to see and new things to contemplate but slowly the nagging of unanswered questions had preyed upon Vorg's mind. He had sensed a shadow-figure, of greater stature than his three podpartners, directing events - yet Ardent, Finwarp or even the Master Guardian could not be the spectre of unquantified apprehension.

Vorg flukeshuddered, recalling his abortive attempt to find the secret access of Wanderer's Cave. Was the Dolphin of Light who had commanded a squid - and placed the cold squideyes he feared in the reefsides of a few - behind all?

The grasp of the giant squid had been so real in the airspace above the vertical shaft - the mindpower of the Bottlenose of Light, so strong!

He had not sought to question any dolphin concerning another possessing such astonishing strength in mind - or to discover the identity of the other Visioner power. Neither had he attempted to mindread, fearing the consequences...

But now he was distant from the Podsherd! Was he out of range from the mind-compassing of the Bottlenose he feared?

Only Crest Spray had the squideye within his reefside. Vorg had extended a slim mind-tendril and seen it watching him! He had retracted immediately... but his curiosity persisted in unholy alliance with a thwarted sense of his own superiority.

The next lightwater he had tried with his other podpartners and found no trace of anything he associated with threat or caution from an influence larger than himself. Neither had Crest Spray given any indication of an awareness that Vorg had used forbidden mindskills!

In their podunit's necessary fishing, Vorg had tested further to see if his dolphin-comrades could differentiate between image and reality...

Gleefully noting Gannet and Mimic make striking-vectors upon the false fish-shapes he projected before them in turn, he became certain that the Bottlenose of Light could not observe his use of mindskills at the longer range!

It would be as well not to mindmerge with Crest Spray as yet - but Vorg felt safe in mindreading both Gannet and Mimic. Indeed, there might be opportunities for self-advancement if both of them appeared to fail or look foolish in some ways.

Joking Gannet and light-hearted Mimic lacked any knowledge of an undeclared leader, greater in status than Gale himself. Perhaps their minds needed a nudge towards imaging which would betray something only half-known within themselves?

How could he prompt their duller minds to give up a secret they themselves did not recognise as a mystery?

Vorg pondered his circumstances and realised a way he could access his podpartners' minds without suspicion arising in Crest Spray - if the Observer was capable of more than just watching him closely. Vorg felt Crest Spray's mindeye in everything he did - the squideye as a menace, but passive so far...

During dorsal-drifting communion beneath the moonglow of the last darkwater before they would arrive at the Spinners' waterspace, Vorg began to make new discoveries...

Crest Spray elected to take first duty as darkwater sentinel. Mimic, Gannet and Vorg sought rest.

Gannet's belly grumbled, digesting an over-indulgence and his dorsal twitched and swayed, marking the progress of fishflesh through his distended gut. There were times he emitted an unsavoury expulsion of bubbles. It was as well to time airsnatch carefully. Mimic and Vorg could only doze...

Vorg spoke in mindmeet, apparently respecting Mimic's Guardian status as Vice-Podleader.

'I have seen more than Nursery Training prepared me for in the waterspace. Truly the seaspace is full of mysteries. I am glad of this opportunity - except I wish there had been training for how to sleep in company with an over-eater.'

Mimic beaksmiled. It would be well to encourage the notion of Guardian comradeship in the young trainee. He could afford to speak in mindmerge without risking over-familiarity, he thought. It would be the sort of thing Beak-Spot would do. He remembered how proud he had felt when Gale had spoken in mindmerge with him during one sleepless watch period...

He said, in mindmerge, 'Yes, Vorg. One of the greatest marvels of the waterspace is that there are still fish left to feed the rest of the warmstream Podsherds. Thankfully, Gannet has less of an appetite for the females. If he sired too many flankers we would be forced to follow our cousins the whales in circumnavigation for krill and sprats!'

They both mindchuckled in a warmglow of kinship.

Vorg paused. Mimic recognised the wonder of the young Bottlenose worshipping starglow in his colour of mindscape - felt the moment himself. They drifted in contemplation.

Innocently, Vorg said, 'What is the greatest wonder you have seen, Mimic? The deepest mystery?'

He asked with the reverence of the young before the learned - of the novice before the master.

Mimic felt flattered. It was a new and rare moment.

How should he answer from his greater experience?

Co-joined minds examined his catalogue of significant responses? Through his reefsiding they mindfinned into areas of recall Mimic was prepared to show: an airthing alighting upon a lagoon and lifting skyward again at speed; a hardside which deep-dived and was thought to be lost but resurfaced five hundred dolphinspans distant; the lightwater which became darkwater at vertical sunrise, and more wonders.

Mimic dwelled long upon the fascination of a porcupine fish escaping the moray eel lurking in the coral. He had seen the striking-vector and the eel's teeth close upon the prey. The rapid inflation of the fish-body and the escape had been comical, even ridiculous. Yes, Vorg would see the same thing one lightwater, he assured, beak-gaping.

'But the thing you regard as the greatest mystery?' came the mindmerging prompting from Vorg...

Mystery? thought Mimic... The greatest mystery...?

... And suddenly he was finstirring with Beak Spot by the reef-angle, observing orca dorsals in trepidation - pinging to confirm five killer-whales but only hearing four echo-returns - and one much smaller, about the size of a near-mature Bottlenose? Intermittent mindscreaming from another dolphin in the mawl of flesh-tearing orcan jaws...!

What had been wrong with his senses in his state of near panic-flight? Had he really seen five orcas or had it been four? Young Gaze could not have been in their company - or had he?

Mimic checked and strengthened the reefside of his mind. Vorg was out of contact, or so it appeared...

That darkwater, Gaze, son of Gale, had fluked out-reef in contravention of the law but had not been reprimanded. Karg, the Storyteller, had met a ferocious end when the bloodlust had come upon the hunters. Why had they not attacked Gaze?

Now Gaze was missing, presumed deep-dived...

It had been folly to tempt Fate twice in fluking out-reef whilst unaccompanied. There were mysteries in the events of that darkwater... but he should not share such images with Vorg. Uncertainty was... disturbing... and Gaze had been the Master Guardian's son...

Gale had become the Master Guardian the very next lightwater and there had been other changes - rapid and unexpected. Yes, there had been a number of 'mysteries' in a very short period but they were not for sharing with a Guardian trainee...

Crest Spray's signal for sentinel-change saved Mimic from further reflection and the embarrassment of silence.

Mindmeeting apology for breaking away, he finned to take his duty period. First things first!

Vorg would have to go on contemplating his 'mysteries' in life alone. Crest Spray would have no time for such darkwater dreaming and Gannet was involved in digesting things more tangible.

Mimic mind-chuckled in his sentinel circuit...

Undetected as a mindpresence, Vorg read all he needed to begin to make a number of connections.

He began to come to startling conclusions...!

Gaze had not foreseen everything.

The Speckled Hump-backs rounded the landmass off the place Gaze called 'Comboyuro Point'. He used what he said was the Splitfluke name. In mindmerge, Gaze warned of forceline anomalies - the stranding risk. Blotch and Twizzle had never found flukingvectors so easy to follow. His mindvoice was a constant reassurance.

'The exodus is near completion, cousins. There will be many surprises. You will need to co-operate with Splitfluke and Bottlenose and be unafraid. Trust me and fluke towards my mindvoice,' came the next instruction.

'Why do you not echo-call, Gaze? Surely we are close enough?' queried Blotch.

'At present, my echo-call would be muted. You will not detect me until you are much closer.'

Blotch and Twizzle did not understand. They understood the next instruction even less! A mindmerge image of a yellow-shape, like a false sun, but a pale reflection of light hung for moments in their mindeyes...

'When you near the coast, look for the false sun. You are welcome at the sign of the sun. Find the sign at highwater and you shall find me. Remember, at highwater.'

The Speckled Hump-backs trusted their leaders; Blotch and Twizzle trusted his mindvoice speaking with evermore certainty to their hearts and minds. The pod of survivors swung in an arc into Moreton Bay, seeming to arrow across the surface. Highwater, at the coast ahead, would be after sun-dive. How would they see a false sun during darkwater?

Gaze appeared too preoccupied to answer their questions - and they needed to fishmuster.

A part of Rick's mind could not accept it was happening. He was a born sceptic - seeking always an alternative explanation of the unusual. Maeve and Gaze had discussed his attitude in unique privacy...

'Why do you not convince him, Gaze? There are ways you could, surely? Why do you allow him to doubt? If you want Rick's co-operation for the Hump-backs - and the 'stars' - then prove that dolphins are as intelligent as man, in their different ways,' Maeve had urged.

'No, Maeve. To do such a thing would be against a law in our natural world for it would cause disharmony through fear and guilt. Few Splitflukes - I'm sorry, few men - are ready to accept the need for 'balance' and 'harmony' in the lifespace. Too long have they assumed superiority over all other creaturekind as if they had rights of 'kingship'... is the word I think you would use. It is as if men want the rights of the White Dolphins or the 'God' of your scriptures in their living present. Men would fear a rival - would 'war' against one. It is best for Rick to have no further insight of dolphins. Let him retain his deep-seated doubt. Let him believe the notion that you have this 'remarkable skill' he talks of - that you can somehow tell what I am thinking. Such represents no great threat to mankind.

'Remember that I could not speak directly to his mind without making him afraid; how I had to alter his memory of contact. You must be the interpreter. You must be 'the gifted teacher' he now conceives. I will not be an enemy he fears for man would destroy all dolphinkind out of such fear. Our sagas speak of co-operation between our species too infrequently.'

Maeve had found herself exposed to imaging of numerous interactions between dolphins and men. All too often they ended tragically for dolphins, the co-operation short-lived, treachery the identifying feature of the men involved.

'Our sagas stretch through ages of time longer than your history, Maeve. Fear of the unknown is more prevalent in man than we mammals of the waterspace. Man's fear of a rival would threaten an end for dolphinkind. At first, he would seek to use us for his own ends - but our shadows in seas would become intolerable. Rick was afraid of me, remember?' Gaze had said.

Gaze had given up all hope of co-opting Rick's help directly. Instead he had fostered the belief that it was Maeve who was 'gifted in remarkable ways'.

Gaze had realised he must hide his mind in a sparkle of light upon surface events. He could not alter the tide-flow but, perhaps, he could create eddies and minor currents...

From the blackwater of the false lagoon, Gaze watched Rick's mind now, filtered images of unconscious dreams and convinced his hand to move...

... Maeve had wanted to paint again. She had persuaded Phil to take the pick-up to the Do-It-Yourself hypermarket. Rick smiled. Phil hadn't needed much persuading and he had been quite the gentleman helping her into the truck - such treatment not unnoticed by Maeve.

Her sweet mock-curtsey had made Rod laugh aloud. Maeve had not seen a rude gesture from behind Phil's back. It was just as well that only the males present had seen. In the moment of quietness there had been dolphin beak-clicking from the lagoon which had sounded uncannily like a slightly contemptuous snigger.

Rick had read embarrassed discomfort in the set of Phil's shoulders but Maeve's brown eyes had been alight with excitement, understanding. Phil had held her hand just a moment longer than required.

Rick knew the contact and, envying his son, applauded his luck.

On their return, Maeve had helped unload a large sheet of plywood, a large can of yellow paint and two or three of different colours. These were taken on to the three-master and Phil had returned to the pick-up for a bundle of timber battening, tools and nails.

What was Maeve at now?

She seemed to know exactly what she wanted and his elder son had been compliant in her needs.

'She paid for all this, Pop. It's not on the 'firm's' account,' Phil had said, seeing his father's questioning glance. 'It's... er... something she wants to paint.'

'Uh-huh. But why the battening?'

'She wants to put her picture near the lock-gates,' Phil had replied. 'She wants me to build a framework for the picture... like a 'tower', she says. It won't be in the way, will it?'

Father and son had looked across the years into the strange matter of human hearts...

'No son, I suppose not.'

What else could he have said? It had been amusing to watch Phil struggling with saw, hammer and nails... but, before long, both 'boys' were hard at it.

Shortly afterwards, so was Rick himself, responding to the enthusiasm in the family. It was a rare zanyism they would remember for years - and Maeve had done some artwork.

They had built the tower to the left of the lock-gates.

Painted red, it supported the large picture which Maeve had painted, facing out towards the bay. Rick could not deny the vitality of what was, essentially, an advertisement but he wondered to whom it was directed.

If the plywood board was divided into thirds, the outer sections showed two different dolphins with an energy of line and colour which suggested athleticism and sporting ability. Rick recognised two sub-species but made no comment.

Maeve had taken a break before tackling the central section but it had not taken long for the outline of a bright holiday sun to become a stridency of yellow. Perhaps to off-set the garishness of that yellow, she had also painted a ball passing across the face of the sun. Not until she had added, painstakingly, letters and words had the picture made sense - or nonsense to Rick and his 'boys'.

'You can't be serious, Maeve. There is no way we could train two teams of the 'stars' to play water-polo! In any case, be practical. The Dolphinarium cannot keep larger numbers of dolphins!'

Rick had paused in his disparagement. He had thought it best to get her to face reality before things went too far... but how could he say the obvious in any way other than bluntly?

'Listen lass, even if water-polo was possible as an added attraction, how the bloody hell would you tell the 'stars' apart? They would have to appear to be two teams. What would you propose to do? Get the 'stars' in tailor-made shirts of two different colours? Give each one a coat of bloody paint before the game? Game? Fiasco more like!

'And how do you see yourself teaching dolphins rules and what is fair and unfair? For God's Sake be reasonable and stop this silliness now.'

He had paused again - those bloody brown eyes and her smile!

She had looked at him as if he was sounding off about nothing of consequence. He hadn't felt quite so fired-up for years! It was ridiculous and he'd allowed himself to be dragged along by the family enthusiasm when he should have had more sense.

Monday was supposed to have been a rest day for them all! True, they'd had fun; felt one, happily co-operative unit, but Rick felt as if he had been tricked. It was a good advertising board - even if it did face the wrong way. There again, a strong gale would probably whisk it away.

He had felt her hand upon his forearm.

Disappointment and disillusion had leaked out of his shoes and the ice around his brain had melted in the warmth of her face.

'Okay Rick, I'll answer your last question first. If you had two teams of two sub-species of dolphins and the colouring was different naturally, it would help wouldn't it?' Maeve had said, quietly.

'Well, yes but where would you get another team from and where would we keep them anyway?'

He had been quite proud of his level voice, feeling a quiet assurance and a sense that it was all about to end amicably without too much loss of face all round. He had not been prepared for the same degree of assurance in her reply. The dolphin paintings were assuming an uncomfortable significance.

'The visiting team is on its way. They will arrive just after highwater. If you let them through the gates, I will show you it's possible. I'll worry about the training if you'll just give me a bit more rope. There won't be any need to worry about food-stocks or all the rest in the long-term.'

'You don't expect me to believe you can sense six or seven dolphins of just the right sort coming towards us? Oh, Maeve, credit me with some common-sense.'

... and then he had remembered a piece of card before the arrival of Gaze - his wild capering in disbelief with his hands on her shoulders. No, it couldn't happen twice?

'Please Rick, we'll simply illuminate the sign at highwater and watch, shall we? I'll make something to eat and we'll take a bottle of wine - well, you can take the bottle you like - and we'll celebrate our tower. You'd like it Rick. When was the last time you had a supper under the stars? You must have had one once...'

... and he remembered a younger time and another laugh.

'Damn it, all right - but there are times I question if you're normal, lass.'

He had heard Phil's voice saying, 'I think you've pushed as far as you should, Maeve. Rod once tried to...' but the rest had been lost in her light-heartening laughter which was an echo of the other time.

Rick had been pacified...

... Rick's hand reached out to switch on the temporary floodlight Rod had rigged to illuminate the tower. In the glow, the dolphins seemed to take on even more life and action. They were very good paintings, although the sun looked a bit artificial. Whatever happened, he wanted to keep those dolphins. One day, he would use a jig-saw and release them from the perpetual orbit of that sun, he thought.

They all took pride in a job well-done - craftsman and artist in each was satisfied. There was tactful avoidance of the structure's purpose. The turning of the tide would bring an emptiness for Maeve - and three male hearts made the little magic they could in the interval.

Rick strummed the guitar he had stored too long - the one his elder son had been set upon, before he had bought his own. Chuckling in accompaniment, some of the old tunes in harmony filled the shadows of his present and past.

Maeve surprised them with her knowledge of the old Irish sea-song, 'Bantry Bay'. She joined in without hesitation...

'As I'm sitting alone in the gloaming,
It might have been but yesterday
That I watched the herring fleet all homing -
Till the wooden boats at anchor lay.
Then the fishergirls, with baskets swinging,
Came running down the old slipway.
Every lassie to her sailor boy was singing

A welcome home to Bantry Bay.'

Rick found himself clapping at the end and found himself not applauding alone. At the lock-gates, a number of the 'stars' had gathered, responding to song and music. The small pod was mimicking applause!

The Dortmanns embraced the magical moment.

Amplified astonishment was to follow.

Below their contented group the 'stars' fell silent but still a beak-clicking persisted on the bay-side of the lock.

Maeve was looking at Rick, her face an expectation.

'Visitors at the gate, my lord. Shall I let them in?' she whispered for his ears only.

Rick was up. He had to see first for himself!

Blotch and Twizzle led the Hump-backs closer to the shoreline which projected an unusual glow into the airspace. Was this glow the 'false sun'? Finstirring, they waited.

'Highwater upon the shoreline is close, Blotch. How will we know a false sun in the darkwater? Any Splitfluke light may be what Gaze means,' came the mindmerge of Dander, so named for quickness of temper in earlier near-maturity.

It had not been his original name. His dam, killed in the reddened shallows, had named him Firth, initially - but had decided his flanker temperament had warranted another.

Recent experience had mellowed his nature and he had come to regret the tantrums of a flanker in the wariness of others of his seasons.

To have lost the calming presence of a dam had not been easy for the young dolphin. Her self-sacrifice, in giving him an escape-vector from that other shore, had tamed his rebelliousness more than anything before.

Blotch knew this - felt, too, disquieting Splitfluke presence nearby. How could he convey the implicit faith he had in their Bottlenose friend?

Quietly came his voice, 'I know your uneasiness Blotch but calm your anxieties. Blotch and Twizzle, finturn and face your pod. They have followed at your flukes when fear would have made them swerve in panic-flight. Trust, in you both, or in the 'friend' you have spoken of, would never have been enough. I could help you in only one other way.

'You have never realised the power of your mindvoices - never wondered why your leadership was unquestioned. Did you not realise that I gave you part of myself?'

Blotch and Twizzle heard but did not understand.

'Examine your own minds, friends. Do you not find a strength different from memory? Blotch, were you always possessed of self-assurance? Twizzle, did you forgive inadequacy in males so readily a season ago?

'Recognise your new confidence? I could give you little for the flukingpassage in exodus but enough of my voice of command. Would the podpartners have fluked in your wake unless you had earned their respect?

'Speak to them now. Part of myself is finning to meet you. No Blotch, there will be no echo-return from this image of myself. Remember the first time you saw me and could not be sure if there was one Bottlenose or more? Now you will meet one of my podpartners. Tell the Hump-backs a guide is coming.'

The Hump-back leaders looked mind within mind and saw the certainty of truth. Whatever Gaze had done - or did from now on - they owed more than a debt of gratitude. They owed him their lives, and whatever vector that life would take.

They finturned again towards the puzzled beak-snouting of the pod.

Twizzle said, 'A Bottlenose guide will lead us shortly. Trust him as you would ourselves. If his mindvoice seems... strange, do not be afraid.'

Blotch added, 'He will have no echo-return when you scan the waterspace but he is the reality and security we seek.'

Both mindmerge voices were complete in confidence and the podpartners could only wonder at what would happen next!

Another light flicked on from the shore. Illumined clearly was a small sun-shape of yellow. Dolphin-forms seemed still-statues either side!

'The false sun!' shouted Dander with a new strength in open mindmerge.

And he was the first to see the Bottlenose finning towards them!

He pinged in echo-location. Blotch did not bother, knowing it would be as Gaze said.

There was no echo-return.

The Bottlenose dolphin finbeckoned them to follow - and they did.

Maeve followed behind him, expecting the shorter dorsals and the lighter flesh he would see. She watched Rick faltering, lowering to hands and knees. Wide-eyed, mouth slightly open, his face turned from looking downward at baywater surging around the stone of the quay.

In a backwash of the seasurge, denied admission by the stout structure of the lock, he counted nine dolphin-heads drawn up as a minor cohort before the fortress of his doubt.

Never had Maeve seen a man in such confusion. No sound escaped him save a grunt from low in his throat.

...Gaze said, 'Be careful, Maeve. Rick is too close to the dread of an underworld of air or water to think or speak clearly. Ask him no questions. Take control and ask Phil and Rod to open the outer gate of the lock. For a while, my Hump-back cousins must be ordinary and co-operative.'...

Phil and Rod quickened towards them. She had to act now.

'Open the gate, Phil. Will you help him, Rod? Your father's fine, just a bit surprised. I did tell you all. Why didn't you believe me?' she said, already moving towards the gate mechanism.

Phil called, 'Okay, Pop?'

Both sons studied Rick. He was getting to his feet. Erect, he faced them - could only shrug his shoulders and nod twice. He turned like an automaton towards the walkway along the lock gate.

Phil moved to join him.

'You feeling alright, Pop?'

The quiet answer was not quite along the lines expected.

'We've got a small promise to keep, son. God help us - I might have to keep a bigger one later.'

Rick hesitated with his hand on the guard-rail.

'That's one very special girl, Phil. You are going to have to keep your wits about you,' he said. 'Well, let's open these gates.'

Phil only part understood. It would take a number of years for his muddied senses to settle to clarity.

They leaned into the heavy beam together. Lighter dolphin shapes at variance to those to which they were accustomed, seemed to be jostling expectantly in the bay-water. The rise and fall of dolphin dorsal and head was less in the shelter of the stone breakwater. Rick could no longer see the ranks of three by three which had given rise to the feeling of a disciplined and unknown force awaiting entry. That had been uncomfortable. Had it been something Maeve had said which had made him feel that his castle and his home were about to be stormed? He couldn't remember.

He watched nine speckled hump-backs swim through into the confines of the lock. They did not seem too perturbed. Or were there ten dolphins? One of them a bottlenose with a larger dorsal and darker colouring? No, definitely nine. He'd better have his eyes checked.

With the outer gate closed, Phil and Rod moved to open the inner. Rick felt Maeve's eyes from across the lock. It was too dark to see more than her shape as cloud drifted across the moon. She was jump-skipping in girlish pleasure and he found it infectious.

'Alright Maeve, calm down. A teacher is supposed to be a steady and calming influence. It looks like you've got your work cut out tomorrow, Miss. When this lot are in, we're having cocoa and getting some shut-eye. I, for one, don't want anymore of your surprises for another twenty-four hours, at least.'

He knew her answer would be the laugh which would echo through his sleep... and he was tired. They were all tired...

Three quarters of an hour later, Rick was conscious of a great deal of beak-clicking from within the lagoon. He could hear an amplification in frequency of the day-time intermittence... The 'stars' seemed to be greatly concerned about something. Were they in dispute about some kind of territorial rights?

He was half-out of bed when it wittered to silence.

Whatever had been the matter, it appeared to have been resolved. Rick felt a further weight of tiredness and followed Maeve's laughter down into dreaming...

Somehow, Fiona was waiting for him...

He woke at his normal time - just after six o'clock. There were no sounds of movement throughout the three-master - just creaking familiarity and the sleeping sounds of his sons from their separate cabins as he moved in habit towards the galley. There was some motion within Maeve's quarters but he did not call out.

Rick made a coffee and took it on deck to sit on a bench with a good view across the lagoon. Out came the short-stub of his pipe. In the calm of a promised fine day, the smoke spiralled the vertical. It was going to be warm.

He studied the lagoon carefully, half-expecting to see two distinct groupings of dorsals after probable disputes of the night. The 'stars' had had little enough time to interact socially. There was no such thing!

Long and short dorsals intermingled in free association of... Of what? Was it wrong to use the word 'friendship'? Rick could differentiate between the two species of dolphins in residence quite easily. Smiling, he wondered if they bothered about skin colour difference.

Perhaps only man equated competence and skill with the colour of flesh. Apparently, it was of no consequence to dolphins, whether bottlenose or hump-back.

When Maeve tried to sort those mingling fins and flukes into competitive teams, he could only wish her the best of luck! The mixed pod appeared to be assuming a corporate identity. Trying to form teams from it would be as useless as endeavouring to marshall balloons re-leased at a fete - or attempting to keep two flocks of sheep with different paint brands from mixing.

He couldn't allow the hump-backs to stay. Rick began to visualise necessary adjustments in terms of rations, water purity and filtration. It would not take long before the filters in the dry-dock area needed changing - or the filters around the lagoon. There had to be a time-limit set for this latest experiment Maeve had persuaded him into.

'There won't be any need to worry about food and the rest' Maeve had said but he was more practical. It was his job to worry about cleanliness and comfort - and here he was jeopardising hygiene!

Two of the 'stars' suddenly performed the 'walking in water' trick. In satisfaction he noted the precision. Both, two thirds of body-lengths submerged, closed to 'shake hands' with imaginary guests like convivial hosts.

There were times he wondered if the conditioning of training had shaped behaviour too far from the natural.

Were they pandering to the crowds too much?

He chuckled. His 'stars' were enjoying showing off. There was no earthly reason for them to perform now - other than a natural excess of energy. Blowhard and Delilah?

His eyebrows lifted. Two paler, hump-backs assumed the vertical and, with one fin extended each, closed with the two 'stars'! At the moment of fintouching, in parody of greeting, the lagoon resounded with beak-clicking. Several dolphins mimicked applause!

In moments the lagoon settled to normality.

Stunned, Rick sat motionless. If he hadn't known better he would have had to assume that bottlenose was teaching hump-back some of the tricks of the Show!

He knew some trainers felt that dolphins often invented or seemed to suggest variations to tricks and that dolphins aped the behaviour of others from time to time.

What he had seen was more than that. There were too many human parallels in humour and social contact!

'Morning Rick. Want some breakfast?'

Maeve was in a dressing-gown at the top of the steps leading to the deck.

'Are you feeling alright? Everything okay out there?' she asked, nodding towards the lagoon. 'I hope the guests have settled in and there aren't any arguments.'

He coughed. 'Yes, fine. Let's have another coffee.'

What else was there he could say?

The near-mature, Spinner males had been the first to hear the approach of a Bottlenose podunit. They had been on herd-flank nearest to their approach vector.

In mindmeet, the message had been passed throughout the Podsherd.

Starshine finned to the fringe of expectant long-snouts questing the waterspace.

In moments, she sought permission, in mindmerge with Bluster, to fluke out-herd to meet the awaited Bottlenose guests. Assenting, he added the caution to stay within echo-location range - and she had gone!

The gap between echo-call and return from the closing podunit had narrowed rapidly.

She pinged identification and scanned the wavesurge visually.

Accompanying a formal acknowledgement, did she detect a brush of mindcontact... similar to her 'bottlebeast'!?

Was Gaze returning!?

Excited, she surged upwards to the crest of the next wavesurge, catching a glimpse of distant dorsals. One dorsal did seem larger than the rest!

Crest Spray felt he was the first to detect the Spinners on vector front amidst the sea noise. He was not.

Vorg detected the mindlights much earlier, feeling more secure in the use of mindskill now. He had not attempted exploration of Crest Spray's reefside block, feeling need of further testing before he could exercise mind-superiority.

He watched one mindlight separate from others ahead.

Briefly, he would be able to mask his mind-activity when Crest Spray was preoccupied with formal identification and greeting. Did Vorg dare?

This solitary Spinner was probably a leader or an elder. The opportunity for discovery concerning the nature of their mission - and, perhaps, confirming the identity of the mysterious dolphin of light - could not be missed!

As Crest Spray pinged identity, waterspace origin and their willingness to assist in the lightwater's fishmuster, Vorg allowed a tendril of mind-scanning to intermingle with the ping-patterning. It was narrowly beamed and directional towards the solitary mindlight fluking out-herd.

The brush of mind-contact and recognition of something previously experienced was all he needed. Vorg locked on to the Spinner mind and was within before 'her?' full awareness attempted token resistance! His power was magnifying!

Vorg mind-chuckled. Crest Spray gave no sign of noticing anything. It had been too quick. The Observer looked incapable of anything Vorg could do! That squideye within the reefside was cold impassive, ex-pressing nothing.

Absorbing, storing the Spinner mind as much as moments allowed, Vorg began to withdraw... sensing an admiration and a debt to himself?

No, not himself, 'Gaze?'. Gaze again! Gaze was alive? When had she seen him? He was supposed to be deep-dived...?

Vorg needed to discover more later...

This Spinner, 'Starshine', wanted Gaze... to repay...! Well, this was too much to hope for... and he could test the squid-eye one last time!

So she wanted Gaze. Mind-smirking, he examined desire and dream; hazy perceptions of her 'rescuer?' - and things Gaze had told her which she held close to the central, misty part of herself.

Watching Crest Spray, Vorg projected a new self-image, glimpsing the long-snouted, Spinner female upon wave-top in the distance.

He was a male, large in heart and mind. His dorsal stood proudly at the rear of the podunit. Crest Spray, Mimic and Gannet were his escorts and owed him subservience. He was the Bottlenose larger than Gaze - larger, even, than the Wanderer of both Podsherds' sagas.

He had come.

He could tune easily to the heartsong of this love-sick female - and none of the podpartners, Crest Spray included, felt his strength of visioning in narrow contact!

Vorg would explore this Starshine, mentally and physically - Ah, yes, the latter first! - and investigate at leisure. Blue Anemone was far, far behind his flukes...

As things developed, he reversed the order of his plans...

Their welcome was whole-hearted. The podnunit might have been flotsam swept along in a current of pleasure!

Many were the invitations in mindmeet to mindmerge.

Not a few of the unattached females - matriarch to recently mature - stirred forefins suggestively as they followed Starshine towards a larger male in company with Spinner elders.

Beak-smiling and acknowledging became a tiring necessity of politeness for the Bottlenoses.

Crest Spray and Mimic mindmerged briefly. They were both puzzled by the warmth of the greeting. It was not until Bluster spoke of Gaze that they realised the young Bottlenose was still alive!

'Gale and his familypod will be as bewildered as ourselves, Mimic,' said Crest Spray.

And they both wondered how Gale had known of the Spinners' Podsherd? Neither shared the imaging behind their reefsides out of loyalty and respect for Gale, the Master Guardian. Could it be that Gale and the Storytellers were privy to secrets they were not entitled to know? Were there things within Wanderer's Cave that pictured distant events for Storytellers' eyes alone?

Observer and Vice-Podleader reflected upon their orders and further examined all they knew of the Master Guardian's son. They began to make connections which could only be dismissed as fanciful. Both required something more concrete for a Guardian mind to assimilate.

And they did not do this alone... Despite a squid-eye...

Vorg as a mind-presence, unsensed by either, reviewed and conjectured. He, however, was better qualified to make an assessment which he did not dismiss as irrational!

Could Gaze have sufficient mind-power to be the Dolphin of Light? It seemed ridiculous but... Crest Spray's mind harboured doubts concerning Gaze in the darkwater of Karg's death! Questions about what he had seen and heard as an echo-return from a dolphin that... looked like an orca!?

Gaze had given him false images of the access to Wanderer's Cave! He had done so without giving rise to the least doubt that he was imaging known realities... which meant he had to have mind-reading skills him-self!

Gaze was another Visioner! And he was far stronger than his smaller stature could have possibly led Vorg, himself, to believe. Vorg recalled the incredible strength of a squid within the reef! Images of other creaturekind within, upon and above an in-reef pool!

Gaze was his rival! And Vorg did not like a rival. Less could he tolerate the belittling of the stature he felt within himself - and wished acknowledged by all other dolphins! Gaze would suffer for the mighty injustice which Vorg now perceived as having been done to him-self.

No dolphin was Vorg's superior! These Guardian pod-partners in no manner approached parity with himself!

Vorg nursed a fractured pride. He cast around for some way in which he could vent the cold fury growing within... Starshine had been close to Gaze! She was conveniently close for pleasure and revenge!

In early darkwater, Vorg asked leave to freely associate with the Spinners. Crest Spray acceded to the perfectly reasonable request. The podunit had completed a demanding flukingpassage and all of them deserved an opportunity of recreation...

Starshine knew he would come. Vorg was larger than the other Bottlenoses. In the simple mindmeet exchanged, she had imaged the great heart beating within the vigorous, young male. Was he the special dolphin the sagas foretold - larger than 'Wanderer'?

Vorg did not lead the podunit of Bottlenoses. He fluked to follow orders like any young mature... but Wanderer had been young once and his influence had grown, and they seemed to respect the younger podmember.

She watched Vorg in the new fishmuster the Bottlenoses were teaching, taking pleasure in his speed and certainty. He was magnificent. It thrilled her when she felt his fin upon her flank as he offered two fish.

'You do not join the fishmuster, Starshine. You seem preoccupied. It is customary for Bottlenoses to tend to the needs of others unable to fluke for fish. Take these,' he had said, in strong mindmerge, vibrant with familiarity.

'Thank you, cousin,' she replied, adding, 'Now let this host show as much courtesy!'

She surged into the shoal and took a larger fish than either of the two he had offered her, returning with the prize.

'You are large, cousin. This is a fish more suited to your size. Is it sufficient for your needs... or is there more you require?'

She finstirred just twice before him and breached to spin in spray and celebration, knowing he understood.

'Perhaps you will see me later, Vorg,' she said fleetingly, beginning and ending in her arc-flight of airspace, surrounded by the glitter of light-lanced water droplets.

Now she sensed him closing from behind her flukes - arched her neck at the rub of his flank against hers...

'Starshine,' he said in polite mindmeet, 'will you show me more of your waterspace in the moonglow? Open seaspace is a wonder to a Bottlenose more accustomed to reefedge and the shallows of the shelf.'

There was a similarity! His mindvoice was calming in its rich warmth just as her 'bottlebeast' had been. Gaze had been disinterested in any pleasure she might have shared in gratitude. Vorg appeared more inclined to the healthy expression of joy.

It was pleasureable to encourage him.

She backfinned to bring her bright eye closer to his.

In mindmerge, she said, 'You are like Gaze in many ways but I feel I understand you more. I owe Gaze my life. Is he your friend?'

She shared, in imaging, her horror of drowning in the weave of the fishtrap and her rescue by Gaze. The muddled images of Splitfluke presences made some sense of Sinu's words before they began, thought Vorg. Evident was her willingness to show gratitude as a Spinner female should. And Gaze had not taken the opportunity?

How could Starshine know she shared much more with Vorg? If he needed any confirmation that Gaze had some strength as a Visioner and a mindreader, it lay within the stored mindlight connections of recall that circled before him, an entity she did not feel. She gave him access to every part of herself...

'We were trained by the same Matrons of the Nursery. Together, we were Inducted to our Podsherd. I know his podfamily well. If Gaze is a friend of yours, you can count upon my devotion. We are like brothers of spirit,' said Vorg. 'It would be pleasure to fluke beneath the moonglow with any dolphin Gaze calls 'friend'.'

His eye was steady and a warmth seemed to generate within. She felt his fin brush her side and pause a moment too long on her lower chest.

He was gone!

Starshine pinged exploratively, dived out-herd and scanned. Was he there, beyond the steeprise of coral and rock? Or there, beyond a sea-shadow and tricks of pale light? Moonlight played impishly beneath the sea and her eyes saw phantom shapes. Dolphins? Sharks?

Breaching carefully in the shimmershine, she pinged again her name and scanned, enjoying the hide-and-seek.

Deep below came an echo-return. Down through the blackwater he had dived ... but he was rising. His speed was increasing...

He breached, leaping into the airspace! Moonlight reflected from his side, the spray in a sparkling starlight and moonglow! Re-entry caused little disturbance - so expertly done.

She waited. Recognising the preliminaries, she knew the dance of courtship and the part she should play... the part she wanted to play with the rhythm in her quickening heart! He was a friend of her 'bottlebeast' but more vigorous - more open.

She waited for his fluke-slapping pounding of the surface as the invitation to join his dance of celebration and need.

Again he was rising, closer to her - strike-vectoring upon her!?

He was so close!

She wanted to finswerve aside but did not know which way!

He burst though the surface into air! Spray and ripple slapped her tingling flank - exciting her further!

His large flukes flapped sideways on entry in cracking air-sound, sending water-sound into the black abyss beneath.

Sound reverberated, echoed from seafloor to seasurface mixed with the ping-patterning of his name... his name... whispering into an expectant silence.

The darkwater music from the depths was a magic she could not resist.

Starshine responded. Her name-sisters sparkled lightfire in the unreachable heavens.

Together, they bi-vectored from the Podsherd to the wave-trough valleys of near horizon. Arcing in air-flight, they were symmetry, broken only intermittently.

In the nature of her kind, Starshine twisted, spinning in compliment... to her love-mate...

And then Vorg was close, tender and close, beak-nipping her neck... finsweeping below... Mind-whispering endearments and suitor's images of joy.

Mind-murmers were light from mind-selves joined; the rhythm of the sea a constant surge in which they were together in rising rapture.

Caught in a surge of seafall and top-shiver, she had not known flesh-fervour so thrilling!

He was... her master in this... oh, and in this... and...no,... and in this?... and oh, my dearest... no, oh? No!

...Nerve-raw, she could not continue...

...Discomfort trebled into pain!

She knew an incursion of self!

She tried to fluke away in overwhelming dread!

Then the shadows, across the starshine in her heart and mind, became denser. Blackness engulfed her!

She could not move her flukes! Feebly, her forefins twitched...

His cold-largeness touched her soul - filled her mind!

Mind-whimpering, she pleaded... begged Vorg to stop!

Her lifespace devoid of everything save his voice...

His voice in waveswell, in dark-depths beneath...

'Know you were mine, Starshine, a pleasant memory of a Spinner waterspace to which Gaze called his friends.

'You will not be lonely for long in blackwaters of mind and heart. Gaze will fluke beyond the lifespace soon. Then shall you call each other your odd names in the dark!'

Harshly, he was mind-chuckling... She felt his teeth close on her flukes, mindscreamed in silence as he tore her flesh. She knew the purpose... scent-staining the surface with her blood!

'Gaze helped you towards an airsnatch for life. I will leave you in airspace for death. Can you feel your forefins turning you to your side? How carefully they hold you there, readily compliant. Airsnatch, while you can...'

Then his whisper of malice much further away...

'You cannot sense the sharks? But they are closing, Starshine, they are closing. Let me show you.'

And still she could not move! Only see in her mind...!

For long, long moments the blackness brightened with an image of sharkfans upon the surface - Large White Sharks about herself, maws red - an enduring image, coupled with maniacal mind-laughter, that became... reality!

So strong was Vorg's hold upon every part of herself, she made no noise, save her final merge-scream in slipping beyond him to expiry. The after-sound was a shriek across the seas...

He heard it from the fringe of the Podsherd at the same moment as four other Spinner males. He joined them in their fluking-rush towards the unknown female in distress.

Five more Spinner sentinels were despatched by Bluster and the Podsherd tightened to circle dams and calves.

In horror, Vorg fluke-trembled at the scene, innocent bottlebeak with other long-snouts, too late to save a cousin who must have fluked out-herd alone.

Eventually, the sharkfanning frenzy terminated.

Many toothed-whales finjerked fitfully in sleep that darkwater.

A near-mature, female White-sided dolphin, far beyond the warmstream waterspace, awoke in terror.

One Pygmy Sperm felt sudden pain of labour and gave premature birth...

Two Bouto, finning the flooded forest of a distant continent, felt scrape and tear of thorn as half-imaged sea-savagery in waterlogged shadows...

Thus were mind-echoes of a Spinner's death signalled to cetacean sympathy... Many were whales who felt their mortality...

Murder is the cardinal sin of most creaturekind, save those species in whom blood flows through cold passages of ambition and power, making them akin to such instinctive killers as man or shark.

In the far landmass of Maeve's 'Australia', Gaze opened both eyes, a cold-fear half-recognised within his heart...

White Tip, already wakeful, fluke-shivering and staring with glazed eye into his own, tried to calm a dread of being alone.

Puzzled, Gaze almost wished he had the developed intuition of Peen, his dam. Somewhere another dolphin knew distress and pain and there was... something of... kinship?

Was his podfamily safe? Oh, Wanderer, let them be safe...!

He could not reach them... and the Hump-backs needed sanctuary this darkwater. There was too much to be done.

He could do nothing else for now.

Chapter Twelve

SPORTING CHANCE

Rick watched her preparing the percolator.
Every movement calm and assured, already she possessed an unconscious fluency in the domestic environment yet her mind was busy with the day. When did a girl become a woman or a son a man?

Ciaran had told him Maeve would not wish to talk about her mother. Was Maeve so self-sufficient that she was able to turn off her feelings like a tap? Rick had warmed to this young woman but there were parts of her nature shielded from him.

Idly, he contemplated her laughter - the happy chiming in company with the 'stars' - with the 'boys' and himself in the evening last. It had been as if Maeve had come to fill a space in the Dortmann family...

Could anyone ever fill the mother void in her own?

Strange for him to think suddenly of problems for the Pearces. Perhaps not - Rick valued support in a family.

Accustomed, outwardly, to solitude he felt Maeve had somehow exorcised his grief... but he guessed the weight of loss within the young woman who had seemed healer unto himself.

Fiona was no longer a spectre in grief to avoid. She was in his night of dream and memory, to live again - in the day, to hear in the concerns and laughter of kinship.

Maeve shared Fiona's sympathies and spells... but were they also there for her own family; Ciaran, Donovan, and, in some small loyalty, for an absent 'mum'?

'Who taught you to draw and paint, Maeve?' Rick asked.

He watched her hand pause slightly before lifting his cup to bring to the table. Those brown eyes were a mask as they turned towards him. The silence was heavy.

Rick waited. She looked towards the lagoon, as if listening for some sound in the breeze. The net curtains were motionless behind the closed port, gull screech muted.

Apparently, not identifying anything, she stared across the silence.

Rick waited for the silence to demand her voice.

She put the coffee on the table. Her eyes were a long way away.

'There's your coffee, Rick,' she said, quietly.

'Well, who did, love?' he asked again.

Completely unexpectedly, they could hear a guitar strumming from Phil's cabin. It was loud and lively! It was early for him to be playing. And why a Country and Western tune?

Astonished, Rick watched her eyes mist to tears.

Half-rising, he saw her raise her small hands, palms outward towards him and gesture him down with three nervous shakes. Her face was creased, eyes narrowed into wet lines.

Words creaked from her tense mouth, 'I'm sorry, Rick. I won't be a minute.'

And she fled.

He heard her cabin door slam.

Noiselessly, he moved outside her door; he listened.

'That's not fair! You can't!'

He could hear blurred words - part-muffled by a pillow?

Who was she talking to?

Rick thought it was time Maeve saw her mother...

He had been a parent too long. Whatever the nature of Maeve's pain, it would be best discussed face-to-face. Ciaran would have his ex-wife's address... He'd phone him later and have a chat. If mother and daughter were ever going to meet again - why not casually, after a 'show'?

Busy with filters and pumps with Rod, the latter dressed in a wet-suit, Rod saw little of Maeve for the greater part of the morning. He knew she was doing something but always at distance - at the far end of the lagoon or, mostly, within the dry-dock. He could hear her laughter and an occasional comment from Phil, expressing incredulity.

Just once he had queried, his question bouncing from the surface. It hadn't got him far. Phil's voice had come back from the dry-dock...

'Maeve says she'll show you later! I'm not sure I believe this but she says 'keep your beak out for now'! And she wants to build something else! We'll talk about it after lunch...!'

The tone stopped him from going - there and then - to investigate. He could tell by Phil's voice there was new vibrancy within his son. The timing was wrong. If he homed in on the pair of them, he would be as welcome as fog on a sunlit day.

Very shortly afterwards, White Tip had arrived, curious and inquisitive. She was the only dolphin in the lagoon! Usually she was within a metre or two of Gaze.

If ever Rick needed proof that she was over the dark period, he had it now. When Rod dived to remove a grating cover, she was by his side and intent. Curiosity, the natural sign of the near

intelligence Rick saw in healthy dolphins, was evident.

Rod, finished with grating and filter, surfaced.

'Dad, how about a break? Don't you want a smoke? I want to fetch... to try something. It'll only take a few minutes,' said his youngest son, an idea-gleam in his eye.

His father recognised Rod would not be denied. There was nothing which couldn't wait a little longer...

He nodded.

'Try and keep White Tip here a bit, will you? I'll be back,' Rod said, hauling himself from the water.

Rick rummaged for his pipe. Barefooted, he dangled his legs over the side letting ripples slap against the soles.

White Tip's dolphin-head surfaced, tilted. For the first time, she finned to bump-nudge his foot. He knew their was recognition. Was it also an expression of gratitude?

The dolphin-head, rising from the water, nodded an emphatic 'yes' and beak-gaped in a grin!

Sheer coincidence of thought and movement, Rick thought - and laughed loudly himself. He reached down to rub her back and side, careful not to touch the melon of her head.

White Tip dived, accelerated underwater. When she broke surface in a joyous leap, he knew it was for him.

She was wallowing close to his feet when Rod came back. He was carrying his diver's plastic board and an underwater pen.

The first simple sketch explained his son's mind. When Rod placed three tools on the bottom of the lagoon, Rick was already party to the experiment.

Rod resurfaced to join his father at the side. They had tried before without real success. If Maeve could hold up pieces of card with no signals - would this work?

Feeling Rod pause, as if uncertain he should try, Rick said, smiling, 'Well, son - go for it.'

Rod held up the sketch of the pliers, made the hand signal for 'Come here'... They both watched, oblivious to everything else.

How could they know the distraction carefully contrived by another mind? For once, neither father nor son turned towards a sound of mirth emanating from the dry-dock...

White Tip's head tilted, studied them. Rod repeated hand-sign - showed his 'sketch'.

Her circuit in a third of the lagoon was rapid and her leap made both feel failure. Her underwater finning passed close to the three tools on the bottom. They did not see the moment of selection, the surface blurring in a short-lived breeze... but she swam close... with the pliers in her teeth!

On taking them from her, Rod saw her head make one short bob downwards and she mimicked applause.

He joined in. Was that head-bob a curtsey?

The experiment turned into a compulsion. Before long, a dozen tools of distinctive shapes lay beneath the surface - some thrown into the lagoon with abandon.

White Tip failed once only. Instead of an open-ended spanner, she 'fetched' a combination spanner - but, shown the sketch a second-time, she retrieved the situation.

During the rest of the morning, Rick shared an excited performance of a mundane - and sometimes mucky task. White Tip proved a capable carrier and retriever - better than a dog. Both saw immense opportunities for the future!

Maeve and Phil were undisturbed...

The 'stars' and hump-backs exited the dry-dock, just before noon, in a procession of leaps and fluke-flips.

'Better get something to eat and get ready for the Show,' Rick said. 'School's out.'

And they could have swum out any time they had wanted to, he thought. Maybe man locked up enthusiasm and trained a conditioned response but could do it only temporarily...

White Tip veered and dived towards the 'stars'. Did she realise she would be required no further? Or was she simply looking for her mentor... and possible mate?

There she was - leaping in tandem on exuberant air cycles. Uh-huh, spring was a variable season this year!

Perhaps a female's needs were signalled on another plane. Gaze had come, her suitor, in response to neither scent nor visual display.

The applause of the crowd had been an ecstasy of shout and clap, prolonged and enduring. Rick had never seen people so appreciative. The noise had redoubled in its intensity after Maeve's encore - a mind-boggling finale.

Swimming in a figure of eight pattern, the 'stars' and humpbacks had leapt and countered in dizzying sequential movement, the choreography reminiscent of motor-cyclists at a town's fete, team-dancing to modern music or... It depended upon taste and dream within the witness...

First, individually, white flank had passed grey flank as two lines of dolphins converged at the waist of the eight - then in pairs - and finally in threes!

The air above the surface had been filled with stream and droplet... in a celebration. Rick had not been the only spectator to see sustaining images of fluttering watery streamers and falling confetti - or sense crystalline water movements of... music?

Dark 'Star' and whiter hump-back had resettled in a stationary chequered-pattern of light-head, dark-head in three rows, mimicking applause - causing child to giggle, mother to gasp and father to wonder at a marvellous nature. This was adaptation of energy and enthusiasm it was hard to grasp. The training was superb - the dolphins, lovable.

Swept by the laughter and delight, Rick applauded the pretty girl and his elder son... and wondered how it had been done in the dry-dock? Maeve had to be behind it but Phil had pleaded for the changed ending to the display.

Rick admitted his son had been right to insist that Maeve be given her head without her 'boss' seeing things first.

The crowd having departed, he told them...

'Bloody fine! Magnificent. Maeve, are you going to tell me any-thing about anything from now on?'

'If you promise not to...' she began, but her head seemed to jerk to look across the lagoon.

For a moment only, Rick and Phil seemed to sense some kind of struggle. They both watched the angle of her chin settle from a jutting insistence... to reluctant submission?

'Oh..., alright,' seemed a weak whisper from her parted lips.

Did she mean, 'Yes, I'll tell you'?

Father and son could not be sure and forgot everything, amazed by her next plans!

'I want to spend some money and build some things in the dry-dock. I want Rod to be released tomorrow morning to learn a demonstration he can put on with White Tip. I... er ... I was watching this morning and I had an idea. The Show can be better than it is if you'll close the Dolphinarium for just a couple of days. Do you want me to go on?'

They sat down on the benches near the table, a close group in the early evening, no longer three but four. Rod had joined them, changing his mind about making larger, more colourful sketches of tools. He felt drawn to the deck and the family chatter.

Maeve told them what was in her mind. Her voice, possessive of a hypnotic quality, made everything seem perfectly reasonable, if it could be made to work...

When she finished, Rick was very quiet. They were all quiet.

Rick spoke first.

'If all that works, Maeve... I have to open the lock-gates to the sea?'

'There's no reason not to Rick. Haven't you felt the harmony? Don't you know already stories of men and dolphins from the past? Partnership is possible...'

Maeve paused.

'The Monkey Mia Dolphins* could be here, Rick, but... better. You could have the best of both worlds and, in the partnership, there could be sanctuary... when it is needed.'

She shook her head, as if clearing her mind.

No-one remarked upon the tears gathering in her eyes - all felt her emotion. Father and sons melted before those tears and agreed.

They closed the Dolphinarium for two days and were very busy, mindful of others about the lagoon puzzling progress.

FOOTNOTE

*Bottlenose dolphins swim regularly in close communion with human bathers in Monkey Mia, Western Australia. Often coming in close to the beach, the dolphins appear to enjoy human contact yet are free and in no sense constrained.

People were too polite to ask, not wishing to be too inquisitive. Not once could Rick find eyes turned towards their working efforts in more than curiosity... but he sensed 'someone watching'?

Ciaran had been uncertain as to whether he should pass Dierdre's number or not. He'd been courteous and concerned. Yes, he'd come and see the new 'show' - and he'd like to meet Phil. They'd laughed at the coincidence of a daughter and a son attending the same University.

Rick had backed away from the desire of meddling further, agreeing that Maeve was old enough to know her own mind. Ciaran had always had the feeling that Dierdre would have invested too much of herself in Maeve to be forgotten entirely.

'Thanks Rick. You know about the risks of giving a son or daughter too much freedom and I recognise your concern over Maeve. She does have a family bond. We found it in the Coral Sea when we were all of us muddled. True, there's a casualty amongst us... but it isn't Maeve, Donovan... or myself,' Ciaran had said, only hesitating in the last two words.

Rick had detected a man as himself, masking a pain in his loss, trying to sustain equilibrium. At least Ciaran had not turned to a liquid comfort, he thought.

His silence after Ciaran's last words must have been puzzling for the Banker for an attempt at jovial friendship followed...

'I'll be there, Rick. I want to hear her laugh again and if she's that much of a 'natural' as a trainer, I want to see it. Maybe we can have a drink at the... whatever that 'watering hole' is nearby. Okay?'

'The 'Red Bottlenose'. Fine. I won't complicate the situation. Look forward to seeing you...,' he had said - and found himself meaning much more in the phrase than he would have thought.

The two men shared much in common-outlook.

It was towards mid-afternoon, on the second day of closure, that Rick felt and spotted the eyes he could feel at his back. True, he had kept looking across the lagoon with the same feeling but there was a change...

Something made him leave the confines of the dry-dock, where he had been suspending a basket net on a rectangular frame which Maeve wanted.

He walked in an indirectly large semi-circle towards the open-air cafeteria adjacent the 'Red Bottlenose'. Whoever the secret observer of the last two days, he felt sure of the vicinity.

Casually, he sought to identify the source.

There were the groupings of mums and kids to which he was accustomed, two pensioners discussing a newspaper article or a crossword...

Mums... and kids? Ice-cream smeared mouths and a wet nappy...

And one woman alone... in sun-glasses?

The sun wasn't that strong.

She had shoulder-length, brown hair gathered behind her head with a wooden clip and pin - the sort of natty clip which was often sold in craft-shops...

Rick walked to the counter for a can of soft drink, half keeping observation upon the woman. Her legs were un-nyloned, her feet shod in thin-strapped leather sandals. Her skirt was full with the blotchy design of 'tie and die' colouring. Nervous hands were bare of ornamentation save a wedding-ring.

Something made Maeve laugh within the dry-dock, the sound assuming a sharp echo. The woman's head came up, her eyes fixed in the direction of the pealing merriment.

Rick was sure. If he needed further conviction, one hand removed the sun-glasses as the other went to the arm of her blouse for a stored handkerchief. The woman's head turned towards him as, unseeingly, she dabbed around her closed eyes. When they opened, they were the brown he expected.

Ciaran had grey eyes. Rick knew the source of Maeve's inheritance.

He took his drink to the empty table just behind her.

He waited for the moment - for the laughter to lift her head.

When it came and echoed into silence, he spoke quietly, letting his meaning filter slowly into her present...

'She's done some excellent paintings of dolphins. You'd be proud of her. We all are.'

'I'm sorry... What did you say?'

Her head turned, the sun-glasses her shield.

'It's your eyes, you see. Brown, just like hers. She sounds very happy, doesn't she? She's a joy to us, too. But that doesn't mean she doesn't have another life and other memories. She's got some pain like we all have - including you. Will you tell me when you want to see her? You don't have to keep buying coffee.'

He smiled at the sun-glasses and felt for his pipe.

During the ritual, he could feel her poised in flight.

If she moved, he wouldn't stop her. He turned his left shoulder towards the sun-glasses and waited. There was a rustle and he thought she was leaving. He kept his eyes on the dry-dock, sucked at his pipe.

The rustling stopped.

Her chair scraped.

Another scrape-noise...

'You won't tell her I was here?'

'Not one word. Down to you... Dierdre, isn't it?'

'Has she talked about me?'

'No. I've asked her who taught her to paint and she cried. She paints very well. She does a number of things very well.'

'Who are you?'

'I'm the manager of an improving Dolphinarium. You've seen me over there. Maeve's the best trainer of dolphins I have ever met but you mustn't worry about her not going to University. She'll be going to the same place as my eldest son. Bit of a coincidence really but I'm pleased. They - er - they like each other, you see.'

'How old is he? What is he studying?'

It was time to counter the questions...

'Dierdre, you can get up to go when you like. I won't make a fuss. Do you want to sit down or do you want to go?'

The chair scraped again and she was sitting facing him when he turned. Her hand came up to take away her shield.

He looked at the same brown eyes. The whites were not as clear - a pinker tinge. She was still an attractive woman.

'Rick Dortmann. My eldest son is Phil. Two years younger is Rod. Phil is studying Marine Biology, starts his third year after this vacation. He's sensible and Maeve likes him. She's given him more... more resilience. He's learned to laugh again but it's not a patch on hers.'

He paused, knowing this was going to be a one-sided conversation mostly. He gave her the chance of intervention before continuing.

'One day she came to look at the dolphins. Apparently, she'd seen some on a sea-going holiday with your 'ex'. I've spoken to him two or three times. Ciaran narrowly escaped attack by sharks in trying to free a tangled propeller. Somehow, Maeve thinks some dolphins stopped the sharks - chased them away. She knows more about dolphins than I do now. It's almost as if she can 'speak' to them. At least, that's the best way I can put it.'

'So she's happy...' came quiet words in the pause.

'There won't be a dolphin at University... She's alive in the Dolphinarium... but she's hiding from something. What, I don't know. Ciaran hasn't told me and I won't be so bloody rude as to ask. Phil will look out for her and you must know that we're all bewitched by her. She will always have a place to come to here.'

Again he let the silence work for him in knocking out his pipe and refilling it.

Again came the laughter on the breeze.

'I let her down...' came a mother's whisper.

He let it hang on the air until it was drowned in a toddler's squawking.

Today wasn't the day for... but she needed something...

'Wait here. If you see anyone with me, get up and leave. I'm going to fetch you something.'

'You won't...?'

'I'm going nowhere near her. If you see anyone with me, go. I won't be five minutes.'

He left.

For the third time, she brought out the simple buff folder. Sleepless, prostrate in darkness, the sweeping surf on the beach was not the lulling hypnosis she wanted. The beach-house was solitude in a lengthy night.

Memories circled the walls and the shore - whispered in empty rooms. With the fatigue came her phantoms - reaching infant hands for cotton clothing - or turning faces to her skirt, disconsolate.

In the dining room was duty, demanding sustenance with grubby hands or joking in trousered legs. Excitement forgot to fasten the gate and it banged in the breeze outside.

The presences were part-exorcised from her studio - the place of escape and isolation which none save one had shared before... until...

She did not want to remember Doug. He paid lip-service to creativity - saw no beauty but flesh - abused even that. She had treasured those pictures of mind and brush by her child - innocent, direct - without deceit!

Doug had torn the folder of her daughter's stumbling expression of growth through to a beginning of statement...

'Forget the little bitch! We matter, not some ghost girl in half-life. Live now!' he had screamed at her.

He had used the torn scraps to light a mirthless barbecue and she had watched fish and bird singe and burn in a blur. It had been the beginning of ending... The flame of passion had died to a curling paint edge around a child's brown eye in self-portrait... The picture, painted so carefully from the mirror on a Sunday afternoon, pencil or brush in her pensive mouth, had not wanted to die.

His hand, feeling for her thigh, had been cold and his tongue a disgust of wetness in her ear. She had reeled away in a misery of the moment.

Doug had worked his charm upon the beach with someone younger; someone else responsive to music which had murdered her motherhood.

Dierdre opened the folder, knowing already the sheet her fingers felt. It was the one which most disturbed her.

Written in Maeve's neat handwriting, on the back of the sketch, was - 'White Tip fins lonely circuits of grief above a rippled sandfloor with the shadow of her mate, deep-dived in pain, an unspeaking podpartner.'

Added, were some notes: 'Water surf too diff. Prhps best if ptng. done and frosted glass over for photo? Lighting needs care. She'd know, I can't.'

The drawing showed a dolphin repeated three times with shadow underneath - each time upon a rippled, sandy bottom. The shadow was distorted by bank and slope of sand with the sense that it was different to the casting shape above. The effect was of a repetitive, circular motion - pencil-line and ink-overlay seeming to bring out overwhelming sadness.

Rick had said that Maeve had brought back one dolphin from a 'dark place' and had quickly told her the story...

There was one thing she might do for her - maybe the last thing she should do - and could she do it...?

Dierdre walked to the studio and switched on the light.

Rick had saved the sketches Maeve had given him. He'd slipped in some photographs he had taken. He didn't know exactly what the four words 'She'd know, I can't' meant - or if Maeve had remembered writing them. He suspected it was some kind of slip which showed she was still thinking of her mother...

'You take these, Dierdre. It's the least I can do. You trained the hand that produced these and that she won't forget. Don't worry about the snaps. I've got more...

'Oh... I can find you a quiet place to watch if you want to see a Show... and Maeve - until she leaves. My phone number's inside,' he had said...

Dierdre spread out Maeve's handiwork and did not feel quite alone...

There was a faint hope and a distant purpose...

Rick had been unable to fault anything. The old routines had been performed impeccably but they had been nothing more than a pleasant prelude to the astonishing.

Maeve had reached for the microphone on the deck of the three-master. Polite applause had rippled through the crowd to be followed by laughter as Blowhard had made noises which had sounded uncannily like 'wolf-whistles'!

He had finned around the lagoon at speed, mimicking applause like a professional 'crowd-warmer' in a T.V.Studio. He had stopped in front of Maeve, standing above him on the deck, and, one fin extended out to the side - the other across his chest, he had bowed whilst walking in water!

Maeve had mock-curtsied and silence had fallen as she had spoken. Rick had listened as attentively as everyone else - he had not seen Maeve teach Blowhard how to behave so slickly!

Some items that had been constructed for the extended Show today, she had given no explanation for. He had been working things out for himself and half-suspected...

'We would like to entertain you further and claim credit for the training of bottlenose and hump-back dolphins in what you are about to witness. However, there comes a point in training where individuals seem to take leaps of learning entirely by themselves. Such is true of you all - will be true of your children. The trainers of this Dolphinarium take little credit for what you are about to see beyond giving an opportunity for its free expression and providing the facilities and the equipment. In the greater part of all that you will see in the last part of the Show, the dolphin 'Stars' have used their own natural intelligence.'

Maeve had replaced the microphone and the crowd had applauded politely as she had clambered down the side of the three-master on to the raft they had made from some empty oil-drums with planks lashed across. She was carrying the loud-hailer.

Sitting on the raft, she raised the loud-hailer...

'Thank you for waiting. I don't move as fast as the 'stars' around water. You will notice I am giving no signals and you are in a position to watch everyone else around you. I urge everyone to keep quiet and you have my permission to throw anyone in the water who looks as though they might be making any signals. Clap if you want to but do not stretch out your arms or you might get wet.

'Blowhard and Delilah, please tow me to the middle of the lagoon.'

Two dolphin heads had surfaced near the raft and submerged.

The raft had moved sedately to the centre of the lagoon. There had been absolutely no signal!

The crowd had buzzed with conversation and Rick had been just as puzzled!

'Yes, ladies and gentlemen, the 'stars' have learned to come to the sound of their names in human speech - and you will notice I am exactly where

I asked to go. Understanding human words, speech however, is just one part of the leap in new learning I am talking about.

'Many of you have a pet. Maybe it's a cat or dog. You speak of your pet as sometimes being quite intelligent. Dolphins are as intelligent as cats and dogs... !'

Maeve had been soused in spray from five or six fluke-flips of water aimed accurately at her exposure upon the raft!

Shouting into the hailer, she had said, 'Alright - Alright! A bit more intelligent than dogs!'

Again water had cascaded upon her and her laughter had been an infection to spread within the spectators...

'The second most intelligent creature in the world?'

There had only been one mild fluke-flip, the spray ending as a light shower across her feet...

'Almost as intelligent us?' and Maeve had turned to look all around the crowd.

There was silence and the water surface rippled harmlessly. The crowd laughed and applauded.

One by one the dolphin heads emerged to nod, beak-gape and grin...

Mums and kids loved it! Dads were smiling knowingly. However the young woman had done it, the family outing was worth the money just to see the looks of sheer joy and enthusiasm in sparkling eyes.

'Well, ladies and gentlemen. It's up to the 'stars' to prove they are as intelligent as that, isn't it? To tell the truth, I know they are... and we would like to show you. Will you follow us to the dry-dock? There are plenty of seats.'

With that, Maeve had placed the hailer into a clip on the raft and dived into the lagoon. In moments, she had been towed to the entrance of the dry-dock, her laughter a 'Pied Piper' trail of invitation to follow. They had.

Two shattering events had occurred within...

Rick was stunned, even now...

Rod had been central to the first. He had performed his 'fetch and carry tools trick', Rick recognising the artistry of Maeve in the larger illustrations. White Tip had responded faultlessly and more...

A mock carriage, towed into the arena and drawn by a team of four hump-backs, had Phil seated upon it. Basic, the 'carriage' had been another raft on an oil-drum base but had the addition of mock wheels at each corner, secured by a large red 'nut' per 'wheel'. Maeve had said nothing about this!

On top of each 'wheel' had been a red sausage balloon curved around the circumference. Rick had guessed correctly - by rubber bands.

A dolphin had surfaced near the raft.

Maeve had stood up in an agitated fashion...

Through the hailer, she had yelled, 'Careful Phil! He's at it again!'

'What?' came Phil's shout in the silence left by the spectators...

A bottlenose, which Rick had recognised as Gaze, had spy-hopped near a 'wheel' and everyone had heard the malicious 'Aaahhh!' in mind and ear.

There had been the 'pop' of the burst balloon as his teeth had nipped it. The crowd had been quiet and watchful.

Gaze had walked in water and his teeth had clicked...

'Justt haftt ttoo popptt balloonstt!' the beak had said in mind and ear - and he had click-chortled convincingly!

The crowd had collapsed in laughter! Rick had joined in, unable to resist the humour. Phil, however, had been outraged, or so it had appeared...

'Gaze! Get yourself here and change the wheel! I've got the spare and a spanner. I'm getting tired of this and I'm not getting wet again! Move!'

Phil had deserved a prize for his acting. Rick had let it all flow around him...

A contrite dolphin head had emerged, tilting in submission with beak resting on 'carriage-side'. Without a word, Phil had handed a large wooden cut-out shape of a spanner to the beak.

In amazement, everyone had watched a dolphin use the spanner to 'change the wheel' - slot the replacement on to the short stub of wooden axle, relocate the 'nut' and twist with the spanner to tighten it? True, it had only needed half a turn but the image of a dolphin using a tool was...?

The applause had been loud and long!

It had died when Maeve had used the hailer...

'We are sorry for that small up-set but at least he put things right. That was Gaze. He has a mischievous streak but he knows when he's been bad. You just have to get used to his habits. Thanks Phil. Phil was going to lead the parade of two teams of dolphins for our next display - well it's more than that. We'll let Phil go and the teams can make their own entries in a moment.'

There had been another buzz of conversation whilst Phil was towed out of the lagoon upon his 'carriage'. Rick, showman himself, had recognised the lead-up to a climax - but had never before gauged such expectancy which had built in the hub-bub.

When Maeve had stood up, she had not had to ask for quiet.

A cloak of expectancy had settled thickly, muffling everything but the clarity of her voice. Why had each ear heard a personal address, including Rick himself?

'A team game requires intelligence and a knowledge of rules. Equally, the players must possess the concept of fairness - be willing to modify behaviour in co-operation. Man plays team games like football or rugby or cricket and develops strategies to win. If dolphins demonstrated the same facility for sport, we'd believe their intelligence, wouldn't we?

The crowd had digested this in murmers - still excited. The children were simmering kettles but the men and a few of the women were trying to qualify capacities undreamed of... Several had remarked the goal-like net structures suspended at each end of the flooded dry-dock and had anticipated in part...

'The game you are about to see has been invented by the dolphins captive here. It's like water-polo but, I think, more exciting because our players swim much better and can jump out of the water. We apologise if you get a bit wet. I did, earlier, and now it might be your turn. If anyone wants to leave the front seats and move towards the back, please do. If the ball is knocked out of play perhaps you would just throw it back. Our dolphins have found walking on land a bit difficult.'

No-one had moved but some had readjusted clothing.

'We will have two identifiable teams. Firstly, may I introduce the Bottlenoses.'

The 'stars' had finned into the dry-dock and formed a dolphin chorus-line, beak-clicking to one side. Applause had crackled around the echoing ampitheatre.

The hump-backs had responded to introduction in the same manner, lining on the opposite side. Rick's heart had begun to beat in quicker tempo. Maeve had had no time to practise anything...

Entirely new - he had feared disaster or... Lockgates had loomed large in his mind...

'I will be their referee but things underwater will have to be observed by a dolphin. Things will move too fast for me. I will ask the dolphins to select my assistant for they have their own ideas as to who is fair and competent.

'Who is the underwater referee? Are you ready?'

Making no signals, she had relied upon words alone...!

Two hump-backs and two bottlenoses had walked in water to shake fins in the middle of the pool. After beak-clicks, they had separated but one hump-back had slapped the surface with flukes.

Maeve had explained, 'They have just decided who will play at each end and elected an underwater referee. I don't know who it is yet.'

Blowhard had fluked into the centre of the pool, his expulsion of air, a fair representation of a whistle!

The crowd had shaken in laughter as Maeve and Blowhard had exchanged whistling noises.

And then it had happened! Rick had been rigid on his feet!

For fifteen minutes, the surface had crazed with surge in spray as a ball, half-metre in diameter, had been passed, nudge-headed, fluke-flipped towards a goal. It was better than three dimensional football, the crowd a frenzy of noise in rejoicing a score - or some in anguish at score against!

It had not taken long for the crowd to identify with bottlenose or hump-back. Rick had become aware of some men laying bets on the result... and he stored that within his mind...

When a goal had been scored, a kind of mass hysteria had gripped the crowd and 'stars' or 'hump-backs' had leapt in wild celebration! Not a few had visions of footballers embracing each other in a victory ritual.

Maeve had not had to blow her whistle once. Blowhard had stopped the game twice, with huge leaps in the air, his large flukes making resounding cracks on the surface.

On each occasion, he had walked in water towards an unfortunate - bottlenose first, hump-back later - accusatory fin extended, beak-clicking noisily. The first bottlenose had appeared to say something and had received a fluke-flip to his side in retribution. Immediately mortified, the chastened miscreant had walked in water to a hump-back which had risen to fin-shake. It did not matter that no-one had seen a sign of foul-play. The crowd had applauded the sportsmanship...

Rick had lost track of the score - had failed to note the result... came to the present through tiers of hypnosis.

He watched the faces of the crowd as they left and reflected upon their comments...

He would open the gates to the sea, believing the word-dreams Maeve painted. A possible partnership could be tried...

He shook himself. There was something else first...

It was over. She knew it was good. Rick's eyes had told her he believed. Hot and sticky, she needed to shower.

Gaze had spoken little in her mind but she felt his gratitude as a warmth within. He was preoccupied again, his mindlight all the time beyond her contact. Others were circling the centre of himself and, try as she might, she drifted on the fringe unable to achieve access. She knew she was not forgotten but who were the new lights near her?

Maeve peeled off wet-suit top, removed the stickiness of shorts. Donning robe and grabbing towel, she raced to the shower before the 'boys' arrived.

She knew Phil would want to go out tonight - found excitement in the prospect.

Were Phil and Rod on board already? She paused.

Had she heard the sound of feet in the passage - a door open?

'Phil! That you?'

There was no reply.

She finished. Wrapping the towel around her head and with robe draped around nudity, she returned to her cabin.

Had Rick's cabin door been open?

There was no-one there but a feeling that someone had been. Nothing looked out of place but there was something not quite the same.

She tried again to access Gaze. Was he avoiding her?

One of the new lights was close and... above her? There was a deep-blue sadness in the mind. Was it one of the 'stars'?

For a moment, she mind-urged along her taper of contact then saw the tendril from the blue-mind to the same centre as her own. Gaze was already aware and in contact. What was going on? Why wouldn't he speak?

Maeve dressed impatiently.

She needed to find Rick. Rick could help identify the source of sadness. Why wasn't Gaze telling her?

Ready to climb the steps to the deck, and fastening a belt about her skirt, she felt and saw a thickening of stronger contact...

She felt her heartbeat deliberately tempo-down to normality from a speeding realisation that something concerning herself was happening...

'Gaze, what is happening? What are you doing?'

'Allowing your heart to be calm, Maeve. I am with you for a while but you must use your words now - and find the way as you did with White Tip before I could.'

From glitter-circles behind her eyes, mindfinned the one she knew best beside Gaze. They closed in contact...

'You helped me in my heart's distress, Maeve. I am stronger now, happier with my Gaze. You remember the tears on your cheeks for my sadness in solitude?'

Avenues of recall opened, images and colours of co-joined sympathies were shared...

'How my mind was the same colour as this other? Can you cry for this one, too? And yourself?'

Her mind-voice was fading...

White Tip was mind-finning closer to his centre... Fading...

The mind-glows of both diminishing from brilliance...

What did she mean?

Her taper was dwindling to a thread!

'Gaze! White Tip! Are you leaving me alone?'

There was no answer - just awareness of nearness to the blue of the new-light...

Rick had found Dierdre in the same place that morning. Again, he had sensed her presence, appearing without fuss, at her elbow. He drew a spare chair towards her table, noting the half finished coffee and her hands tightly clutching a folder.

'How did you know I was here?' she had asked, a weak, tight smile wrinkling the corners of her pallor.

'I just felt you were watching. I can't explain it either,' he had said. 'Is there something you want?'

She had known her eyes were red with sleeplessness had felt a wreck.

'Two things, please Rick. You said I could see Maeve without her knowing. May I?'

Rick nodded. 'This afternoon. No problem. But you need some sleep first. Come with me and trust me. Maeve is busy in the dry-dock with Rod and some 'stars'. She won't be able to see you.'

He had reached for her hand, almost paternally.

'And the other thing is what?'

'When I'm gone, would you give her this?'

'No, Dierdre. I won't be a go-between. If you want to give something to her - then you will have to do that for yourself,' he had countered. 'You know I'm right.'

She had wanted to argue... plead... but she was too tired to think straight.

She had slept in Rick's cabin.

Sleep had overwhelmed her... Grateful of surrender, she had descended the blank shades of grey to a warmth in a darkness unpeopled in dream, with no discordant music or voice...

Nothing but the dark... another rhythm, comforting, steadying the throb of her heart...

The clear sound, of the voice she needed, awakened her. Was there something new in the tone?

Maeve was talking to a crowd, her voice encompassing an unseen audience?

Assertive and assured, with lightness of humour, it was a mature voice, embodying hard-earned experience - not the least hint of uncertainty quavering confidence.

Was this really Maeve? - the daughter who had trembled before exams - or was so blighted by sundered parents?

There was movement above!

Hurriedly, Dierdre ducked from sight of any casual glance through the port. The noise of someone clambering down the side alarmed her. The unseen audience clapped.

When Maeve's voice began again, she risked peering through the net curtains.

Maeve, aboard a raft, was still talking through a speaker of some sort. She was cheerful... pretty in the bloom of maturity which came as a shock. Wearing a wet-suit top and shorts, she was fit and graceful.

Tears welled easily within and behind Dierdre's eyes, mixing with a saltiness of guilt and loss. They ran with a thick, broad slowness across her cheekbones.

The high, chiming laughter was not for her. She heard the belling notes in lower tones of solemnity - a sorrowing down of merriment, distant through a fog.

Meaning of words was lost - the sound of her voice was all...

When Maeve swam with the dolphins, somewhere out of sight, she left emptiness upon an abandoned raft...

Dierdre communed with self and thought. She could leave her farewell upon Maeve's pillow. Rick had suggested the option... but the sound of Maeve's voice... censure or not, was...

Was she sapped of strength to seek forgiveness?

Time became a torment of indecision...

Ciaran was strong - dutifully efficienct, his practicality was arid, lacking imagination - leaving little to nurture...

Yet, he had tried. He had been provider in many things. There had been a time of loving but years took tolls of tenderness. Now Banker and wife were bankrupt.

Oh, she had been easy meat for Doug! His brand of red-wine had seemed so fresh and tantalising - togetherness apparently so complementary and savoury...

She had succumbed to dreams, suppressed so long, finding nothing but horror in her daughter's face.

Nothing was what she deserved!

Mechanically, she tidied and straightened the bunk, sat clutching the folder for Maeve, needing to speak for the last time...

Then there were the footsteps she knew!

Staying very quiet, apprehensive of confrontation, she waited for the sound of Maeve's door to open and close - for the sound of the shower. Not knowing if she could face it yet, Dierdre left Rick's cabin and went on deck. There was still time to fade away...

Two dolphins finned beneath her, raised heads and fixed her with knowing eyes. She recognised one!

The white tip to the dorsal was identical to painting and photograph in the folder she held in a tightness of hand. Both creatures raised their heads and opened their mouths displaying small teeth in even rows. They reminded her of inquisitive puppies with grinning mouths... No, not puppies; they were... too aware?

White Tip, as Maeve called it, finned closer and raised its head further. How did she know this one was female?

Quiet beak-clicking came from her mouth.

Was she trying to speak? - To reassure?

The head tilted and the eye facing her seemed... to wink!?

Dierdre stepped back, her own movement masking the sound of Maeve's entry to the deck. She moved again to the side. Both dolphins raised their heads.

'Are you trying to tell me something?'

Dierdre's whisper was confidential and nervous. She did not expect a reply.

'I think it's me they're trying to tell something.'

Dierdre whirled! The warm smile she wanted to show, unworn in the moment of shock.

Maeve saw the loneliness and the fatigue - not the falseness her mother would have wished as a mask.

They studied each other.

Maeve walked to the side. Her mother followed her gaze. Maeve looked thoughtful, deep within herself.

'You're really not going to say anything?' Maeve said, looking into the water.

'I don't know what to say, love. I needed to... wanted to see you, to give you... this...'

Maeve turned. Dierdre saw the turmoil, wanted to reach for her... but couldn't. Maeve's eyes were too inward.

Then a daughter's eyes misted...

'Hello... Mum,' sobbed from below, within...

Dierdre found some words. 'Hello love. I didn't mean to upset you.' The tears were flowing from her own eyes. 'I wanted to give... To see if I... Oh, Maeve, please try and forgive me. Please, I don't know how I...'

But it was her tears that spoke louder. Maeve stepped closer and joined a folding of arms... murmers of moisture intermingling and a desolation of clasped hands...

Words were 'Forgive me' on the cover of a folder and the content within...

It was then Gaze began to glow in Maeve's mind and his whisper was confidential...

The crowd had been a long time leaving. Bright-eyed, question after question had been asked, parried and answered with all the patience in politeness he had been able to muster.

Rick was much later than intended as he walked towards the 'Red Bottlenose'. He had seen Ciaran and a young man in the crowd, applauding with an energy equal to any there.

This was going to be dicey. Whatever was likely to happen between mother and daughter aboard the three-master, he hoped Dierdre would keep her distance. The young man had to be her brother, Donovan.

This was Maeve's triumph, recognised by her father and brother - to say nothing of Rick, himself. He had been wrong to give Dierdre access to Maeve - a fool of a man!

What had possessed him? How could he prepare for the disaster he felt looming closer?

Ciaran spotted him - got to his feet. Rick waved him down. Getting his own drink would give him time to think.

There really was no other way. He'd have to tell him.

Perhaps Dierdre would simply leave, unremarked.

He walked towards father and son. Had Ciaran read his discomfiture? Out-stretched hand gripped his own...

'Wonderful Rick. I had no idea Maeve was capable of such presence in front of an audience. She's tended to be a little reticent when meeting people. Locking up her feelings has been a characteristic she probably inherited from her father. You were right to insist I should be here with Donovan. The pair of us wouldn't have missed this.'

'Glad you liked it. I told you she was a 'natural' - no, more than that. She's taught me more than I dare think about yet. I feel I'm seeing things from a completely different viewpoint. Maeve's pointing to potential I've only dreamed of.

'Sorry. I'm being rude. Hello, Donovan. Good to meet you - but I hope you won't give me the same shake-down your sister has.'

'Hardly likely, Mr. Dortmann.'

'Rick's the name boyo. There's not a deal of formality here.'

They grinned at each other and the gap of years sharply narrowed.

Rick turned to Ciaran, wondering at the thoughtfulness behind the Banker's eyes.

It had to be now...

'Ciaran, Dierdre's here. She's aboard the boat I call 'home'. She wanted to see Maeve. I found her here yesterday afternoon - sort of felt her watching. I don't know how she found out about Maeve being here but...'

'It's alright, Rick. I know - we both do. Whatever happens is not your fault.'

Rick studied both - saw the slight flush in Donovan's cheek. He knew before being told.

Donovan said, quietly, 'It was me Rick. I told my mother what was going on three days ago... I suppose I went to sort out my feelings at the same time as going back to the beach-house with, er, a friend. I thought that... It might have been interesting for... Things weren't the same. I told Mum before you phoned Dad.'

'Yes, Rick. Don't worry. Dierdre's parked somewhere else. Her car wasn't in the car-park. Probably it's in a side-street somewhere. That probably means she doesn't want to cause any kind of scene,' said Ciaran, in a level voice.

Too controlled, thought Rick, sensing a practised and professional detachment - but he had looked for her car...?

Ciaran was still speaking, '... we've talked to Maeve, we'll be off. I'll just make sure she's alright if she's met her mother. I want to congratulate her anyway.'

Rick smiled at them both.

'She'd want you to meet the dolphins - especially Gaze. It ought to be like meeting an old friend for you.'

'How do you mean?'

'Maeve's convinced you met the same dolphin on your holiday and it saved your lives. I don't know. It would have happened a bloody long way away. There again, your lass has been full of surprises. She even sensed Gaze coming before she saw him. I don't want to tell you more. It's best you have a longer talk with her.'

Rick stiffened. Maeve was coming towards them.

The conversation died. They watched her approach.

Rick asked, 'Everything alright, love?'

'Yes, everything's fine. Hello, Dad - Donovan.'

'That was one heck of an entertainment, Maeve. I'm proud of you,' said Ciaran.

He warmed to the readiness with which she embraced him but her smile had a sad edge. Something had happened and he couldn't ask.

'Not bad sis,' said Donovan, clapping a hand to her shoulder. 'More like that and you'll end up in show business.'

Rick wanted a clue - they all did.

She turned to Rick. 'Would you mind if we went back to see the 'stars'? I'd love Dad and Donovan to meet them.'

How should he answer? Was the coast clear?

Her eyes were disconcertingly direct. Was another comment behind them? Both lids closed briefly with the slightest of an inclination to her head. The nod was barely perceptible... and the smile was for him...

Rick knew how to answer.

'Yes, of course we can. Would you like to come aboard Ciaran?'

...and it was her father's quandary. If only he could read her mind - or she could read his in turmoil of need and anxiety. Had she seen her mother or not? What had happened? How did Maeve really feel - and how did he, for that matter?

Courtesy demanded an answer...

'Yes, love. We'd like to very much. Thanks Rick.' He might need a way out... 'We'll stay for a short while but then there's some paperwork and Donovan might have other plans.'

Rick thought suddenly of the 'boys'!

'Maeve, Phil and Rod...' but her hand was on his arm.

'They're getting a take-away. All you've got to worry about is the state of your drinks' cabinet. Do you want to buy anything here? The take-away's paid for.'

'Okay, okay! So we're having another evening supper. Lead on woman,' and Rick was laughing in relief. Ride along with it, he thought. She's on top of everything. But how, beats me...

Half-way across the grass, Maeve laughed for the first time.

'What's so funny sis?' asked Donovan.

'We all are. Don't worry.'

They were all mystified.

'You sketched and painted all these?' Ciaran asked, fingers lingering over the last.

'She certainly did, Ciaran. I vouch for it,' Rick interjected. 'What's the last one you're looking at?'

Ciaran held up the sketch which he found far less... now what was the word?... 'effervescent'? Yes... This was the odd-one-out. It was so...

Rick was speaking, '...first time Maeve came. The dolphin is called White Tip, a female. I think her young mate died as a result of chemical poisoning. They'd been captured... Let's just say both were ill-treated through the ignorance of a man more concerned with finance than the welfare of a couple of unfortunates. White Tip was in a dark place after the young male died... Well, it was more than that... She was locked in circles of grief, Ciaran. By all my Irish ancestors, Maeve brought her back to life and that's the truth of it. You'll probably think I'm foolish.'

'More concerned with finance than welfare...' reverberated in Ciaran's mind. He continued to look at Maeve's sketch...

Yes, he saw the constant circling - aimless, the mobility going nowhere - the staring at the shadows of what might have been and now was lost. Smudging shading brought out the sadness... and made him feel his own...

Rick wanted to ask Maeve why it had been returned to her and dare not.

Ciaran had to ask, 'The note on the back, Maeve - you thought about your Mum. She's been here, hasn't she?'

He'd expected a sudden silence - not a calm reply.

'Yes, Mum's been here. She wanted to give me something and see me for the last time... but it won't be the last.'

'You've seen her then? Was she - you weren't upset?'

He noted Rick leading Donovan tactfully away; was grateful.

He looked at the younger brown eyes across the table. They were understanding... just as attractive... and seemed to fix him within their orbit.

He did not hear the arrival of the pick-up or subdued chatter.

'We were both upset, Dad. Mum asked me to forgive her and I... I realised something. How many of us really know how others suffer their private griefs? Or when we will need each other again?'

A father marvelled in a daughter attaining maturity. When had she taken the leap, ascending to adulthood? The silence was there to be filled...

'Did Dierdre - your mother - see this? Did she help you?'

Maeve was quiet, looking beyond him. Was she listening to another voice somewhere inside?

'I tried. Perhaps we can still help each other,' came the voice recognised from twenty four years.

In utter confusion, he turned. Dierdre?

She was handing him a folder... The action saved the need to touch...

He watched her sit closer to Maeve than he had ever thought would happen again - and did not know how he felt. He fumbled the folder, his administrative hands betraying him in a tremor of clumsiness.

Looking at the content was an escape, removing a necessity for words...

Mother and daughter were silent. He could not look at them.

There was a painting... It was Dierdre's work and it had astonishing power, extending a theme recognised in Maeve's sketch. Subtle choice in shade and hue magnified the solitude. To portray such sorrow in happiness denied could only be achieved... if an artist identified with the theme, he thought...

He reached for the photograph. If anything, lighting and the medium of black and white, emphasised grief. It was discomforting; too real, too close to himself.

Ciaran raised his eyes...

Dierdre spoke. 'I came to give Maeve these. Rick gave me some sketches. He's afraid he might have offended you. We were together too long not to understand that we can't be cut-off from our children - and I needed to see Maeve. I won't interfere. I'll be going shortly.'

Maeve said, 'Not until you've had the take-away. You are the one who chose it with Phil.'

Dierdre could not be strong for long. She needed a reason to avoid the eyes of her wronged husband... Was there something else behind his mask?

'Yes, love. I'd better help those boys dish-up.'

Maeve waited. There was a beak-clicking from the lagoon. She turned her head...

When she looked at him again it was with sadness.

'Neither you nor Mum have always said what you mean, have you? Mum tried another photograph first. She hadn't wanted to give it to me but I guessed there were two or three attempts before she would have been satisfied.

'I've kept one. Do you want to see it, Dad?'

It was important to her... 'If you think I should, Maeve.'

She reached to a blouse pocket.

'Mum rejected this effort because of the reflection of light across the plain glass sheet she put over my sketch. She hadn't liked frosted glass - it ruined outline. This is the one I will keep.' (She couldn't know, at that point, that all photographs and paintings would be taken by Deirdre back to the work-room and, absent-mindedly, poked between layers of half-finished items. No, she didn't know then. But Gaze would decide...)

There was a pale reflection of part of Dierdre's face in the glass above Maeve's sketch!

What had caused her to take a photograph when she had been too close? He knew she liked to use a rigid tripod and a remote shutter device...

'Mum wanted to keep it for herself. I wouldn't let her.'

Beneath the one eye of the reflection - wetness?... Maeve was watching his expression. Was she also reading his heart?

Maeve said simply, 'He's gone, Dad. He made her sick. The tears aren't for him. They're for what she has done to us all, including herself. I see that now. Do you?'

He had to think about that... and was glad they were called below deck. Ducking his head to enter, he was, for an interval, on a small cruiser upon the Coral Sea - could almost wish himself there...

As the meal progressed - but this time with laughter and other personalities for shelter in convivial chatter - he sensed another beginning, if he could suppress the pain...

Later, in the night's peace from the noise of the day, Maeve asked, 'You were in each mind?' She hesitated... 'Were you also in hers when she took her first photograph?'

Gaze said, 'You saw what mind and heart wanted to see... and heard discord or harmony. Few 'men' can do this - fewer still can alter attitudes.'

'You haven't answered me. Why did my mother bring those photographs and her painting? Did you make her do everything? Did you,' there was a fateful hesitation, 'cause Rick to give her mine? What did you do, Gaze? Tell me!'

She had to know if he could alter feelings! That was close to a violation.

It was too much power... To love or to hate were matters of self...

White Tip mindfinned closer, mindvoice expanding...

'Are you afraid, Maeve?'

The mindlights of Gaze were fading in brilliance, turning within as if... Maeve realised he was confronting himself! Did he feel guilty about something...?

White Tip said, 'Gaze is patterning, Maeve. He knows your love for him... but he senses your fear. He is... deciding what to do.'

The taper of contact broadened with White Tip, her bright light touching and encompassing her own. Maeve knew it was for comfort. They were a twinned-star close to his centre.

It did not take long. The brilliance of his mind seemed to intensify and he was reaching filaments for them. They were entwined closer than ever... but Maeve wondered why the filaments were blue? Why was Gaze... grieving?

His mindvoice was strong... so strong... so...

White Tip's mindmerge was expected. It came in the false-glow before sunbreach. Gaze heard it from within the centre of himself in the inviolable junction of heart and mind.

'The gates will open in the lightwater? Maeve will forget save in her heart? Why Gaze? You have love for her as you do for me? What of these other Splitflukes who mean no harm?'

'The Splitfluke religion teaches 'man shall have dominion over life in the worldspace'. Falsely, he grasps, in his tool-using hands, notions of superiority. He has sought to impose his will and to destroy that which has made him afraid. Maeve began to fear me... even as you knew terror, my love.

'In her fear is discord. If Maeve spread apprehension here, the Humpbacks would face another red-stained shore - here, the 'stars' would drown in fishtrap weaves.

'Let 'men' see our mindskills slowly, taking care not to cause their fears. Maeve felt the beginnings of 'violation'. It was not intended... quite the reverse. I cannot bring myself to cause the destruction of Maeve's and her dam's 'paintings' and 'photographs'- but Deirdre will mislay them. These Splitflukes must forget much of our existence in late lightwaters... only remembering slowly. They are unready - unable to sustain a partnership without... floundering in fear.'

White Tip said, 'She will not be able to mind-leap the waterspace as she did?

'For some time, only in her heart. She and the crowds will see the skills retained by 'star' and hump-back in ways to cause no fear. The games can continue without risk, I feel. The new, mixed podsherd we shall revisit. We will see Maeve again - but there is danger for both her and dolphinkind if held too close to her mind. Like Rick, she began to sense a primitive dread...'

'And that is why you are sad?'

'We feel sadness. These Splitflukes must not be allowed to feel many things yet - beyond superficial sympathies. Splitflukes are too dangerous for us...

'Maeve is, perhaps, the rare and limited exception...'

Rick opened the lock-gates in the morning before Maeve was up. He felt impelled to honour a promise...

She was pleased when she discovered, rejoicing in the new freedoms for all the dolphins who had responded so marvellously to her unexpected gifts as a trainer. She regretted no particular absences as she watched a distant pair of bottlenose dolphins leaping into the air above Moreton baywaters in something like celebration... For a moment, she felt like she had on the holiday with her father and Donovan, remembering the bliss of swimming with a young bottlenose in its joyful innocence...

'I know in my heart they'll be back, Rick,' she said, seeing the concern in his face.

At highwater, they were - eager for the tricks and the Show. It seemed Maeve had been right all along. A kind of partnership was possible.

No-one noticed that two bottlenose dolphins were missing - everything seemed normal... even to Maeve herself.

Crowd attendance at the Dolphinarium increased. There were adjustments to schedules to take account of highwater each day. Rick allowed some supervised swimming with the dolphins, off the beach area nearby. Here, he had to worry more in educating people about dolphins but he recognised such free association proved incredibly popular.

Phil and Rod, both astonished, saw their father screw the old name-boards back on the three-master. They didn't help him. He wanted to do it himself. The 'Fiona' looked much better as a result.

Maeve was looking forward to University - and so was Phil. They told Ciaran when they went for a meal together.

Ciaran said that they really ought to arrange another meal so that Maeve's mother could have a chance to get to know Phil better.

His daughter puzzled at her father's motives...

So, temporarily, Maeve forgot a strange bottlenose dolphin's name and the unique experiences they had shared. But there would come a time when her heart would cry out...

Chapter Thirteen

ABOMINATION CONFRONTED

White Tip was puzzled. Gaze and she fluked bi-vector towards the far steeprise, only recently detected by herself as an irregularity in the forcelines.

His vectors were positive in seaspace.

In finning from the new, mixed podsherd of Hump-backs and Bottlenoses, he had hesitated only once...

'Dance with me White Tip,' he had said, in a closeness of mindmerge tinged with blue. 'Leap in vectors of love, twist in airspace above. Scatter the waters in joy and celebrate your freedom. We fluke for a new home with dear friends to welcome you.'

He had spy-hopped before her, beak-gaping a smile - investing an enthusiasm - willing her to wild cavorting capers in spray and foam. That part of herself, nearest her racing heart, had not understood.

It had not been until he had spy-hopped further out that she had fathomed the tinge in his blue.

A Splitfluke, close to the 'false sun' in the sign of 'words', had been Maeve. Had they been dance-fluking in farewell to her heart?

'Yes, White Tip. We have given her heart a means of recognition. She will know of our gratitude and of our joy. Maeve will know us in herself and of our return, if we must. She shall know our hearts - even though our minds she may question,' Gaze had said.

She had said in wonderment, 'Her mind will forget what her heart remembers?' She added, unable to help herself, 'You are sad to do this - regret the loss of her affection?'

White Tip had stumbled in imaging. Gaze had not yet declared himself ready for... Her mind had shaded pinker than she would have wished him to see!

Hurriedly, she had reefsided and camouflaged her indiscretion of imaging with other mindmerge... Thankfully, there was no awareness of her small jealousy in his mindlight cluster, seemingly involved in last, deep instructions to Blotch and Twizzle.

Later she had said simply, 'Your heart is as large as your mind, Gaze. You love her.'

For a fleeting moment, had she seen a flush within him?

Then she had not known what to do as he had mindmerged,

'But there is greater space reserved for you... a time and a place for expression of love, and it is soon.'

Her mind had been an uncontrollable pink for longer than she had liked, her warm-glow embarrassingly persistent.

Puzzled now, she wondered how Gaze knew the vectors to skirt confusing force-flux. When her lateral sensing was chaotic confusion, he was unerring. She felt he must have known of the steeprise ahead. Was this the waterspace of his Podsherd of friends?

'No, my love,' he was saying - 'my love' in greater confidence? she thought. 'This place Splitflukes call 'Cato Island'. Our Hump-back friends made flukingpassage here... so did I, more than a mooncycle ago. Here we will share much imaging for we must pause in our voyaging. You have new things to learn.

'Of all Bottlenoses I know, you are the one who is closest to myself.'

White Tip was mindpink again!

Once more, the mindmerge took an unexpected fluketurn.

'You have great mindstrength. Party to what we can achieve, it is possible that your mind is capable of similar skills. We need to learn much more of each other for the good of dolphinkind - and for ourselves. The time for your self-awakening... and of joint-discovery awaits us in the lagoon ahead.'

Gaze paused in his earnestness...

In some way she felt him scanning the steeprise of rock and coral. He was not echo-locating. What was he doing?

She was becoming accustomed to his mindreading - was not surprised when he said, 'I am mindscanning, my love. This skill I feel you can... learn.

'There may be more. Fintouch me now...'

Complying, she saw part of his mindglow expand to encompass her.

Enmeshed, intertwined, they were racing through a black void, outside anything... but his voice was there...

'You are safe. Here, between now and moments before, are the echoes of minds. Here, there are mindlights in their colours of mood. These narrows of awareness are too difficult for most to vector in conscious passage.

'Co-joined as we are, we float inside this narrow band. You are not looking around, above or below...'

White Tip felt mindtendrils tug to turn her in the darkness.

It was like an interface of air and water, light above and dark beneath... stretching to infinity all around. She had never seen it before... except in darkwater dreaming - or, perhaps, in her grieving? It was nowhere and everywhere. She began to panic!

She felt the peace of his touch. Calmness spread through her... spinning eased... mind-circling visions slowed...

His voice was quiet, soothing...

'That was your second disorientation, my love - the first, prolonged after Bloom's deep-dive. This time I am here.

'Now look above and below...'

Again, tendrils took hold in turning her. Then she was stationary and mindflow settled to a kind of constancy...

Wave-shapes appeared in translucence above which she recognised as the white-glow of present! In odd airspace, a ghost-gull transparency, lukewarm mind of dull orange, was gliding an unseen air-current!

She tried to mindfin adjustment, apprehensive of dizzying nausea...

Below in the darkness, unobserved before, there were echoes and whispers from shadowed shapes! Point pricks of light perforated the blackness - minds in the deep!

They were 'others' - but not dolphins! What...?

'Well done. Now you are curious, watchful. You are beginning to scan the mindscape. Watch my mind.'

It was command. She could not resist.

Growing from his cluster of self came a filament thinner than tendrils of contact.

Seemingly intertwined as his mindlight extension she was swept at speed towards... the steeprise ahead... He was looking, examining...

And all so quickly!

They were seeking and questing myriads of mindnoise murmers... Light-flickers, most no larger than grains of sand, dazzled in concentrated constellations...

'Watch for a larger light - especially those of cold white. There... and there... Do not be afraid. These are sharks.'

Centring upon one such light, she seemed to see it magnify...

And there was a ghost-shape, sharkfanning the force-flux of reefedge, white-light cold, predatorial...

Suddenly, the white-light flared and a smaller, erratic winking terminated. White Tip heard a mindwailing echo...

She knew what had happened. At times she had heard the same noise in fishmuster before the fishtrap and separation from her own podsherd and podfamily...

'That was the beginning of your strength of mind, my love. But it had no chance to flourish. One lightwater we shall seek truth of your podfamily... when we seek the reason of our difference to dolphinkind.'

They were leaving, filament retiring in retractive reversal towards their own thinking forms. She was free...

'You can learn to project your own mind. Image the steeprise ahead. Reach out and seek a warm-light. Tell me what you see.'

She realised 'Cato Island' was closer now. They had been fluking bi-vector, in reflexive motion all the while!

White Tip tried to solidify a mindray - to make a passage for energy in curiosity...

Twice her mindself stuttered. Gaze saw the first as a light-loop bubble on her mind - the second as a curling extension growing further before turning back into herself. He knew what to say...

'Nearly... but you are trying too hard. Seek to float the passage, a gossamer of filament whirling within calm wind - but under control. Image where you intend - not where you are. Avoid distraction from other minds.'

He saw the third attempt in satisfaction - watched a filament of herself bisect the waterspace, hesitating only once...

White Tip saw ghost-swell surging alongside reefedge! She could discern above and below! In her excitement, the light of air, dark of water - shaded to grey...

'Careful, keep calm. Mergelink with a mind. You need to fix a reference in another space. Then you will see more clearly and understand.'

She concentrated, sensed the passage bordering light and dark. Reefedge and surf-speckled lines reappeared. She sought an 'other' and found a ghost-gull, orange mind alert, bobbing upon the surface she could not yet see.

Her filament of self she brushed against the lukewarm glow - and moved within!

Motion she sensed first. The sea rhythm was pronounced as her new form rose and fell - tilted and swayed.

Webbed feet maintained wholly instinctive station upon the surface.

It, 'she' - had fed recently but not to repletion. There were some familiarities in sensing but sharper, higher pitched.

This gull... she could not read her name... had lateral sensing! She could feel the forcelines... but her eyes were clearer...

The worldspace was a magnified in clarity...

It was beautiful!

Her feet moved in rapid long-sweeps and her strange wings thrust against - a solidity of air? Co-joined, they left a sucking weight of water. It was like a lengthened dance-leap... but it did not end...! She was finning the airspace - and so high!

Looking down was her undoing... The worldspace turned grey!

She thought of safety, was out of contact, retracting through the narrow band with light above and dark beneath...

She was dizzy. Gaze did not speak - watched her whirl of mind-glow. He waited for stability...

'Gaze?' she whispered.

'Yes, my love.'

'I was... I saw...'

'I know.'

'Did you...? Were you... there?'

'No, my love. You were. You never tried before.'

'The steeprise is... beautiful,' she said.

'I know, my love. It is the place,' he said, tenderly finsweeping her side and beneath...

She fluketrembled, her mindglow more than moonglow.

Her mindrays were joyous sun-breach as he began the dance she recognised and needed!

Their dance-leaps bounded the distance. She was willing to teach now - and he, to learn.

Later, they finned the blue lagoon - spiralled prisms of watery light - watched many others fish-flick or crawl-creep coral in the truce period, feeling life anew...

She played, making bubble-traps to confuse in the mind-flares of air-fearers... beak-nudged a bottom fish to wakefulness... watched his flat-fluking sand-mist settle like dry rain... finturned to Gaze again, touching in intimacy his flanks... his mind...

'My love... you knew of this place? How? Were you here before... before we came?'

'Once, but alone. We are not the first to find the way in each other. We have a heart's home - where, no matter...

'Here is merging of two in one and our need. The seed of a dream is an image kept forever; here is within our hearts...

'Blotch and Twizzle were here before us. Already they make a saga in the new podsherd like Storytellers of my own. Their hearts fin another lagoon, as we shall be in our memory.'

'Forever is long enough to forget, Gaze,' she said.

He said nothing.

At first, her heart thought he could not reply - but she shared his dam's imaging, further within the warmstream ... and her constancy...

...'It is also my need to love... beyond demand... even to the time of the deep-dive and the sharks... Remember always, I love you...' Peen had said, in dorsal drifting...

White Tip felt his touch in body and mind - the same sun upon their basking backs in companionship. She felt an affinity with his distant dam, the certain warmth... in her loving... and of his...

In a darkwater, they finturned an alignment, just as he had done to contact the Hump-backs closing this place she could never forget.

White Tip felt the mindenergy build - joined the arc-lancing leap across the blank horizon.

She recognised the infinity of half-light and darkness but, at greater speed, the 'others' were fibres of fleeting existence - shading lines of colour as they passed, and new point-pricks of minds ahead. Somehow, she sensed the rapid flow of forceline flux but he did not need their reference. How...?

'We image where we wish to be, not where we are or the flow in our passing. Remember the image we shared and hold to that!' he mindmerged quickly.

She sensed a growing separation, panicked and Gaze was absent! Faster than a heartbeat, she was back to the lagoon...

Gaze was gone! Visually, she scanned the lagoon's waterspace.

A large jelly-fish, with hanging tendrils she knew could sting her eyes, was a dolphinspan away close in the reefedge foam! She finned further away.

Where was Gaze? She circumscanned, slowly with care...

In relief, she heard the quick return in her short range, identifying his shape and size, from...!

If had not been for two shapes she saw then, visually, behaving like dolphin sentinels breaching and twisting in air-flight, she would have been desolate in isolation.

Her fresh stability of spirit saved her.

She recognised the Bottlenose visions as the dancing podpartners of Gaze - knew their purpose in protection.

White Tip trusted her dolphin senses and finned towards the alien jelly-fish... Her echo-location had not failed. His flank was there to touch - but his bright mind-glow was diminished.

'Visualise this image and hold it in your mind,' he had said, showing her a dolphin-shape of greenish stone in a niche between coral and rock. 'You are safe, both here and there, but I cannot hold you close. The distance is great and I will need nearly all my mindenergy. It would be easier if you could use your strength as well but you have need of confidence still.'

She knew where Gaze was - did she dare the distance another time?

White Tip took the leap...

Gaze felt her mind falter... slip to recede in other vectors behind. For an instant, he wanted to return but clung to the image of the jade carving, in the niche to the side of Ardent's cave entrance. He had to ration mindenergy to complete the passage... It was an act of will...

It would take several lightwaters before he would be able to leap this distance again. If White Tip could have held to her image, the energy debt would have been less - but it was too soon. He had asked too much of her, despite the rapidity with which she learned. Too long had he been without news. Helping the Hump-backs had taken longer than he had thought... and now there was his White Tip.

He had to know of the Watcher Guardians - and of Vorg. What had been the mindscream in the junction of heart and mind he had heard in darkwater dreaming... echoing through the border-channel of there and then? He feared a strange connection with Vorg - his magnification in malice.

The ghost-grey of the reefedge he recognised ahead - and the galaxy of mindglow in the Podsherd. The satellite orbit of smaller podunits were the darkwater Guardians...

He kept the image intact... ignored fruitless questing which would force him back...

Through lagoon unseen and across, tight-blind to anything but the jade in a niche...

Through the maze of water-passageway to beaksnout the dolphin-carving...

And facing within a grievous sin, behind the eyes, so coldly dull, in a yellow-skin's ageing Splitfluke skull...!

Ardent's last mindmerge was cautious but, coupled with all before, his meaning - starkly clear:

'Fishmuster easier in open-sea...

All have safe returned and he...

Winking light in a sad demise...
Darkness now our one disguise...
Sister's risk can be as cruel...
Absent-minded - I seem a fool...'
The out-fluking podunit to Spinner waterspace had aided and advised in new fishmuster strategies and safely returned to the Podsherd - Vorg as well...
Starshine had deep-dived tragically!
Gaze recalled the darkwater of distressing mindscreams echoing woefully through the narrows of empathy...
He guessed the suffering and knew the sin - Vorg had murdered his friend...
Ardent... no longer believed in the efficacy of the squideye deterrent! Vorg was reading minds which meant - he knew the identity of a seeming 'Dolphin of Light'!
Vorg knew of himself - and Vorg would tolerate no rival!
Gaze recognised the Cleric's fear for the safety of his own dear sister, Gape!
He guessed the Watcherguardians would not allow Vorg to be alone with her now... but no Bottlenose would be safe. Guardian training and alertness could not safeguard against a Visioner of Vorg's distorted desires!
The few Watcherguardians were having to cloak action and plan under cloaks of subterfuge... which Vorg would penetrate easily, the moment he wanted, with mindreading! Was he too late already!?
Rick's fears and poor Maeve's were being realised in his own Podsherd, in his own podfamily!
In a futile attempt to avoid close examination by Vorg, Ardent was attempting to appear the absent-minded, bumbling old Bottlenose that Vorg and Gaze, himself, had first encountered in their joint Storyteller appraisal... It was pointless!
Vorg would have already read his father's mind!
Gale would have revealed the secret of the niche in Ardent's cave entrance quite unwittingly...
Gaze did not know what to do! He cursed his own compassion and the optimism that malice could be curbed. Rick was right to dread an evil under worldspace...
In his fears for others, and for himself, he saw the dizzying greyness from inside the Splitfluke skull - felt the backwards force of retraction...!
He fought... to keep the reference of a niche in place... strove to clear everything... to sustain the image he needed...
A new reef-system swelled in ghost-line! There were many dolphin 'others'...
This time she remembered the image, ignored the constellation of minds... Her forward vector juddered slightly, but she continued...
White Tip crossed the lagoon in mind-proximity to a podsherd of

dorsal drifting dolphins...

She felt they must be Gaze's friends...

A mindlight, brighter than the rest, she noted... The image of the niche blurred.

There, on the fringe of friendship, was Gaze! Gaze would be her reference in this place!

Mindsmiling, she brushed his mind-orb cluster in tenderness - and entered...

It was wrong!

This was a real 'other'!

She could feel real motion in this other's waterspace - hear airsnatching dolphins known in this place!

This was a real Bottlenose... with the mind of Gaze!?

Fixed in the fringe of this 'other' Gaze, curiosity stronger than apprehension, she dallied...

This Bottlenose was sleeping...

Quietly, she called the ping-pattern of her name in her mindmerging. If Gaze was there, he would reply...

She linked a little closer to the 'other'...

The mindlight cluster seemed so nearly the same... Could this be a cousin, or brother?

His Bottlenose limbs were larger - the muscle and flesh, a far firmer athleticism...

This 'other' was very strong...

From some level of sub-consciousness, she felt a stirring... like a growth of need... a hunger...?

She whispered the ping-pattern of her name, mindmerging her need of him...

Was Gaze here?

There was recognition of her presence!

She watched the incandescence of regrouping orb-lights at a level closer to consciousness, closer to herself...

'Gaze,' she called, quietly. 'Where are you?'

Briefly, there were flashes of red and white-heat in the 'other's' mind-cluster as if... Anger she had thought was there... was not...

Her Gaze was speaking! He was here!

Relieved, she heard... 'White Tip? You leap-linked the distance by yourself? Well-done! Come closer to my... this centre. I am here... my love.'

Joyfully, she moved in, between and within the circling brightness to find him...

His voice was the calm she needed... mind-clustering identical to memory...

She heard his voice... did not resist as tendrils of contact grew to lock her to himself...

Happy, she allowed the intertwining to tug her towards his warmth;

pleased in his tightness of mindlimbs about her...

'Gaze, my love,' she sighed in his embracing.

There was silence in the circle of warmth.

'Gaze?'

'Gaze is at the place you have left, White Tip...'

The mindvoice was different! It was... colder!

'He wallows near the steeprise you call 'Cato Island'.

You thought... he was here but he is not. That puzzles me.

I am his 'brother in spirit' shall we say. My name is Vorg.'

The colour of the mind-circle changed!

It was sharper, fiercer... more livid!

'You need to share more intimate knowledge of me... and I desire to come closer to you. You are welcome... if novel and unexpected.'

A harsh mind-chuckle struck discord in her heart...!

'Share my dreams, White Tip. But first, learn the ping-pattern of a different name... Yes, let us call you Starshine, a romantic Spinner who once desired your Gaze. Learn the ping-pattern of her name!'

White Tip struggled to escape - found herself locked in mind-chains utterly unbreakable!

In horror, she knew mortifying danger greater than any she had known possible! Where was the greyness? - the force of retraction to the safety of the steeprise across the horizon?

Her horror became a starkness which was now... and enduring!

'Ah, White Tip, little stranger Bottlenose with such a big heart! You waste time thinking of escape.'

Suddenly there were his images of a close and intimate touching... a deep and sickening fin-intrusion felt physically across her mind!

'You have fixed your reference, as Gaze has told you, here in the Podsherd... More I shall learn, later...'

Again came an intrusion... painfully penetrating... such sharp sickness that tore within! She mindscreamed, squirming!!

'You have some puzzling images in your mind... but you wake a need... Oh, yes...'

He was hurting her! She tried to reefside against the forcefulness... could not!

'Yes... there is time for sharing... some real images in dreams. You have a strong mind and this 'Cato Island' is... a beautiful place. Let me wear the face of Gaze in your dream... You can be the live mind and heart in mine...

'Learn the ping-pattern of Starshine's name!'

He tugged at her mind, distorting the shape - plagued her with images of suffering! She could not resist him!

Her last use of mindvoice was her screaming! It came from the junction of mind and heart...

'Gaze, help me! Voorrrgggg...!'

Powerful mind for a female, thought Vorg... enjoying...

Then she was another called Starshine mindmerging the pattern of... her name... her name... Hearing the stronger voice... Obeying...

'That's better, Starshine. Now let us play our game of hide and seek in the water-shadows of open sea. Do you see me here - or there? Do you care if the white-shape is a dolphin like me? Or am I a shark in disguise? It does not matter, my tender love. The moon is above and the stars to shine on our loving.

'Do you feel me within, wanting you? That's so nice... my supple sweetness. Do you feel our oneness?

'I caress you with my teeth... Do not think of the others to come... no, not yet... yes... Aaarrhhhhh... Ah, yes..!'

And white-shapes were shark-shapes and the mindsea red.

Unaware of White Tip's torment, encompassed within the spectral Splitfluke skull, Gaze fixed again to the dolphin-carving... clung grimly to jade, unhearing... unseeing...

The greyness lifted. He could stay barely moments... not long...

Rapidly, he left mindmerge messages for Ardent...

Squideyes in reefsides of friends, no longer deterred; served only as markers. They had to flee before turning to fight Vorg...

Gaze could recognise a time for killing; did not know how...

No Butting Pod could find or face such malignance magnified in murder... less, the distortions Vorg would achieve in quest for domination... his lustfulness...

Leaving only commands... residues of self within the niche...

he mind-grimaced, combating the force of retraction, weakening...

With fleeting urging, ripping past the known mindlights outside... he was finished... and gone...

Both eyes opened in horror! Mindscreaming pushed Ardent from an unnerving, despairing sleep. After-echoes of deep suffering were within the melon of his head... his dream...

He felt so cold in the cave's darkness...

Again there was the death... sharkfanning frenzy and... the rending of female dolphin-flesh!

Twice he had had the nightmare! But this second was... different?

Had he heard the ping-patterning name of his young master... and of Vorg!? Was Gaze safe?

Ardent finned rapidly to the niche at his entrance, beaknosed the jade carving and offered mindmerge...!

Within the lagoon, several of the Watcherguardians awoke simultaneously - none knowing clearly why. They woke others and finned surreptitiously towards the few friends on Guardian stations, puzzled, but sensing a need... to draw together... to face or flee a danger...?

Peen suddenly flukethrashed involuntarily, limb-jerked in strange discomfort! Her violent movements awoke the familypod.

Gale's mind, alert to the unusual, ascended to consciousness in quick mind-breach. Gape stared wide-eyed!

'Gale, something is wrong. Gaze is in danger. He is fighting hard to... to stay... to make us...' Peen said, in stumbling images.

Her mindmerge was insistent, confidential - but it made little sense to the Master Guardian.

She knew his mind.

'Gale, we're all in danger! I... I know it!'

Gale circumscanned the Podsherd.

The darkwater Guardians were patrolling as usual. Everything appeared normal...?

What was the strange clustering of dolphin dorsals on the fringe nearest the Storytellers' Caves? The Watcherguardians?

Gale felt a kind of impulsion to fin towards them... to gather together... Why?

Peen read his thoughts in mindlink. Companionship and love in the seasons made it easy...

'I don't understand either, my love, but... we must join them...

I feel it too,' she said. 'We fin quietly - now!'

And Gale recalled his son's imaging, in certainty, that his dam would know if something was wrong...

'Gape, we do as your dam requires. In this, she is the Master Guardian,' he said.

He beaksmiled, feeling less confident than he tried to look.

They finned and drifted towards the gathering Watchers...

Ardent withdrew from contact, felt change within...?

The squideye was gone from his reefside block! There was something else... He could read the flukingvector he would need to meet... a Bottlenose he had to meet... in a distant waterspace. Why did he know the name of a landmass rising to break surface from an underwater ridge? Why was it called 'Hunter Island'?

He heard the finningpassage of a dolphin in the maze... His heart beat faster! Who!?

Tinu ping-patterned his stacatto name, paused politely but shortly entered. He looked grave and perplexed.

'Old friend, the Watchers are podforming. They gather quietly, drifting... like controlled bubbles linking in one. I woke from... a bad dream, saw their finningpassages and came to ask you what... you know...'

Tinu stiffened. Finturning a beak-to-beak directness, he demanded, 'Ardent, where is the squideye in your reefsiding?'

Ardent fin-pointed abstractedly towards the niche as if he could not find images to convey understanding.

'I beaknosed the jade-carving. My squideye has gone. I only know it is important that all... 'all friends of a young Bottlenose, known in our hearts, must do the same'...'

Ardent had not finished... Tinu heard, like an order...

''Bring the friends and the podfamily, known in your heart, here. Let them, too, beaknose the jade'.'

Tinu found himself indecisive. He did not know what to do. It was seasons as a Guardian, and his faith in Gaze, that made up his mind.

A Storyteller had given an order - even though Ardent the Cleric was an unlikely source. This was his old friend...? Perhaps Gaze was behind this in some strange way...?

Tinu finned in obedience towards the waiting Watchers. Not one friend was missing - nor any of the podfamily.

It is as if they are waiting for me, Tinu thought.

He led them, co-operative ones and twos, to Ardent's cave-entrance.

Faithfully, the Cleric saw to everything else...

For Peen and Gaze to see Wanderer's Cave was a break with tradition. They knew it but no-one questioned Ardent. All felt in some awe as they finned above Wanderer's sandfloor signs - but all seemed in a kind of trance; remembered so little...

Gale and Tinu were discomfited by the break with tradition but Ardent was so firm in leadership - neither challenged... Beneath the benevolent overlay of apparent absent-mindedness was a new dolphin - one charged with a crisis mission over-riding everything else...

There was a pause. They heard his mindvoice seeming loud in authority in the smaller space...

'Two of you, untie the net holding the rocks there. Finning will be awkward in narrow places for a while. You will adopt line-ahead. Keep close and make no noise.'

The net fell to the sandfloor, spilling a few rocks. The surface splash was slight, the net already immersed.

'Follow me. When we emerge, Gale will lead our flukingvector in the seaspace. He will know our starting place from his memory. The... a Bottlenose we need to find... is many dolphinspans distant but we fluke as fast as we can.'

With that, he was gone... and so were they.

Later, Gape confessed to her dam that the second cave bore strange resemblance to a place in a horrid darkwater vision she had once had - when killer-whales had come close to the Podsherd.

Gape told her when the friendship-pod was hundreds of dolphinspans distant from the leap above a coral wall and a kelp curtain. Yes, it was a few darkwaters before... before a Bottlenose they loved had gone missing... Was it the same Bottlenose they were seeking now? What was his name?

She questioned Ardent but he wouldn't - or couldn't - tell her...

Peen knew.

She also knew she was the only dolphin there to know - and that she must keep his name only to herself, deep within her heart.

A dam does not forget the ping-patterning name of... a son...

Thus, Gaze sought to shield them from an enemy now.

Would Vorg notice their passing? He hoped Vorg had not discovered the secret entrance to Wanderer's Cave - that the absent-minded Ardent had not been quizzed too closely. Perhaps Vorg had been leaving such to his leisure? Gaze had tried to leave enough of his voice of command as a residue in the jade-carving to invest something new in old Ardent...

Vorg, however, was taking his leisure somewhere else! He was finning a blue lagoon wearing the face of Gaze pursuing White Tip... beak-scarring her flukes... imaging blindness to her eyes...

And she could not escape... never escape...

Vorg mind-chuckled a sweet new melody of madness.

One lightwater, he promised her, she would have flesh to put around her mind... they would play for real...

He took pleasure feeling White Tip or Starshine squirm and wriggle in the network of his mind-cluster. Who was who... didn't really matter...

Casually, he thought it nearly time for his dam's deep-dive... Blue Anemone had out-lived usefulness...

What if he held White Tip's mind in his dam's able flesh?... MMMmmm...

Gaze was back in 'Cato Island', dizzy in a red-haze of bloodflow... Dimly, he perceived a warmth beside him...

He dissolved the 'man-o-war' camouflage, knowing the circuiting podpartners would have dissolved already in his increasing energy debt. The jelly fish had been shimmering in a ghost-glow before disappearing. He had clung to the jade in the niche far too long...

At least White Tip was safe beside him, doze-drifting. He fin-touched her tenderly, ping-patterned his name...

There was no response. He offered mindmerge...!

A filament of mindenergy was arcing the distance from her mind-space. It began from her low-glow of diminished mind back towards...!

He recognised the vector! She had leapt to fix a reference in...

Nooo...!

In that moment, his mind flared in blue-glow! His grief sapped his last energy...

He knew of only one other dolphin capable of resisting the awesome force of retraction...

If his White Tip had leapt the distance to warmstream waterspace... Vorg had her!

Inexperienced, she would not have been able to stay long. She had dared the distance alone! He knew it... and she had expected to find himself...

Noting a mind-cluster bright in the Podsherd she had been unable to ignore the temptation to fix her reference within the Gaze she thought she perceived...

She had not continued the few dolphinspans to the image of the niche...

Intuition it might be in part, but he knew it surely in his heart!

Vorg had his love!

His sudden anguish from the centre of himself, echoed in empathy through the blue lagoon!

It startled crabs to shelter, gulls to flight and even the living coral seemed to cringe. His heart-rending did not travel far beyond the reefedge for his mindenergy was all but depleted.

It was sufficient to stop a mini-universe for an interval...

A shark-shape seemed to sink to shadow above sand, sharkfanning stealthily. Guilty, its conscience seemed troublesome. Tight-mawed, it hid its teeth...

A crab reached from behind a clam-shell to hide the cadaver of a half-eaten concubine...

The Moray Eel, out-reef and facing open-sea, retreated further within a rock cleft, reluctant with easy prey...

It was long moments before fish spiralling ceased and gulls began their glides to land...

Only slowly did his mind hue lose the tired blue-shade.

Then it took on a sharper, livid redness...

Gaze began to think like a killer, wallowing within waterspace adjacent to 'Hunter Ridge'...

He rested, dozed and patterned by the half-alive form of his Bottlenose mate...

Part of a sire's iron-will asserted itself.

White Tip was lost to him for now - perhaps for the rest of his life in the waterspace - but other dolphins depended upon him.

Vorg had to be faced, cave-trapped, if he could, and killed.

He could keep White Tip alive for a while... but he needed help. Perhaps the Spinners would help him?

When he had the energy to ask - he would.

That was one difference between Vorg and himself... Gaze had real friends he could call upon. Vorg bent others to his will...

What other differences, however slight, were there between them?

He had to best Vorg by power of mind for he would lose in any physical encounter...

For two whole lightwaters and half the third, Gaze tended to the needs of White Tip. He fished for her, half chewed her food, nudged open her dolphin-beak - partly by controlling those basic body functions deep within the cortex of herself; partly by physical force in lifting her head. All the while, she was silent... absent from now.

It was a little easier, in the second darkwater than in the first; the 'man-o'-war' did not ghost-shimmer and one podpartner could be constituted to fin the lagoon in the deep, mid-blackness...

...but in the first, energy debt allowed no luxury of a reflexive Guardian. He had finned as sentinel, alone...

Before sun-breach, in the false-glow of promise, Gaze was more tired than he had ever been...

He had finned tight repetitive semi-circles and he must have experienced a kind of self-hypnosis...

It had been somewhere between the borders of sleep and mechanical watchfulness that he had felt... had felt... had half-seen another... fluking a Guardian circuit... He had been grateful of the presence... whoever... the... white... the...

In sudden sun-breach, he had scanned for the stranger who had helped with no request, guilty in drowsiness...

Was there a white flukeflip in a foam of moaning surf-murmers in the lagoon entrance?

He felt the stranger had gone...

He had finned attendance to White Tip.

Now, in vertical sunlight of the third lightwater, Gaze felt strong enough to dare another distance. He needed help from friends...

Spinners, wide-eyed, wallowed as the ping-patterning came again!

The larger males and a few elders finned to podsherd fringe... Most could hear the pattern of Starshine's name! It was a persistent whispering from far flukingspans...!

It was unnerving...

Bluster, himself, felt a cold dread - the patterning sent shivers to fluketips...

Silence settled across questing long-snouts. Not one Spinner breached or twisted in joy... Orienting to source, they waited...

Bluster, as much to keep up appearances as anything else, finned a few spans out-herd...

He pinged his name; identified his herd... waited...

It was all Gaze needed! Fixing his reference to the isolated mindlight from herd-cluster, he entered Bluster's mind...

No Spinner was ever so possessed as Bluster then...! He heard the polite invitation to mindmerge from within the melon of his own head!

'Who speaks to me? Identify yourself!' he imagewaved, striving to project gruff aggressiveness.

The answer was a series of imagevisions within himself - proving, emphatically, contact most extraordinary.

There was no ping-patterning of a name now, but Bluster guessed the source of Spinner wonderment none-the-less...

Images within his melon spoke intimately of himself - Spinner sagas - of a kinship with Starshine, before her demise... This dolphin knew things which only one who had fluked with Spinners could know...

Bluster said, in mindmerge - sensing a strange affinity with the distant dolphin, 'Have our flukingvectors crossed before?'

'Yes, Bluster. Know me by a name that Starshine gave me. I am her little 'Bottlebeast'. You know I helped her once. You know as the leader of a herd knows - and notes - these things. Is that not so?'

Bluster knew him - felt flattered in the respect for his status. Would that pushing Spinners, nearer his age, afforded the same respect. When he was younger, he would have... A herd-leader was oft subjected to challenges by younger, fitter males of ambition... He was digressing... He felt only mildly surprised when his thoughts were read...

The friend of Starshine was saying, 'Then perhaps we may help each other again, Bluster. I need help to support an injured Bottlenose... or she... will deep-dive...'

Bluster heard his heart-plea in the hesitation. He was still young enough to respond!

Again, his mind was read - which was disconcerting... He strengthened his reefside, automatically...

'I am many dolphinspans distant, Bluster - at least half a lightwater's flukingpassage at speed. You are too important - have too many responsibilities to leave the podsherd for one Bottlenose. There are several Spinners who are younger and could help me. Will you help me as I have helped one of your own?'

This Bottlenose speaks like a leader in his own right, thought Bluster. Had Starshine's 'Bottlebeast' friend been large or small? He really couldn't remember. Perhaps it would be best not to take any chances. In any case, some lightwaters of rest without the bickering of a few he could mention would be a good thing, perhaps...?

The last mindreading was too uncanny to question!

'Exactly, Bluster. By all means send those. You may find a few return somewhat chastened. I understand the sort but I need their energy and spirit. May the White Dolphins bless you for your kinship.'

Suddenly, the leader of the Spinners knew exactly where to send assistance - flukingvectors had never been so clear. Equally, he knew exactly what to say and how to say it...

He is a special dolphin, he thought. You'd better watch yourself, Bluster my old flanker.

A regenerated leader faced the long-snouts of puzzled Spinners...

'Dart, Meridian, Equinox, Tumbleturn, Snout-twist - and you, Rayrender! Out-herd at flukespeed. Go!

'Move it, or by my flukes, you'll be finning out-herd stations for a full mooncycle!'

His tone - his bearing - his stature - were the younger Bluster. None questioned him. Too proud to flukequiver before him outwardly, they relearned their place in the heirarchy.

Fintouching each in turn, this new Bluster mindmerged all they needed to know. Strangely, each Spinner male looked at him with new reverence. They would not let him down...

In the early darkwater, the Spinners raced through the lagoon entrance, pleased at arrival in this new waterspace - even if it was in the shallows of reefmass. They preferred the open-sea - but it was a novel change. Their airflight twisting above the lagoon terminated abruptly...!

In lagoon centre was a huge Bottlenose, studying them gravely...

The Spinners finned quietly before him and spy-hopped.

'You are on a mission of mercy, Spinners. How would your leader, Bluster, view your conduct on arrival?' said a strong voice in mindmerge.

Long-snouts lowered in a line...

But the Bottlenose was not finished, 'You are supposed to be fine examples of dolphins of the open-sea but have not leapt into maturity. Your bodies are muscled - you show vigour in life but each head is that of a Nurseside flanker.

'Do I have mature Spinners here? Or do I have light-headed limpets clinging to flankerhood?'

So strong and certain was the mindvoice they heard, each snout lowered further...

'I wonder if it is worth meeting your minds,' the Bottlenose, paused... 'I can only hope your hearts are larger than the minds I have just seen. Flukefollow and attend me closely.'

Without a word, they formed dolphinline and finned to follow.

'Here is my mate. She lies still, hovering near the deep-dive. There is only one way I can help her.

'Come closer. Let each fintouch me now.'

A chastened podunit, they clustered about him, none noticing he was smaller than he appeared...

'I need the hearts I see that each has. I need mature minds. I offer you mindmerge...'

It did not take long...

Gaze did not need to give any further instruction. Their hearts were large in deed.

Rayrender - who Bluster felt 'was getting above himself' but Gaze recognised as the most capable - was the last to let his fin drop away. He spy-hopped and shook his snout. His eyes were misty. He was waiting to gather his imaging - needed to...

Finally, he said, 'It shall be as you ask Gaze. Believe us, we never knew. We shall care for White Tip for four vertical-sunlights. If you do not return, we shall ensure she takes the deep-dive. We understand the reasons. She must deep-dive... to end suffering.'

Rayrender had to ask the questions... Killing another dolphin was so alien to everything his light-heart wanted to believe and live by...

'How can a Bottlenose be so cruel to another? How can he kill without regret? This cruelty must be stopped - but can you kill, Gaze? Can you... vanquish him, anyway?'

Gaze surprised them.

'Answers to your questions, Rayrender, I have not yet found.'

He paused and they sensed him needing to leave...

His last imaging was, 'I know only this. I have a reason for finning this waterspace and as large a heart as yours, Rayrender. I do not know where the help is that I need in facing Vorg, but I fluke to find it.

'Spinners, thank you. In the fourth lightwater - expect my return, or not at all.'

They watched him fin underwater towards the entrance. He was out-reef quickly.

Rayrender said in open mindmerge, 'His heart is larger than mine, let alone his mind.'

Each Spinner finturned towards the wallowing White Tip whose airsnatching seemed so shallow and laboured...

They donned the mantles of protectiveness with a greater heavy-heartedness than they had known.

Vorg awakened sluggishly, both eyes opening to scan the Podsherd visually. His beaksmile was tight. Only a very astute dolphin would have seen the slightly leering quality.

Guardian now, his mustering was soon. He acknowledged comradely greetings, the awed simperings of those who ought to be senior in status but were not, in his estimation.

Soon Beak Spot would meet an unfortunate accident and how he would console the pretty Gape! But not before a delightful double experiment with Blue Anemone...

'Oh, yes, White Tip... My dam has the flesh to put around both your feelings. You will find it pleasureable,' he imagewaved - noting the mindsquirming within his own.

'You still struggle, my sweet? You miss your own flesh and harbour hopes of Gaze? Foolish female - he is too far away. I can remove his memory if you wish... Perhaps not, for it would alter your dreaming. Your pleasure can be mine and the pain is worth savouring,' he mindmerged sickeningly.

The silent mindscream within was an afterglow of his satisfaction. Wonderful!

'Enjoy your life while you can, my sweet. You have cause to be grateful. Gaze is, shall we say... too little experienced in matters of flesh-fervour. The shrimpcalf has no large appetite in comparison to mine. Really, I fail to understand his attraction to you. We surge in passion-waves so well together, do we not?'

He beak-gaped, mimicking the mindscream, casually scanning the Podsherd again - this time questing mindglows.

Something was different? Some Bottlenoses were missing from the clustering...!

Where was the Master Guardian, Gale - he who had spawned his only rival? Or Gape? Peen was missing! Where were the dorsals of the Watchers?

He scanned the Storytellers' Caves - one place in particular. Ardent? Where was Ardent? Or the watchful Tinu who kept a lonely station in the cave nearest the lagoon?

He turned within himself. Quartering, bisecting her captive mind, he examined every stored image, tugging at memory - distorting feeling. The only puzzling image was the same from the darkwater...

Ardent! He had been wondering about the old fool! There was something to do with Gaze in this!

He studied the image again...

A green dolphin-carving in a niche - within Ardent's cave entrance...! He recognised it vaguely from the lightwater of his appraisal!

Vorg dived. His finningpassage was direct and purposeful. There was no Tinu to block his entry. Unerringly he finned the maze. There was the niche; there, the green carving...

A captive mindlight saw the same, tried to reach with a thin filament...

'Poor sweet,' he said. 'This was the landing of your leap? It was just too far and you stumbled into me? No, you thought I was Gaze. Don't be disappointed. After all, you found someone better!'

He clamped her mindglow - swamped it in darkness...

Finning towards the niche, he blocked an anticipated image of a hidden squidbeak and tentacles and nudged the... she called it 'jade'?...

Immediately he withdrew! The Vision stored within startled him! No squideye - a skull! A Splitfluke skull, with empty eye-sockets had loomed momentarily...

A Vision - but that was all. He nudged the jade again. The same skull with emptiness, a blackness inside...

He knew. Gaze had been there but was not now... Unless that small whiteness finning like a dolphin far back in the skull was...

A sense of foreboding overwhelmed him... He withdrew from contact.

Had it been a warning to some small part of himself?

For just a moment two minds in the melon of his head had shuddered in fateful synchrony...

He reasserted himself. It was important to find Gaze before he was found. It was time to kill - time to make his dream of domination real and now!

How would he find him? The Watchers and the podfamily of his last obstacle had fled - but where? Vorg guessed enough of Gaze to under-stand he would try to protect his own in some far place. In puny opposition, he would try to interpose himself between Vorg and them. Vorg had but to flukefollow... But where?

A wriggle within gave a clue!

Gaze loved this captive of pleasure. She was linked to her own physical form beyond the horizon... and Gaze would not desert the captor of his heart! Gaze would be near the weakening White Tip... ceding to some mythical White Dolphins on her behalf!

The mind within his own was straining between now and retraction to herself... All he had to do was yield slightly - feel the force of retraction and flukefollow mindflow!

Beautiful! White Tip could do nothing but lead him to the place of killing!

There was a prolonged mindscreaming, so silent but so savoury in high-pitched quavering!

Vorg was a leer across the mindscape. It was time to be the Voyager he had desired. So many dreams and desires merging to one!

From the lagoon, it was much easier now to drift through lagoon entrance as seemingly innocent weed. Vorg noted Gannet's complete indifference.

233

Content in expanding mindpower, Vorg headed out-reef, towards the horizon in open-sea. Idly, he mindchortled at the undoubted consternation the Podsherd would experience at so many Bottlenoses going missing in such a short interval. Perhaps he could return later - the only survivor from an epic struggle in the deep-sea. It would be easy to convince the small-minds... and female gratitude might be worth it?

Away from any Observer - that was another Bottlenose missing, for he had not observed Crest Spray - he relaxed against the force of retraction a little and progressed at a leisurely rate to eat the flukingspans...

The flukingpassage would be long - but there was time.

Oh, yes, my sweet... there are darkwaters of time...

Gaze followed the forcelines of 'Hunter Island Ridge'.

Seaspace to right forefin was 'The South Fiji Basin', the deeper... He paused in patterning... He was using the Splitfluke names - could visualise the 'maps' of Mark the Navigator. There was an advantage.

Vorg had never seen the inside of Wanderer's Cave... did not know... but wait!

There was something else... Vorg had not shared the imaging of Splitfluke minds... knew little of killing in Splitfluke terms...!

Splitflukes were more aggressive, violent in fear... They used killing machines far outside the knowledge of any dolphin - were experts in murder!

Killing machines...? And Vorg had not read Splitfluke minds... might not be able to tune to...!

Did he have time? He dared not mindscan on vector front... Vorg would be following the fleeing friends by now, or using the force of retraction to beak-snout towards him. He could risk scanning across deep-water to right forefin...

Gaze ceded to the White Dolphins in his dilemma... reached out a filament of himself... By Wanderer, let one be close...!

In the third darkwater after Gaze had gone, Rayrender doubted that White Tip would still be airsnatching at sun-breach. He mindmerged his doubts to Snout-twist and was not surprised he felt the same.

'She is a carcass in all but shallow airsnatch. You have not failed Gaze,' Snout-twist said. 'She is all but deep-dived already. Sometimes I wonder at the point of it all. Do you realise how hard you have worked? How hard you have driven us? I can only hope it is worth it.'

They shook their long-snouts in the blackness...

Both were reluctant to let heart and mind dwell upon... that which had to be done at vertical sunlight.

Neither Equinox nor Meridian were sleeping. They gave no sign of hearing anything. They too were troubled by the dreaded images of holding the Bottlenose female down beneath the surface until she flooded her lungs. It looked like an inevitability.

Such was the time of their severest testing - the time their hearts were heaviest. Hope was an aridness, a drying desolation in a pitiless sun on the shores of reality.

Only slowly did Vorg sense that things were too easy. Yes, White Tip's trailing retraction would lead him to her real flesh - and Gaze - but would his rival realise and have time to prepare?

His enemy had as bright a mind as himself... It would not do to meet Gaze near any kind of reefmaze... He must draw Gaze into the open. There he would have full advantage of physical strength and agility for, in the end, it would come to butts and teeth...

Out of range of any echo-scanning certainty, he could see the fleeing mindlight cluster of the Watchers and Gale's podfamily...

Already he guessed probable vectors towards White Tip's wasting form - and his main protagonist. What Vorg needed was a location.... needed to see the bright mindlight and, hence, his foe...

Gaze was probably shielding a glow of mind in some way like Vorg. Yes, hider and hunter they approached... neither ready to show himself. Neither would attempt echo-location and nothing beyond short range mindskill for thus would advantage be surrendered. Vorg mindchuckled, convinced his wave-crest camouflage effective in its ordinariness.

Gaze would have to face him for White Tip would surely expire soon. Also, he had to distract any shark's cruising attention... Such a pity that Starshine had seen the sharkmaws so quickly. White Tip was seeing them regularly for Vorg liked her silent screaming...

The Watchers - the rest, were reducing flukespeed as if trying to find a last vector towards a destination.

It was vertical sunlight...

Surprising that a fog-bank had drifted much closer when there was little wind... Fog did not normally hang its shroud for so long in the lightwater...

Vorg knew where Gaze was!

Quite good shrimpcalf but not good enough. Both of us can do that! he thought.

He broad-beamed mindmerge through his own fog to that other fog-bank ahead, confident he was close enough and in open-sea.

'Another game of hide-and-seek, Gaze? I thought you'd guessed I'm expert at that. Starshine enjoyed a game before... well, should I say, before a greater thrill that your White Tip knows about now?'

Vorg leered across the silence...

'Lost for images or visions Gaze? Why don't you show your bright mind like any mature Bottlenose should?'

Still there was silence... but the fog-bank to his beak-front cleared a little.

It was enough for Vorg to see ghost-glow shimmering around a very large jelly-fish through the mist!

Vorg recognised the kind - stinging tentacles beneath...

His first instinct was avoidance but...

'Oh, better still Gaze. Unlucky. We both had the same Nursery training. We both know that your small phantom has a predator, don't we?'

The fog-banks were closer. Vorg played with mist into tentacles of streamers, feeling to intermingle with mist ahead.

Gaze spoke from somewhere else!... Beneath...?

'Wrong way, Vorg. Your mist tendrils cannot fix to my mind. We are sparring with Visions. You know as well as I that they cannot harm us. You need my fear to fix through a Vision. Neither I nor my 'man-o'-war' fear your mist.'

'Then what of this!' came a mindblast from Vorg.

Suddenly, a large turtle was making a striking-vector at the jelly fish. Immediately the 'man-o-war' was gone...

So was the turtle... The fog-banks rolled against each other... parted.

Vorg was enjoying the strange conflict. It was as good as a dream...

'What next Gaze? A killer-whale to be countered by a giant squid? Know more fear each time... and through it I will come closer...'

But was there something else within the mistiness...?

For the first time, Vorg pinged in echo-location. He detected Gaze immediately... and a hardside behind? So that was it! Gaze was trying to draw him towards the twistingfin of a hardside!

'Cunning little flanker. An unlikely weapon, Gaze. Very clumsy. Small-minded, indeed.'

On the point of strike-vectoring upon his prey now located, Vorg checked. Gaze was well clear of the hardside forewave...

The shoal of small squid rose unexpectedly between them. Vorg pinged again to verify reality or Vision.

There were numerous echo-returns from real not Visioned squid...

'A shoal, Vorg. My mind separated into each and too many for you to counter in Vision or reality alone. Make your striking-vector if you must but my mind will be all around you.'

Now what did he mean by that? Vorg, uncertain for the first and last time, located Gaze precisely and met the challenge...

He made striking-vector upon Gaze as a Sei Whale, fluking through preposterously small squid shapes, all the time, aiming his bottlebeak at the real victim. It was fast, furious... fantastic!

And there was Gaze, fluketurning in panic. He was utterly terrified!

In the turn, Vorg saw the chance of Butting the blow-hole of his enemy... It was too good to miss a disabling opportunity!

The juddering connection was pretty well on target!

Vorg sank his teeth in Gaze's flesh, twisting in separation to tear like a shark. It was triumph! He noted a feminine mindwail from the melon of his head.

...Perhaps it had been the sixth sense of which he boasted that had moved his feet towards the bow. He didn't know. There had been nothing from location equipment - nothing to see in the fog. Fog of all things!

Suddenly it had lifted. One moment he had not been able to see the creaming of foam around the prow - the next, it had been bright sunshine and there had been the big, fat Sei!

It was the most unusual shot he had ever made...

The Sei, moving at speed towards him, had appeared to judder to a halt and sink into the surface. He had fired... or something had made his hand move...

Watching the snaking rope had given him the same thrill!

When the explosive harpoon had detonated, he had not believed the evidence of his eyes...

One bloody dolphin ripped asunder and another, belly-up on the surface? What a bloody waste! How-the-hell was he going to live that one down?

They hadn't explosive harpoons to waste. There were less expensive ways to kill dolphins.

He'd told the skipper there was no point changing course two days ago. They'd argued and now it looked as though he, first harpooner, was in for a rough ride...

...Peen flukestopped, wide-eyed.

Gale guessed immediately, a strange veil lifting.

They all remembered, finturned...

There was nothing save the far distant hardside which had made a sudden noise...

Gale asked, 'Peen?'

She said nothing but she was fluking for the distant hardside - or towards just behind it. Hearing her mindscreaming he flukefollowed, her urgency infectious...

The others were quick to form pursuit...

...In the middle of the lagoon, the Spinners faced each other and looked deep into themselves. Each awaited another's mindvoice.

None seemed to have the imaging...

Finally, just after vertical sunlight, Meridian mindmerged openly.

'Rayrender, you have led us fairly and with understanding. We are all committed to Gaze in our faithful promise. We know our part in what must be done. Will you cede for her spirit and for our own?'

Rayrender floundered. In the face of awesome duty, he could find nothing to say...

In the sober silence, punctuated only by inrushing surf through the reef-opes, he said, haltingly...

'I have no imaging - only a heavier heart than I have known. This should have been a place of mercy for this Bottlenose to fluke free - a place of life, but it will be a shallow sea of death. If we could give breath to help her live, we would. There are forces beyond ourselves who deny her seajoys. What we must do is based in kinship and love - we all know that. We must... just hope the White Dolphins see our hearts in the parts we play. We know each other... we are brothers in spirit. Kinship must be our strength... in consoling one another.'

He despaired... 'I cannot find the imaging you need, Meridian...'
There were long moments of thoughtfulness...
Equinox mindmurmered, 'You just have, Rayrender. Thank you.'
He finned to grasp the forefin of the Bottlenose female in his long-snout. Without comment, the others took fin or fluketip.
Rayrender and Snout-twist stayed clear. They would follow the group down, press her against sandfloor until her lungs were flooded, freeing the other four to keep shark-stations.
Rayrender said, 'It is time.'
He ping-patterned her name... watched as four Spinners descended, tugging her down...
He dived with Snout-twist to press reluctant masses against her back... her powerless flukes...
Spontaneously, the four surface Spinners began the echo-lament... There were no females present yet they knew the patterning...
It seemed fitting...
...Through blood-red kelp curtains far back in his mind, blackness, below and behind...
No pointpricks of light... Nothing but blackness...
Deep blackness where he must go...
Away from red light to dark below...
It was time to know... to see the sea mystery...?
Pale glow...? Weak white...? Three shapes growing...?
A patterning of... a name he seemed to know...
The pain? Where was his pain? Did he feel it now... or had it always been there?
More speeding shapes sharkfanning the watery greyness... in a frenzy to a stained surface nearby...?
White dolphin shapes, ping-patterning a name... His name...?
The deep-dive already? The sharks were... for him?
A much louder ping-pattern he recognised...!
Starshine? And others... Cyrene sadly singing?
Pinging from others of warmstream waterspace?
A sense of being turned into air... Yes, he needed air...
He had to airsnatch!
Should he ping-pattern his name? What was his...?
A close white-shape ping-patterned his name... added her own...
Two others joined her... Cyrene... Yes, he knew her... Why was she so insistent? She was one, the other was... Wanderer...!? But his shape faded, was gone... Cyrene faded, pinging a happier song...
A white-shape fluked across a shark's striking-vector aimed at him!
He was in bloodflow!
He finturned towards the nearest landmass, still dazed. Flukethrashing weakly, he felt the other white-shape behind...
She was protective... His mind perceived a debt repaid by the White Dolphin female...

Not once did she come into full view but he knew her.

Twice, sharks veered from attack-vectors dissuaded by Starshine's fleet interceptions...

Gaze ping-patterned his name, joyfully! He patterned hers, acknowledging her in gratitude... but she was gone in breeze-blown surf...

Gale was there! And a mindsobbing Peen. The others came quickly.

So many names to remember...

White Tip!

Now was vertical-sunlight...? No! Not now, nnooo!!

They gathered to help him but he was unapproachable... pushing them back...

He tried the distance desperately, sputterflaring in dizziness...

Snout-twist felt it first... a weak flukethrash. He bore down harder, quashing the guilt-tremble deep within.

Rayrender felt the after-ripple through more solid flesh in her back.

The mindvoice was barely audible... They could have so easily missed it in the murmurming of aquamarine...

Rayrender was closer to the melon of her head...

'Gaze...? My love... we live...? We live...!'

He let himself ascend, mindurged Snout-twist to do the same!

His order to assist a dolphin to the surface was never so willingly obeyed - nor at such speed!

They would disobey the special dolphin they knew as Gaze!

This was a real time for Spinner celebration and five of them shook off mindtears in a welter of spray...

Rayrender stayed at her flank. She was weak still and he was determined not to let the strange Bottlenoses down...

There was guilt enough this lightwater. Joy was redoubled later when the pod of Bottlenoses fluked tiredly through the lagoon entrance with a wounded Gaze in their midst. The Spinners were not surprised at their coming. White-Tip had known of their approach long before Equinox had sensed their echo-returns from his out-reef station. How was any dolphin's guess.

Chapter Fourteen

AWARENESS AND MINDWEBBING

They separated from the faithful Spinners in deep waterspace with profound thanks. Rayrender would not learn of a surprising new command duty until Bluster told him...

In joyous passage, Ardent fluked bi-vector with Gaze. White Tip communed with his dam; Gape in close attendance. Gaze admired his sister's restraint of high spirits in recognition of White Tip's weakness. His sister grew faster in empathy now, he thought. Also, he perceived Peen donning the matriarchal mantle in ways far larger than sympathy or recognition of the pairing bond. Already, affection and trust deepened the relationship. Dam and mate seemed impelled towards a mutual junction of mind and heart...

Startled, Gaze recognised, for the first time, similarities of light-clustering within both minds... wondered if his dam, too, might have mindskill greater than she realised?

He was distracted by lateral sensing and Ardent's mindvoice.

From a host of questions, Ardent asked, 'Must we fear further Abominations in the warmstream, Gaze?'

There were long flukeintervals before he had his reply...

Gaze said, 'The seaspace is changed, Ardent. Our laws of harmony were constant only in older seas. We have changed nothing; Splitflukes alter the songs some dolphins sing, even the sea itself. Where there are Splitflukes, there is discord. They are the ultimate predators... perhaps, the unwitting source of some Abominations... but I have much to learn, much to pattern upon...

'Rare Splitflukes are capable of living in kinship with ourselves... but only so far as deep fear of an equal can be quashed ... an alien 'superiority' they dread...

'Abominations have existed on land as Splitfluke religion teaches. For some reason, perhaps due to Splitfluke discord or poisoning - or something darker still - Vorg... his sire... were different to dolphinkind... as are White Tip and me... What may be the cause, I do not yet understand...

'Splitflukes have teachings called 'chemistry'. They begin to fear disharmonies which 'pollute'... alter the whole worldspace. They have begun to dread 'pollution' as we do recent Abominations.'

Gaze seemed to be faltering but then Ardent heard, 'No, Ardent. My hesitations are because I have had little time to pattern upon things I have seen and encountered. There are contradictions between Splitfluke life and learning, and their faith and belief...

'Soon there will be welcome and needful rest...

'Maybe there are Abominations deep within every creaturekind... Maybe a changing seaspace has given a new Black Dolphin birth from an undersea of dark desires within our minds...

'I only know I do not yet understand. I do know I will need to be a Voyager again... a lightwater when, perhaps, a Splitfluke I... have come to respect... when this Splitfluke learns more herself. That may be seasons hence...'

Ardent tried to follow closely imaging in his young master, noted an emotional hesitancy - but was too polite to enquire. Guessing unstated affection, was it more?

Gale continued to set steady flukingpace, taking account of the two weaker dolphins, in the flukingpassage homeward. Trusting that Beak Spot would deputise as Master Guardian, he knew the heavy burden and that his deputy was not quite ready.

Crest Spray's utter confusion after learning the whole truth of Karg and Vorg - and his profound horror in two dolphins' cruelty and evil - had been evident to all. He had broken from the circling communion of minds, in the first darkwater, and finned towards a pensive watch station... Conditioned cynic, he had wrestled with his own patterning...

In sunbreach, before their homeward vectoring, it had been touching that he, older and more experienced, was the first to have brought fish-gifts to the new podmembers, Gaze and White Tip. It was done with a kind of reverence, almost worship...

Gaze had said carefully that 'they would not be treated in any way different from any other dolphin of the pod' - which served only to confirm marked respect in the practical Observer.

Seasoned, watchful in everything, Crest Spray's sense of appropriateness and awareness to unusual seadrift had felt the 'unexplained' in association with Gale's son. Knowing little with certainty until the astonished now, seasons of practical, reserved detachment from others had suddenly been challenged in a way which was a shock to his good old heart. But that heart responded to the courage, hope and love he saw in Gaze...

However 'different' Gaze or his young mate White Tip might be, there would be no other Bottlenose more ready to accept the young 'master' dolphin's orders - whether he was to be acknowledged 'leader' or not, he thought.

Crest Spray's sharp senses failed to note fleeting, white shapes abreast their flukingpassage as they closed known waterspace. A realist does not become a mystique within a few mooncycles...

Gale's anxieties concerning a diminished efficiency of Guardianship were not realised. In warmstream waterspace, he had expected no out-reef Observers and possible laxity in the reef and lagoon-entrance sentinels.

Pleased by the challenge pinging from an out-reef site rarely used, he identified himself gruffly and the names of his podpartners were added in glee...

With astonishing speed the whole Podsherd formed an avenue of reception. Joyclicks reverberated in heartfelt welcomes and there were not a few airleaps from the more unconstrained. Not one Bottlenose unaware of their arrival - or unprepared for celebration? thought Gale.

His son's beaksmile loomed... He knew.

'Then also know, sire, that Beak Spot behaved most wisely in your absence and others to whom he might have fluketurned for needful advice. Both he and Sinu the Inventor you have to thank for the continued safety and welfare of the Podsherd - and this without any thought of personal gain or interference from myself. They have formed just the kind of bond that has always existed between Ardent and Tinu.'

Gaze added, 'Tinu has still more cause to be proud of his Inventor son... and you have justification of your secret pride in a trained deputy. Yes, there was uncertainty... a certain unpreparedness of mind but there is nothing to fault in the way Beak Spot has been honest with himself and Sinu in seeking to plan for others' needs. They have maintained the Podsherd's cohesion and co-operation despite the inexplicable disappearances of so many key Bottlenoses.'

Gale asked, 'When did you know all this?'

'I guessed it would be so. I have not read minds until lightwater last. Do you not enjoy a surprise?' was the reply, and sire and son laughed in themselves at themselves, glad to be home...

Flab was there, faster than she used to fluke. Finwarp closed quickly... Peen observed the weight loss - guessed only half the reason. Flab had lost her large appetite for fish in concern for dolphins disappeared. Although party to the fraud of Gaze's earlier disappearance, she had known a weight of grief in departure this time in the inexplicable 'absences' of friends... Peen had not been there to share her confusion and sorrow.

Peen heard... 'Yes, Flab has worried - especially about you. But do not concern yourself. It seems we might have aided in her secret vow of 'not to eat as many fish'... And Finwarp looks impressed with the result, don't you think...?'

Peen found control of beaksmile difficult. Her son had matured rapidly these mooncycles...!

All knew contentment in reunion with the Podsherd...

Here was a dutifully respectful Beak Spot, not quite managing to hide his huge relief at their return - making formal report to the Master Guardian and stumbling in imaging, observing Gape finstirring provocatively... If Gale noticed, he made no comment.

Sinu mindmerged, 'I did not expect to have to be both minor guardian as well as Storyteller, my sire...'

And in pride, Tinu said, confidentially, 'But you were Bottlenose enough to rise to it, my son...'

Esu added, 'Don't voyage too far again, my sire, for my brother is louder than yourself giving commands to a wing muster! We heard, in confusion, on another wing!'

Their joyclicking laughter was but small part of the rejoining of all...

Greater was sobriety in late lightwater as the Podsherd, at insistence of Storyteller and Guardian alike, herded for formal communion of minds...

Most guessed matters of import on the breeze but none the extent nor the forms of revelation...

Few knew the narrator's name...

At first, none recognised... All were amazed at strength of imaging; sensed the urgency...

He told them of Abominations...! As much as he knew of dangers to dolphins in their malignance... but not everything. He made no mention of Karg and the despair of Cyrene, mindful of Frolic and Dapple still. Neither did he make mention of 'Australia' or Maeve... but he did imageline the dreadful end of Starshine... the power of Vorg as a Visioner...

At that point, mindmurmuring disbelief intruded. Some minds began to close against him - too many for him to monitor and hold all at once. Guardians finstirred restlessly fearing for control...

'Visioning is just Storyteller fancy!' said a dolphin in the assumed cloak of anonymity.

'No Bottlenose would be so cruel!' said another.

'Vorg would not do those things!' came a loud female mindvoice - which not a few males recognised. 'He was my son.

You are mistaken!'

Three Guardians began to fin purposefully towards the sources of disturbance.

'Wait!' came a command, and three pairs of puzzled fins were motionless.

Even Gale's faith in his son faltered. Surely, Gaze was attempting to be too honest... too open...?

A rapid mindwhisper said, 'Precious few Bottlenoses here have seen Visions... know of the terrors they can hold. It is more comfortable for most to believe in such as fiction.'

'Then show them, Gaze. Let them see the reality,' Gale insisted. 'Can you hope for understanding in any other way?'

'But then they would learn to fear the Visions,' came the reply... 'and in their fear is greater danger still. No, my sire. First we try a personal persuasion...'

Sensing a kind of victory, conscious of some support, Blue Anemone's mindvoice carried clearly... 'Who are you Bottlenose? Show yourself and prove your story of images against my son!'

She fluked for the centre of the communing herd, quite magnificent in outrage. Dolphins finned aside to make room for her display of false, dam pride. She thrived on the moment.

The eyes and senses of all sought the cloaked defamer... They all knew of Blue Anemone's caustic nature - had seen even Guardians embarrassed by her public mindmeet ridicule.

She finfaltered as Gale breached three dolphinspans from her...! Her silent self knew the unassuaged longing... More uncertain than she dared show, she wallowed momentarily... Masking her hunger for him, she was a mocking parody of injured innocence; felt herself drawn closer...

'You, Gale?' she asked in too sweet mindmeet - adding, in confidential mindmerge, suggestively, 'Perhaps we should be alone after all, to share... our imaging? I did not know...it was you.'

It had not been Gale's mindvoice...? She knew it. Who then, was Vorg's accuser...?

In utter silence, where only sea noise was the continuum, the Podsherd strained for Gale's answer...

'No, Blue Anemone. It is my own son you need to face.'

There was shocked mindwhispering, some quickly stifled beakclicks...

The melon and eyes of Gaze broke surface, waited... Then he was finning forward to touch her respectfully...

She had no opportunity to ridicule him - not with 'her Gale' so close.

Before she knew what to say, he was within her mind...

In moments of fretful quietness, he shared knowledge of her intimacy with a son, not judging, but reminding her of discomfort and later pain; her sense of violation and being used for pleasure in sickening images! The image constructs they had used that were... so real...

In such was the beginning of self-disgust...

He knew the identity of her son's sire! To her alone, he showed the sadism of both... The tragic ends of mutilated... unnamed females...!

It was almost enough, for Blue Anemone was not without pity - a sense of shame within superficiality.

He showed Visions a sire and son had used...!

The Podsherd were amazed to see her flukethrash wildly as if in extreme need of an escape-vector! They checked for...?

Young Gaze appeared to be doing nothing...?

She was still, heart rhythm tempoing to steadiness as... his mindlights changed through sorrowing hues...?

She realised he was... asking for forgiveness? Of her!?

And here was a conflict... The bloody end of a son...! A victor's wounds; near loss of a mate...?

A Bottlenose, the Podsherd recognised White Tip, was finning towards Blue Anemone and Gaze. Why?

They clustered, a near static trio. Still there was silence.

And Blue Anemone learned of stranger suffering still; torture to a dolphin's sanctity of spirit... A son's threat to her own life...! The manner of an envisioned ending...!!

It was enough!

Gaze had a dam's forgiveness.

Darkwater beneath moonglow was filled with her mindvoice, the echoes returning from great distance and depth! When had Blue Anemone used such intensity - had such range? thought the Podsherd.

The trio of Bottlenoses separated.

'He speaks the truth!' she imaged in mindmeet. 'My son was a Visioner! He deserved the sharks in his deep-diving!' She seemed... so certain? 'Vorg was like a shark himself!'

Amazed, they watched her pass to the fringe of the herd, fins and flukes barely controlled. She was churning within a turmoil of self. She wanted no dolphin's approach.

Before Bottlenoses had time for too much gossip-clicking, Gaze spoke again. They all heard the authority...

'Some among you credit not the power of Visioning still. Your doubt demands more. I must show you the strength of a Vision without causing your fear. Know, too, that my mate and I fear rejection of ourselves in consequence. The Podsherd has exiled Bottlenoses before, perhaps for lesser reasons...

'Be still, Bottlenoses all... Stay calm...'

The moment awaited the event... All were watchful...

'Now is sunbreach; new awareness... Be not afraid...'

Moongleam paled...! Horizon burned in orange glow...!

And here their minds saw the sun lifting incandescently above home waterspace, etching the wavetops!

Here was the warmstream light with greedy gulls wheeling airspace above in anticipation...

And the sounds of normality: swell-surge through cave and reef-maze; fluid pressure in foam against known barriers; gull screech, and a sighing breeze in fronds of trees...

A warning pinging from a Guardian as a small hardside was closing the entrance...!

But no call of danger...

Suddenly, new dolphins - Hump-backs? - fluking the small forewave... leading the hardside within the lagoon...

Some could not resist finning towards the new interest. Politer 'hosts' offered mindmerge with new arrivals - were amongst the first to suspect, to realise...

And suddenly a long-haired Splitfluke jump-entering the water... Her laugh-sounds magnetic, many were inquisitive;

finning in excitement to see and nudge...

Sudden darkwater! Bottlenose bumpnudging another and apologising reflexively... Bewildering distance between a friend and self... The first calls to podfamilies... Some echo-locating in disbelief... Slowly the realisation...!

The silence filled with awe...

'Yes, Bottlenoses. That is the conviction of a Vision.

A few finpairs of you realised quite quickly. Many more of you were lost in your own lagoon! And I have shown nothing in which to be afraid. I must teach you the differences between what is real and what is manipulation of fancy. Differences there are! There may come a time when your very life may depend on the knowledge - a time when you will need sufficient courage to master the terror some Visions can bring. I have to teach you much.

'You must learn for your own defence. We must fight any Abomination

- learn to recognise them. Fear not my mate and I for we seek only refuge with those we love, friends we hold dear... and time to unravel the differences between ourselves and others to hold in greater dread.'

Gale, Peen - all friends of Gaze - watched the Podsherd. Saw the struggle for direction; the search for consensus in... judgement of Gaze and mate. How would they react?

They knew Gaze to be good... White Tip, too... But...?

Of all dolphins to give the lead, it was she with public cause to hate him most!

Her finningpassage was slow yet purposeful, approaching Gaze directly but with unaccustomed humility.

Ardent was the first to guess the reason. The Cleric had seen Bottlenoses before face down darker sides of self in his quiet ministrations. He recognised her 'waywardness avowing better of self in greater care for concerns of others'...

But even he was surprised...

A confidential whisper said, 'Indeed Ardent, the ways of the White Dolphins and female hearts are strange...'

'I trust this young Bottlenose,' said Blue Anemone. 'I know he means no harm... harbours no ill-intent.'

Her fin touching his, she sensed his... gratitude?... and her redirected heart swelled with joy and pride...

In ones and twos, they did not express homage, although it seemed part of it, but acceptance of 'special dolphins', the son of Gale and Peen... his young mate from an 'elsewhere' podsherd origin...

Thus was his truth revealed in all but the harmful...

The greater truth was shown when Gaze - sometimes White Tip - communed individually with Bottlenose after Bottlenose, assessing strength in mindskill capacity, ever watchful for signs of other Abominations. Finally, to the relief of all, there were none apparent!

Such preliminary screening, although of immense relief, caused Gaze to pattern more deeply still. How had Karg, Vorg, White Tip and himself arisen to bring potential for discord and evil within the warmstream? The answers seemed to be out of beakgrasp, unattainable... but they had to continue the search, perhaps the fight...

How busy they all were as her son showed his discoveries! Peen had thought. Thus far, no change had been asked of the time honoured heirarchy or patterns of respectable behaviour. Bottlebeaks were heartened that he did not seek to bring power and status unto himself, respected known leaders or tradition. It was in exploring and assessing their powers of mind that they were most preoccupied.

A Bottlenose would be asked unexpectedly to report to the Storytellers' Caves to be met by Tinu and Ardent. After a short period, the beaksmiling 'unfortunate' would reappear and be led deeper within. No dolphin had found any experience discomfiting. Many had found strange and exciting things to see and nudge. Some talked in mysterious terms of

246

having been on a 'fast voyage' to 'somewhere else'. A few of these were able to describe fleeting sensations of 'a different motion' or 'a different form', whatever that might mean. A very few seemed to have sensed or seen more... but they were extremely tight-beaked about it and tended to be capable of exceptional reefsiding... Every Bottlenose was convinced that these short experiences were for the good of the Podsherd - so each dolphin co-operated. And then Ardent had sent for her!

Peen realised her son's - embarrassment? It reminded her of her own feelings of guilt in flankerhood when she had been discovered doing some daft thing out of sheer excitement or insatiable curiosity, close to an infection for all dolphins. Sometimes, beaknosiness assumed epidemic proportions for she had seen the whole Podsherd in abandoned pursuit of the minor and quite ridiculous...

White Tip's arrival seemed to shade the pink glaze in an area of his mind to normality... Her daughter-in-tradition was a calming influence upon her son, thought a proud and grateful dam.

He shook her again with knowledge of her minddrift...

'How should a son feel anything else but uncertainty, knowing a dam's earlier dread of his abnormality? White Tip is here for more than my reassurance...' He beaksmiled, a slow beginning to a broad gape. 'I have found the joy you know with my sire... in all its expression, all its need.'

Peen could not help her maternal beakbeaming.

In the broad good-humour of understanding, she felt the mild fluketugging of herself... mature understanding of her need for his sire...

No need of reply in such rapport.

As if prompted by her own imaging, he spoke in close mindmerge; so confidential she was sure that even White Tip was excluded...

'You have known of my distress, my pain and danger before any other, my dam. You told my sire it would be so... and you were proved correct. 'Rapport' is how you qualify this gift, continuing to believe in a mystical connection between a dam and a son rather than anything unique within yourself.'

Gaze paused and she sensed struggle for ordered imaging. At that moment, she understood the stress Storytellers spoke of when engaged in particularly difficult patterning... But what was he patterning?

'Yourself... myself, my dam... White Tip... I see similarities... Sense potential... Read probability... But, I cannot be sure of anything,' he said, carefully.

Peen found herself drawn reassuringly closer within the brightness of his mindlights... inexorably pulled deeper and deeper between incandescences of connections...

She surrendered self; was not disturbed, feeling no violation. He was radiance and warmth. Had she ever felt as secure with Gale?

Was there someone else...? In the dazzling brilliance of the clusters in Gaze's mind, was there a separate entity?

'Well done, my dam!' she heard him say.

Peen heard, 'I am here.'

White Tip's mindvoice was clearer than ever! And so startlingly close! The radiance dimmed and there was the recognised light-cluster of her son's flesh partner. She seemed so happy - like a young near-mature excitedly on the edge of self-discovery.

'That's what it feels like being with him'... and a strong image of a dolphin swimming the airspace like a gull raced through Peen's consciousness, coupled with White Tip's laugh-clicking.

Peen, soon to realise the significance of a contrived image in following events, heard Gaze...

'You may have mindskills which you have never identified within yourself... one skill may be emotionally based... an empathy which is heightened by your own feelings. There are other dolphins who... appear to share this mindskill.'

Again, hesitation or patterning? thought Peen.

'I have to do something which may shock you. That is why I am cautious. Remember that White Tip is with us. I want you to tell us what you observe. Do not be afraid for you are accompanied all the time... everywhere...'

What in the waterspace did he mean? thought Peen... and felt mind-hold tighten... by Gaze... and White Tip?

'You are safe, Peen,' mindwhispered White Tip. 'We are starting a small voyage... just like the gull I showed you. Tell me what you sense and feel.'

Suddenly there were twinned filaments of light redness racing, piercing a grey-gloom ahead...!

Peen was immobile between these mindlight extensions - enmeshed by Gaze and White Tip? - but speeding through voids of dully illumined waterspace? A sudden darkness... sense of water pressure? Slow movement... under weight of shallows?

There were three mind-clusters about her! She recognised Gaze and White Tip, felt relief... The third? The third was not her own...?

Peen did not see the absorption; the coalescence of their minds into weaker radiance from 'another'... Gaze called it 'fixing a reference' but she did not understand...

White Tip mindimaged, 'What do you sense, Peen? What is this new body telling you? Already you have felt pressure and guessed the shallows... but what else?'

...and Peen was shocked! She had more limbs! But... nothing she could move... no reassuring pushpressure for fin or fluke... She needed food, did not know how...? Legs...? And claws! This other was a crab!!

From Gaze came the whispered, 'But you are not alone...

Remember, my dam...'

It was as if he was fintouching to reassure her. She did not allow panic to overwhelm her.

'You are reacting like a Bottlenose within a different mind. This 'other' will continue existence unaware of our presence. Yes, feel the new body but can you detect anything from the mind?'

White Tip's mindvoice came, 'Typical, isn't it Peen? Male dolphins are always trying to rush us into things! Let your dam take her time, Gaze.'

It was followed by pleasant, but slightly suggestive laughquivers... which did as much to calm Peen down as any of her son's mindvoice imaging.

She tried to sense what she could...

There didn't seem much: a relentless scuttling of legs forever searching sustenance... periodic motionless searching for... danger? She could sense weak waterflow and these eyes seemed effective in dimglow now that her mindeye was adjusting to strangeness...

She was - 'they' were - within... something? What or... where was this place?

One claw seemed to scrape against a hardness which seemed odd. This crab could almost be a prisoner within whatever... And then, unbidden, came a kind of feeling that the place had seen occupation... by a dolphin before now...?

Peen felt overwhelmed by a sense of longing for company - could feel despair in solitude. She began to panic again!

'We are here Peen. You are safe.'

White Tip's mindvoice brought a second salvation. Peen tried hard to concentrate... not on the 'other', this crab, but... on the place...

It was sad and lonely... and not of the waterworld but meant for it...? A hardside! They had not been the first dolphin here...? Finwarp had hidden in a deep-dived hardside! And she knew... She knew, but did she guess it or feel it?

Peen was not alone in asking the last question. So began the 'pursuit of the red herring' for Gaze, which he might have recalled was in the teaching of an evil Karg. Peen had asked to go back to the Podsherd because 'she didn't like it in the hardside and wanted lightglow and company'...

They had left, Gaze perplexed. Did his dam possess sufficient mindskill for some accident of birth alone to be his basis of difference to others? Was there potential for a greater mindgift within her... or was it dam intuition to be respected and listened to... but not especially remarkable?

Or was there need still to voyage to seek some possible Splitfluke origin in 'chemistry' or 'pollution'?

Already, Gaze knew his sire's mind to be trained and methodical - almost the 'conditioning' which a distant Rick had placed so much importance upon, and which belied the true skills and abilities of the 'stars'. Yes, he would have to examine his sire further - as with all other Bottlenoses in continuing search and appraisal - but there seemed no answers to his patterning...

And his patterning would continue through lightwater and mooncycle...

In several mooncycles, growth in awareness of the few to whom it applied - very few and to varying degrees - was all but complete.

One or two Bottlenoses had small success mindscanning the waterspace over limited range. It had been Crest Spray who had performed best, surprising himself greatly. Perhaps it was all those darkwater periods as an out-reef sentinel that might have helped? Gaze said that he thought it was a bit more than that. Gale, too, seemed to have an 'awareness' of other minds and creatures within an area. It was not as developed as in the Observer but the skill was there, deeply latent. In Gale, nothing else seemed out of the ordinary...

A few Bottlenoses seemed to share an ability to sense the purpose behind an object; to sense past history in fleeting sensations. Peen was amongst these. So too was Dapple, Cyrene's dam! Fortunately, Frolic, the sire, had skillgifts only within character insight. Guardians were informed to discourage discretely any finningpassage by Dapple which was close to Wanderer's Cave - more emphatically, anywhere near to the recently discovered 'Entrance of Gaze'. No risk could be taken that she might discover, accidentally, evils resulting in a daughter's demise. Frolic could fluke unimpeded.

A greater number of the Podsherd seemed to know how other Bottlenoses might be feeling despite no obvious mindcontact. Now and then, Gaze would stumble upon fortuitous mindreading but explainable in terms of the empathy between friends or podfamily ties. In the ways of predators and prey, some could sense intent or whether another was aware of oneself...

Gape, his sister, was one of many with this kind of instinctive foreknowledge often knowing her brother's mood and general minddrift - but it was not remarkable...

In small podunits, they were all exposed to Visionary experience with the greatest care taken to ensure that the detectable signs were thoroughly learned. This would occur in a small cove, in open waterspace, at the reefangle, deep upon the shelfslope poised above the abyss - in as many known and strange localities as possible. The podunit would be within a cordon of Guardians who Gaze insisted should be in attendance 'to reassure and safeguard the Bottlenoses whilst otherwise engaged...'

They learned to look for signs of shimmering in the periphary of mindeye; never to look directly upon a suspected vision. Later, the best detectors learned not to look upon anything directly but from slightly obtuse mindpoints. As with all Bottlenoses (perhaps all creaturekind, thought Gaze), some were much better than others - and some hardly made any progress at all. Strongly emphasised was the hypnotic effect of direct Vision exposure - a mesmerising effect which slowed down thought and reactive ability...

The latter teaching was most clearly understood by a Guardian named Ebbstir. He had been one of the Guardians asked by Frolic 'to teach some trainees a lesson in a float passing game', a game in which Vorg had duped them all with a minor Vision...

Amused, Gaze heard in sudden mindmerge, 'So that's how the little sprat cheated! He starfished us! We didn't know our own heads from fins and flukes! We looked directly at his Vision float, kept looking at it and for it... We were blind and mesmerised... Sweet Wanderer, we were so flukeweighted - dumbstruck and slow!'

From that moment, 'starfished' became a new image in Dolphinese. Ebbstir became one of few Guardians to add to communication with a new image - a duty normally discharged by Storytellers who occasionally formalised image-slang into the respectable. Far more important to Gaze, he had found a most reliable Vision detector and someone who could aid in training others... which was set about immediately.

They were twelve Bottlenoses from the whole Podsherd, tried and screened by Gaze. He vectored the whole podunit to the shadowed side of the islandmass. It was there that for a whole mooncycle he taught and terrified and taught again.

A mixed minorherd of males and females, they experienced a strict regime of discipline which none dared or wanted to challenge. They knew their mindskills were being honed for the defence of all they loved - knew the need for absolute dedication of self to the common welfare... Gaze kept reinforcing their commitment to that aim. At times of weakening for an individual, it only needed small access to - they named it 'Gaze-recall' - for them all to know the need to prepare against evil.

There were periods of relaxation and joy; always a strong sense of harmonious congregation. For the most part, they were a tight mindweb of instinct, emotion and new awareness.

Within each was a contribution to the whole. An act of knowing or fearing was imaged reflexively in open mindmerge using the abbreviated short forms of images he taught them. But the movement of the podunit was much more than instinct -

more than event and reaction. They were monitoring, seeking, quantifying and qualifying... Measuring, judging, planning, responding, assessing, guaging... All with the new imaging's speed and the added skills he was teaching them to use...

He would leave them in dancing communion. They would know he was gone... know that he intended to terrify... was watching their cohesion... his mindeye open for weakness or inefficiency...

At first, he scattered them with furious assaults in which they knew panic!... forgetting everything...

Phantom sharks, orcas or giant squid would melt cohesion like ice under his external raging heat of blinding Visions!

They forgot to check for shimmershine... He would calm them, reassure and admonish... They learned, slowly...

Gale, Crest Spray, Ebbstir, Frolic and Mimic learned faster, aided by training in Guardianship. Widefin, a fish- herder by choice rather than a Guardian, was a little slower - as was Sinu the Inventor and Finwarp. The latter seemingly quite-at-sea away from the practical Flab, but Gaze knew the iron beneath. Slowest were Peen, Gape, the nervous Dapple and the even more fluketrembling Cornice, a recently mature female with an uncanny sense for imminent peril. She seemed to sense danger within waving weed fronds, around any rock or reefangle and was surprisingly accurate, Gaze had found. The fact that her nervous energy brought her to the point of flukefleeing at the first hint was her drawback...

Gaze had his greatest problems with Cornice... until he noticed the hovering presence of Mimic mesmerised by an older and, perhaps, stronger influence than...! All that was required were a few shared watchstations in the darkwater... Gaze did not have to whisper in the dreams of either. Each found greater stability and a new kind of magnetic influence strengthened the weakest part of the mindweb! Peen and Dapple both beaksmiled independently, remembering... Gape felt her loneliest and came to a decision - whatever her sire, dam or brother might say!

Towards the end of the necessary absence, mindscanning was so automatic for the 'Awareness Pod' - Gaze's joking name - as to be almost instinctive. They made the occasional mistake, sometimes in over-reaction or tardiness, but they were much better prepared. Above all, they were hardened in Vision exposure... There was an excellent chance that if the Podsherd was indecisive in terror of a Vision, the Awareness Pod would see through falsehood to reality, act in concert and, if necessary, fluketurn to fight...

A son mindmerged to his Master Guardian sire, 'It may be necessary to share your authority at some time. Inform the Guardians of mindweb existence. Bottlenoses of this awareness pod must have Storyteller' status. Sinu will inform the Storyteller heirarchy.'

Gale understood the reasons - had to beaksmile as he heard, 'It would appear that my dam and sister will have the same rank as yourself from now on. It is very hard to be a son or brother in a podfamily of such influential dolphins!'

...And Gale was proud to serve his son just as Peen had said he would be. He could feel the good-natured laughter of all the mindwebbed podpartners...

'Awareness Pod' was not adopted into Dolphinese; instead, the agreed concensus amongst the Storytellers for the purposes of the sagas was for 'mindweb', Ardent told Gaze. It was felt that the image was more illustrative...

Ardent asked, 'How did you conceive the idea for the mindmerge linking of key dolphins with various mindskills and the short-form images, Gaze?'

Gaze said, mysteriously, 'From a Splitfluke's sire, a 'banker', who uses a 'computer terminal', 'networked' with similar 'terminals'... but mindweb is better for realities of life in the waterspace...' Thus causing a bewildered Ardent much unanswered patterning in turn. He patterned that the 'computer' things did imaging and sensing for Splitflukes... implying subservience for which?...

Slightly maliciously, Gaze confirmed or denied nothing.

For several lightwaters, Gaze finned Wanderer's Cave, explaining his need to pattern upon many things. For once, the rule concerning females gaining entry within was relaxed and, occasionally, White Tip accompanied him. There seemed little point in objecting, Ardent pointed out in general. Wasn't she of Storyteller status now? Did not her mindskills far outreach those which Bottlenoses could normally achieve? As it was, there were no objections for White Tip was perceived as one who brought greater strength to Gaze himself. Surprised, other females noted that White Tip was to be seen finning mostly with Peen. Apparently, even his flesh-mate was a distraction he felt he could not afford whilst finning so pensively above Wanderer's sandfloor signs! Gossip-clickers began to mindvoice rumours as to why?

Why? thought Ardent... and asked her when perhaps a good Cleric should have bided longer.

'But I am never absent from him,' White Tip told Ardent. 'You have forgotten he is an image away.'

Ardent heard the accustomed mindwhisper he recognised,

'Ardent, dear friend, your questions can be distracting. Did you not realise it is also distracting for the mindweb?'

Suddenly there was Sinu's voice!

'Mindimaging, even certain feelings, passes quickly to us all, Ardent,' said Tinu's son. 'As Storyteller to Storyteller, let us all do the tasks to which we are assigned.'

And Ardent realised that the new mindweb had found the politest way possible to tell him to mind his own business!

Mindsmiling, Peen said, 'Gaze will tell you what you need to know later, dear Cleric.' She was there in moments to fin for a while in bi-vectoral companionship.

The mindlaughter of recognised Bottlenoses was something he could only join. Things were changing. He supposed that beaknosiness, however well-intended, was something to be held in check...

In early darkwater, it was Gale who came to escort Ardent to the gathering mindweb, out-reef of lagoon-entrance, away from Podsherd observation. They needed no sentinels. Only Gannet remained on entrance watch, extremely careful to remain unobtrusive sensing the Master Guardian close.

'Be part of this pod for some answers for now, Ardent. There is need, perhaps, for your sensitivity to the moods and fears of others... perhaps, later, a need to guide myself,' said Gaze, mysteriously and unexpectedly.

Ardent did not understand. New commands, terse and clipped, were given. He watched the rapid finstirring which formed a new alignment in a shape which was vaguely familiar. It was some moments before he realised quite what it was...

'Yes, Ardent. Here is a Splitfluke symbol of religion and power just like the cross you showed me at appraisal. Holding such fascination for you, it means so much more than any dolphin could have known. Splitflukes recognise the cross as meaning a wisdom and a love far greater than themselves.

'We believe the White Dolphins fin as intermediaries between ourselves and a greater Divinity. Splitflukes believe that Divinity sent his son into their landspace world but most did not recognise him. They killed him upon the cross. The few who believed kept his teachings alive in the sagas of their kind. There is similarity between such imaging and that of our revered Wanderer. Perhaps that is another reason for using the cross-shape in what is to pass...

'We have need of news concerning our dolphin cousins...

Spinners, Hump-backs and the Bottlenose 'stars' I have told you of. We need to reach beyond ourselves to learn and discover more... There are so many creaturekind - so many disharmonies. We cannot fin in contentment and ignore such suffering and injustice. To move closer to a Divinity of all the worldspace, many kinds of predators must learn the meaning of pity... There are other sorts of Abominations who make the darkwaters darker than death...

'We must learn a new positiveness... ways of reaching beyond our needs to the needs of others for then our fluking- passages will have greater purpose. In addition, I have to find a way of contacting other podsherds and other cousins to prepare against Abominations in elsewhere seaspaces. That is what we begin; I know not where it will end.'

Ardent said, 'A worldspace of despair and pain is too great for a Bottlenose to have any influence, Gaze. Such an earnest desire to help creaturekind, much less dolphinkind is beyond all save a Divinity of which you image. Your desire surely outflukes even your capacities.'

'Just so, Ardent. And your mindvoice is my foundation in reality. In such I need you. Censor and counsellor, you will seek to dissuade me from over-reaching myself if you feel the need. Uniquely, you and Tinu hold Wanderer's imaging in your hearts... but you have the greater sense of humility never realising the enormous stature this gives unto yourself. I fluke in need of your wisdom.'

Few Bottlenoses are given the chance to recognise the high point of life's leap. Ardent knew it then. There was no question of changing any facet of his old allegiance to Wanderer, seasons deep-dived... There was, quite simply, a magnification of commitment and dedication to the younger dolphin. The irony that he, of no especial mindskill ability, was given formal right to image from his own mind and heart concerning future actions by Gaze did not strike him until much later.

Ardent finned to his station in cross-shape alignment, knowing they were embarking upon strange contacts across wide openseas without having to be told. The mindweb partners simply adjusted to and absorbed his welcome presence...

He was not surprised to witness the loud and directional rehearsal of a ping-patterned name across the waterspace... only puzzled at how Rayrender could possibly reply?

'We are modelling this call upon Splitfluke 'radio', Ardent. Alone, we ping-pattern 'omnidirectionally' but skewed to beakfront. Aligned like this, we become a 'beam array' and, hopefully, increase our range and our 'receptive ability'.'

Ardent, almost regretting his half-formed question, said nothing... He flickslipped beneath the waves with the rest, holding orientation...

The ping-pattern built volume in repetitive chant-sing. There were moments of silence and the last call was made with such intensity that the darkening blackwaters of distance seemed certain to split apart! Red mindenergy impulsions, from Gaze and White Tip, seemed to accompany their pinging... Were they mindscanning within the call, wondered Ardent...?

In Spinner waterspace, Dart was finning his outstation circuit. He had just finsteered two near mature males back towards the herd. One of them, a bit too melon-headed for his season, had needed a sharp flukeslap to get him moving. With the greatest of pleasure, Dart heard Bluster and Rayrender giving the pair a thorough mindblasting. Longjaw, the melon-headed sprat, gave a sudden mindscreech as the joint leaders gave a fin each a sharp beaktug. That ought to reaffirm the dangers in seeking to fin outside the protective circuit!

Dart, beaksmiling in recall of younger lightwaters, heard old Bluster's mindvoice berate both juveniles. The leader of old could still make many flukeshiver in embarrassment and guilt. Then came Rayrender's voice, pointedly reminding the pair that they could be beaks on to sharks who wouldn't be so polite as to remind them with some fin-nips before twisting chew-chunks from their sides.

The two miscreants were quailing visibly before the assault.

Dart warmed to hear the next mindmeet imaging, felt too the justified mild criticism of himself, knowing a minor watch duty failure. He had allowed himself to be distracted for too long...

'Dart has finned in obedience to a special dolphin, one greater than any here. If you think he, an experienced and careful sentinel, has time to be distracted by empty-headed and over-excited sprats then perhaps we should just point you towards the nearest shark vectors!

'Report to a Nursery Dam in the lightwater. Perhaps she will have tasks more suited to your calf-brains. Be assured I will check on you. For now, fin off to your dams who will be worried by your absences,' said an extremely stern Rayrender, through teeth looking so dangerously sharp.

Every Spinner who overheard, and there were not many who didn't, knew the reality behind the imaging. Silence settled between nervously finstirring spectators, serving to heighten the embarrassment for Longjaw and friend...

Dart felt the eyes of Rayrender and Bluster, knew he was required to give sign of his own understanding... He raised longsnout and beakclicked twice; resumed the sentinel circuit.

There was no need of further dialogue. Sentinel duty was demanding in needful concentration - they all knew it.

The silence did not die. It hung above, floated between and drifted below the Spinner herd.

Such was a measure of the discipline imposed by the joint leaders. No one was surprised by Rayrender's sudden elevation in status. The herd was benefiting from Bluster's experience and Rayrender's leadership. Unique as it might be for two Spinners to have equal senior status, the herd had greater cohesion. Bluster was realising a long felt need for a confidant without fear of ridicule; Rayrender was learning the arts of leadership with closer support than he might have had. Dart knew the arrangement. As with all Spinner males, he was finding it agreeably acceptable...

A confusion of whispering ping-patterning passed below the herd.

Several longsnouts stirred restlessly. Dart stopped finning, waited.

It was almost as if dolphins were calling from far flukingspans, trying to attract attention...

The singing pinging came again, a little stronger, almost decipherable. Dart finstirred to bring the dome of his head in concurrence with and to confirm the songline...

Dolphins were calling a name he knew well!

Twice he flukeslapped surface, the slapcracks reaching Rayrender, already puzzling the strange whisper pinging...

Rayrender fluked for the sentinel circuit - came at speed to Dart.

'Your name!' mindmerged Dart.

They waited, already guessing the strangeness.

Sudden strength of echo-call was confirmation!

Together they pinged acknowledgement, feeling slightly stupid. How could they hope to span the wide seaspace to the echo-call origins?

'Your answer was all we needed, Rayrender... And Dart as well. That is good.'

The mindvoice was from within themselves!

Both Spinners were not as shocked as might be supposed - had to beaksmile as White Tip's mindvoice echoed in mindmerge conflux...

'My! Dart, what a sensible and strong dolphin you have become! If I hadn't my Gaze, I could fluke the moonglow with such a lovely Spinner as you. MMmmm...'

Dart's mindlight shaded pinker but his joy in contact outshone all else - save that within his friend and leader.

Rayrender mindimaged mock-threats... What did Gaze suppose he was doing 'arranging' the unexpected elevation of an unworthy Spinner to a position of leadership? Such things flew in the face of sea-tradition!

He said, 'Now I can't give Bluster a few butts to make up for the many he gave me!' He added, seriously, 'Thank you, Gaze. Have you need of 'some light-headed limpets' again?'

'Conduct yourself as I see you have been, Rayrender, and no dolphin will outdo your dedication to duty - few will lead half as well. Deserving of recognition, you have it. You understand the strain leadership has

256

imposed upon Bluster and I note you count him now as friend and counsellor. That is good...

'I need you again, my cousin, but in a different way... Rayrender, please assemble those Spinners to whom I am most indebted. Bluster, too. Replace Dart on sentinel circuit. There is something for you to learn... something to spread and share with elsewhere podsherds. In this you help me - perhaps all dolphinkind.'

'It may take a little time,' said Rayrender.

'We understand,' came a feminine mindvoice. 'This time, Gaze and I are protected by a pod of Bottlenoses more prepared to face the unexpected than any dolphins have ever been... We'll stay close to yourselves and Dart really doesn't mind... do you dear?'

Her mindgiggling was infectious but an added spur.

Spinners, whom Gaze needed, podded together remarkably quickly...

In warmstream waterspace, the cross-shape alignment broke apart. Crest Spray fluked bi-vector with Gale further away from the reef. Mimic and Cornice finned thirty dolphinspans to one side of lagoon entrance; Finwarp and Dazzle moved to the other side the same distance. Frolic and Ebbstir began the recogniseable Guardian circuit whilst Widefin and Sinu made successive passes beneath the remaining Bottlenoses. The whole series of fluking movements was so perfectly precise that it was spellbinding.

It took Ardent several moments to catch up with events.

He guessed that Peen, Gape and himself were to watch over the fin-drifting forms of Gape and White Tip, both of whom seemed to be finning tight reflexive circles. He wanted to know what was happening; asked Peen.

'Gaze can't answer, Ardent. He is here but somewhere else... and so is White Tip. They are safe. If it were not so, the mindweb would feel the gaps. I know it is puzzling and I cannot explain what they are doing and how it is done. The mindweb knows it is very important,' came Peen's voice and he felt her fintouch in reassurance.

Later, finning bi-vector on Gaze, Ardent looked directly eye in eye. The phospherescence within eye centre of his young master seemed a diminished intensity. Waiting until he felt he was unobserved, Ardent touched briefly fin to fin. There seemed no sign of awareness in Gaze. Was he well?

Sinu's air-leap was so startlingly close that Ardent felt the swash of his breach-wave as a physical slap!

'In Wanderer's name, Ardent, stay clear of Gaze and White Tip! You just touched Gaze and nearly caused mindweb partners to attack you!' mindblasted the Inventor.

Gape and Peen surfaced! For a fleeting moment, Ardent was transfixed by the sight of Gape's teeth! Her eye centre was very wide. He realised, intuitively, that Sinu must have intercepted to turn Gape's striking-vector! There could have been only one target... himself!

Ardent is learning about the mindweb painfully slowly, thought Sinu.

Mindmumbling, the Cleric whispered, 'I'm sorry. Gaze didn't look quite right. I wondered...' Mindvoice trailing away, he was grateful of the Inventor's mindmerging presence.

Sinu said to dam and sister, 'Ardent was inquisitive, worried for Gaze. He doesn't understand how closely linked we all are, even Gaze and White Tip in their mind-separation. I think he's learned a lesson, Gape. Your anxiety is needless, Peen.'

Ardent felt Sinu's stern look rather than seeing it.

He felt Peen's fintouch again... heard her in mindmerge...

'Oh, Ardent, you did frighten me!'

Pausing lengthily, she added, 'There again, the mindweb could just have been tested by my son again... We were all scanning near distance and beyond... Perhaps, Gape, we have relearned why Gaze insisted that we concentrate watchkeeping in the close proximity...'

Sinu beaknodded thoughtfully... joined Wide-fin beneath.

Gape's maw relaxed to a beakgrin. She couldn't help herself; needed the humour...

She mindmerged, 'I wonder what Cleric flesh tastes like?'

Ardent decided it was safer to say nothing and was careful to keep at least two dolphinspans away from the central figures of new awareness...

The mindweb soothed and settled itself and waited in continuing watchfulness...

Chapter Fifteen

LIFE CHANCES AND BETTER ODDS

Ciaran paused in the boring process of archiving and dumping data from the quarterly record of share dealing. True, he could have delegated the task long ago but he liked to keep close to the perpetual process of buying fortunes and selling broken dreams.

Popular demand, political legerdemain, obsolescence, innovation or plain bad luck affected the market. Tasked to pick up signals preceding triumphant profit or defeated loss, he recommended buying or selling the Bank's share holdings.

He missed some indicators, made the occasional 'wrong' choice, but steady application of 'safety first principles' in research and appraisal had swelled the percentage of reserves he husbanded. 'Husbanded' caused him deeper introversion.

Judgement respected, he was admired for objectivity in monitoring the market. Making no enemies, non-involvement in the frenetic scurrying of dealer and broker made no friends. He supposed a material world viewed him as successful and sound. Weathering divorce, he was conscious that colleagues felt he had been more than fair to an ex-wife. Hadn't he ensured that the lion's share invested within the bricks and mortar of a marriage went to... the lioness? Friendship for him now, a male of middle years, nodded across the canteen or half-smiled from a passing car. Old 'friends' maintained distance, shunned his solitude, apprehensive his contagion might infect their own comforts in companionship.

He missed the beach-house at Redland - the sound of sea surge, the wind sighing or raging in the night. He missed domestic challenge and purpose - could not feel whole in his well-appointed office. Clambering between the cold covers of the double bed he had had no real reason to purchase still seemed abnormal.

Damn it! He missed her! He could see some reasons why it had happened - oversights and blinkered ignorance which magnified in time to colossal diversion and separation of selves. Too late now to forgive himself or Deirdre.

Ciaran remembered Deirdre's wan smile as she had driven away after the meal shared with Maeve and Phil. Safer to talk to the youngsters in their obvious excitement, there had been nothing of small-talk between themselves. Joining, rejoining University days away, there had been abundant opportunity in dialogue without coming close to wounds and scars for Maeve's parents. Parting with her old-acquaintance smile, the rear lights of Deirdre's car had passed down a short drive between the beech hedges, leaving the shadows deeper. Maeve and Phil had driven back to the Dolphinarium; solitude had sat in his passenger seat on the way back to the flat.

Soon, Maeve and Phil would be coming home; the end of their second term was very near. This vacation Maeve intended to spend time with him, having spent the previous one with Deirdre. It was about time he tidied up his...

'Home' - huh! It seemed a lifeline for himself was strung across an artificial lagoon in Brisbane Dolphinarium. Such was a place of neutrality - and an opportune friendship. Ciaran found some solace in meeting Rick there. At first, it had been a decision 'to keep in touch' with people who had somehow become of central importance. Then 'home' had moved across the city away from the flat.

Ciaran had found himself stopping by 'The Red Bottlenose' on occasion... and again. Less to do with need of a drink; more to do with walking across the grass to 'just say hello'.

But Rick had been too worldly wise not to understand craving for human contact. In the ways of men of solitude, Rick had understood... and found consolation in companionship himself?

Despite mood, Ciaran half-smiled. The reflection of his face on the monitor mockingly agreed that there was nothing else to do for the day. Cancelling the program, he accessed another which was hard to keep from mind. He needed to do some things before meeting Rick for their 'real business'.

Another routine had established itself. Ciaran tapped the keyword 'Dolphin'. Practised fingers brought his new other-interest to life. He was careful not to use bank time; vocational dedication to his Lord High Finance demanded it. The monitor glitzed jiggery-pokery and the accounts for the Dolphinarium showed up. There were only a few entries to make and it did not take long. He would take the weekly summary over with him.

Perhaps it was time Rick had a word processor himself - and an accounts' package? The Dolphinarium could afford its own paper, too. Yes, the whole concern was becoming a lot more profitable, thought the Banker - and then deliberately removed that 'financial hat'. This was one enterprise where profit was going to be used for the real 'stars'!

There was a wholesome breadth of smile beaming back from the screen in front... as if the monitor was enjoying things. He remembered, good humouredly, his discomfort when Rick had said quite bluntly...

'If you think this place is only about entertaining and making profit, you can take my whiskey bottle you're toying with and ram it straight up your arse. No, not yet. Pass it over here and give me another shot first.'

Pushing across the bottle, Ciaran had waited.

Rick had assembled thoughts and insights. Coming out in a rush, Ciaran had been caught up and swept along in a current of wild enthusiasm which had seemed more than the 'whiskey chatter' it was. That was the first night he had slept on the three-master. Two days later, he had brought sufficient clothes and toiletries, wary of another bout with the bottle. But that was just the excuse. He couldn't recall the pair of them hitting the bottle hard again. Only later did it dawn on him that Rick had planned that first and only time he had gone to the Bank with a hangover.

Starting out as an Irish remedy for sickness of spirit, they had breezed around the notions of outrageous ventures - having yet to agree on how best to use the windfalls...

Ciaran wondered what Maeve and Phil would make of the weird alterations at one end of the old dry-dock. Such had seen him taking a few days off work to help in erection and fitting out. The fact that Ciaran had used some of his own savings to help start the project spoke volumes for the gifts of Blarney bequeathed by Rick's ancestry - but then both men shared something of Irish descent. Perhaps that was why they found the racing and sport so enthralling?

What was utterly amazing was how the dolphins seemed to be so prepared for things - the ways they adapted to required variations in Rick's showmanship! Well, it was either Rick or his younger son, Rod. It didn't seem to take very long for either to be able to shape behavioural response.

More astonishing, once a breakthrough was made with one dolphin of either species, one could almost guarantee that all the rest would get the message!

'Well, it's obvious, isn't it?' Rick had said when asked.

'They bloody well teach each other. Cetaceans are intelligent mammals and they have their own ways of spreading the word. Once they get the idea there's something in it for them, they co-operate and pass the message! Come on, Ciaran, you've seen enough of what's been happening to face that truth, haven't you?'

He began to consider the evening's problem. What to do with the profit from their escapades in the Dolphinarium? The evening would probably stretch into the night hours.

Keying 'Starspor', Ciaran accessed the separate account figures for their joint scheme. Already the total stood in four numerals before the dot! And that was after having paid himself back for buying and equipping the 'Tote-Office' shed! It seemed 'Ord Aussie' was very happy to bet on the outcome of the water-polo between 'Hump-back' and 'Bottlenose' and steady income accrued from letting the kids get towed around the lagoon in what they called 'Tug Races'.

Very careful to stay within the gaming laws, the Tote took only a small percentage. Nevertheless, the income had been steady. Strangely, what Ciaran had feared might happen had not. He had expected the fastest dolphins or the best team to be quickly spotted by discerning punters - but no 'predictable' or 'reliable certainties' had emerged. Despite the know-all tipsters that abounded, events had produced a genuine 'lottery'.

The oddest things sometimes happened in the 'Tug Races'. He recalled the fat girl he had seen towed rapidly to victory when most had wagered on the lightest lad. Her sheer joy in waddle-wiggling up the steps had touched not a few mums and dads. One could almost have suspected some kind of dolphin conspiracy.

Then there was the time the cerebral palsied boy, a leg in a caliper, was put down for a 'dead cert' winner by a crowd who really believed in dolphins sensing human needs. For a time, it looked as though there might be something in that for the lad was first around the buoy marker at half-way. No, he ended up third out of seven starters. If the dolphins were out-guessing the crowd, the Tote was doing pretty well!

And that was another bit of awkwardness that would pose a little difficulty soon - the Tote-Office decoration. When Maeve got back, how was she going to react to Rick setting about her peculiarly placed advertising sign with that small electric saw?

When the shed had been erected and weather-proofed, it had looked a bit bald and uninviting. Both of them had pondered how it could be 'brightened up'.

Rick had said, 'Right, got it! The thing was always in the wrong place anyway. She won't like it but I am still the Manager around here.'

Rod had been despatched for claw hammer, pinchers and jemmy and the wooden tower near the lock-gates had disappeared speedily.

Staring at the huge pair of dolphins - one Hump-back, the other Bottlenose - and a stridently yellow sun, Rick's profane criticism of Maeve's artistry centred only upon the latter.

'Your daughter paints dolphins better than I've ever seen but to lock them up in perpetual proximity to that ******* sun was an insanity! She hasn't too much idea of a good location for advertising either. God alone knows why I let them talk me into building the tower. Well, I promised these 'beauts' I'd cut them free one day - so it might as well be now!'

With that, the saw had gone to work and, shortly after, the panels to either side of the Tote-shed window had looked very much better. The sun had been burned in a more realistic fire - whether Maeve might object or not. Ciaran could only smile at what he sensed was a Manager's reassertion of self, admitting that the relocated advertising was functionally appropriate - but wondering how the artist might feel. Artists and art-lovers were unpredictable.

Ciaran looked at his watch - which another artist had bought him. The previous mood started to flood back but he dammed the flow.

It was time to go and see Rick. He packed up to leave, not for a moment anticipating more than a long evening of convivial argument.

'I think that's his car. Are you sure you can face meeting him more often?' Rick asked her.

He watched her tired eyes turn inwards - was surprised at the certainty of the reply.

'We're all past being pink-cheeked cherubs, Rick. We were man and wife, father and mother for a long time. You learn how to win and lose in the card game without having to draw a gun like some of life's cowboys. It all depends on how Ciaran thinks and reacts, doesn't it?'

Then she wasn't so sure. He watched an indecisive hand straying towards a bag - the fingers upon a coat lapel.

He kept quiet; moved towards the kettle. Tyres crunched gravel outside. Engine noise stopped. The car door opened. There was no slam.

He's seen her car, Rick thought.

They both knew that he would either drive away or climb the short companionway.

The car door slammed. The engine did not restart. Slow footsteps.

Rick, grateful of a sizzling kettle in silence, decided to surrender the escape route. He pointed to the mug rack.

She nodded, rose as he moved quickly to face a friend on deck.

'Bring it up, Deirdre. We'll have a coffee up there before we start bargaining with the unofficial treasurer. Avoid being specific. 'Moneybags' worries about spending.'

Ciaran was looking out to sea; didn't turn as Rick walked to his side.

They both saw Rod standing near the site of the old tower where he had been levelling and raking patches of new topsoil. His son appeared to be looking intently towards - something much closer than distant vessels?

'Deirdre's here then, Rick.'

The tone was factual - gave nothing away.

'Yes. It's more than just a social call. I asked her to come.'

Ciaran wrapped thought around that - asked, 'What are you up to?'

Yes, he could take the straightforward answer. It was the truth anyway, thought Rick.

'She's got some skills I want to use. I'm going to have the dry-dock redecorateded - give it a facelift. Maybe other things, too. If I went somewhere else it would cost a bomb.

No, I didn't tell you about contacting her but she's preparing sketches for next time. I'm surprised, you being yourself, that you didn't see her potential for earning dosh in her own right long ago. She could have some good ideas.'

Pausing meaningfully, he added, 'I'm too old to be a sentimentalist - or a match-maker.'

A pair of half-smiling eyes turned towards Rick. There was no clue as to how deep meaning might have gone.

Those eyes read him. Ciaran took several moments to digest everything before answering.

'You - not a sentimentalist! I'll bring a tape recorder so that you can hear yourself when you've had a few drinks.

Alright, Rick I hear you. I'll look 'n listen. Incidentally, I haven't forgotten who is Manager around here.'

The friendship deepened with Rick realising just how good Ciaran probably was in unravelling personalities from within financial knots. He still hadn't a clue, though, how the man really felt about Deirdre. Did he keep those feelings in a double-locked, safe-deposit box?

Ciaran clapped a hand to Rick's shoulder. It was a brief slap, more of decision than confirmation of friendship.

Both men smiled and then two things happened quickly. They could hear Deirdre bustling before the climb up from below - just prior to Rod shouting urgently!

'Pop! Ciaran! Quick - over here!'

Deirdre found herself saying, as cheerfully as she could, that she had made some sandwiches - to an empty deck.

Both men were running the short distance towards Rod.

There didn't appear to be anything of grave importance.

She sat down, hands busy automatically placing plates on tops of mugs.

She wondered when the last time was that she had seen Ciaran running excitedly. When was he ever excited?

Rod was pointing towards the bay, his angle of arm indicating an area close in. Both men prepared themselves for anything. Capsized dinghy? Floating corpse?

There was nothing unusual. The surface was clear of flotsam. What was the cause for excitement?

'What is it, son? You've got me expecting to see the water on fire!'

'Wait a bit, Pop. They'll do it again, I think.'

Rick's eyebrows raised and dropped in a glance towards Ciaran. The apology and puzzlement did not need verbalising. They stood watching rise and fall of water, the older men's pulses slowing.

For Rod, the moments of unexplained waiting became an embarrassment. He knew what he had seen. How could he start to explain it?

'Okay, son. I give in. What did you see? Somebody swimming in a birthday suit around here?'

'Give it just a bit longer.'

Rod's face was flushed, Ciaran noted. The lad was practical and down-to-earth normally.

He nudged Rick with a knee and tilted his right hand, back uppermost, whilst not allowing it to move very far from his thigh, signalling the universal 'Hang on a bit'.

Both men, breathing steadier, made the connection that they were waiting for dolphins to surface.

So what could be so remarkable about dolphin behaviour that they hadn't already seen?

The surface punctured slowly with dorsals. They were perfectly aligned with the lock-gates of the Dolphinarium but remarkably stationary. Apart from six dorsals, three on each side of an extended line of slowly bobbing, almost triangular shapes, no other fin, fluke or snout was visible. Neither did spacing appear to change. It was almost as if a cross of thorny wood was part submerged in front of them!

Then there was movement - but nothing like Rick had ever seen.

In precision of purpose, dorsals turned about to realign in an easterly direction. Six at the sides moved backwards, little by little - until appropriate concensus seemed agreed? A new cross - a perfect crucifix -

was aligned with distant ocean across the bay!

The dorsals slid slowly beneath. The surface rose and fell as if nothing had happened.

'Good God,' whispered Ciaran, and then thought it an unwitting reverence.

Rick and Rod stared disbelievingly at each other.

They were all lost for words; watched the whole thing once more. Whatever was going on, after that the 'stars' seemed to have decided to call it a night.

It became obvious there would be no further unusual reappearances.

Ciaran turned to find Deirdre a few paces behind. She looked as astonished as themselves; had obviously witnessed the second, slow-motion alignment and realignment.

Sleeping on board that night, reflecting upon events before finally dropping off, Ciaran realised that conversation between all of them had been easier than he might have expected. On the whole, watching what one said - thinking before putting your foot in it - the evening had proved very enjoyable. The dolphin cross shape had served to break down a few barriers. The talk of future plans had been fun.

Miles away in the beach-house, Deirdre turned out the light. In the darkness, she heard the gate rattling in a stronger breeze.

She found herself turning up new ideas from under the stones in her mind. Shapes, colours and textures were whirling as they used to long ago. It was going to be exciting planning a new look for the dry-dock. Maybe other things would come along if this was a success?

Well, she hadn't thought about things on quite this scale before. It was certainly different.

And maybe an ex-husband and father, could stay a friend? She knew it far too late for any other possible future. She had hurt him too deeply - murdered marriage.

Her kind of guilt could expect no forgiveness.

The last image before sleep cloaked everything was the disturbing dolphin cross she had seen. It would be pointless trying to paint it. Movement of the kind she had witnessed could not be portrayed... unless in film...?

On canvas, nothing she could bring out or emphasise... and yet... she had felt... something...?

Matt Summers would find this one hard to credit! Probably Dawn's dreamy eyes would widen with that rapt look when she saw it too, thought Pete.

He carefully guaged the descent to the landing pad.

The 'Tin Can Tuna' had a decent enough man as Navigator, provided it wasn't your sister or wife he was chatting up. Summers was a wolf with calm sheeps' eyes. The sort of eyes that looked gentle in firelight, without lascivious intent. He was sure Summers was bed-rolling his cousin, Dawn, but she wasn't exactly the virtuous choir girl she appeared!

As soon as the helicopter was securely dogged down for the night at sea, he made his way up to the bridge, carrying the camcorder. Good shots, he wanted to show Matt - who had been talking about dolphins and whales a lot lately. Thinking back, Matt's fascination with cetaceans seemed to date from that first cute chat-line given to Dawn: 'Bottlenose dolphin on the bow for days - a man and young woman to welcome it to Brisbane Dolphinarium holding up a sign - and whether dolphins might be able to sense they were needed. Then the punchlines about loneliness, feeling incomplete, seeking someone or something to help him feel spiritually home.' Blood-ee hell! And Dawn had listened! The conversation had broadened and the drink had flowed - towards sexual surrender and conquest?

But this video was something else! This could mean hard cash from some film company? What would Summers think of this behaviour?

He'd been well out to sea at a thousand or so altitude. The mail and some 'odds and sods' pieces of equipment was all they carried. Chas was kipping and to wake him up would have been heartless, knowing the anxiety for a mother in hospital. The chemotherapy had slim chance of success.

The sea calm, depth vision surprisingly good, he had been startled by the formation. He'd expected it to be a fleeting trick of movement and imagination but the dolphins' assemblage had remained stationary... better than photographs he had seen of Belukha whales, with their haphazard gregariousness white pocking the grey-green of an Arctic sea.

He had grabbed the camcorder... filmed coincidentally as the formation had carefully reversed, in uncharacteristic slow motion, to a counter realignment... There was absolutely no doubt what the formation was! It was perfectly representative - readjusted in reversion to precise geometry! He had hovered above a superb crucifix comprising a hundred and fifty plus deep-sea dolphins! He didn't know the species - Matt Summers would...

Water plop was the only noise in sharing his imaging... patterning his plans. Ardent had lost mindvoice... remaining mesmerised before proposal and explanation. Fincircling above sandfloor signs they guaged potential within chaos...

His master's mindlights were not the confusion they appeared... The haphazard could have harmony over time...

'Splitflukes are creaturekind with whom we cannot hope to communicate in depth for long. They feel superior; regard the worldspace their own. Their hands and minds create chaos when their hearts demand harmony. So vast is their influence, so enormous their ambition, they are swept upon isolated shores of indifference to decay in self-stranding.'

But Ardent wondered before the marvels of invention and the imaging of landspace achievement he shared from within...

The completeness of such a savage history he viewed... and the startling revelations of an alternative Deity!

'Yet we cannot mindmerge consciously with them... blind conceit reefsides against us and their fear. The only way for these 'men' to truly appreciate what we are is to influence an event... to work within their needs... to imply our congruity of spirit in the symbolism of their faith, making partnership possible on our own terms... but indirectly, striving not to reveal our true capacity...'

Ardent wasn't sure... yet could detect nothing which he could condemn as violation on Gaze's part. He marvelled before the new 'songline network' - another new image for Dolphinese - and at the immensity of worldspace.

'But we have no contact with White Tip's podsherd still,' said Gaze.

Ardent reflected the mindfrown, knowing the importance Gaze attached to keeping a promise he felt had been made...

as did the hardtasked mindweb...

Deirdre uncovered the draft proposals.

Rick, Ciaran and Rod went down on their knees to see things more clearly in the Sunday afternoon sunlight.

Deirdre stifled a laugh.

Tuned to the sound, Ciaran looked up.

'What's so funny?'

'You haven't taken in part of what you're looking at yet.

I've only used colour here and there to begin to work out tone and texture... er, things in my mind,' came the reply.

Ciaran looked down, thinking it had been a long time since she had smiled properly... and then realised, guiltily, that he hadn't shown this much interest before...

Rick asked, 'The dry-dock? Half of it covered over?'

'Yes. Keep looking.'

Rod said, 'If these are display areas for exhibits and not just photographs, there is a Sea Aquarium and Museum already which is nothing really to do with us.'

'I know that. I've looked around. You don't have enough space for showing up-to-date photographs of all the things you are doing and what you will be doing. There are also areas for historical records and exhibits of all the interactions between dolphins and men throughout history. One display is deliberately with the back facing the pool. An age limit will have to be imposed for admission there.'

She paused... expecting the first of many questions.

'Why? What do you propose in there?' asked Rick.

'The Black Museum.'

'The what?'

'Rick, we know you love your 'stars'. It's also true that you want the unnecessary slaughter of dolphins to stop. With a voice in legislation to stop it worldwide, you would. This place isn't just about entertaining now... It's becoming a place of interaction between two unique species who share the same oceans which men are turning into 'killing fields', to mix a metaphor. In your heart... you'd like to portray reality, as well as a circus, to mobilise opinion to help the many more 'stars' out... there.'

When had she been quite so eloquent? wondered Ciaran.

The breeze pressed her blouse emphasising her breasts, still well-formed and full. He directed his eyes to sea.

Before a financial mind asked the obvious questions..., Deirdre kept going. She might as well finish the whole of it - even if they pulled it apart in dissembling.

Rod interrupted. The young man was astute... gave her the opportunity.

'Why did you nearly laugh at the beginning? There's something here, near the lock gates. Was this it? No, it couldn't be... a chapel?'

None of the men spoke.

She smiled briefly, ruefully.

'I wondered when you'd spot it. Yes, Rod - sort of. When you all got down on your knees, I couldn't help myself. You see, I know that's what we're going to argue about most of all but... I just know it's right...'

The financial eyes were swinging back. She didn't know if she could meet them, fearing accusation. In quietness, she glanced at him, not daring an expression of any kind.

Surprised, she read mild interest - not the censure she half anticipated. There was no hint of ridicule.

'And why is it, your word, 'right'?' he asked.

No, not the start of a row, she thought. Not precursive to argument, it was puzzled request.

'Don't you understand the effects a dolphin cross formed every day will have on people? Before you know it, this is going to be a place of pilgrimage. It's as if the 'stars'... share the symbols of Christianity. The way they form up, the slowness... the pointing to the East before they go away... It's so full of mysticism, people will flock here to see it.

'It's like a minor miracle. Oh yes, the cynics will say that you've trained them to do it somehow... but it's such a powerful symbol... a kind of... a reaffirmation of a Saviour. It's like another Covenant... another Rainbow.'

They were still silent.

'Some will need... to pray.' She finished, weakly, 'No,

Rod, it's not a chapel. It's... let's call it a grotto by the sea with some religious imagery. I've got another sketch.'

She produced the drawing which had proved the hardest to do. Laid it above her ambitious scheme of... an improved Dolphinarium?

Rick cleared his throat. How the hell should he react to that lot? Knowing the personalities, what the devil could he say?

'Wow!' said Rod, just as speechless, and walked to the rail. He blinked before looking into the water. You never knew what you were going to see next lately.

The smile growing across Ciaran's face completely and utterly left-footed Rick.

Deirdre waited for the sarcasm which might well be justified; felt marooned by her creative temperament.

Rick had to say something.

'Look, Deirdre, the whole thing is brilliant. Only a fool couldn't see the opportunities but it's too big and we're too small. There aren't funds. It would mean more visitors, the need for more employees and bigger car-parks for a start. That would mean traffic prob...'

'Not if the visitors came by boat,' said Ciaran.

What? Bejesus, not him as well! thought Rick.

Deirdre looked at Ciaran; could not believe the slight back pats confirming alliance within protracted and lengthy argument looming like a cliff ahead.

Rod decided to make some coffee before the first salvoes were fired.

Three photographs of a huge dolphin cross, in deep sea from great height, which appeared in some newspapers shocked America. Astonishing definition and resolution spoke volumes concerning a 'spy in the sky' camera. The camera's existence was not allowed to shake the world for overlong, however. There was a rumour that the photographs had been sneaked out of somewhere surreptitiously, categorically denied by the White House spokesman.

An Air Force General was overheard to remark to a Senator, 'We've been taking camera shots like these for years. I could show shots of a World Leader's wife sunbathing with nothing to prop up her superstructure - but it wouldn't be politic or polite. You can bet your ass Ivan's got shots of some of our best butts minus denim. Smile and wave, boy, show 'em your having a good steak on the barby. Ain't nothin' new.'

Which pretty well doused the fires around a great new scandal - so the ball bounced towards the Church.

Beyond wonder and marvelling in the Lord's handiwork - long experience taught that the Press preferred crucifixion to circumspection. White collars, anxious of over constriction within their heirarchy, were markedly guarded. It was most strongly pointed out by the Catholic Church that miracles were subject to severest scrutiny over time. The Pope, practically unreachable, kept his own counsel - which was probably wise.

More newsworthy items - progress towards the Superbowl in America - a member of the Royal Family in the U.K. receiving a threatening letter from an obscure leftist group - a Swedish, blonde sex-symbol claiming rape by a film mogul, a director and a Bank's Chairman 'on the same night and in the same bed of an Amsterdam hotel' - served to swamp a public mind with real life drama.

But the photographs continued to exist: made into posters with watchword titles like 'Our Lord in the Sea'; made into calenders; packaged into good-luck symbols, or miniaturised beside eye-smiling sweethearts.

One of the most obvious places to market these was in the Dolphinariums of the world - although small shops, near and alongside Catholic churches worldwide, sought small supplies. Natives within subsistence economies - ever hopeful of profit in reach of card and cane technology - began to cut and carve, seeking new acquisitions with ancient skills.

Pete, the helicopter pilot, cursed all Space agencies above both hemispheres - but more particularly the northern. He was Australian, after all. Having a small crock of gold snatched from his grasp was good for neither ego nor pocket. A windfall could have paid off the several hundred owed to the finance company for the camcorder.

Matt still thought the shots were good; a mixed herd of spinner and spotted dolphins. He'd commiserated concerning lack of sustained interest by any advertising agency.

'Why don't you take the video to Brisbane Dolphinarium?

They might be interested in buying it from you. They might ask you to do other sorts of filming... You could take some shots from the air for publicity purposes... All you've to do is point the thing and pull the trigger. They'll probably have all kinds of ground and water shots... but you fly-by or over-fly several times a week.'

So he decided to do just that. He might have missed out on filming dolphins the first time but things could improve...

Happily, his timing could not have been more fortuitous.

Ciaran had sensed the pick-up's return from the station long before it came through the gates to the beach park. Some sixth sense appeared to excite the 'stars'. Looking over the rail of the three-master, he had observed the dolphins circling ever closer to the lock-gates. A few had passed into the lagoon already - indeed two dolphin heads had emerged and begun beak clicking inquisitorially - or conspiratorially? - at the same time. Then there wasn't a dorsal in sight - quite simply vanishing... as if a game of hide and seek were taking place?

Maeve leaned across the cab roof of the pick-up, waving and laughing as they negotiated the gravel drive. Obviously Phil had hungered to get behind a wheel for Rick was in the passenger seat. Ciaran watched the vehicle veer very close to lagoon side - a daughter's stare, her hands trying to shield strong light. Becoming more attractive with maturity, he felt astonishment, gratitude and marvelled in the seeds of life.

Maeve's hands dropped. She looked disappointed. Last vacation, Rick had said that the dolphins had swum along the lagoon following the pick-up's progress... but not this time.

The pick-up stopped. The engine stalled as unpracticed hands and feet failed to find and sense neutral. Moving to go down the companionway, an ungentlemanly expression floated to Ciaran's ears, followed quickly by an apology. Then Maeve clambered down, stretched out her arms and closed for a hug.

'Hello, Dad. I hear you've been spending a lot of time here. You after my job?'

He laughed. 'No, I'm out to make money in other ways than getting wet, love... and for different reasons than you might suppose. But more of that later.'

They separated but he felt her hands leading him back towards the deck.

'Where are they, Dad?'

'Don't ask me. You're the one who's supposed to know the answers. They were here - went away again. Minds of their own, haven't they? Things seem a bit un...'

A piercing wolf-whistle made them both jump! It was followed by a loud splash.

Maeve's eyes jerked towards the lagoon's surface. It was crazed with ripples. Her laugh was low, assured. Her eyes held the merriment he remembered.

'Blowhard,' she said, quietly emphatic.

As the ripples flattened, the dorsals emerged. They heard blow-holes exhaling, inhaling. Small plumes of water droplets hung in adjacence to wet backs. Beak clicking began in a teasing twittering...

'They do know I'm back! They've been playing with me!'

On some kind of cue, they were up! Walking in water, they were all mimicking applause!

Her laughter rang across the surface. Everyone smiled, gave her space on the deck. It was her stage.

Rod on deck, wet hair from the shower clinging to his neck, saw it first. He was already half down the hatch before giving the warning.

'I wouldn't stay up here. They're up to something!'

Too slow to avoid a sousing, they cringed behind the gunwale.

'You can't say I didn't warn you,' came Rod's voice from the sanctuary below deck.

Rick watched Maeve's wet hair raise cautiously above the rail. When she stood up, she was sodden - moreso than himself or the rest. Her sweat shirt clung to obvious femininity - more pronounced than in the Maeve of six months ago. She still reminded him of Fiona. The vision of Fiona on the honeymoon beach came to mind...

Phil was unfastening a bag and reaching for a towel.

Aha, still mesmerised after all these months, thought a father.

'Don't bother, Phil,' came Maeve's voice. 'It was me they were after - me they want. They might as well have me, just as I am!'

Ciaran caught sight of her unzipping a damp skirt, clambering agilely, with length of leg, up and over the rail!

They all saw the reunion. She was towed at speed to lagoon centre, with sleek shapes dance jumping above her in celebration.

They knew her laughter would come - smiled in synchrony.

Phil felt the ache down deep in himself; wrestled with growing desire, lost in her conquest.

Five minutes later, they all heard a helicopter hovering overhead. They waved; saw the jinking acknowledgement. The helicopter moved off, out into the bay.

They realised the 'stars' had disappeared, one by one, to leave only two, Blowhard and Delilah, in Maeve's company.

When she clambered back on deck, Phil had a towel and wrap ready - claimed a kiss for his trouble. Her response was in the closeness of embrace but her eyes held a question.

Releasing herself quicker than his hot blood hoped, Phil heard, 'Where did they go, Phil? What are they doing now?'

She read his disappointment - kissed him again and reached for his hand.

Maeve would not have an answer until the evening.

'You needn't look like that. I haven't touched the Sports' Fund. I paid him out of my personal account,' said Ciaran. 'It's cheap at the price. You are going to need more publicity material and documented film evidence for all sorts of things. Pete could be a heaven-sent opportunity - your own 'eye-in-the-sky'. Although he'll have to be careful about charges of moonlighting from his actual employers, I don't think it's a problem in the short term.'

Rick didn't answer, heard the video player stop after automatic rewind. He pressed the play button again; watched the few minutes of film as transfixedly as before. First, a huge deep-sea 'crucifix' comprising two species - spinners and spotted, he thought. Then the air shots of the Dolphinarium and Maeve's swimming with a diminishing number of 'stars' and hump-backs.

He could see what had happened - as Maeve had seen in wondering astonishment.

The dolphins had left Maeve in ones and twos to swim through the open lock-gates into the bay beyond. Purposeful reformation into the 'crucifix pattern' had significance he felt unready to admit. Too early to concur with Maeve's opinion or her family, Rick felt the mystique nevertheless.

She had voiced the thoughts of a mother immediately.

'You see! Dolphins are capable of faith and belief! They can recognise symbolism within... a religion.'

Then she had stopped, her eyes suddenly introverted. When her eyes had refocused upon his again, there was a strange, rock-hard certainty within... as if something only half remembered was being recalled? As if there were new purposes in the truths of memory?

Rick, certain she had not spoken everything in her mind, found her words not so ridiculous in the light of events...

'The 'stars' are showing us something of far greater significance than their intelligence. Awareness of faith and love in the symbolism of a cross makes the whispers of our bloody violence... shouts of murder. Don't you see how human consciences will work... from within? People will want to stop killing dolphins in horror of what they do before a God and a Saviour... And your 'stars', Rick, are keys to a new conscience a world needs.'

The sound of her approaching car heralded a mother. Still unsure of how the evening would develop, Rick said, 'Your mother's been coming over a little more often from Redland, Maeve. She's got some ideas that have interested your father and me. 'Moneybags' thinks we have some cash to use in redecorating the dry-dock. Perhaps there will...'

She interrupted with, 'Do they talk to each other, Rick?'

It was no time for anything but directness. Her eyes were puzzled. Did they contain also... something more than uncertainty? Hope?

'I think they speak more as equals than perhaps they did before, Maeve. Dominance or submission are out of the roles they play now. Perhaps they are learning how... to be simply friends?'

Rick saw the brown eyes kindle in a fresh warmth that wrapped about something in his throat, choking him with closeness.

Then she was gone to meet a mother and brother. He felt for his pipe, sought Ciaran to distract him with comradeship.

The conversation between Deirdre and Maeve gave a new slant to an idea that evening. 'A grotto by the sea with some religious imagery' solidified in form and line in the minds of both - and broadened the aspects of 'dolphins in distress' to include 'something tangible for visitors and those who would seek to pray'...

Together, they sketched quickly - began to cut card and stick with glue. The ideas within minds took shape for fathers and sons to see and touch... for practical tool-users to assess mechanical problems, strengths and stresses... the effects of winds... Donovan sketched clamps and wall bolts...

The idea was not new. The Chinese, inheritors of ancient arts and wisdoms, had many 'firsts' which a modern world chose to overlook. The entrance to the grotto might be perceived in half existence as a sculpture in an ornamental pool outside the guest house in the riverside city of Tongling. Maeve recalled Tongling had adopted the Baiji, the Chinese River Dolphin, as a municipal mascot from her wide reading. The city had constructed a semicaptive holding facility to breed and conserve the species at risk from incidental capture, illegal fishing, injury from propellors in crowded waterways and increasing pollution of the river. A photograph she had seen of five sculpted dolphins soaring an arc above a stone wave was stored in memory. The moment of recall had come...

Ciaran asked, 'It's impressive Maeve but are you or your mother capable of that kind of sculpture? Who will do it?'

Deirdre surprised him.

'Any sculptor in need of a theme more than the money, 'Moneybags'.'

His ex-wife's attempt at humour and her laughter were not lost on him. He smiled wryly... awaited explanation.

Deirdre looked at him confidently, fully in the face. She was capable still of an emotional armlock within a lovely smile.

'Put an advert in this magazine, offering free board and lodging, reasonable workshop facilities and promise regular viewing of the finished product and you might well be surprised at the numbers of young, enthusiastic and skilful hands just aching for this opportunity.'

She handed him a slip of paper with the name of the magazine and a smoothly worded advertisement. Their fingers touched briefly and something seemed to flow between them...

He raised his eyes just in time to catch her blink - the furrowed forehead that smoothed too quickly in camouflage...

It was best to notice nothing for now, he thought.

Within days, work on the grotto began. The men worked on the functional aspects of wall-building and woodwork.

Simon, an art student, responded to the advert by turning up on a monstrous - and loud - motor cycle. He explained 'how he'd tackle the problems of the unusual shapes'. If they wanted rapid results, he'd use 'materials ideally suited and quite cheap'. A Treasurer approved, politely masking doubt.

A week and a half later, a mother and daughter painted half life-size 'dolphins at risk' carved from polysterene and coated with several layers of glass-fibre.

The results of teamwork excellent, Donovan quietened Simon's 'monster' and gave it an engineer's thorough overhaul to show their gratitude. Everyone was grateful. Then, Rod, Donovan and Simon began to talk of motor cycles a lot...

All co-operated in fixing ten differing but realistic shapes to the concrete block structure with strong brackets

to achieve what Simon called 'the sense of a communal curve'.

The ten most endangered species of dolphin formed the arch, through which a grand view of Moreton Bay could be obtained ... of precisely the area of water where the 'stars' formed their crucifix shape each evening.

There were two small 'chapels' behind the archway. They had flagged floors and glass canopies set in stout timber frames. Both 'chapels' had small altars. On the back of the concrete block structure, above one of the altars, was an enlargement of a 'dolphin crucifix' photograph under glass.

In the other 'chapel', for no clear reason that the men understood, Simon had been asked to place a pure white bottlenose dolphin 'sculpture' above the altar. Uncannily, the white dolphin seemed to catch and contain the sparkling reflections from water surface nearby. Young Simon seemed to be most pleased with this last effort, suggested by Maeve. He was gratified by the write up in an Arts' Column of a Brisbane newspaper with a large circulation which mentioned him by name. The article served to advertise Brisbane Dolphinarium to a different kind of sober citizen than the racing punters or the doting parents.

Rod referred to the new visitors as 'C.C.s' explaining that it meant 'Curious Christians' and that he looked forward to a day of a '1000 C.C.' attendance, 'all revved up to give for the good of dolphins worldwide'. He did not amplify upon novel ideas for new kinds of dolphin races they were hatching as a trio in 'The Red Bottlenose' of an evening.

Unpressurized, visitors began to drift towards the grotto seeking the best vantage point to view the 'Dolphin Cross'.

Deirdre's prediction proved correct. Numbers of visitors did indeed pray, a predominant Catholicism obvious in the many genuflections towards the simple 'altars'. Despite small signs clearly stating that the 'grotto' was not consecrated as 'hallowed ground' - it made no difference. The white dolphin was often touched by a supplicant and needed regular cleaning. Allowing no lighted candles, Rick was asked - often.

Evening saw a steady passage of pedestrians walking the pathway on the grassbank between the old dock and the lagoon. The conversation was always polite and pleasant as passers-by edged closer to the grotto and quiet minutes of witness. For some peculiar reason, even the lager-tin lobbers seemed to seek the bins for something sacred seemed to have invaded old haunts. Jeering shouts died quickly in irreverent throats... There was the guilty feeling that someone was looking over a shoulder at doers of misdeeds...

Ciaran stared at Rod, Donovan and Simon across the table. Rick and himself had been invited for a drink. Novel that sons should offer to pay, both fathers had agreed, walked across the grass towards 'The Red Bottlenose', sensing motives larger than filial loyalty. Ciaran saw self-satisfaction in an 'entrepreneur' in the way Rod had rubbed his hands with a satisfied smile. The two others of 'Simon & Sons Ltd.' had shared the looks of open warmth and innocence, oft the masks atop convivial deception.

After the niceties, Rick had skewered Rod with directness of eye; demanded they drop the embarrassing preamble...

'Why?' had barked Rick, thumping right fist into left hand.

'To make more money for the Dolphinarium?' came back Rod, precisely apeing hand movements and tone of voice.

'How?' had asked Rick, quieter and deciding not to use histrionic gestures.

'This,' had said Rod with complete calm and strength of conviction in consequence.

The model had been revealed and the dialogue had begun.

Now Ciaran met Rick's eyes and a deal was struck before the lads finished talking. It would not do to let them know they could win a round so easily.

'You want how much!?' said an incredulous Treasurer.

'Enough to buy materials to make three of these for a start. We'll aim to become self-financing after that,' came the positive reply. 'It's sound. We'll more than double the Tote's take!'

'No,' said Ciaran. 'It's ridiculous, isn't it, Rick?'

Both fathers watched the downcast expressions, the teeth tapping and the foot shuffling.

Rick said, 'Yes, ridiculous. They'd have to make six to make it viable. Can we afford that?'

They watched the fidgets cease and the eyes come up.

'I think so,' said Ciaran, 'if somebody fills a Manager's glass and the unofficial Treasurer's.'

Which happened rapidly...

The first prototype needed very little in the way of modification and was superbly buoyant. Constructed from glass fibre and polysterene, the two cylindrical floats formed a twin hulled raft. Lightweight aluminium framing provided solid support for a mock motor cycle made from the same main ingredients and mounted on top of the raft. Meant for just one rider, it promised an exciting experience. Careful checks were made to ensure no sharp edges to catch tumbling human flesh. Somebody was sure to go for a spill!

For once, Maeve had no part in the painting. Spraying the glass fibre with salt tolerant paints was well within the capacities of 'Simon and Sons'. The mock trade name had stuck. It even appeared stencilled on the raft.

At least one entrepreneur was thinking ahead, noted a Banker, beginning a train of thought himself...

The method of propulsion was quite simple. The dolphins would have no trouble at all, Rod assured them.

'It'll take two dolphins minimum to move and steer effectively but three D.P. will give much greater efficiency and speed.'

'D.P.?' asked Rick.

'Awe, come on, Pop. What do you measure an engine's out-put in?' asked Rod.

The light dawned in Rick. His hilarity ignited all.

'Minimum: 2 D.P. / Recommended: 3 D.P.' was stencilled on a float.

A long aluminium bar, underneath the front 'wheel' of the sea-going 'motor cycle', passed through both floats. It had stout rubber grips fixed either end and between the floats.

'We'll need the grips to protect the 'stars' mouths,' Rod said. He added, 'That's my one anxiety. They'll have to work in real partnership or they could hurt themselves smashing through a wave.'

Rick said, 'Well, you've come this far - keep going son.'

So Rod took to the lagoon with the raft.

And was ignored.

The whole 'Simon and Sons' labour force took to the water and swam, pushing the raft before them - and were ignored.

No interest appeared to be taken in the raft at all - apart from a couple of dolphin heads appearing and clicking disapprovingly... as if to say, 'Do you mind not parking this piece of rubbish in the main waterway.'

'Simon and Sons' felt obliged to ask for Maeve's assistance...

While they were asking, pleading with a giggling Maeve, the dolphins disappeared for the evening 'crucifix ceremonies' and, presumably, communion of greater importance.

The last thing Maeve said that evening was probably the greatest bit of sense all day.

'Why don't you leave the raft on the lagoon, free floating? That way they can get used to it and work things out themselves without too many dunderheads in the way!'

It was late and there wasn't much else they could do. 'Simon and Sons' retired to 'The Red Bottlenose' to ponder the bitter tastes of defeat. Ciaran and Rick consoled them with a mixture of old Irish remedy and occasional melody.

They realised the dolphins must have become increasingly curious during the hours of half-light

Rod said, 'I heard a lot of beak clicking around dawn.'

Ciaran and Rick noted the redness of eyes. Unready for anything but a strong dose of coffee, 'Smith and Sons' were trying to face the cold light of day. Both men realised the need for tolerant sympathy.

Occasional beak clicks could still be heard from the lagoon. Rick had reported that the 'stars' seemed to be nosing and nudging around the raft. He'd seen Blowhard jump over it a bit disdainfully - thought it wise not to say so.

Ciaran prepared to leave for the Bank. Looking at the slumped heads, he knew they needed something to hold on to.

'For what it's worth, I still think you've come up with a good idea. You need more cash injected so you might as well know the first production model will have to sport the colours of the best Bank in Brisbane. I'll arrange a donation to the Dolphinarium in return for advertising rights this morning. It's possible a few of the larger accounts will be interested. I'll ring around - if you wish.'

Donovan was looking at him with the widest grin he had seen in years. Words were not necessary.

Rod, acting as spokesman, said, 'Thanks Ciaran. I don't know what else to... I just hope it works.'

Ciaran, walking up the steps towards the deck and trying to disguise the light-hearted spring he felt, muttered aloud,

'Well don't waste any more breath. Get out there and train some 'D.P.'! This time, ask Maeve to help. See you later.'

Rick, found himself in debt to a friend again, smiled inwardly and acknowledged a funding wrinkle he hadn't thought of...

He could hear Donovan knocking at Maeve's cabin and the brotherly sweetness in, 'Would you like a coffee, Sis?'

She was smiling when she opened the door - and already dressed in a wet-suit?

How much had she overheard of Ciaran's comments?

As the sound of Ciaran's car diminished on the gravel, they all heard a light thumping noise against the quayside, conducted as muted vibration through wood and concrete.

After a light breakfast, Rick solved the mystery of the bumping noises. The prototype was snugly alongside the three-master - could only have been manoeuvred there by the 'stars'. Indeed, Blowhard appeared to nudge it occasionally to counteract the effects of a slight breeze and maintain station. Either some elementary notions of seamanship had sparked in his brain overnight - or he was clearing the lagoon of rubbish by pushing it back towards 'untidy despoilers and dumpers who fouled the waterspace'.

Maeve gave up trying to follow reason in the welter of suggestion and counter within 'Smith and Sons'. Obviously, they wanted her help - but they weren't too clear how or in what exact way. Not sure either, she didn't let on...

Choosing her moment, she went over the side and simply sat on the prototype as if it was a motor cycle in reality.

On a calm surface, it felt quite secure. Deliberately, she pushed away from the three-master to let herself drift in aimless circling.

Within seconds, the dolphin heads were up, observing - and waiting?

She heard the argument on the deck falter to silence; felt quizzical stares. Sensing a need of something positive to be signalled, she held aloft her left forearm three separate times, pointed directly towards the three nearest dolphins which happened to be two hump-backs and an original bottlenose 'star'.

The response was immediate - the three 'walked in water'.

Only when they were aloft did she recognise Delilah and the two hump-backs they had named Blotch and Twizzle. Well, in for a penny in for a pound, as a transported ancestor might have said... She gave the 'come here' signal.

It was far easier than even she dreamed it would be! Three beak gaping maws surfaced close alongside. She made a 'maw with hands' and mimed grasping the end of the pushbar pointing to Twizzle. Twizzle beak clicked a few times and Blotch seemed to answer or agree. The pushbar grip was nudged by Twizzle... and then her beak opened to grasp it securely.

She wallowed in parallel with the left-hand float!

When Maeve pointed to Blotch, unhesitatingly he mirrored Twizzle's former movements and her position. Watching with a feeling of immense relief, she saw his teeth close around the right-hand, pushbar end!

Delilah was even easier; Maeve only had to point to the central grip. Delilah finned between the floats, directly underneath the seated human laughter which pointed towards the lock-gates... She knew everything was going to be perfect... There wasn't any need to fear failure...

The prototype moved, gaining speed steadily!

It swept through the lock, holding a precise centre line, and out towards the bay. Around the stone quay the sea-going 'motor-cyclist' met the first waves!

The bump-bouncing made handlebar grabbing obligatory!

There was an adjustment of speed and she felt a slight twist in the direction of the raft... as if some kind of compensation was being made... for current or tidal drift?

Then she was three hundred yards offshore!

'Simon and Sons' heard her laughter as a faint tinkling on the breeze.

'The outboard! Quickly!' Donovan yelled.

Simon decided to stay near the lock-gates; grabbed binoculars and raced towards the grotto. Donovan and Rod swept through to the bay with all the speed their excitement could muster.

They discovered quickly that they couldn't close the gap on a straight run! They got closer if the 'motor cyclist' was turning... but that mechanical advantage diminished as the dolphins adapted in teamwork to the weight and drag of the raft and in timing of fluke thrusts!

In the end, Rod cut the motor and they watched the bounce and spray; both saw her joy and wondered at dolphin endurance.

The 'D.P.' output seemed greater than they had hoped and the actual limitations around their scheme were not with the dolphins but with 'strength to weight' ratios in the design of the raft, thought Donovan. He sensed the dolphins could move the thing faster but were holding back... sensing weaknesses in the raft's shape and structure? That was... ridiculous?

The pushbar was loose in the float sockets when she returned at reduced speed!

The first production model would need strengthening. Something best done before glass fibre encased the basic polysterene shape, pointed out Simon. He also proposed an interesting modification to the general shape of the floats.

'Five feet long cylindrical shapes might be functional as floats but they're bloody boring to look at and make. You could almost make the raft look more alive if you gave each float the appearance of... say, Dall's Porpoise! Now that shape must be nearly hydrodynamically perfect! Why didn't I think of it before?'

Rod looked at him. Simon was full of surprises. Since when did he know about Dall's Porpoise?

Simon saw the look. He said, 'I was reading a magazine yesterday. If you've got ten dolphins most at risk shown in the grotto arch, what about Dall's Porpoise? That's another cetacean cousin that's in real big danger, you know. We could make the floats have real advertising purposes, couldn't we? And the shapes would be more streamlined... present less in the way of drag...'

His voice petered out but he saw the beams of concurrence lighting the faces of new friends with whom he shared so much in common.

Rod said, 'Did you know that Dall's Porpoise actually leaves 'rooster tails' of spray behind it when it's fluking... I mean, swimming flat out? I wonder...?'

Chapter Sixteen

A SIRE'S
SICKNESS AND SPLITFLUKE DRUMS

F ar less tiring than it had been, the songline network saved much
needless expenditure of energy, Gaze told him. Ardent could only
marvel at the experience! The much older Cleric, whirled with
recalled sensations of speed. Had they really been so far? Or been so
close to Splitflukes who were unaware, it seemed, of manipulation?

The 'Dolphin cross' of their own mindweb, that of the deep-sea Spinners
(in recent alliance with Spotted cousins as happened from time to time)
and the 'crucifix' of the mixed podsherd of 'stars' in waterspace - known
as 'Moreton Bay'? -comprised 'nodes in a larger network of friends', Gaze
said. Ardent did not understand but patterned generally that the 'crosses'
amplified echo-calling, served to channel mindenergy for Gaze (and/or
White Tip) and provided temporary 'fixing of reference' in the vastnesses
they had mindleapt.

Now Ardent could see the importance Gaze attached to such precise
positioning for dolphin cousins forming the 'crosses'. Not purely to invoke
imaging within Splitfluke minds, accuracy was necessary to maximise
receptivity and power in the minor mindwebs of other podsherds.
Lately, he had found himself 'quantifying' Bottlenose friends as potential
'directors', 'reflectors' or 'amplifiers' as he began to understand some of
'the functions of the cross'.

What a shock 'out-of-his-body' experience had been!

They had 'skip-leapt from cross to cross' finding the mindglow
congregations easy to find in the planes of empathy. Each mindweb
had adjusted network in absorption of mindenergy, finned to required
realignment and helped to give springing impulsion for the next leap. It
was amazing to feel the energy within common purpose; the mindpower
they all shared.

Gaze had beaksmiled and said, 'Splitflukes only sense what you have
felt, Ardent. The nearest they get to achieving the same thing is in the act
of prayer within buildings they name 'churches'. It seems incredible that
they sense a way of life as we know it but have not achieved beyond an
elementary mindmeet...

'Even more difficult to understand is that they are capable of much
they call 'progress' which leads nowhere... but towards a kind of mental
sterility?'

Before Ardent had had time to pattern further, they had arrived at and
within the much smaller 'crucifix' outside the strange place Gaze called
'The Dolphinarium'...

Apparently, he had regarded dolphins in waterspace here as to be so unfairly constrained by unthinking Splitflukes as to be prisoners or specimens for 'human curiosity' and little else. They did not appear anything less than overjoyed by Gaze's presence...

Ardent found himself nudged within a mindlight cluster; sensed Gaze's mindtendrils detaching, unravelling. Guessing a new reference had been fixed for himself, he did not realise the 'other' was feminine until she spoke softly!

'Well, so this is what it's like to have the imaging of a Cleric held actively in mind! I'll have to watch what I do and say... Ardent, is it?'

Ardent managed to stutter a greeting of some kind but, in all honesty, was completely out of finstroke with himself.

'Hello. I am Twizzle. I promise to be good and tease you only a teeny weeny bit. He's nice, Gaze - but uncertain of himself, isn't he?'

He heard Gaze's mindmerge - 'Behave, Twizzle. I remember a Humpback who was suspicious and nervous of males once... and for too many seasons. Where did that female go?'

Ardent heard a mature, middle-aged laugh.

'Blotch stole her quite away, Gaze... and you know it!'

The small mindweb shook with laughter.

Ardent felt the humour trembling around him. He liked the Humpbacks and Bottlenoses here.

Then there was serious communion of minds...

And they were not just dolphin minds!

As the cross realigned with the strange lock-gates, the dizzying sensations faded away at last. He was able to share Twizzle's sensing.

Gaze's mindvoice said, 'I'm sorry about that Ardent. You have experienced disorientation of self due to the strangeness and speed. During our mindleaping, I could do nothing to help you directly. It will get easier for you in future leaps.

'Now play your part of observer in all I do. Remember that I do trust you - seek the same trust of myself. Already I have explained the reasons for manipulating Splitflukes indirectly. I need a Cleric to caution me of violation if you sense it is necessary.'

Splitflukes were in close proximity... but unthreatening. Gaze was mindscanning them! Their hopes and dreams were being viewed dispassionately; how advantage might accrue to dolphins or other cetaceans at risk in the worldspace if...

...Gaze was not being selfish; he was manipulating desire and intent without changing them. Accepting without bias the emotions and needs of individuals, nevertheless he arranged circumstance or event to maximise opportunity to protect and safeguard cetaceans generally - dolphins particularly! It was obvious that the thrust of his scheming was to improve the quality of Splitfluke life and experience through interactions with dolphins. The Splitflukes would appear to be the main beneficiaries... but their views of dolphins would be forced to modify in reviewing 'partnership' or 'the congruity of spirit' of which he spoke.

Gaze's patterning possessed a kind of plausibility but Ardent felt the magnitude of the task as a crushing weight. How could another species - these Splitflukes - be convinced to change life-style and behaviour when claiming superiority and an inheritance they did not have as 'a Divine right'? Whatever his mindskills, Gaze was doomed to fail... or he would be tempted to twist Splitfluke will to attain his aims...

Gaze mindmerged, 'And that is exactly why I need you Ardent. If I seek to bend Splitfluke will to my own desires and ends, I become the Abomination we must fear. I came so close to attempting to alter human emotion once... It shall not happen again. The Splitfluke, Maeve... began to fear me and had cause. I altered her memory of me which was small violation enough. I lost... I lost feeling close to love across the species' divide... Few dolphins have experienced this in the sagas... In such short lightwaters, so much joy, my dear, old friend...'

Ardent risked request with, 'And shall I know this Maeve more clearly, Gaze?'

They watched her approach in Gaze's mindeye.

She was alone. The nearing mindlight cluster which meant so much to his young master was as close as another Bottlenose in bi-vector... yet their presence was not conscious awareness in Maeve.

She touched the shape of the White Dolphin!

Immediately they were within, unobtrusively observant...

Ardent joined the flow of image evaluation, amazed in rapidity of absorption...

'That's what it is, Ardent. I let my mind become dry sand and absorb her imaging like moisture held in storage.

Together we will pattern concerning many, many things later.'

Ardent watched the image associations, formed by Gaze, enter Maeve's recall... be recognised as memory of a dancing duo of dolphins loved; not as a farewell...

They both felt the smile grow upon her face; both saw the grotto blur in the present.

Gaze mindwhispered, 'She is remembering feelings of the past and the joy we shared. It is all I could leave her heart to image... She feared me too much...'

But Ardent knew he was wrong... Something below one eye cried Gaze was wrong!

Perhaps it was wiser not to tell him? But Ardent was always truthful...

He mindmerged carefully, 'Sometimes to be truly happy, all creatures need to feel a depth of sadness. How else is happiness realised? Is Maeve happy in imaging alone of joy?

Podpartner 'stars' may help her to laugh but your absence is an emptiness she feels without knowing. Your mindskills could not take away all her sadness. Feel wetness upon her face.'

Gaze was silent a long time...

Eventually he mindmerged, 'But Phil loves her. They will find each other as White Tip and I have found ourselves...'

Ardent said, 'Perhaps when she forgets to feel for you, Gaze, it shall be so. Your effect upon her was so immense, was it not? You have left a hole in her heart. Indeed, Gaze, this was 'violation enough', a lack of empathy in yourself.'

He added needfully, for he detected the horror within his young master, 'An Abomination would feel no pain of guilt... Young love is oft blinded by good intention... You are trying to minimise harm you may have caused.'

Gaze imaged a beaksmile. It was forced but the warmth was there.

'Ardent, the passing seasons make us wiser. You <u>are</u> the sage I need.'

Several lightwaters after their return to the Podsherd, Ardent and Gaze were patterning within Wanderer's Cave. There was much to review. The songline network was efficient; the mindwebs of other podsherds prepared in readiness to face the unexpected. Even in the brief absence to 'The Dolphinarium', White Tip had stayed with the deep-sea Spinners and Spotted cousins to continue awareness training. She had mindcarried the Guardian Ebbstir in mindleaping, much to his confusion and delight; enmeshed him with tendrils close within Rayrender's clustering where Ebbstir proved able assistant in training...

So now there were three mindwebs becoming increasingly hardened to horror in some vision exposure... But there were no signs or rumours of further Abominations...

Gaze still patterned between differences in Bottlenoses generally and White Tip and himself. Reasons seemed just as elusive. And the truth of his mate's familypod...?

There were times Ardent sensed the growing frustration and complete bewilderment in his young master - sometimes manifest in occasional flukejerks and twitches of fins which threatened to disturb the more fragile of Wanderer's sandfloor signs. Gaze would be mortified if he actually did destroy something in Wanderer's legacy of sign and self.

Ardent watched Gaze finning pensively above the last series of signs and map which Wanderer had made before he had deep-dived in so much pain... That had been shortly after the tragedies of others who had suffered so in finning through hardside debris and deep-dived to escape the agony...

Ardent finstopped...?

A pod had gone to puzzle the strange illnesses and deep-diving rumoured by visitors from distant waterspace... Who had been the Bottlenoses of that pod?

In a strange excitement, Ardent sought to remember...

He was not alone. Gaze caught his mind-drift...

Ardent recalled Wanderer fluking out-reef through the lagoon-entrance with some Guardians and... Karg the Navigator!

One young Guardian had been Gale, Gaze's sire...!

When the pod had returned, Wanderer and one of the Guardians had been suffering internal agonies...

Karg and Gale, weak for several lightwaters, had been unable to fishmuster or eat at first...

Wanderer had struggled to make his last sandfloor signs; had firmly extracted a promise from Tinu and himself. He had made of his patterning, predictions through clenched teeth...

Tinu and himself had wondered if Wanderer had been of sound mind in the end for so wildly unlikely had the things been that he had said... But he had been a special dolphin...

Wanderer had endured longer than the Guardian, the latter deep-diving two lightwaters before the Voyager. Karg and Gale had recovered - Gale quicker because of greater strength? - but it had been mooncycles before full fitness returned...

Ardent saw Gaze wallowing motionless above the signs and the map... What was odd in the sandfloor signs?

The old Cleric focused on the sprinkling of orange sand. The original small pile had spread to encompass a wider area - the orange colour mixing with the commoner yellow shades. It was dilution of colour... just like Wanderer had said would happen in time? Why had he said that? Why had there been such insistence that Tinu send for samples of orange sand which could only be found in one cove on the other side of the islandmass? What was it supposed to signify?

What had Wanderer said...? Something about the sand's significance of time...?

Ardent's age was never more apparent to Gaze than in his mind's meandering between memory, dream and fact in those quiet moments above Wanderer's last signs. It required some prompting to let the past breathe in pain through years... to have Wanderer's imaging breach in conscious recall...!

Gaze watched the imager fin the present, marvelled at the wonder of 'seeing' Wanderer living near death in the past!

Wanderer it was! He recognised the gasping mindvoice in extremes of urgency... Fleetingly, Gaze recalled the voice of a white dolphin and the manifestations at the time of his own near demise... when Vorg had disintegrated in the harpoon's impact... The voices were the same! The dolphin features were miraculously identical!

There was a message across the seasons from the Past to the Present... The riddles and signs and clues all fused together with startling clarity...!

Missing only was Gaze's name...

'When orange absorbs in these sands we know,
Another may safely finsearching go.
Poisoning accesses visions strong -
And power can hide within a throng.
Corruption knows no guilt within -
Love's countenance only knows no sin.
Love shall come, strong at least as they,

Teach dolphinkind to guard and pray.'

Wanderer had given Tinu precise statement... something which formed prediction in prosaic prose... 'who shall know before he is taught'... 'He will know your imaging behind your reefsiding'... 'One dolphin will come, at a time of danger, to find another entrance to Wanderer's Cave...' Straightforward commonplace statement was avoidance of complication which suited the personality of the retired Master Guardian...

Ardent, however, had been given riddles in rhyme... a mixture of faith and love in near metempsychosis... but the imaging was so deeply buried in layers of memory and emotion that it was camouflage of mind within mind! Stronger than reefsiding, in which all dolphins were capable, Wanderer's transmigration of self within Ardent, gave no clue for a mindreader of hidden messages from any special dolphin of the past...!

How mightily Wanderer had struggled in full certainty of his eventual deep-diving! In short lightwaters with Ardent, Wanderer must have achieved Merge with the Cleric! Such was an act of astonishing faith and will! Unless something had happened to Wanderer to magnify mindskills...? But what could do that? Was this part of a message across the seasons...?

Gaze had been looking in the Cave at Wanderer's sandfloor signs of the present! The real Cave to examine was locked within the memory and recall of Ardent's mind, faithfully true to the Wanderer of seasons ago! Answers to all he needed were finning no more than two dolphinspans from Gaze himself... but locked away in fragmented capsules of the past. To achieve answers he had to compare purpose and intent with a Wanderer he sensed in the present and the Wanderer recalled from the past in the old Cleric!

Truly, Wanderer had predicted his coming! Had he also struggled to protect him from others before he was ready to reveal himself? Intuitively, Gaze felt that Wanderer's struggle to retain life and breath despite an agony of distress had been to strive to protect him! But how did he know somedolphin of his mindskills would come and need to fight against new terrors in the waterworld?

Unless... he suspected that offspring of survivors from that fateful flukingpassage to 'a place marked by orange sand' would sire Bottlenoses... who were different!! Like Karg...!

Or that a 'poisoning would access visioning powers'...!?

Gaze began to understand! Clues for the origins of Abominations were assembling in his patterning...!

He had to go to the 'place marked by the orange sand'!

The map of the present gave the general location - but the map of the past was precise. Gaze knew where it had to be by flukingvectors indicated... and because of maps from the minds of Splitfluke navigators...!

There was more... The reason for placing orange sand upon yellow was to give an indication over time of when it would be safe to investigate the area... when the 'poison of the place' would be diluted to 'safe' degree!

Suddenly, Gaze guessed what would be found - the Splitfluke 'pollution' which they feared!? But what kind of 'pollution' could cause such awesome effect upon Bottlenose mindskill?

There seemed no answer to the last question... Probably Wanderer had not known... What was clear was that strange changes had occurred within Wanderer, Karg... and possibly Gale. The effects of exposure to the pollution were lethal - or triggered rapid mindskill development of latent ability...

Wanderer had achieved Merge with Ardent a few lightwaters later... Karg had developed Visioning - and magnified in malice inherent within?

What had happened to Gale who had sired himself? thought Gaze. Neither White Tip nor himself had detected any kind of remarkable ability in his sire... but something had been transmissible in the seeds of life...

Karg had sired Vorg - and the power of visioning had been transferred. Gaze had to accept the inevitable. The quest of 'the red herring' ended... Although Gale had no mindskill of note, nevertheless, his degree of exposure to the pollution had caused some kind of change in mechanisms of procreation!

As his sire had recovered first from dire illness - it was indicative of least exposure to poisoning influences...

But what of White Tip?

It seemed he was near to an explanation for Abominations arising in the warmstream - to be challenged in patterning by the existence of his own mate who was sired by no Bottlenose of the warmstream Podsherd...

Gaze mindmerged, 'I felt... feel we are closer to an understanding, old friend... But my mate breaches to scatter spray across our feeble reflections...'

Ardent concurred... finned above the sandfloor, twisting bottlebeak to follow the ripple and flow of sandmarks...

He was comparing the maps of the present to the past which, he realised now, he had vouchsafed for seasons...

Gaze watched him drifting silently across the length and width of inreef pool... Ardent was looking closely, or trying to with myopic determination, at each rising ridge and fall seeming to flow around warmstream waterspace...

'Watching the ripple and flow!'

Ardent's imaging screamed inside the melon of Gaze!

Sometimes it was Ardent's patterning - sometimes...!

They were of the warmstream which divided around the islandmasses the Splitflukes called 'Fiji', further towards seaspace of the sun's deep-dive at end of lightwater. The Splitflukes called the warmstream the complicated name of 'Pacific South Equatorial Current' and it flowed across the vastnesses of the 'Pacific Ocean'. Born from the warming of the 'Humboldt Current', it swept 'westward' majestically to divide around Fiji... The 'southern divide' had helped his flukingpassage towards 'Brisbane and Maeve'... The 'northern divide' flowed across the 'Coral Sea' before turning 'south' and, co-joining with the 'East Australia Current', bustled with remnants of the 'southern divide' and lost themselves, cooling in the 'Tasman Sea'...

It was the warmstream which sustained them in comfort and plenty... Carrying necessity it sometimes brought the unusual in strange flotsam or signs of distant catastrophes...

Could the 'northern divide of the warmstream' have carried pollution towards another podsherd in which White Tip had been unborn as yet...?

Ardent was frightened in Gaze's flukethreshing!

He watched his young master power across the pool... Saw him closely examining line of current flow and islandmasses marked... the emergent atolls...

Then there were sudden orders! The mindweb was summoned.

Beak Spot was placed in joint authority with Sinu again. They could manage without Sinu.

Gape did not have to ask... She, too, would stay to give 'assistance to Beak Spot' for the family of Gaze and the whole mindweb knew it their time of needful harmony...

In close communion of minds, this time the Podsherd were given the reasons for departure. Many volunteered to join them but were refused, politely but firmly.

Gale setting flukingpace, they left in the darkwater, all conscious of the unexpected across vectors ahead...

Familiar seawhispers of warmstream waterspace faded...

Wanderer's signs were explicit. What helped even more was his sire's remembrance of the flukingvectors of the seasons before.

'I remember how proud I was to fluke in company of a Voyager and a Navigator. Whitegraze, he was my Pod Leader at the time, had said that 'I deserved the opportunity of extending the range of my fluking experience'. Perhaps he thought he saw something of potential in me...?

'I know he thought I was one of the stronger of my pod. He didn't have 'favourites' but I think he was assessing me for promotion when the time was right. Tinu listened to opinions expressed by all his Pod Leaders and I felt optimistic of my future as a Guardian. I have regretted always that I was too ill... not strong enough to fin with Whitegraze before his deep-diving. He was a fine Bottlenose,' Gale said.

'Indeed he must have been to have commanded your respect - and so to command it seasons later,' replied Gaze.

They were silent...

As a leading quartet, Gale, Gaze, White Tip and Ardent were 'fluking the diamond'. Ardent, as the elder Bottlenose could make 'the tail of the diamond' and have passage eased through the press of water. It was a common enough formation and sometimes adopted to break waterpassage for pregnant females, or as a sign of respect for revered elderly dolphins.

Ardent was not about to complain, recognising the worth of sea tradition and accepting the compliment...

Eventually, Gaze mindmerged openly, 'The Splitflukes have a name for this place marked by Wanderer in orange sand. They call it 'Swains Island' - although it is not truly an island according to Wanderer. He indicates an atoll above steeprise from the abyss. This youngland is owned by a Splitfluke herd called 'Americans'. Ardent remembers a white-skin Splitfluke in a saga...'

Ardent beaknodded once... The mindweb was attentive...

'The white-skin was American, old friend. They are a herd which is ambitious but slow to anger. If they do intend violence, they possess weapons which are fearful. They are responsible for much death in the waterspace - even when not actually warring with other Splitflukes, in things they call 'War Games'.'

Gaze paused, sensed the mindweb's puzzlement...

He mindmerged, 'A 'War Game' is meant as a practice opportunity for killing and using Splitfluke weaponry... but it is practice and not actual spilling of life-blood. I know the expression seems odd.'

He shared some further imaging and, finally, the mindweb appeared to accept a concensus and strove to banish doubt clouds. Gaze continued...

'Splitflukes I have mindread in 'Brisbane' know of a war for Americans in another herdspace called 'Vietnam'. Much killing took place in Vietnam but it took a long time for the reality of horror in the war to breach into conscience for the ordinary Americans at home in their herdspace. The Vietnamese fought in non-traditional ways - hiding in the jungle or the peasant throngs of apparent innocence. The Americans sought to destroy the hiding places and used chemical weapons to 'defoliate' the jungle... to create vast tracts 'Of No Hiding Place'. I believe that at 'Swains Island', we will find the cause of the Podsherds' recent Abominations... and partly the reason for my own difference to other Bottlenoses.'

Fluking reflexively in mindmerge as he had taught them, the mindweb communed leaving only Ebbstir and Crest Spray to monitor seaspace.

He told them the significance of Wanderer's orange sand!

The Americans called it 'Agent Orange' but it had a more complicated chemical name of 'tetrachlorodibenzopdioxin'... Gaze told them only the abbreviated chemical name 'TCDD' which was easier to beakclick. Over eleven million gallons had been sprayed from airthings to cause trees to shed their leaves... Such a vast number had no significance to the mindweb... until he helped them 'see' the area encompassed by the liquid to a depth of one dolphin body!

He told them of the persistence of manufactured 'dioxins' in soil, sediment and water... Of landspace and waterspace poisoned for seasons and of absorption and intrusion of the food-chains. He spoke of Splitfluke fear, discovered lately, that dioxins could have mutational effects upon the natural world... of poisoning and evil which could result!

The Americans might not have used all their stocks of 'Agent Orange', said Gaze. They would not wish to contaminate their own herdspace, store-up danger and horror for future generations of familypods...

Gaze mindimaged possible dumping of excess and unwanted stocks of 'Agent Orange' in the seaspace...

'Splitflukes worldspace-wide abhor dumping of poisons within their own herdspaces. Americans may have looked to the islandmasses held in 'herd name' to store hazardous wastes... Perhaps they have stared into the abysses of the deeps...?'

There was a lengthy pause... as if Gaze was hesitating to hurt someone close to himself?

Finally, he said, 'Share deep images of recall in my sire's reefsiding.' Gale heard, 'Forgive me for reliving something suppressed so long... Hidden almost from me...'

Gale felt the briefest fintouch from his son... before they all flukestopped, wallowing in amazement of a young Guardian's past... glimpsed through waves of seasons gone...

Peen had been pregnant, growing larger with the unborn and unnamed Gape... She was missing her mate, far too many dolphinspans distant...

Crest Spray had watched them go, his beak tracing an assumed vector beyond the horizon... He was waiting, a little enviously...

Mimic was a calf striving to keep pace with the Nursery Dam's right forefin... And Gaze and Cornice were unborn...

The mindweb adjusted to difference in space and time...

From and within Gale's memory, they shared the vectoring towards... the atoll ahead...

Wanderer cautioned the need to check the steepsides and reefrises thoroughly. He suggested two bi-vector units and they split accordingly. Karg and Gale moved upcurrent of steeprise; Wanderer and Whitegraze finned downcurrent. They intended to repod on the further side of the atoll.

They ping-patterned and sang to maintain contact and send awareness of progress towards repodding in quartet.

When they met, both podpairs reported nothing of great import - except that Whitegraze had drawn attention to the 'threads of odd staining' drifting through the waterspace on the downcurrent. Voyager and Guardian had finned though the phenomena without apparent effect.

Karg reported nothing upcurrent, verified by Gale.

Then Gale fluked reefside and airleaped to observe the lagoon across the reef. Stained, the surface had been fluid blotching on the skin of the sea! From crack and ope of reef, thin tangled tendrils of alien oddness intertwined. All four Bottlenoses examined them further.

It was Wanderer who decided that he and Whitegraze should fluke the lagoon to ascertain their cause of mystification...

As senior Bottlenose present, he gave instructions that Karg and Gale should fin out-reef of entrance. Thus, unwittingly, he saved two lives; sentenced a Guardian Pod Leader and himself to death.

Gale and Karg watched them fin across the stained surface and saw the first airsnatches. Signs of irritation were immediate. Both bottlebeaks lifted but not for long. Voyager and Pod Leader dived below.

Later, they confirmed that their eyes, blowholes and mouths seemed to sting and burn - that they had dived to allow coolness of water to alleviate discomfort temporarily. They tried to airsnatch in unstained areas.

When eyes and senses had cleared a little, they searched lagoon bottom visually and in echo-scanning... In moments they detected the alien cylindrical shapes resting on lagoon floor. Most seemed neatly placed - so neatly that they knew of Splitfluke involvement without further investigation. Storm disturbance had caused some cylinders to topple - and of these, many leaked a dribble of globules in response to water eddy and movement. Some toppled shapes were fractured badly or broken in half, witness to a storm fury or a freak wave which occurred in the warmstream occasionally. These broken shapes had stopped leaking to aquamarine.

Wanderer was debating how long it would take wave action to intermix the sea with Splitfluke fluid when the haunting stillness impinged upon their consciousness... The patterns of light ripples dancing on coral and sand gave illusion only of normality and sanctuary...

There was something else which should have been there but was not...

More alert, Whitegraze saw them first for what they were. Light playing across their carcasses made them appear to move. But they were incapable now!

The lagoon bottom was stippled with death! Predator or prey, all were unmoving in the light's illusion of living!

Shells gaped. Anemones linked languid traceries of stillness across wide-mouthed flat-fish staring fixedly from twisted eyes.

The Bottlenoses finned closer to reefside shallows, noting death in weird images of horror. The darkwater would bring them again... and magnify fear. They finned aside from a shark in weed, its gape-grinning maw decomposing slowly.

Then there were gulls - corpse after corpse in twisted postures of silent agonies. They lay upon the sand or turned in the eddies of shallows.

Whitegraze told Gale later of foreknowledge of his death coming like cloud shadow across the rigid wings of one of those gulls. He and Wanderer had looked eye in eye... both known it confirmed.

They had fluked rapidly from that place, desperate to warn the other podpair; wondering how long they had...?

The mindweb's silence was stunned shock!

Gale's memory of sickness - his despair in personal helplessness and his uncertainty of recovery had such intensity in recall!

Peen said, fluketrembling, 'You did not tell me. I did not know it had been so awful. Why did you hide you thought you would... that you were afraid you...? Oh, Gale, you had to know I would have shared all the pain... needed to be close and there!'

Emotion in Cornice was felt by all. They were too dazed to understand immediately whether the youngest mindsobbed in recognition of the horror, or the bravery of Bottlenoses past or the strength of love between the Master Guardian and Peen. As it was Cornice, it was probably all three at once.

Gaze mindmerged, 'I do not know yet what we may find at 'Swains Island'. For this reason, in a short while, White Tip and I will mindscan ahead. It will be better to see if life exists there now. If it does, we can assume that risks to ourselves will be minimal in finning there. Understand from Gale's imaging, we dare no chancing with Splitfluke poisoning, this 'pollution'...'

And so it was that they formed the crucifix in deep-sea and aligned with a place of old catastrophe...

White Tip and Gaze leapt to scan, fearing mindlights of 'others' would not be discernible to fix reference upon...

Such worry was needless it seemed. The atoll's lagoon was populous, light clusters visible as speckled densities in the planes of empathy. True, there were not the similarities to swirling shoal patterns of other islands they had seen... Life, not quite so abundant, was surviving and multiplying...

Hopeful, less apprehensive, they both fixed to 'others' and moved within...

Prioritising, they tried to sense the waterspace; the sandfloor and coral towers, and attempted to share the vision of their temporary hosts... or whatever sensing was available and appropriate...?

They both recognised lateral sensing and awareness of mass proximity. Both recognised motion through water of some kind...?

Thrusting aside the need to know if Splitfluke canisters were still there, both found it far more important to qualify their hosts at about the same moment...!

Gaze realised he was pulse jetting in motion with six limbs redundantly trailing, or swinging slightly to give or maintain direction. Stopping, the strange limbs spread an undulating stick-suction to coral and crevice...!

He knew the creature but it had to have been mutilated in some struggle with another...? There were no signs of wounds or scar tissue; no memory of conflict...?

Did the 'other' have vision? There was concentration - acute deliberation within the senses...

Why was it necessary? Gaze moved closer in cluster...!

One eye only? No depth vision - only detection of strong light or colour... Everything was blurred and six tentacles, when there should have been eight, sought constant feedback to reinforce weak visual cues... No second socket for another eye...? A horrible suspicion was born...!

White Tip's host was a fish. She mindmerged reassurance to Gaze who was somewhere beyond the shoal dancing of which she was part... Gaze replied tersely...?

Did he seem uncertain? That was silly - they were both uncertain in

this place. They needed to know if Splitfluke
canisters were still there, he reminded.

Lateral sensing allowed her to adjust and monitor her placement... The
eyes of the 'other' were more efficient than she expected. She began to
influence change of direction... Saw in mindeye, three of the shoal detach
to follow...

Something was odd about them. What was it?

She concentrated on the waterspace in the lagoon. It was more
important...

There seemed no parallels with the awful imaging which Wanderer
and Whitegraze had described to Gale and Karg. Whatever cadavers
had littered the sandfloor, they were gone. Anemones, sea grass and
sandworms she noted, though fewer than she would have expected.
Creatures were claiming crevice and niche. The 'other' finned wide
avoidance from a moray.

There was no sign of 'the tidy Splitfluke piling of drum or canister'...
And then there was - but just a sign...

The broken canister leaked nothing. It was part covered by a patchy
coral crusting; the first resident shellfish and very small crabs. Looking
so innocent, it was impossible to equate the metal shape with deadly
imaging in Gale.

She mindsummoned Gaze and waited; turned her attention again to
the tiny podpartners following her, fin-flickering in a graceful curve...

Fin-flickering! How could she have missed something so obvious?
These partners - her own host - did not fishfan in motion... It seemed
their fishtails were stiff, lacking elasticity... Looking like fish, moving
oddly...!

They moved with two pairs of pectoral fins making odd, semi-circular
motions which did suggest a flickering and fluttering... like tiny fast-
beating wings!

She mindsummoned Gaze again, keeping the mindwhispering constant,
urging him to fix a new reference upon her host and herself.

There quickly, he shared short-form imaging for speed...!

'Mutational effects' were recognised...!

They allowed the force of retraction to rejoin them with the mindweb
and their own wallowing bodies...

Poison, despite water clarity, might still deny entry to the lagoon by
themselves as physical entities. Using senses in these 'others' - who might
have developed immunity to the 'poison' if it persisted as a threat to life?
- was the only way to discover anything else.

The mindweb reached concensus - although several doubted if much
could be achieved by investigating further.

Gaze waited for the darkwater truce period before the second
mindleap, alone. This time he fixed to a cold, white light he recognised.
The cruising shark was but recent in residence - showed no significant
variation of form or sensory ability. Digesting a food-find from an out-

reef fissure, it was sharkfanning elegantly; half comatose... but allowing a waterflow through gills...

Hypnotic, the motion soothing... there was nothing to disturb natural rhythm... nothing to shake an indolence of a waterdreaming continuum... they could sharkfan lower in the freedoms of fluidity together... perhaps forever... spiral down... beyond starshine... below darkshades... to rest in the sands...

Gaze saw dark sandfloor loom upwards in a curve!

Realising the imminence, he unfixed, withdrew to refix upon a near 'other' alternative! Splitfluke poisoning was still killing... but insidiously, over lightwaters...

He could see the mindlight of the shark as a diminishing glow - a tired ebbing away from consciousness. He could not see its unblinking eye, staring through a scatter of sand.

Neither could he see the rolling straggle of weed catch in the vacant maw which seemed less vicious. He sensed the carcass prostrate on the lagoon floor; felt this 'other', a tiny crab, tentative in exploration of the unexpected food source - and then the tiny claws sought to scratch and tear.

Within the mind of the crab, Gaze patterned... The shark had succumbed... to something in itself? The ending had been an accumulation to a certainty... tired acknowledgement of ping-patterning heard beyond the beachbrush of wavebreak... distorted, until in depth, final sound echoed in expiry...

The shark had scavenged out-reef... happened upon another predator... or another seeker of sustenance feeding upon an unfortunate... for 'all' consumed each 'other'...!

In a leap of understanding, Gaze knew the poison hidden but active within the food-chains!

Many more would dive to death before the natural rhythms decreed. But how far would Splitfluke pollution spread?

How far already? He imaged the mindweb fishmustering in the lightwater... The darkline of horizon seemed not so far away... and fresh fears breached!

He would have to caution the mindweb. Merely feeding could cause White Dolphins to ping-pattern Bottlenose names...

Locked in apprehension, he did not monitor the movement of his crab host closely. Dimly aware of the scurrying movement, a claw holding aloft shreds of sharkflesh, Gaze read an intention to seek a sanctuary to consume and digest...

Paying little heed to the place of refuge which the 'other' chose, it was not until tiny legs slipped on a hardness of surface that an enclosure, away from stronger watermovement, registered. It was just sufficient for him to try to identify location...?

Too dark for cues of colour, sound was hollow. Curious, Gaze opened mind to further sensing in the crab... reminded of how his dam had sensed solitude and despair in the hardside tunnel, the place of Finwarp's self-imposed exile in guilt. Peen had sensed something merely from clawscrape upon metal. Ironic that her son, after framing such mindskill appraisal, should be faced with a similar conundrum.

Sand covered a side, or wall, as evidenced by the crab's locomotion, assured for most part, despite a slipping drag occasionally. The curve of metal rising from the sand gave insight.

A Splitfluke canister or drum! Instinctively, Gaze knew the colour of the metal; that his host 'other' was within a broken canister as described by Wanderer!

Gaze became fully alert; waited for the next scraping touch of leg or claw...

The vision images came in rapid confusion... Mixtures of other times and places... He could focus on nothing but a

whirling kaleidoscope... opened absorption of mind to store, having no opportunity for qualifying... The patterning could come later...

He could sense intent... Strangely, there was sense too, of... hesitation?... no, a sense of Splitfluke apprehension...of fear of danger to self in 'hands' that had touched this metal?

The 'other' was sensing the waterspace. It was questing for danger in preparation of re-emergence. Gaze detected the eddyflow of temperature difference as strange feelers waved above eyestalks. The waterspace was glazing early dayglow...!

He had over-stayed! He had to warn the mindweb!

Gaze allowed retraction to tear him backwards.

'Splitflukes took away the 'drums' and 'canisters', Gaze?

But where would they take them? And why?' asked Ardent.

The mindweb did not pause in flukingpassage. Fears in fishmustering too close to the atoll they had expected to vector upon had been understood. The new vector was towards waterspace to meet Spinner friends.

Fatigued in mind, Gaze had left it to White Tip to request assistance. Rayrender and Bluster had agreed.

'We have only one clue to where Splitflukes may have tried to hide their chemical poisons, old friend. White Tip herself is our guide. She is a mutant as am I. We have no outward signs as did the surviving species we have seen... and shared knowledge of with friends. Yet our mindskills have accelerated and magnified... Some change in Gale himself has made my mind or brain inheritance different to dolphinkind. Something similar happened to Karg, was seeded to Vorg, his son. If there was evil in sire, that too was magnified... became evident in maturity for the son.'

Gaze paused, patterned...

Mindsmiling in contact, Ardent heard, 'A Cleric would be better to advise on whether evil is transmissible from sire to son in the seeds of life... I can only pattern that Karg may have ingested slightly more poison than my sire. Remember, Gale recovered first from the sickness and suffering. This makes me pattern to try to understand if Splitfluke poisons may have effects that are unqualifiable for dolphinkind.'

Gaze added, 'Splitfluke chemistry strives to be precise in predicting interactions between substances they call 'inorganic'. Precise effect upon living flesh or form, which they call 'organic', is not so readily determined. This much I know from Maeve's learning... and of others... but I do not understand everything, Ardent.'

It was Ardent's turn to pattern.

Peen asked for him, knowing all the mindweb wanted the answer. The network was vibrating in confused anticipation.

'White Tip, Gaze? She is the clue to where other Abominations might be found? She doesn't know her podsherd origins...'

Peen tried personal address to her daughter-in-tradition, aware of mindweb attentiveness... and also the deep sympathy felt... 'Forgive me dear, you do not know whether your sire or dam still fin the... We have had no contact with...'

'But my mate has half images of the podsherd waterspace

of her early seasons,' answered Gaze. 'White Tip already knows I have been comparing remembered feature of reefrise and steepslope, line of deep abyss and arc of sun in dayglow with Wanderer's sandfloor signs. Certain possibilities may exist. That is why we are co-opting Spinner assistance... From a calf's memory there may still be a chance to find answers for my mate.'

White Tip mindmerged, surprising Bottlenoses again, Peen included, with her strength of self. 'Gaze has tried so hard to keep a promise he has felt made to me to find out the truth of what has happened to my podfamily. I love him all the more deeply for this. But there is greater urgency now. If, as Gaze fears, my difference to dolphinkind is also a result of Splitfluke poisoning, then that poisoning could have brought Abominations... to my podsherd waterspace...'

Ardent finned first alongside her; both Gale and Gaze were there rapidly.

Ardent said in open mindmerge, 'Then for both reasons we fin as your podfamily in all good faith.'

It was contact heart to heart, short but needful. Ardent finned aside to let a sire-in-tradition show his respect and affection... For Gaze to fintouch and console...

They were reinforced with selected Spinners and Spotted cousins who had raced to converge. Rayrender, Bluster and Equinox they knew already. All cousins had rudimentary mindgifts tuned to cohesion in mindwebbing.

Numbering twenty two of mixed podding, they progressed in the direction Gaze called 'westerly'. They declined an offer to herd with melon-headed whales, politely. Maintaining their single-mindedness was imperative.

They decided upon search methods. All were warned to check for mutant creaturekind before seeking prey. Belated sign of food-chain poisoning, it would be the only clue they would have.

Recognising the line of trough in the abyss was the first indication that they were closing the second possibility known from White Tip's calfhood memory.

For half a mooncycle they had searched, finding the first area of congruity between memory and Wanderer's signs in five lightwaters. Diligence in Guardian search techniques by two main groups, led by Crest Spray and Gale respectively, had revealed no sign of mutant or anything discordant in the normality of seaspace rhythms. They had come upon a small podsherd of short-snouted Whitebellies but these cousins, as usual, had declined association and had fluked divergent vectors. At least they had appeared healthy.

Continuing their established method of operation, White Tip had accompanied Gale's pod; Gaze had fluked with Crest Spray's. Both podunits had further sub-divided to allow a wider search area, with due regard for the safety of all, but with nothing of note reported.

Each darkwater, they had come together for Gaze to continue to monitor events far 'west' in 'Brisbane'.

They would form the dolphin cross for a short period only, for all were needful of dorsal drifting relaxation after periods of arduous exploration and search. Ever constant was the anxiety of fluking seaspace which might reveal unknown and unqualifiable terror.

They had tried to joke in the network... but the image of each fishbite taken as possibly hastening the deep-dive was an ever present fear. That their mindmurmurings might already be reaching an Abomination, raised terrible spectres around each reefedge or seashadow.

Cornice, in her over-reaction to weedtwist or darkshapes of uncertain outline on seafloor shelf, often sent a pulse of panic to the rest. Gaze had to intervene quickly, despite the presence of Mimic, for they were increasingly sensitive all.

Crest Spray confided that he was glad Gaze had ruled that Cornice should fluke always in company with Mimic... and never far from Gaze himself.

'She is like a lobster alone on the migrant march, fearing each shadow a fishbeak to snap off a limb,' he had imaged in confidentiality which Gaze allowed a leader during a darkwater rest period.

The mindweb was conditioned in sacrifice of privacy to facilitate instant response. There were no secrets for the mindweb partners... beyond those to which Gaze was privy and sanctioned. But leaders were allowed greater independence and freedom to act within procedure. Gale and Crest Spray were satisfied to see Guardian tradition respected in this way... and felt the compliment.

Just before vertical sunrise - on what the sagas were to record as 'Discovery Lightwater' - they sensed it!

Ardent was to name it later as 'The Slopes of the Void'.

For void it was indeed!

296

Gaze immediately ordered flukehalt. They vectorcurved away, upcurrent. When Gaze felt a prudence of dolphinspans of distance, they formed dolphin cross.

They knew his intention - most of all White Tip...

'No, my love. This leap I take alone. You will stay close to my flank. Feel impulses of myself through my flesh. This time I deny you know emotion... only my constancy.

'Ardent. My dam. Fin close at her side. She will know of my need... if need there be... but I forbid any dolphin here... to attempt to fluke or fin waterspace above this void. Whatever may be found, I doubt the presence of an Abomination as we have experienced. This must be Splitfluke intervention in harmony... a different kind of abomination...'

Mindvoice command was felt, recognised. Not even a sire dared counterimaging.

When White Tip heard him again, it was deep at junction of mind and heart; a close whispering within her flow of self.

'This once, I must sense to see a history alone. Tragedy you have known enough. I would shield you from more... but... the truth you will have of a podsfamily... as I have promised,

... with care, my love, with care...'

The mindweb felt his leap... He was gone...

Slower... as slowly as he could project mindscan forward through darkness and light... yet fast enough to free himself from fierce ebbtide of retraction...

Never had he found forward questing such a delicacy of balance... He felt himself dizzying between the barriers of empathy... pushing forward in distance, striving to use the lightside for reference, aware of the gulf beneath...

It was too slow. Nothing to mark the motion, he had to quicken slightly... to sacrifice a little of accuracy... to see any lightglow in passing...

Like initial outherd flukingpassage, at first there had been mindlights... 'others' of existence... He had seen them pass in periphary... but the scattering had widened... the mindlights, diminishing in brilliance with suddenness, a few on a fringe, winked a solitude... until there were none...

He needed to fix upon an 'other'... some 'other'...?

He must have passed above a trench... had sensed awesome depth beneath... But even in the deepest abyss there should have been mindlights from some...?

Gaze faltered, felt the tugging... increased impulsion of self... searching in desperate need, the sense of solitariness threatening to drown his purpose...!

Tiny lowglows ahead... to fix... upon...?

White Tip formed the images before she knew them...

The mindweb reacted to the trembling. She felt Peen's fintouching...

'He's fighting something,' White Tip mindmerged through contact of flesh.

Peen's wide-eye spoke as loudly as any mindvoice...
I know... Himself... Wait...
Nothing to sense with? Nothing of limb extension?
Fixed within a lowglow of living... but nothing...?
Unless...?
Gaze told Ardent later of the personal terror he experienced then. He was fixed to an 'other'... Could be fixed to nothing else but a living 'organic' thing... and desperate had become the need...
It was the motion that saved him from unfixing in dread. Whatever... wherever this 'other' was, waterspace placement reassured, gave stability for his unstable self.
A motion-sense was there. He could feel the rise and fall of seasurge... but not a wholesome wetness?
Assertion of his own self-will was possible... but it took effort to expand, to encompass more of the lowglows... to identify... to qualify...
There was dampness and darkness...? These 'others' had limited experience...?
They were so small!
If the 'others' could give no clue... what of the thing around them...? The thing they were... consuming?
And patterning was his final salvation! That, and the strange residual images of landspace, in uprooted, stormtossed tree debris!
Grub-like creatures feeding on flotsam torn from a tree!
Most part submerged, the tree remnant drifted through waterspace devoid of life... These 'grubs' fed upon wood exposed to airspace...
Increasingly sodden, the debris would sink and these creaturekind would not develop form; never grow through...
'Metamorphosis'?... Was that the 'word' in Maeve?
Even now, some lowglows were diminishing. One winked out in expiry as he monitored...? Why? The wood... the 'branch' was not sinking yet...!
He knew!
The branch was damp with water from the splash of wave or dipping immersion... A poisoned waterspace that was killing! Struggling for freedom from a wooden birthplace, even these small 'others' would die.
Gaze knew where Splitfluke canisters and drums had been taken. The 'pollution' was still active... Splitflukes were still sinking their poisons - their 'industrial residues'... or 'nuclear' waste in the deep!? Intuitively, Gaze knew that Splitflukes might use the same place for similar activity... How much waste did one hardside dump in 'sailing the seas'? And if they kept coming here...
Gaze gathered himself. He needed another kind of final truth... White Tip...
He nerved himself for another leap...
Gaze shared as much as he dared... He showed them the pale hues of sorrow... The bleached bones of remembrance... The flaking sharkfans... Dorsals sunk in sands...

Fixed to the four-legged crab-creature, he had seen the litter upon the upper slope, far downcurrent in misty flow. Light had flickered an intermittence. One eye immovable, tracking dimly a searching claw, the second had scanned an endless semi-circular in reflexive motion. The mindlight was low and expiring.

Some weed seemed twisted in frenzied shape; crystalline and brittle it had broken to brushscrape of claw.

Shortly after had come the skeletons in the quiet of the flownoise... the sound of sandslip and detritus tumble...

Not seeing all... eye blur of image mere indication of immensity... confirmation of desolation from leg or claw...

The fringe of farside... an edge of poisoning potency...?

Upcurrent, from there, grey opaqueness... The doomdepths of blackness beneath...

Unillumined was lifeless whiteness he knew was there, teeth white, bone white hidden from...?

He told not of white shapes, distant in shadowplay...

ping-patterning, acknowledging a mind's last moan...

Such cautions were for a self, alone...

Leaving the 'other' crawlcreeping the precipice above the steepdrop down, he had unfixed and retracted.

The mindweb was quiet; the trembling of network, pulse faltering in each.

From Crest Spray came the questions, doubting nothing in the imaging, striving for practicality and aware... the awful dilemma for her... the unknowing...

'So many... Gaze, so many? And how far?'

Gaze answered, in fintouch with White Tip - as close as her mindblank allowed, 'From upcurrent fringe of the trench...across and within... From downcurrent slopes, above shelf and into distant seaspace the c... signs are scattered. Silent densities of... the signs thin slowly to pockets in eddies around seafloor rises... Further, is isolated indication...'

He stopped as White Tip's fluketrembling and unvoiced mindscreaming wracked the mindweb with force. Bottlenose, Spinner or Spotted cousin alike, all put up barriers of reefsiding to mute her distress, the network fixing them in her torment.

Cornice's more audible sobsounds were totally understood.

Mimic finned closer to her.

Peen was at White Tip's flank; Dapple ready behind.

Imaging still fitful, blurred by his mate's power in grief, Gaze tried to continue...

He knew the pain; knew it had to be beakfaced... and, in herself, she was strong enough now...

'I do not know how far. Perhaps three times as far as the signs? Or five? Splitflukes have poisoned food-chains for all... Weed-eater or fish-taker, all will succumb... Predators fin or fluke over distances greater than the homespace of each... and prey flee from sanctuary to hiding place...

'It will be very, very far, Crest Spray.'

Gale said, carefully, 'And next Gaze?'

And a son was grateful for his Master Guardianship.

They were all wallowing, safe from the void's brink for now... knowing they could not go on...

Beaknodding to sire, Gaze mindmerged, 'We have finned above the signs taking precautions we could. Between two poison-places as we are, the first... and this new... we must make left forefin vector...

'I can guide us to fringes of Spinner waterspace we know as safe. Bluster will lead from there, I trust?'

Bluster snoutwaved acknowledgement, feeling an immense pride but remembering an obligation. To his lasting credit, he said, 'Rayrender and I will do as you ask.'

He finned bi-vector with Rayrender immediately and the joint leadership for Spinners was sustained. An oversight by Gaze was forgiveable... in such circumstances...

They all saw him nudge White Tip's fin against that of Peen... All knew Gaze and Gale would lead from vector front. He would be there in her mind when she needed. For now, it was a time for female consolation... and, moreso a dam.

Peen responded without mindmerging necessity.

Finning a few dolphinspans away, Dapple began to sing the echo-lament for deep-dives... and, they knew, for Gaze's mate. Quietly ping-patterning, Bottlenose and cousin joined her in sending haunting echolalia across silent seafloors and into the trench...

The echo-returns were sibilance from vast depths of sea, as if malignance hissed venomous reply.

Their song faltered... and died, lost in the immensity.

Chapter Seventeen

MIRACLES AND MINESWEEPERS -
Part one

❚ Perhaps I hope for too much, old friend... Disruption of harmony in
waterspace cause catastrophes Splitflukes wish not to recognise. More
numerous than shells on the homespace beach, they know no predator
to govern multiplying... except that of their warring... or pestilence which
affects us all. Possessing learning of 'medicine' and 'science' for the good
of all, 'all' rarely includes other creaturekind. It is as if they regard 'joy in
life' or 'range of emotion' as motivation or qualities for Splitflukes alone...

'Such is prime selfishness... deliberate and wilful, it is refusal to accept
the rights of other creaturekind in the balance and cadence of species'
co-existence... Little is taught in their 'education' to parallel awareness of
needs for sharers of worldspace which we know as necessary. What they
learn is detachment - an acknowledgment of an 'other' only in shallows of
interdependence... They domesticate and demean an easily 'conditioned'
herbivore or co-opt the energies of a minor predator like...'

Mindpictures of several creatures, which Gaze named, entered
successively the mindlights of both. Gaze seemed to make a choice and
focused upon one. Ardent noted four legs, teeth and claws... a redundant
tail that seemed to have a flicking motion - but not for fanning or finning...

Then the creature was shown in loose co-operation with Splitflukekind...
running to herd herbivores which the sagas mentioned but few had seen...
performing 'tricks' in 'shows' - or aiding Splitflukes in flushing or fetching
prey...

Gaze said, 'They would make dolphins their 'dogs of the sea' - believe
us free in the fallacy created. True symbiosis outreaches them...'

'Their need to maintain superiority and their fear of an equal...
The desire for more taken to excess... Loss of real joy in a blindness...
selfishness which calls no kind of truce to hear a music in songs of all...
These bring the windnoise of torment to seaspace; the silence of stillness
in emptiness.

'You image a 'hole in one Splitfluke heart'... I fear voids in a world
they claim!

'If there was anything which ought to force dolphinteeth against such
unseeing or uncaring malignance in 'the heart of their barren world', it is
the injustice... the evil of their voids!'

Ardent saw the fluketrembling in Gaze; knew the struggle for direction
within. Sharing the horror, he strove to beak-
clutch to tenets of faith. Anger and despair... desire for revenge?...
hopelessness... pulsed in lurid shades around the mindlights of the younger
Bottlenose who was master of much... Was he still master of himself?

In the flukingpassage to Spinner waterspace, they had not shaken free from threats at the brink of the void... It had hissed in their souls... stayed grey afterimaging, oppressing the mood of each...

Mindmerging carefully, a little tentatively, Ardent said, 'The sagas tell of no attack by dolphinkind upon a single Splitfluke, Gaze. Long, long ago, you know we left the land to claim homespace and the sustenance of...'

Yet again, Gaze felt his mind-drift, read his heart...

'From mammals Splitflukes do not recognise in the same way they do not see us now! They deny the parallels of life we take for granted!'

It was irritation. Gaze paused. Starkness of mindglow suffused to gentler hues.

'Oh, Ardent... Gentle Ardent... You sense my desire to fight unjustness in Splitflukes... to change trend and force them to conformity... I know that cannot be done in conflict for I honour the White Dolphins as much as yourself...

'To sink teeth in Splitfluke flesh, I dare not. Neither dare my heart bring them suffering. My love of harmony... the love I sense possible in Splitflukes few... pulls me back from acts, understandable to their vanity... in their insanity...

'But it is hard, dear Cleric... It is hard...'

Ardent imaged a sire's respectful treatment of a wounded Splitfluke from an airthing... Guardianship of Bottlenoses unto the creature's time of deep-diving...

Would Gaze see the importance of the tradition? Despite the sacrifice and Splitfluke abominations? Were the hardest things of all, tolerance and forgiveness, possible for him?

Fringing the mixed podsherd, Spinner and Spotted cousins were aware of Gaze and Ardent patterning in the strange manner of Bottlenoses. Bluster and Rayrender had given strict orders that they should be given freespace to fluke alone.

Few of the Bottlenose mindweb finned Guardian circuits. The rest were digesting food-snatches in dorsal drifting dozing, safety guaranteed by Spinner watch-keepers. The long flukingpassage had created an energy debt for they had been reluctant to fishmuster in transit, afraid of poisoning still... and the overwhelming sickness of spirit that had shadowed the waves.

'Three lightwaters we shall fin an association here,' came the imaging of Gaze, 'and then return to homespace.'

'And the Bottlenoses and Hump-backs of 'Brisbane'?' asked the Cleric.

'We change nothing. We leap to continue the influence of the dolphin-cross. We await opportunity, Ardent. Each fall of darkwater will tell us more... allow access...'

Ardent waited.

The lightplay within Gaze's mind indicated there was something else. His years as a Storyteller had trained him to observe many things... and he was always ready to learn and adjust to strange phenomena - even the brilliance within a... Trainee?

The Cleric mindlaughed at the notion of Gaze being young enough to be Trainee still.

'Allow access' was imageplay of various interpretation?

Was he thinking of Maeve?

He was not surprised when Gaze said more.

'Yes, Ardent. I have a 'hole in a heart' to repair, old friend. She has gone to this 'University' which teaches her much. When she next returns to 'The Dolphinarium', we shall meet her heart there.'

Ardent pictured the flukingpassage of vastness with tired trepidation! His heart wanted to go but his flukes felt weighted enough!

Gaze's mindchuckling had richness for the first time in lightwaters...

'No, Ardent! Not you. White Tip and myself... that is the 'we' I image!'

Then Ardent knew Gaze as tired as himself. Duality of meaning in imaging stood markers to their needs of sleep...

'So if you don't mind, Rick, I'd like to bring my tutor here. I haven't been sketching and making notes for work assignments over the last couple of months because I hadn't really known where to start. I mean, where do you start with a guideline that says 'Function and form in the world of nature are often sources of design and art'? It was so bloody general, I didn't know where to begin. Fed up with bloody theory and no 'hands-on', I was close to dropping out when Deirdre put that advertisement in 'Art in the World'. I was looking for a job, as well as a way out of stupid studying, so I leapt at the chance.'

A rueful smile crossed Simon's face.

'Coming here has shown me ways to work and survive there. I don't know how it happened but I want my tutor to see the results. I'll plough myself through writing an essay about it all later.'

Rick, Ciaran and Simon looked at the bobbing line of rafts that had been modified by 'Simon and Sons'. They were pleasing to the eye and moved quickly under 'D.P.' thrust. The mock 'motor cycle' had been dropped due to effects of wind and inherent risk to riders in 'coming off'. Rod's bruise was still evident to forehead.

Now a low platform straddled the 'dolphin floats' with a spray shield in front. The 'rider' lay prone on the raft with stout rests for the feet. Two arm sockets allowed a kind of bracing support for the upper body and there were rubber-clad handgrips.

Nothing had been sacrificed in exhileration. A rider had the sense of being part of a pod of dolphins bumping across - sometimes 'through' - small waves. The feeling was reinforced by the realism of the floats and the fact that the central dolphin in 3 D.P. was visible through the 'floor' of the raft.

Wearing a wet-suit was essential!

Important to assess wave height before each race, the 'stars' had managed, nevertheless, to cope very effectively with sea surge of up to just under two feet. They could manage beyond that but the strength/weight ratio of the rafts themselves became a limiting factor... as well as the need to remember the strains imposed upon dolphin beaks.

The desire for speed in modern man had provided more than enough volunteer riders. A 'waiting list' for hopeful participants was kept in 'Fiona's' small office and they had felt it necessary to impose restrictions. Not so much a question of age, experienced swimmers and sound surfing experience had seemed sensible prerequisites.

Riders were developing small 'cult' followings although there wasn't really much they had to do. The dolphins were the star performers. For all the arm dangling and shifting of weight on the raft which some riders did for show, dolphin sense corrected for drift or tidal flow.

The profit from more adventurous forays across the bay on a marked kilometre course had swelled enormously. Ciaran had had no difficulty in finding sponsors for rafts. Indeed, numerous offers of financial contribution had come from other firms who wished to supply buoy markers, a 'stake' boat, a rescue inflatable and outboard motor and so on. The latter also saw use in allowing 'peace of mind' for swimming in free association with dolphins off the beach area.

Both men knew profits for the Dolphinarium were on the up even though four more 'dolphin fads' had had to be found. Working flat out in the afternoon shows, it wouldn't be long before two more would be necessary.

Rick smiled at Ciaran - saw his eyelid flicker agreement.

'No problem Simon. When do you want to bring him?'

'The weekend. Saturday afternoon would be best... if that's alright?'

'After the work you put in with Rod when Maeve and Phil went back to the 'brainbox academy' you deserve it lad,' said Ciaran. 'You'd better go to Rick's office with him.'

Simon looked puzzled. 'Er... why?'

Rick said, 'It's a matter of the agreed five per cent of income from the races split three ways for 'Simon and Sons' as agreed with the treasurer around here. The only problem is that the 'Sons' told me to put it 'I'd know where'. I can't think my 'boys' were trying to be rude. Ciaran and I take it they meant giving their shares to you. Phil said something about Art Students needing more money for paint and motorbikes ... or something.'

Simon's look of utter confusion; his later delight, were high-spots of their day.

Rick heard her car first. He tapped Ciaran on the shoulder; saw him return to the main menu on the computer's hard disc and turn.

'Your turn to make the coffee. You know how she likes it anyway.'

'If it gets awkward, I'll flit back to my flat. I know this is...' Ciaran began...

'Stuff it, treasurer. She's put a lot into this. You and I know that she needs to be on site tomorrow now the painting starts. She's probably all keyed up about whether the thing's going to look right and both of you have been jockeying along with a bit more understanding than your average marriage separatists. Why don't you just relax and let it... flow around you?'

Ciaran nodded, got up to move to the galley.

Eyes, the same old mask, thought Rick.

'The foreman said we ought to give exterior walls months to dry out. Texture paint to partitions; stain varnishing won't matter. Any soft board base can be decorated as you see fit. They promise they'll be back in six months to make good settlement cracks. I've had excellent reports about this lot. They've a good reputation.'

Deirdre looked at him, at the building work which had been put in hand with astonishing speed. Already her scheme for 'the new-look' was quarter completed!

Even the raw block and stone work looked appealing from the outside. The display areas were roofed. True, the place needed a thorough cleaning but the tiled floors were...

'Where did the money come from?'

Ciaran had expected it. How was it possible to explain the enthusiasm of planning officials, co-operative good-will in the consortium of interests which surrounded 'Brisbane's Dolphinarium'? It had been so easy. Red-tape had been cut as if a powerful mower had made a path. The Bank had granted the loan at concessionary rates, recognising spin-offs in trade for other small businesses in the area - the hidden but real opportunity for growth. The 'boat-park' for visitors had been the clearest example of co-operation.

His eyes drifted towards the bobbing walkways and buoys.

Some cruisers were moored for the night, their lights already coming on as twilight approached. No doubt they were talking about the thrills of the day. The fingers that had held a dorsal fin... the toddler who had been towed a small distance under maternal watchfulness... were busy with tea and biscuits now.

He saw the dorsals of the cross quietly emerge; heard the breathless amazement of spectators seeing for the first time. Others, the regulars in the evening's adoration, were quietly explaining.

There was something a little different. He found the alignment a slight variation. The dorsals were in line... with them? Normally, they pointed directly through the lock gates. Perhaps... perhaps the moored boats altered things?

Or perhaps... the object of their worshipping had moved across the sea?

Ciaran chuckled. She was still waiting, her eyes trying to fathom his thoughts...

'Well, the Bank you see... It's a worthwhile investment.

They approved a loan and the planning authorities have been very helpful. I suppose they feel they want to encourage the 'Moneymachine' to put in more for the good of the social and natural environment. They've all got a bit excited. It's as if a new good-will is prompting a kind of consensus in mutual concerns and co-operation...'

She looked amazed.

'You arranged to finance all this?'

'I sowed a few seeds. You know the way the Bank works. There are all kinds of ways of funding new ventures and being supportive without losing an opportunity for profit.'

'Rick told me what you did for young Simon. That was a good thing.'

'He had some good ideas... So do you.'

He pointed to the sign near the builders' cabin.

"Art and Design: Deirdre Pearce, Redland Beach..." was fifth in a lengthy list...

'No sense in wasting an opportunity is there?'

He saw the light flicker behind the brown. She didn't know what to say. He decided they were too close - made to walk towards the chapel. He realised that 'chapel' was much more pertinent than the 'grotto' she had called it to shield an embarrassment.

There, he touched the White Dolphin in the ritual of habit it had become. Somehow there was peacefulness in just closing one's eyes for a moment...

In the pounding of his heart he felt her hand...

Her lips touched his cheek, daring no more...

He heard her voice coming from a distance of self.

'Thank you, Ciaran. You have done so much and I don't deserve it.'

He looked at her; reflected the sadness of smile.

'A way to say, 'things I regret I didn't do before'...'

The years of companionship said the rest.

She reached for his hand and felt the trembling...

'I'll make something to eat. Rick'll wonder what's taking us so long.'

And walking back, she knew his hand hadn't wanted to lose contact... whatever that 'not-so-dry' mind was thinking...

Three nights later, Rick found it harder to drop off than he had thought he would. Nightfall had been anti-climax after the evening's excitement, he supposed.

For Deirdre it had been vindication of creative insight. confirming a prediction she had made. For himself and Rod, there had been bewilderment - yet the feeling of possibility.

Ciaran had smiled in the shocked silence. The smile had grown to warm laughter - and a hand on Rick's shoulder during the applause of on-lookers.

'The car-park needs to be larger, Rick. You had better have some more space available for some coaches - especially on Sundays,' he had said.

Rick knew what he meant...

They'd watched the attractive young woman being pushed along towards the best vantage point. The young man, finding the grass easier than the gravel path, had had to have help from one of the 'regulars' to lift the wheelchair on to the jetty's concrete.

Rod had seen it first. The tone in his quiet voice had brought them all on deck. But Rod had not expected what had happened next. None of them had.

Fortuitously, it had been one of the best viewings of the dolphins' cross for several days. It had seemed to maintain position longer - had 'sunk' and emerged regularly. Whiter shapes of the smaller hump-backs had made the terminal ends of the cross. This, if anything, had given more striking realism in the slant of sunlight.

The girl had stared at the cross in earnestness. There had been something about the set of her shoulders and the angle of her head that had seemed as if she'd been listening - but not to the young man?

She had fumbled nervously with blanket covering. She had pushed aside a caring hand - from a husband? - which had tried to insist on warmth.

Swaying, steadying herself on the wheelchair, she had levered herself upright! Still the arms of the man had wanted to reach for her... to stop her falling...

But he had stepped back. And another step away?

She had shuffled a turn; his hands had reached out palms uppermost... Hopefully expectant, they'd encouraged...

Even from the deck they had felt him willing her... the insistence that if she could stand, she could walk those two or three steps toward him...

And she had - she had!

Her sobs of joy on the breeze - his exhultation - had affected everyone! Beginning as a light ripple, it had soon become the hub-bub!

She had walked the length of the jetty!

He had had to offer the wheelchair again. Stepping down and the gravel path had defeated her. Onlookers had known by stance, tight small fists, not for long... not for long...!

Several smiling faces had been behind a triumphant chair on the way over to the 'chapel'.

Rick supposed the papers would be full of it. The first reporter had arrived as her entourage had made the car-park. Three others had arrived within five minutes. Somebody had to have phoned from 'The Red Bottlenose'...

They had talked it out. Ciaran's portable processor had been switched on. They'd had a nightcap and they'd left him to it...

He's up too late, thought Rick. On the verge of padding along to remonstrate, he heard another cabin door open... the scuff of soft slippers...

He climbed back in his bunk. There were quiet voices.

The sound of the kettle being filled.

Drifting, with eyes closed, sleep still illusive three quarters of an hour later, he heard the scuff again. Behind them was a firmer tread.

He heard the cabin door open. It was Maeve's cabin but Deirdre was using it in temporary residence.

There was lengthy silence.

An indecipherable whisper.

The cabin door closed... There was no tread outside...

Soundlessly, Rick reached for the whiskey bottle, held it aloft in silent salute and took one mouthful.

About bloody time, mate, he thought.

Fiona was very close as sleep came...

In the cave, the Cleric finstirred to edge eye to eye.

'How, Gaze?'

'Her mind could not accept the healing. Their 'medicine' is truly wondrous but they failed to strengthen mind.'

Ardent patterned upon the answer.

'Her joy was immense... and her mate... You are using them... but not... altering?'

'No more than their minds were capable... no more than their hearts cried for... Would you censure me?'

'No, I cannot, Gaze... But the other Splitfluke pairing?

Is that a matter of heart's need... or base desire?'

'Do you ask the same of Bottlenose pairings, Cleric? Allowing opportunity for expression of their feeling... of their need... Would you censure in this?'

Staring into phosphoresence, he saw only good intent...

Five weeks later, Deirdre and Phil watched Maeve and the personal tutor they shared at 'Uni', walking along the beach.

Seated on the porch at the beach-house, they were enjoying the fine fresh day. It had been decided the youngsters would overnight at Redland before going on to Brisbane.

Something of a surprise that they had been driven by Doctor Saxonby and requested a bed for the night for the lecturer as well, Deirdre asked the obvious.

There was a look of uncertainty, even of quashed hope in his eyes... There and gone in a moment.

It took Phil time to frame the words.

She waited.

'Maeve apparently shook Saxonby up with her depth of knowledge about cetacean behaviour... physiology... courtship and social structures... and so on. She's red-hot on it all.

When she started talking about interactions with man through the ages, it was if she'd taken over his lecture. Well, so others say.

'Saxonby just let her go on - asked a question here and there. She had the answers too! Apparently, she told them all about a thing called 'empathy'... You know, Dad's used that word - but I don't think he's ever really thought about it in the way Maeve was talking. She says its 'transposition of minds and feelings between interactants'... that the nearest word is probably 'telepathy' but it's more than that.

'Saxonby challenged her naturally. For the first time, in what was supposed to be his lecture, he demanded some kind of 'scientific proof' for her hypothesis. Perhaps that was a bit unfair but I suppose he felt he had to drag Maeve back to sticking to facts. Other people there say he was interested, though. He wanted her to answer - or try to - but she clammed up...

'Afterwards, he sent for her. Maeve says she'd expected to have the difference between theory, hypothesis and wild conjecture well and truly rammed down her throat. But he didn't. He congratulated her and said he was particularly interested in her last remarks, only telling her that she should have clearly stated she was 'hypothesising'. He was more interested to know how she had absorbed so much before they'd even tackled 'Cetaceans'.

'She told him about 'The Dolphinarium'. Although mates knew about us meeting and working there, we hadn't let on to lecturers. That's our affair.'

She felt the sudden stop and the silence - knew there was more.

'And?'

She watched his face. He was inside himself. It was something between Maeve and Phil? He was trying to find the words for something difficult?

'Look, Mrs. Pearce, you might...'

''Deirdre' is my name, Phil. Your family's too close for you to call me anything else,' she said, grateful for it.

He half-smiled back.

'I love her. I've never been more certain of anything in my life. Oh, don't worry. I promise I'm being a great big brother.'

He watched her face; the eyes that reminded.

She dipped her forehead - encouraged him to go on.

'I know she likes me around - enjoys being with me. Pop once said 'listen for a girl's laughter'... Maeve makes me feel good. But sometimes... she almost blocks me out as if she's frightened to feel too much.'

He's still struggling to define it, she thought. Surely it was more than Maeve drawing a line? There must be more.

She touched the back of his hand.

'Go on.'

'I... er, it's been hard to concentrate at times. Not as easy as it used to be. She's a big puzzle. My last essay... It was a bit of a pig's ear. 'Too superficial. Insufficient support from background research.' First time I've had a 'D'. Saxonby called me in - wanted to know why.

'Alright, we're both young. Unsure of ourselves and all that. But... well, Maeve's got a straight-laced reputation. I'm glad she isn't free and easy... like some... but I don't understand her; if she's hurt somehow.'

He looked at her. Deirdre hid discomfort.

Phil said, 'She's not talked about your divorce... loves you both very much. If I'm close to treading on something I shouldn't - I don't know anything. I can't talk about it with her... I'm not sure I should with you... but I don't think her parents' lives are the reasons for her distance inside.

She loves and respects you both very much; talks quite freely about what you've both done with her.'

In the pause, she felt relief; recognised his maturity.

'She's not a prude. Being open and warm seems second nature... but, now and then, it's as if we're talking... and suddenly she can't go on. She's never short; there's never a scene... But she just freezes as if she's somewhere else in another place. It's as if she's trying to remember something else, or someone else who was close to her... very close.

'Has she ever been close to someone else she hasn't told me about?'

It was out.

Phil was worried about 'someone else', thought Deirdre.

Simple jealousy, was it? Maeve involved with someone else!

Hardly likely. She'd have known... Or would she? Had she been so wrapped up in her blind infatuation with... She didn't want to remember that slug! Had Mum missed some signals?

He was waiting; deserved an answer.

'She's not been one for boy friends and heady romance, Phil. If you think there's competition, you're way off.'

He was watching her intently; hanging on every word.

If there was a time for honesty, it had to be now.

'Emotions are funny things. They can make you make mistakes, Phil. Let's say her mother made a whopper and hurt her family and herself... embarrassed a good few others as well. Now it's possible that it's affected Maeve - I don't know. What I do know is that she's attracted to you. You've just got to give things time, haven't you? You do have fun together, don't you?'

He shrugged, smiled a bit more wholesomely.

'Yes. We both can't wait to get back to Brisbane. Things are always better with the 'stars' around.'

'Things are going to be a lot different, Phil. Ciaran and your father don't want me to say too much. You'd better stand by for some surprises.'

He was wanting to say something; missing the reference to Maeve's father. There was no point in repetition...

'I'd do anything for her, Deirdre. There's an emptiness in her that I seem to sense. I won't be dramatic... but will you talk to her?'

'I'll try, Phil. Mothers don't always understand you know. I'd advise you don't let her know we've had this conversation. It never happened.'

She couldn't help the thought, it's bad enough trying to understand oneself! At the same time, she felt flattered that he was being open. Dimly, she perceived that the rift she had feared between herself and Maeve had closed up... wasn't there anymore...

Could she winkle out any problem in Maeve? Was there anything anyway?

The earnestness in Rick's son said... there was?

A shout from down the beach turned both their heads.

The photographs he had seen misrepresented nothing in the odd phenomena. Doctor Saxonby was excited if not disturbed.

Never had he heard or read anything to give him guidance for interpreting the behaviour of the hump-bank dolphins they had seen offshore. The pale shapes had definitely been that species, even if they were too far south from areas of normal habitat and distribution. Slightly darker on top with paler undersides - a hint of spots - indistinct dorsals surmounting evident humps - length of snouts: all had confirmed it.

Amazed, he had heard Maeve name them - not just the species but individually, as if known intimately! He couldn't have distinguished one from another.

He'd been steering the conversation around to discovering how Maeve and Phil really felt about each other. Phil had an academic record heading for a good degree classification but, lately, he'd gone off the boil. Work was being completed but he'd had to give him a jolt with a grade for an essay which was harsher than deserved. In Phil's formal record was the justifiable 'CB', although he wasn't about to let on.

Maeve's results had been consistently high in her first year.

No, neither young people were 'laid-back' but something was troubling Phil - and he was worth that bit of extra interest.

You had to be so careful with students' relationships and their rights to emotional experience and development! He had made the decision to go and see the Dolphinarium, which held such importance, the moment Maeve had told of association with the establishment. Intrigued, he had heard Phil's description of Maeve's ability as a 'Trainer', when he'd asked after that unusual lecture where Maeve had held the floor, spellbinding the rest...

On the point of beginning to delve how deeply she felt about Phil he had seen her stop. Her head had turned as if expecting the event...

Ten yards away, the nine small dorsals had surfaced; 'jetting blows' occurring simultaneously.

Remarkably, dorsal alignment had been precise geometry and stationary - a cross-shape obvious!

Maeve had kicked off her shoes.

'Excuse me, Doctor, please! I know them! Blotch, Twizzle... The hump-backs are here!'

Her skirt had come off and she had plunged in!

Watching her swim directly towards the dolphins had brought an unexpected lump to throat; certain knowledge of her attractiveness for Phil! Twenty five years had fallen away and he had wanted to be swimming out there as well!

He had shouted down the beach.

Phil had come at the gallop with Mrs.Pearce trotting behind.

'I'm sure I've got some stills of their cross outside the lock-gates. They form it every ev... Oh, please forgive the mess. I've been doing a lot of work lately.'

Deirdre felt Maeve's glance - continued to clear one end of the large flat work-table, shuffled sketches to one side.

'Yes, here they are. I don't mind you having one or two. Take your pick... Take the lot. I've got the negatives of most,' Deirdre said to him.

'Thank you, Mrs.Pearce. These are better than a lot of the shots released in the press. Some are taken from above.

A helicopter?'

'Trade secret, Doctor... Or rather, somebody's job might be compromised. A regular flight schedule, I think.'

'Say no more. Have you anything else of interest?' Maeve said, 'The video, Mum? The deep-sea spinners...?'

'Oh, yes. Ciaran made... Your father made me a copy. Over on the shelf. Would you mind watching a video, Doctor? It's only a few minutes, I'm afraid... but it's worth it...'

The weight of Maeve's eyes was heavy on her back.

'I'll just take this folder with me, though.'

She turned to face a daughter; looked directly at her.

'I promise you'll see everything in here tomorrow. But not now, love. A surprise package. Okay?'

The brown eyes were puzzled. Was there also a fleeting flash of hope? She hoped not.

'All will be revealed tomorrow,' she said, turning to steer Doctor Saxonby to the door.

Maeve said, 'I've seen it lots of times. I'll tidy up in here.' She added meaningfully, 'You look as though you've been very busy, Mum.'

Her mother's laughter gave her no clue. As soon as they were outside. Maeve set about 'tidying'.

Whatever her mother had been up to, there was no real evidence of anything.

After some minutes, she leaned back against the worktop which ran the length of one wall. The call from the lounge made her jump.

A pile of old folders cascaded on to the floor.

She left them there, ready for the chocolate drink...

'Amazing. Start hypothesising, Maeve. What do you suppose they were up too?' her tutor said, as she came in.

Maeve thought about it - had to say something...

Suddenly she was talking - and he was leaning forward.

'Ever heard a child's voice in a church trying to sing and the sound getting lost in a big space? Don't you remember a teacher telling you to project your voice in a school hall or 'the ones at the back won't hear'. What a difference when there's a choir of voices... or a large group chants aloud...

'I think they're singing or echo-calling in unison and it extends their range. If they point in the direction they want to send a message... or if they want to have greater chance of hearing another message... they might arrange the melons of their heads in some kind of fixed pattern... Perhaps it's to do with amplification of signal and greater sensitivity in...receiving mode...?'

'What would you call this behaviour?'

The reply came much quicker than he'd expected.

'Probably the best description would be something like 'Orienting to songline'. We know Cetaceans have a language based on regular patterns of song - we've all heard tapes...'

All listening to her, Deirdre and Phil felt it best to stay quiet. This seemed important to Maeve herself...

'What do you think they might be saying?'

She gave an impish smile.

'How could I possibly know? Maybe they're calling for mates. Open-season for pairbonds from other podsherds in other waterspace? The latest joke? Have you heard the one about the octopus with only six legs?'

The Doctor's eyes flickered.

'Podsherds? Waterspace? They seem unusual words to use, Maeve?'

'Sorry. They just seemed appropriate. The meaning's clear... isn't it?'

'Perfectly - just unusual. How would you attempt to verify and support that notion?'

Maeve thought about it. He didn't think she could answer and was about to ask another question.

She said, 'We could only do it two ways. We'd have to have sensitive equipment across a songline to listen... a kind of big ear in the sea. At the same time we'd have to be able to monitor huge areas of sea visually so that... so that we could check for other podsherds in alignment with each other.

It's not something you could hope to validate in a small area like the lagoon at the Dolphinarium.'

He was nodding, encouraging her to go on.

'Co-operation between the Military and those concerned with environmental research would be necessary. The scale of the thing would demand it. How far does sound travel through water? It's a lot further than sound in air. The first... those first satellite photographs from America from the 'Spy in Sky'... or whatever you call it... were the sort of thing we'd need. If we could tie in visual shots in a pass above two crosses with a way of picking up sound between them, we might be able to... prove something? We could check if they were 'Orienting to songline' for a start... couldn't we? Which way... I mean, where the crosses are pointing to?'

'Well, I suppose I asked for thoughts but that's a bit ambitious, isn't it? Do you honestly think you could get that kind of co-operation?'

She didn't say anything.

He was still thinking.

Eventually he said, 'Well, we could try to see if the two crosses we know about ever form reciprocal bearings on each other, I suppose. It would need a polite letter of request from our Government to the States. I'm not sure what the reactions will be... when I ask.'

Maeve looked at him. Phil was sporting a smile of real pleasure.

Phil asked, 'She's got you that interested?'

'Damn it, Phil, yes. But there's another thing that's bothering me. The small cross we saw this afternoon changed it's alignment. It seemed to be pointing towards us for some time and then it altered or adjusted to point out to sea.'

Deirdre spoke.

'You'll see the same thing if you come with us to the Dolphinarium tomorrow. The 'stars' do exactly the same thing in the bay, a short distance from the jetty. It's more than a simple and odd bit of...'

''Stars'?' he asked.

'It's what we call the dolphins there - 'stars' of the 'shows' that are put on.'

She felt Maeve looking at her again, turned and gave her one wink. The smile that came was like warmth in spring.

Doctor Saxonby began to voice a suspicion... which was wild conjecture in himself... surely?

'You don't think they're trying to communicate with... Trying to show that... No, that's ridiculous! I'm sorry. You've certainly given an older man food for thought, Maeve. Interesting. I'll look forward to tomorrow.'

Ardent finstirred, patterning hesitantly. Gaze was... trying to go too fast? His warnings of Splitfluke envy; their murderous nature, held barely in check, seemed stormnoise in mind. Alone in his cave, he wondered at wisdom in revealing too much of themselves too quickly...

Was breeze strengthening to a wind to whip events into tumult? Gaze was attempting too much... and yet...?

He was repairing the 'hole in a heart'... He needed to rectify imbalance. The disharmony within this Maeve was cause enough in short lightwaters ahead but...

The feeling of weight in flukes was growing...

I am tired, so tired, he imaged... and found within himself the knowledge... quiet acceptance of termination... Not yet... Soon...

After breakfast, Deirdre took back the folder of sketches for the new-look in the Dolphinarium. Today was going to be a real surprise for Phil and Maeve. They had been kept in the dark quite deliberately. She found herself looking forward to the look on Maeve's face when...

The old folders had fallen down. She bent to pick them up. Shuffling and reordering, she noticed the corner of a photograph... drew it out to look at it more closely...

A dolphin with a white tip to a dorsal? When had that been taken? There was no dolphin with a dorsal marking like that at the...

Welling down like tiny drops penetrating a porous barrier...like rain through plasterboard under a faulty flat roof...hidden memory in tears was recalled...

She had to give the photograph to Maeve... later, after the fun of the day...

314

'Quite a number of people - more than you might think,' said Rick. 'Art students, building inspectors, coach drivers, and weird men in business suits just like your father, lass. We've got a real cross-section of the community coming through the gates. It's going to take you time to readjust.'

He turned to Doctor Saxonby. 'Now it looks as though we'll be having lecturers and head-shrinkers and God knows what.'

His smile of welcome was readily returned.

'So you want to show your - Doctor, is it? - the 'stars' and what they can do. Right, Doctor Saxonby, my wet-suit will fit, I think. You do swim?'

'A little. I'm out of practice.'

'Don't worry, the 'stars' will do all the work. Phil, get the outboard started. Not the old one - the new one over there.'

He pointed, watching his son's face light up.

'You'll want two teams of three 'stars', Maeve. You'd better get suited up as well.'

A Manager was thoroughly enjoying this...

Shortly afterwards, he watched two race-rafts, 'Bouto' and 'Baiji', cruise unerringly through the lock-gates with Maeve's laughter reassuring her tutor that he 'just had to let it all flow around him'.

When they came back in, hair plastered to heads, they were grinning enthusiasm.

Rick had to field all manner of questions from a most appreciative lecturer concerning training technigues. It was obvious that one answer puzzled him more than the rest put together.

'Once one dolphin gets the message, the rest understand rapidly. They teach each other as well, you see. Maeve's the most successful trainer I have ever known.'

'You're saying they tell each other how things should be done? That they teach each other?'

'How else can you explain the kind of co-operation that exists between them? You felt that team-work on the raft, didn't you? Don't under-rate their intelligence...

'Curiosity they definitely have. Enjoying games and human contact is well documented. Why the hell shouldn't they be able to accumulate knowledge? They've got that indefinable extra bit inside their heads that makes you realise you can't just treat them like... like pet dogs...'

Doctor Saxonby was looking at a dolphin beak making clicking noises a yard or so away. There was an uncanny sense of the beak emphasising the Manager's words...

It was then that he decided to ask if his brother could come and see for himself. It was unfortunate that a distant mind had chosen to monitor someone else at precisely that moment...

Even the most alert can be distracted by parallel events in which beguiling 'other interest' destroys prime intention.

From the display areas, Deirdre led her past the shop. Some customers were examining souvenirs and gifts which Ciaran had bought in. There was rapid turn around of all kinds of things. Steve's Art College friends were only too willing to try a market with paintings and pottery. They all centred on the 'dolphin theme' - even the basketry from overseas. She glimpsed the first of Steve's quarter scale dolphin models neatly mounted on a mahogany base, a spinner leaping into air. She wouldn't mind that one herself. If he could use porcelain shards - or coloured plastic? - to create a greater sense of spray... She'd have a chat with him.

'We can't go in the old-dry dock,' she said. 'The workmen are in the process of part roofing it with a half dome of steel, aluminium and clear laminated plastic. There's rope and chain everywhere.'

She guessed the question and what it would lead up to.

'It's great, Mum. I can't believe it's happened in just six weeks. Where did the money come from?'

She had to join the drift.

'Your father's arranged the money side. There's a loan from the Bank and local firms have been contributing a lot.

Rick says he doesn't know what he'd have done without your father.'

She added, 'I don't know what I'd have done, either.'

Brown eyes turned to brown, saying nothing at first.

'You've been seeing more of Dad, then?'

'He's a good man, Maeve - as well as being a good Banker.

It can't be the same - I've hurt him too much - and Donovan, and you. There would always be the memory of what I did when I went off the rails... What you saw your idiot mother...'

The words were hesitant but they came from somewhere very close to the hearts of each...

Maeve had to ask.

'Are you going to get married again?'

This was the difficult bit. She reached for a daughter's hand.

They were at the chapel. Deirdre sat, pulled Maeve down on the seat alongside. Looking at the White Dolphin, it was easier to speak... to avoid her expectancy...

'Part of us will never be unmarried. I forgot the years of knowing him and feeling the care he showed, Maeve. Your father is... he's been closer and more supportive of me than I've ever felt before. But I don't think we'll remarry. Your father wouldn't ask me and I don't think I could live with myself if he did...

'You know we tried the married way all through, Maeve. Yet I'm not as... conventional as I thought. Your mother's got a bit of the oddball about her. Maybe that's part of you as well. No, I'm not going to freak out and go Arty-flighty - but I can see new challenges that there wasn't time for...

'It's exciting... more exciting than you'd understand, perhaps... And Ciaran is... Your father is a wonderful man.'

This was the worst bit. Value judgements of a young woman sensing love... or a daughter in love? she thought...

can be puritanical in the extreme.

She tried to smile, saying, 'I know your father is there if I need him. He knows I'm around to help him. He didn't trust me or himself after what I did; he feels he can now.'

She tried the reassurance of, 'We both love you even if we might seem bloody stupid to you.'

Maeve's eyes were focused on something deep inside her mother - Deirdre was sure of it. Then they were turning inside herself. They blinked shut.

When they opened, Maeve was not looking at her but at something behind ...

She watched her daughter get up quietly and move unhurriedly towards the White Dolphin mounted above the 'altar'. Her pupils were very wide, indicative of stressful self-searching within.

Did her words cover irresolve? Were they avoidance?

'This is marvellous. The light and reflections seem to make it move... Is it one of Steve's? Yes, it must be...'

Her mother watched her daughter's right hand feel the smoothness; saw the hand stop in rest and Maeve's head tilt forward. It was like watching a supplicant.

Deirdre swallowed hard, daring no sound.

It took a minute - seemed longer. Maeve's head came up and her eyes were moist. If she was crying, Deirdre had to have wounded her. She felt destined to bring pain to the one who was closest.

Tears gathered in her own eyes. She tried to reach for Maeve... could not give hands and arms motion, paralysed by the weight of not knowing...

'Do you love him, Mum?'

'Yes. More than I did before. I won't hurt him again but neither will I try to live the old way. I think it's good Ciaran has this interest here. He's supported me - recognised me in ways he never did. He's a very clever man, Maeve. He's come alive. He was dry and methodical and little else - apart from when he was with Donovan and you. He seemed to expect me to act out a role - and I tried... all the time Donovan and you were growing up. I loved you then and love you now. Your father and I... we lost it... in mundane habit, I suppose... I convinced myself he'd lost interest in what was important to me. The way he's been over the last few months is the way I always wanted him to be... the way I felt he needed to be... but I couldn't influence him.

'I'm sorry for what I did because I know, despite it all, that dear man - your father - he loves me... I risked losing everybody who mattered more than anything just because someone turned my head pretending to take an interest in me... me, inside... But Ciaran is the man I want and need. I'm not about to lose the man I love by living the way we did. If living the unorthodox way is the path ahead, I'm going to run down that path laughing all the way and drag Ciaran along by his hair... and to hell with what the world thinks - Bank, Universities - the lot!'

She looked at Maeve, a vague outline against brightness through tears. With as much control as she could muster she added:

'We can talk to each other again, Maeve. Dad has found ways of financing me in a small business. It's more exciting than you can imagine. He's encouraging me, supporting me in what I want to do to fend for myself. And, God alive, that means so very much. I actually talk about book-keeping... and finances for the Dolphinarium... and feel as excited about it as he does...'

Maeve's outline was still. Deirdre had to see her face.

She produced a tissue, dabbed to restore vision.

Maeve had her back to her when she had finished. She was looking at the new buildings, the emergent half dome above the dry-dock.

She turned and said, "Art and Design, Deirdre Pearce'?

You've kept your married name then? Well... it saves money.'

Their laughter turned the mens' heads on the 'Fiona'.

Ciaran, turned to Rick.

'Manager, Sir, there is reason to celebrate. How about bringing that secret bottle up? Doctor, have you ever tasted 'the finest whiskey from the oldest distillery in the world'?'

Rick leered a grin; made for the hatchway.

Doctor Saxonby left before the afternoon show, having stayed longer than intended. Promising to witness the reality of photographs he had been shown in the display areas, he explained he was hard pushed to make it to the Airport for his flight. He was profuse in his thanks to all. Yet he was no nearer to understanding Phil's dip in academic achievement. It would have to wait.

The race programme took priority and the show.

Breaking a pattern, the 'stars' made no appearance after a 'welcome home' and a brief period showing Doctor Saxonby and Maeve what 'thoroughbred' dolphins could achieve. They had simply vanished into the distance as if someone had declared 'Rest and Recuperation'. The hump-backs had been seen by no-one. Rick was wondering if they'd bother coming back if they'd been at Redland but, sure enough, they responded to Maeve's whistle and wave from the jetty, swam through the lock-gates in a bustling surge with the rest of the 'stars'.

Everyone was busy. Easier with Maeve and Phil to assist Rod with the show, Rick heard whoops of delight as he oversaw the marshalling of 'riders' and rafts.

In mid-evening, when the bustle had subdued a little, straggling knots of people waited for the dolphin cross to emerge.

Maeve said, 'All those people, Mum - every evening?'

'On Sunday evenings it's packed love. We don't open the shop and the only refreshments are at 'The Red Bottlenose'. Not many people bother until after the dolphin cross breaks up. I agree with Rick and Ciaran.

We don't want to make a big commercial thing of it. The cross has all kinds of meaning and significance for all kinds of people. In the evenings, there is nothing to distract attention. There are times when you can feel the rapport between the 'stars' and the onlookers. We haven't told you about the miracles that some people claim have happened. We wanted everything to be a surprise - but they are claimed to have happened.

'A young woman with a spinal injury who had not expected to walk again - and she walked the length of the jetty. The boy who was having difficulty learning to speak - but he did after several days of swimming with the 'stars' in shallow depth off the beach. A woman with a history of agoraphobia who walked to the chapel without qualm. She comes at least once a week now. There's another three or four people who claim something. The first one was in several newspapers. We wondered if you might have read about it.'

'Missed it, Mum. 'On campus' is another existence much of the time. I must have had an essay to do or something... Can we go over there?'

She pointed to a space on the grass bank between the dockyard and the lagoon. The cross would still be visible.

'What about, Phil?'

'He's doing something with Rod on the new rescue boat. He'll find me if he wants to. His radar's infallible.'

Maeve laughed - but was it altogether wholehearted? It wasn't quite the laughter they had shared earlier; the warm certainty in each other...

Deirdre reached for her clutch bag; remembered an unusual photograph... a question in her mind... But she'd wait...

Sitting on the bank, looking at the cross, they both saw adjustment to new alignment.

'Isn't that different to anything before?' asked Maeve.

'It changed once, a little. That's not the same as... anything before.'

They both stared the length of the cross. It could not have been more perfectly viewed from another vantage point.

The breeze dropped away. Sea surface unruffled, low angled sunshine highlighted whiter dolphins at extreme ends of the cross; one alone at the intersection...

A chattering crowd was muted... became silence...

Both heard whispers... but were undisturbed...

Positive the time was right, Deirdre reached into her bag and placed the photograph on Maeve's lap. Her daughter did not look at it immediately - was staring beyond the cross with rapt intentness...

Deirdre saw Ciaran on the 'Fiona'... There was something she wanted to ask him... Now was a good moment...

Quietly, she rose, not wanting to disturb the pleasure for Maeve. The cross is beautiful tonight, she thought.

Beyond the cross she saw two airleaps... Two dolphins in shimmershining spraydrops; both waterdancing for her...?

Nearer now to the cross, she watched them finsteering... resuming known places at centre...

Two Bottlenoses, one each side of a paler Hump-back she knew was Blotch... The cross submerged but they were there, beneath or behind...

Her brown eyes dropped to... a photograph, down upon her thighs...?

Murmurs of memory breaching... relieving heartscape grey, lightening darkslopes... heightening high hopes...!

'White Tip...! Gaze...! Why did...? Gaze...?'

Chapter Eighteen

MIRACLES AND MINESWEEPERS -
Part two

Welcome back to the Land of Hope then, son, thought Rick. He couldn't have been more jubilant! Fiona would have been delighted. They'd have got on like a house on fire.

He fumbled for the start of Phil's letter again.

He never wrote letters! The odd card, now and again. Opening it, Rick had already guessed content. A treasurer had better start putting coins in a piggy bank!

Not like last time, he thought. No plunging into the unknown and tearing himself to pieces!

He was thinking about getting engaged to Maeve, if you please.

As if they didn't all bloody well know where things were heading!

Good God, the way they are with each other! Not clinging but always supporting. The way Phil's glance across his shoulder always sought her; responded to her laugh. They'd all been there; they'd all read the open books in son and daughter.

But had the mid-term break added something else? Veils of reserve had dropped away in Maeve. There was conviction and confidence in the way she leaned against Phil in moments of rest; an arm around his back, companionable union, clearly not a claim of possession they all saw on the beach.

Maeve was writing to 'Deirdre and Ciaran'. Now that was interesting - not 'her mother and father', but first names of friends known already. Using Ciaran's name he understood for they used first names whenever Ciaran was around. So Phil uses Deirdre's name as a friend - confidant too? There again, what was so odd? Phil hadn't known a mother figure except as a toddler. Yes, Phil would be likely to talk to 'Deirdre' that way. 'Mrs.Pearce' would be too formal. Intuitively, he guessed it would become 'Mum' for both of them in years ahead. And he really didn't mind in the least.

Deirdre was an able person if just a bit unpredictable at times. He smiled. Maeve's mother loved her treasurer much more than she'd known and she wasn't about to lose him again. Just as independent as Fiona, that's what she was.

He visualised a breach of barriers in his son talking about some deep anxiety and couldn't think of any objection to Deirdre or Ciaran listening and responding.

He realised the family had got bigger over the last twelve months - grown as the Dolphinarium had expanded.

There wasn't any point in being long-winded. He reached for a postcard;

addressed it and scribbled on the back the family encouragement - 'Go for it, son.'

He'd post it after he'd read this next 'thing'.

Posted from Jervis Bay, the correspondence looked very official, bearing the Naval Insignia. When he'd opened it, however, there was a neat, handwritten letter.

He read it closely. Ah, Doctor Saxonby's brother - in the Navy? He'd like to come and see some things for himself at the Dolphinarium. Well, that was no problem. What the devil was the connection with the Navy? He'd write when he got back. His fingers were already picking up Phil's letter again.

'Okay, okay. I accept the need to close the place down for three days a week. None of us thought - well, at first,

I didn't think it would grow like this.'

'Good,' Ciaran said. 'There's more than enough turnover on Saturdays alone to cover what you were making and more, just six months ago. You're getting extra profit from the other sources - mooring charges, voluntary contributions and the collection boxes in the chapel. All that on top of the tote office, shop and admission charges. But there's a thing called overkill, Rick. What's more important is the fact that you and Rod have been working flat out just to ride with it. You need some rest. How do you suppose the 'stars' feel about it all? They're not dogs to come to the whistle day after day, are they?'

'You after my bloody job?' Rick said, the outstretched cup of coffee belying anger. 'Okay, you're right.'

More right than he realised, thought Rick. But he more than likely did. That business brain opposite was advising an application of a brake and it was needful. Continuing to whistle the 'stars' at 'show' or 'race' times, they'd have to have a truce in the war of entertainment...

Deirdre was saying nothing. She was simply smiling at the two of them.

Rick said, 'And how does middle-aged 'flower-power' feel about it?'

'He is right, Rick. You could give Sunday over to the dolphins and they'd probably conduct community singing off the jetty or have a church service... In any case, you've got all kinds of maintenance to keep on top of, I know. And you have been looking tired. So has Rod. What time is he getting to socialise with other young people? His brother's just got engaged. I know how that takes some sisters... In Rod...?'

Rick turned away, winked at Ciaran. Trust a woman to put in the last word to hit home. Yesterday Rod had asked for some time off... as he had the week before...?

'How quickly could I get the paperwork sorted out, bloody advertisements and all that?'

'Are you asking me as a friend or a client of the Bank?' came the reply he was used to.

'Whichever one helps me do the paperwork before I dive over the side and hope the Good Lord replaces these fingers and thumbs with a set of decent fins!'

'And flukes,' said Deirdre.

'Oh Jaysus!'

They were all grinning.

'Right, my secretary will be over tomorrow afternoon. She will be glad to earn a bit extra and is due some holiday entitlement. She's very good and it could all be sorted in three days if you let me use the Bank's Publishing contacts.

You'll pay the same print-rates - and pay my secretary cash-in-hand. We'll stretch the law just a tiny bit this time.'

'You thought all this out before, didn't you!?'

'Brought to you for approval Manager, S...'

They all heard the car draw to a stop on the gravel outside.

'Nine thirtyish on Sunday - just like he wrote,' said Rick. 'I'd better go on up.' And left.

'My ex-husband can be pretty cute,' said an ex-wife.

His tongue came out. She decided she wanted to stay on board overnight, whatever his reaction might be.

Mike Saxonby turned out to be just as much a civilian as themselves. He was responsible for taking a key role in the training of Naval divers at the Royal Naval College. Of particular interest to him was the possibility that trained dolphins could be used to assist divers in search and rescue or, indeed, in helping to 'ferry' small pieces of equipment and sundry items from sea bottom to surface.

'Divers are forced to adhere rigidly to decompression procedures and that brings a time component into play for many things. Cetaceans have us well-beaten for free swimming at depth and for the facility to replenish oxygen when needed.

If a diver runs out of oxygen or gas mixture - he's dead unless a 'buddy' can help. Whales and dolphins take down the oxygen they need and if they run out of breath, as it were, they change over automatically from aerobic diving and utilise anaerobic metabolism. If you think of...'

'Robic what?' interrupted Ciaran.

Mike grinned. 'I'm sorry. If you run out of air under water, you can't breathe. Don't get to the surface, you're dead. Whales are capable of using oxygen stored in muscle tissue all over their bodies, not just their lungs. It's called 'anaerobic metabolism'. They'll incur an oxygen debt in this state but they can replenish it later. They have lots of small storerooms of extra oxygen all over their bodies and along come the blood workers and unlock the doors to get more of what they need. It's even thought that their brains might be capable of storing some as well.'

'Thanks. Now this simple sailor half understands.'

Again that grin; Ciaran decided he liked him.

'So what with another advantage in good old 'blubber' which has terrific insulation properties and avoids them having to get overcoats on

DON'T DOLPHINS CRY AT ALL?

for work, they could help us a lot. Our problem is that we haven't had much success in trying to train dolphins - and believe me we've tried! My brother wrote to me about coming here.

'I know how careful he is about jumping to conclusions. He said enough to make me wonder if you'd been making breakthroughs in training we'd love to know about.'

When Ciaran arrived in the late afternoon, he was just in time to confer with his secretary in the 'unofficial capacity' she wished she had known more of earlier. Her 'boss' had sides to his personality she hadn't realised were there. The work was fun too. They conferred over wording and... ideas which had occurred to her in assessing the task. Ciaran's enthusiasm and praise for her initiative did more to ensure 'thoroughness' than he realised. Time-proven magnetism in a 'good boss' and an admiring secretary was at work - was not allowed to affect planning...

Going on deck, after the impromptu conference, Ciaran heard Rod's voice explaining.

'No, Maeve didn't try it first. Dad and I did. One of the dolphins, I forget which one, seemed very curious when we were working on the filters in the lagoon. That was when we didn't have the lock-gates opened very much. Now we do, the filters don't have to work so hard. Anyway, I decided we'd experiment with some display cards like Maeve was doing in the 'show'. I sketched some big outlines of tool shapes and threw an assortment of real tools in the water.

'Only made one mistake that dolphin did. Soon, the rest caught on. That's what you saw this afternoon. You can try it yourself if you want.'

Mike had witnessed the pale shape finning underwater from the lock-gates even as Rod was speaking. He was not surprised to see the dolphin's head emerge alongside... Not then - but later he realised no signals had been made by anyone observed. It had been one of those odd coincidences...

Ciaran watched an 'encore' of Rod's part in the display.

Mike asked casually, 'Have you tried this at real depth. Say, over fifty metres - even seventy?'

Rick intervened slickly, 'There's no reason go that deep. What would the crowd see? They'd suspect we were con-artists or something. Where do you suppose they'd sit? There's been a few panic stricken when they've been splashed a bit. You're suggesting taking them out to deep water?'

Rod played on, 'He's not thinking about the show, Pop. No, we haven't tried it deep. You're thinking about poorer light and finding things by echo-location or lateral sensing, aren't you?'

Mike smiled. 'Yes. That would be more useful.'

Rod said, 'They'd do it, whatever depth in your range.'

The smile didn't change. 'Prove it.'

A father and son heard the drop of an invisible gauntlet to the deck. Their eyes met but only briefly. It would have taken a high speed camera to record the twitch of Rick's left lid. Rod saw it; Ciaran rumbled them.

'You doubting my 'stars', Navyman? It'll cost you,' growled Rick. He was ex-Navy himself.

Ciaran didn't know exactly how much - guessed a bottle at least, and knew the 'brand'... He guessed the next request.

Shortly afterwards, he watched them walk to his cruiser now moored alongside the bobbing walkway, feeling a little uncomfortable. He was sure father and son were conning the brother of a university lecturer they both knew.

'The innocent to the slaughter...' he thought.

Two hours later, Mike was thoughtful as Rick 'divvied up' the 'booty' from 'The Red Bottlenose', a true 'Buccaneer'.

A week later, Rick was convinced that the Pearce family were all descended from some tempestuous coupling between a whirlwind and a water god; that they were carriers of a curse to inflict torment upon himself. Events were occurring which they all might have foreseen in the light of some of Deirdre's comments, articles in the newspapers and the testimonies of some of the regulars to the 'chapel'.

First had come the polite phone call requesting a visit.

Rick had felt obliged to agree - found it impossible to refuse or insult 'the Cloth'. Not one 'to pass the buck' normally,

he had pleaded with Deirdre to 'substitute' for him. Ciaran had excused himself because of 'pressure of work' but his laughter had been deep and round. The bloody treasurer really enjoyed the discomfort for him, thought Rick - knew that, if the roles had been reversed, he would have been just as full of commiseration on the surface but rocking with pleasure in the cradle of his gut!

Deirdre was with them now, a Cardinal, two Bishops and a Parish Priest! He could guess most of the conversation and was dreading the moment of facing the conclusions. His bunk had seemed the safest refuge. Maybe they'd go away and write a letter? No, dedication to 'Mother Church' on arrival, had shone in hopeful and trusting radiance from their sunlit faces. They'd be back for tea and 'one lump' and a biscuit. Picturing an open-air service around the chapel and on the jetty, he was sure what they were after. When did the 'stars' decide that evangelism was an appropriate addition to 'shows'?

You might have bloody well asked the Manager first! he thought, quite irrationally.

He heard them come aboard; wondered if he should have covered his hands with oil and looked harassed in a boiler suit.

Two minutes later, a polite knock at the cabin door told him that Deirdre was fetching him to face the music. Sounds of organ music - intermingling with whale song? - echoed about

the secret halls of himself...

She came in. Was that smile, in the lips of her mouth,

pleasure, sympathy or was she taking the p... ?

'The Cardinal would like to speak to you Manager, dear.'

'What's it all about 'flower-power'? You're enjoying this, aren't you?'

'Don't worry, 'sweetie pie', it's all sorted, apart from one teeny-weeny problem.'

She was grinning broadly.

'Go on or I'll be really rude with you. I can't be with them - you're different.'

'It's a matter of 'the collection boxes and contributions made by the faithful for the futherance of God's good works'.'

The light dawned! 'Tell 'em to put their mitres down points uppermost and sit down on 'em - hard!'

'Really, Rick?'

'Sod it, no. What do they want?'

'It's quite easy and you can't really refuse. They want to sanctify the chapel. There'll be an open-air mass - you expected that, didn't you? Fortnightly, on Sunday evenings, the Parish Priest wants to hold short masses. Contributions in the collection boxes must be divided between the needs of the local parish and the local churches. After all, members of 'the flock are donating as part of their duty to God and His Church'.'

'Those donations are for Dolphins of His flock, woman!'

She was smiling. He knew he was beaten.

'For Christ's Sake, we'll give 'em the right hand side of the chapel. Any money in that box can be their's to st... to do what they like!'

The smile was still there.

'They'll provide their own candles, Rick.'

'Jaysus!'

It was now. The ping-patterning of his name was growing louder... He wanted to mute the call; to fin the warmstream a little... longer...? But he could not ignore... the mindvoice or the name he recognised...

He sensed his whitebeak nosing into the entrance he had found so long ago...

Ardent watched, through half closed eye, a White Dolphin fin into the Cave... which bore... his... name...

And then two more...? White Dolphins...? 'No, Ardent, but special and friends...'

Yes, the mindweb... would know now...

The blueminds of Gaze and White Tip confirmed...

His flukes were so heavy... Could he fin the passage to sunlight outside...? Would he feel the tear... of teeth...?

Again the short range pinging of... his name?

Could they see Wanderer? 'He is... here... Gaze,' he tried to mindmerge.

'Yes, Ardent, I am here - White Tip, too,' imaged Gaze, seeking a way through the Cleric's blackening mindcluster...

'There is no need to fin the passage. The place is here with all who love and honour you. There will be no shark maw to fear, old friend...

'Here is close to Wanderer who you honoured best of all.

Here is closest to his heart and your own.'

Dropping gently from White Tip's mouth was the jade...

They saw Ardent's head tilt to follow it down just two dolphinspans... to settle upon sandfloor...

Dimly, Ardent wondered where... on sandfloor signs it... and he had rest...?

Ardent felt them at flanks... the peace and love in both.

There was... something to say...?

Something Gaze needed to hold in... He felt it... important to... Or Wanderer felt...?

'He will know later... faithful, old friend...' merged Wanderer, whitebeak the warmth of old comradeship. 'Answer us now... What is... your name...?'

They were all... there...! He saw his sire fin from the jade... watched the broadbeak gape the white smile... And heard the voice of his beginning... Another... his dam... was comforting... recall patterning... his name...

Tinu came in, flukes thrashing in urgency! He saw them two dolphinspans down; dived for farewell...

Head and beak close, he looked within Ardent's eye for a sign of recognition...

He saw it deep inside, mindmerged, 'Not for long, Cleric.

We'll fin bi-vector again... You'll show me more discoveries then...'

So many shades of Bottlenoses... So many in such a small cave... imaged Ardent. And so many to greet me...?

The next call of his name was so loud!

Weakly, he pinged acknowledgement... heard it whisper in the tunnel... rebounding from reefsides...

He pinged his name... surprised in pinging clarity and

resolution... Was strength in Gaze making... the patterning stronger...?

Gaze! He wanted to warn... risk within him... self...

They saw his mindflare; flashing awareness of Gaze within ...then his benevolence fading and paling to weak whiteness!

Gaze opened himself to absorb... to pattern the weakness, later...

And Ardent was gone.

The echo-lament of the Podsherd filtered through the maze passageways of the Storytellers' Caves... down the mysterious dive to Wanderer's entrance and the secrets within.

Tinu knew the mindweb had felt Ardent's gap... That his son Sinu, Gale and Peen had been first to sing...

He knew, too, that Gaze had summoned him to be at his old friend's side at the time of mattering most...

Respectfully, he fintouched them both...

They rose slowly to airsnatch, finhovering... above the dolphinbeak of the faithful Cleric. His body would sink soon to settle on sand. When it did, they would remove the weight of rock they had nudged across his flukes.

'Such a friend...' mindmerged Tinu.

They both heard a mindsob in the crusty old Bottlenose;
shared the lights of grieving.

They finned aside to leave comrades undisturbed.

Gaze mindwhispered to his mate, 'A friend and a sage, my love. Now we fluke alone...'

White Tip imaged, 'He was afraid for you even at the end, Gaze. There was a warning... It was too weak... What...?'

Over a week before Phil and Maeve would be back, the two, grey vessels arrived. The minesweepers were berthed in the dock alongside an old quay seldom used. Some hurried dredging had been done and they had come like grey ghosts through the morning mist.

The 'stars' had accompanied them. Rick had seen them in lines ahead of both...

Playing at 'frigates and destroyers', he had thought.

Then they had disappeared to reappear at the beach for swimming association with expectant youngsters and some adult hands reaching down in wondering trepidation which was quickly relieved.

Somebody high up must have listened to Mike Saxonby for the Navy only moved that fast if things were felt important.

Visualising the communications and co-operation which had to have been necessary between Civil and Military authorities, the importance attached to 'something' spoke of an involvement of the War Department at least, in Rick's mind...

He couldn't help wondering if there was more involved than Mike's earnest desire to see if dolphins could be useful apprentices...

The sailors wouldn't mind being tied up alongside for the couple of months Mike said he had been allowed. Rick grinned.

He could see two ratings looking towards the Dolphinarium and beyond.

Yes, my lucky lads... 'Like a naffin' holiday camp'; 'There's the Bar'; 'All that beach crumpet', and 'There's a Golf course'... Rick read the arm pointing...

The Bar ought to do well at least. Quite cynically, he realised the 'bikini bouncers' would wobble over to the bank the other side of the lagoon. He'd better make sure of more litter bins within reach of laconic arms and painted fingers.

Sure enough, the evening adoration of the dolphin cross had a number of naughty nauticals hip-close to feminine wonderment on the jetty. Sailors were the same world over - or maybe the girls were.

Rod was at his side.

He echoed his father's thoughts. 'Doesn't take the Navy long, Pop.'

'Takes the heat off you, boyo.'

Rod grinned, 'Me? I'm spoken for.'

Rick's eyes shot round. He said nothing, waiting.

Rod said, 'I'll take my time. I'm just glad I can get regular time-off.'

'Uh huh. When do I get to...?'

'When I'm ready.'

They looked at each other, deep down. There was no point saying any more.

'Where's Ciaran, Pop? There's something I'd like to have a chat about.'

He wants to talk to a Banker? thought Rick. He knew Rod was careful with money. Taking the long term view already are you, you blossoming Don Juan?

'Not coming back tonight. Deirdre was worried about getting Maeve's room decorated and ready if she wants to stay there. Ciaran thought he'd give her a hand. He'll be back here tomorrow.'

He read Rod's face.

'Must be something Deirdre can't do on her own, then,' said Rod. 'Ciaran's a helpful bloke, Pop.'

They both burst out laughing. Rick wondered when his son had taken the magical step into mature awareness...

They had finned longest with Peen. The mindweb had been blocked from contact. They had watched the tri-vector circuit of the Podsherd. All Bottlenoses had sensed the love in flukewake; known the tearing within farewell.

The trio had stopped alongside the Master Guardian with the mindweb a cordon of respect. Many Bottlenoses had known mistiness of eye as they had familypodded with Beak Spot close to Gape.

Gaze and White Tip had vectored to open seaspace as the last rays of the sun's deep-diving had been the pathpassage 'westwards' towards the Spinners and beyond.

The Podsherd knew their voyaging necessary.

Sinu, mindmerging with his sire, imaged, 'Gaze senses another mind beneath event. The Splitfluke, Rick, wonders at purpose in the unusual co-operation between authority within the grey hardsides and other Splitflukes of peace. Gaze needs to know what they... plan... And this Maeve returns soon...'

He shared the imagery of the sagas... the violence within waterspace... disruption of harmony and mindscreaming in many.

Tinu mindmerged, 'He is afraid?'

A Storyteller son said, 'Not for himself, sire. He fears for other podsherds... all creaturekind, Splitflukes as well.'

There were moments of deep communion. Both surprised, they realised they were closer to merging than they had ever been...

Sinu added, 'For the first time, sire, I feel Gaze fears a loss of control.... He was trying so much... but Ardent's dread of Splitfluke warring... has transferred to Gaze... Yes... he is afraid for seaspace... and almost... angry?'

Admiral Carson acknowledged the piping, watched his pennant rise. It was less than deserved - but in time...

'Thank you, Lieutenant. I trust you can find quarters for Commodore Dwyer, despite short notice.'

'We've plenty of space, sir. I've given leave to most of the crew. They're regarding the Navy as being all heart.'

The Admiral's face didn't change.

He had the reputation of being one of the 'old-school': rigid, applying regulations as by 'Jehovah's right' or so the medical orderlies had told him. 'Eye for eye' was what they had called him in training.

The Lieutenant, deciding he had no sense of humour, led the Admiral Surgeon to his cabin, wondering if a sharp scalpel would 'enjoy setting about his hide'.

The orders were puzzling. On the verge of trying to tease out snippets, Lieutenant Glynn saw the closed stare in the pale, expressionless blue. He knew compliance was the only thing expected.

It was confirmed with, 'The Americans coined the phrase 'Need to Know', Lieutenant. Exactly that mode of operation exists on this ship henceforth. Is that clear?'

'Aye, Aye, sir. Clear as mud.' The cold blue eyes flashed a withering look. Lieutenant Glynn hastened to add, 'My apologies, sir. A slip of the tongue.'

'Commodore Dwyer has some gear aboard the transport. You will arrange stowage of electrical items in your workshop. The explosive charges will be stored in an ammunition locker aft. The three marines will come aboard. Find them berths. They will form no part of your crew - will take their orders from Commodore Dwyer or myself.'

The eyes were demanding the expected courtesy.

''Eye, eye', sir.' The bastard couldn't read his mind.

Almost as an afterthought, the Admiral said, 'Lieutenant, the dolphin cross Mr.Saxonby mentioned - I'd like to see it.

My respects to the Manager of the Dolphinarium and request a visit by myself this evening. Put the area off limits to ratings. I'll go alone.'

'That might be a little unpopular with the crew, sir.'

The eyes said he couldn't care a less.

Glynn left to fetch the diving teams from both ships.

''Well-trained fish'! I tell you Ciaran, I'd like to get that yellow-ringed water snake in a dark alley, pull out his front teeth with pliers, and slit him full length to see what he had for breakfast! That bloke's the kind of bastard that would still have keel-hauling in the bloody Navy! I've seen enough of his sort weaving up the rungs of ladders. The cheek of the jumped up, self-important... He's a bloody 'Medic'!'

Ciaran wondered if the hurricane would blow itself out.

'I'll bet that little pennant hasn't flown on a sea-going command! There's nothing human about that lanky monkey, the two-faced turd!'

Ciaran reached for the kettle. Rick was in exactly the wrong mood for a snort - except the snorting he was doing.

He'd risk it. 'One lump or two, Manager darlin'.'

The hard points of his friend's eyes focused, welding to the present in sparks. The grin didn't come.

'Mike Saxonby and that 'thing' are as different as chalk and cheese. Jaysus, that man - no that's too dignified - that produce of an alley cat and a tiger on a dark night in Sydney should have been...! What are you grinning for, Banker?'

'Tigers in Sydney, Rick?'

The eye of the storm at last, thought Ciaran.

Rick grumbled, 'You know what I mean.'

The flash and clash of the spoon still carried the threat of lightning strike.

'What did he say to unsettle you, sport?'

The answer came from under a lowering brow.

'Showed me two letters - 'by way of introduction', if you please! One from Naval Command; the other from - wait for it - The Bloody Prime Minister's Office! The first pointed out to me that I still had a year to go on the Reserve List and I'd 'signed the Official Secrets' Act'. The second was an open letter requesting 'all assistance be given' to that thin-lipped son of a whore! He put both of them in his fancy medical case.'

Rick watched Ciaran's expression change from an initial surprise to thoughtfulness. It took about thirty seconds.

'You didn't happen to mention to Mike Saxonby that you were on the Reserve List?'

'I think I did, on your boat. Why?'

Ciaran didn't answer directly.

'Seems on odd thing - a Surgeon - 'Well-trained fish'. He must know the difference between a dolphin and a fish. What's the Navy slang for a torpedo, Rick?'

Expressionless, they looked at each other.

Rick said, 'That's bloody ridiculous.'

Ciaran said, 'Yes, it is, isn't it? I'm sure Mike's trying to help divers but I can't see the need for an Admiral Surgeon to be around two minesweepers - can you?'

Across the distance of a thousand Splitfluke miles, the Spinners' cross surfaced and separated. Sensing overwhelming dread on their return, the Spinners' mindweb knew that Gaze and White Tip had witnessed something to fear in their leaps of seaspace. Along unseen connections in empathy had come the tremble and a mindscream...

'Hunter Island Ridge' was close; stretched 'westerly'.

Gaze could flukefollow the steeprise dip and fold with ease -

but still the place disturbed him. Above this rise, Vorg had been confronted - died in the harpoon's detonation... even as his clustering had flashed intense, primeval red...

Gaze recalled the butt so close to blowhole; the greater concussion as Vorg had been torn asunder.

White Tip mindsobbed.

He fintouched. She had been in panic, fixed to Twizzle in the 'Brisbane' cross...

She mindwhispered, 'His clustering, Gaze... so like Vorg?
I felt... the coldness... The need to hurt... to kill?'
He knew. They had fixed briefly to the new Splitfluke as he had stared at the mixed podsherd's cross, entering within to examine... to learn...!
Similarities had flashed in recognition instantly...!
She had mindscreamed fearing a trap - enmeshment with no escape from the voice of his mind...! Intrusion of self and pain were living memory!
Gaze had tried to reach her to stop retraction - felt her terror of his whispered tenderness... felt, too, the deep shudder of the Spinner mindweb... But they had kept station, whilst they had not! They had unfixed for rushing reversal!
Bluster and Rayrender were finstirring close at flanks, waiting and puzzled... fearful...
Rayrender saw Gaze become aware of their presence...
'Gaze? There is something terrible in 'Brisbane'? We... felt the networking trembling... Here, both - flukethrashing! Bluster had to threaten a few - I had to snoutsnap a friend to keep her still.'
They were both concerned.
His mindvoice came quietly, 'An Abomination is there.'
He saw longsnouts gape wide; knew their willingness to fight... and their apprehension...
He heard Bluster mindmerge...
'I am old, sometimes slow for a Spinner, Gaze. You know this better than the herd... Yet you have given purpose and meaning to these tiring flukes... a young friend to train in skills half forgotten. Instead of rivalry, ignominious defeat in a butting contest, you showed me another way for podsherd security... security in ourselves. My old flukes... these ageing teeth are yours. Rayrender feels the same...'
Gaze and White Tip saw both longsnouts open and then drop in formal submission to their will...
It was White Tip who spoke first. 'We are friends, not leaders to crusade against dolphinfoe. It is not cousinkind of which we speak...'
Gaze imaged more clearly; conjured the Splitfluke who had terrified so...
He showed them the 'visions' within the twisted mind, glimpsed in distortion...! His mate had been too shocked... Now, quicker than the Spinners, she knew other terrors!
She scanned his lightclustering... Something altering, changing in Gaze...? Even as he showed the things to dread, she saw whiteglows of coldness harden... a mindlight turn bloodscarlet, frighteningly vivid...!
Were the mindlights 'Gaze'...? They were so sharply defined like...?
And Ardent had tried... to warn... something inside his 'young master'...? Something inside... himself...!
White Tip knew the warning!
The lightpattern was larger than the great white shark! It was not

cold... not the instinctive, unfeeling habit of killing... Colours of other emotions contrasted too much... But it was worse! Capable of deep love and pity... he was pitiless now! Already, a hunter's vectoring stretched relentlessly across a hissing sea!

And she could understand... But would the Spinners?

Gaze showed them... He took time patterning, for himself as much as them, to explain that mind... awesome 'weaponry'...beyond their experience and evil to dread...

'In their warring, creaturekind suffers, chaos reigns... A 'God of Peace' is usurped... by a primitive 'God of War'... They seek his aid to 'Victory'... They will use... whatever weapon is effective in shortest time, for 'best' result... despite disharmony for worldspace...'

He imagevisioned the warscapes of land and waterspace...

They fluketrembled, each an insignificance, before the vastness of suffering...!

'Splitflukes, such as he in 'Brisbane', can do all this with weapons from their 'science'...

'This Splitfluke begins 'research' for a new kind of weapon... one which needs less of the thing called 'money'... One which can be used in 'first strike-vectoring' risking no retaliation...'

He showed them visions of dolphins, Splitfluke hands busy about the melons of their heads... The 'devices', in a darkwater dream, placed inside...

The last imagevisioning was the worst...

...The 'nuclear device' did not look like a 'bomb'. Dropped overboard, months ago from a 'merchant ship', it had settled snugly on the rocky bottom off the main channel...

Encased in glass fibre, the bomb was camouflaged to look perfectly normal, similar to the rocks around, for great care had been taken by divers to photograph this environment... Retrieval of human eye and camera lens had been easy.

Detonation was only possible by preset squawk signals from the two small beacons on the seafloor a mile from the 'device' which was bigger than an aircraft's load capacity...

The beacons, too, looked innocuous and innocent. Close observation in the murk would detect nothing that looked man-made. The nuclear trigger had been set before the bomb's arrival - just two things some 'local' anglers had 'thrown back'.

The bomb had brothers. They had travelled far along the 'target's coast', settling close to noisy, coastal cities and towns - in places that were accessible to the merchantmen...

It didn't need to be further, for when the brothers shouted in united voices, they would quieten everything.

The submarine captain knew it was true - knew the enemy's capitulation would be immediate. Beautiful that they wouldn't know to whom to surrender! The victor would be hidden in the throng of shocked and outraged innocence. Naturally, those at home would be the first to offer help, prepared already for assistance in the massive aid required - to be seen as 'real friends' to help unfortunates in their need. The 'homespace' would become much larger!

The waste there had been of financial resources in former complicated and expensive delivery systems! The savings had brought pleasurable reward. The captain thought of his secret income - the 'extras' to which he was entitled for observance of silence. The large estate was worth it alone - but the services of such capable femininity; the acquisitions plenty could afford, were sweeteners indeed.

In the old days, the enemy saw who was reaching for the trigger and would try to shoot back. Invisible assassination was possible now. The life of the sea could be shaped for a greater destiny, the water a cloak to pull across a face.

All that had been needed was secrecy and some ultra-smart computer chips with a surgeon's skill; those, and the little 'sea-dogs of war', the hidden 'pets' in part flooded tubes... The crew thought the creatures were being ferried to replenish depleted stocks; were convinced a warm-hearted Naval force was deploying on an errand of environmental mercy.

He pictured the dolphins, set, primed and ready to go.

The adaptations to the torpedo tube had been nowhere near as complicated as a surgeon's task; the neurologist's assistance. When he'd been told and trained, he had marvelled the skill; applauded the sheer audacity. The guidance systems, hooked to responsive cetacean brains, had been most efficient in test procedures.

He saw to the simple needs of the 'sea-dogs' himself. Requiring no more than unlocking the panel to the buttons, he'd press the self-cleaning function for the filters and another for food. What else did they need! They would not be in the tubes for longer than three days - normally only two.

He'd watched them manoeouvre themselves within, compliant to avoid the pain of the 'shock-sticks', as they were called. It had all been done under the most 'humane' of conditions in deep sea from support vessels. One after another the ten, old submarines had loaded, all looking perfectly innocent from any 'spies in the sky'. They had been so far from any potential target and what threat could 'diesels', carrying no missiles, possibly pose?

They had made towards 'release points', each captain knowing they would close the unsuspecting enemy coast at no nearer than two hundred and fifty miles.

They'd loose their 'well-trained fish' as the 'C.in C.' called them - the captain used 'sea-dogs' because it seemed more 'buccaneer'. He'd relieve sonar to 'listen-in' hours later, remembering to 'down' sensitivity. Those silicon chips knew the terrain. They were capable of correcting course as well! If a 'sea-dog' veered to left or right, sought to deviate, mini-amps of current to vital nerve centres brought 'doggie to heel'.

334

A 'sea-dog' would swim between a pair of designated beacons. At the moment of crossing between, three things would happen. The small squawk attached to the dolphin would emit one burst of coded pattern. Poor 'doggie' wouldn't last that bit; a small charge which exploded the melon to leave a wound just like a shark bite. The beacons would emit a short, powerful belling pattern. 'Brother bomb' would arm; prepare to leap out of hiding to shout on cue!

No warning - it would be so beautifully unexpected...!

The submarine would be running deep, a thousand miles distant, at least, and on course for home. They were first in the 'Age of Biological Science'. The 'C. in C.' had seen wonderful possibilities in using toothed whales to assist in marine operations. The man was brilliant!

It was unusual for an Admiral - originally a surgeon he believed - to resign a commission and take another in a different state's Navy. There again, there wasn't a nation in the world that wouldn't have been interested in what he had offered their own...

Gaze answered Rayrender before he asked.

'These visions are not the future but 'possibilities in his mind'. I read no more. Know that all the signs within Karg and Vorg are manifest in him. He seeks power and he is strong. I need to be closer still... To touch, if I can...'

Bluster said, not doubting the young Bottlenose, 'Such a creature deserves to die, Gaze.'

White Tip waited for the reply, her heart knowing the strength of the sagas in her mate. Could any Bottlenose kill a Splitfluke? But Gaze wasn't any Bottlenose...

His colours in mindlights proved poor Ardent's warning!

She wondered which one was right?

Gaze imaged, 'This discord is not of our making... may be beyond our resolution... We continue to try to sing inside Splitfluke hearts... remind of harmony and joy... But he...?

'This Splitfluke is too distant from songs of the sea...

Deafened by noise in demand for power, possession and pride, our whispering of things forgotten will be scorned by him...

'Forlorn may be hope... but this dreaming must not become real! He leaves for several lightwaters. Maeve returns soon. We have little time.'

They knew he was leaving - White Tip, too. He refused escort. The Spinners watched their flukingpassage, knowing conflict within... and ahead.

Dark cloudshadow seemed to follow their flukewake...

Lieutenant Glynn emerged on deck close to Mike Saxonby.

The last days had been pleasant without 'Eye, Eye' and that creep Dwyer around. Off to some 'hush-hush' laboratory, he believed. They could bloody well stay there! Maybe some enterprising Doctor Type would put 'em in little cages and try some shock treatment to shape behaviour and personality.

Mike Saxonby was different. He belonged to the human race. The lads liked him and the divers welcomed him like an old friend. It didn't matter that he was a non-uniform type - the man knew his onions and they responded to that wry grin. The man had to be liked by the dolphins, too.

Mike was looking beyond the jetty, scanning for a sign the 'apprentices' were around, he supposed. They both saw the leaps of two dolphins a couple of hundred yards away.

Two other 'non-uniform types' could be accounted for so the rest had to be about.

Glynn said, 'Time to play teacher, Mike. Whistle for quiet in the playground and get them in, then.'

Mike turned, 'Morning Dave. You crept up on us.'

Glynn asked, 'Where are the lads?'

Mike pointed, finger down over the side.

'All in, lined up and ready.'

Sure enough, a quick glance revealed six diving ratings in the water, gently finning to maintain position close to the ship's side. One face turned upwards.

The voice echoed and rang in his head.

'Skipper! Come on in, sir. The water's lovely - or is that the last bit of a hangover we spy?'

It was true. He'd met the two older men from the Dolphinarium in the Bar. That bloody Manager was more used to hardstuff than he'd thought. They were good fun, though.

He grinned. 'Just had a shower, Evans. I've used a very expensive body talc. Wouldn't do to waste it, dear.'

It didn't need more. They laughed.

He watched Mike raise whistle, winced at the piercing blast. Amazing that the dolphins had responded so quickly!

For the last four mornings, they'd come to the whistle like sheep-dogs ready for work and treating everything with an endearing curiosity. Mike felt that they sometimes had a conference because if they didn't understand immediately, sure as hell they did the next day!

'Why are the men wearing swim-hats of different colours?' he asked.

'Can you tell the dolphins apart?' answered Mike.

That wry smile was demanding the young officer to think it out for himself.

'Ah! You're making it easier for the dolphins to sort the men, one from the other?'

'Well done, skipper. Your prize is another whiskey.'

'Get stuffed.'

Rick felt good. A day off. Rod leaping at opportunity to go wherever he was going; Ciaran at work, and Deirdre tidying up at Redland - the hours stretched, a contented luxury, ahead. All that paperwork had disappeared as those quick fingers of Ciaran's secretary had done conjuring tricks! Now that was money well spent!

And they'd be here tomorrow! He stared around at the almost finished building work. Deirdre's ideas looked even better than the sketches. Change of light, the sound of the wheeling gulls brought life to the rawness of new roof and concrete. The landscape gardeners would be in soon. Maeve had been stunned last time. This time he was sure her spirits would soar as high as the gulls. Unless they were so starry-eyed with each other that...

The tannoy was loud across the narrow water between the grass bank and the old dock. Rick recognised, through the distortion, the climactic rejoicing of cannons and bells in 'T's 1812 Overture'. It cut off in fifteen seconds or so.

There was brief shrieking as volume was killed.

A voice said, 'My compliments, Rick. Thought you ought to suffer as well!'

A figure appeared on the bridge of a single minesweeper, waved once. Rick knew who the noisemaker was - guessed the other ship had slipped whilst he had been showering after an unaccustomed two hours of extra sleep. Nobody had wakened him and he hadn't heard a thing. He had to be losing his touch for a 'night out'.

Age comes to us all, he thought. There once was the time my perky captain - there once was the time.

Acknowledging, he wondered where the 'stars' were today.

Lieutenant Glynn must have read his mind for the tannoy, with efficient clarity, came to life briefly.

'Care to come aboard? We're going out.'

The 'sailor' was skin deep; Rick doubled away.

'Haven't a clue, Rick. We're diving at less than twenty metres, trying to get them used to light and arm signals, and they were responding. The lads were getting more excited in 'fetch' and 'take' exercises - and suddenly they were gone!

They all vanished together. I snatched a compass bearing. They headed out to sea, I think.'

Mike sounded disappointed. Dave Glynn was quiet.

Rick realised they had to have arranged the trip together for his benefit. His own 'stars' had thwarted things.

'A Shrimp sale,' he said. He watched them digest it...

'They'll be back. It's just excitement... How did you react when you heard the ice-cream van as a kid? Never takes long. Time it if you like. You say they vanished a short time ago? Let's see now... inside ten minutes? Any bets?'

Mike's grin was back.

'No way!' He turned to Dave. 'I think he's saying it's tea break all round. Can we fix it? The divers need a break. We'll give it an hour.'

Dave raised his eyebrows. No comment was easier. With both these men, 'you watched radar carefully'.

337

Lips had barely touched the mugs when the look-out said,
'Flamin' 'ell they're 'ere! Er, 'Dolphins to Starboard', sir.
And if you don't mind me saying, full of bounce too!'
Two hours later, Mike wanted to speak to Rick.
'It gets hard to distinguish one dolphin from another for the lads down
there. They seem to be able to sort us out.
'One diver says he's working a different 'apprentice' to the one he
teamed with this morning. He says it's got a white tip to the dorsal.
Another lad isn't sure but, if there was a change over, he's got a 'Champ'
now.
'Do you have a dolphin with a white tipped dorsal, Rick?'
For the life of him, Rick couldn't remember...
He took the safest way out.
'There's always been a few that come and go, you know... We run an
open establishment. It's never really mattered...'
Not mattered? thought Mike. What a bloody marvellous under-
statement that is!

Ciaran and Rod were watching the entrance to the park and the lock
gates mid-morning next. Both convinced that riotous movement between
either entrance would signal the arrival of elements of both families from
the University in Sydney, neither was prepared to wager. You just couldn't
predict it.
Families? thought Ciaran. Somehow they were all one family. It
wouldn't have seemed possible eighteen months ago.
But it was real and they were. There was magic in this place.
A dead-heat! At the moment the mini-bus swung through the gates,
the 'stars' entered the lagoon in their leaping exuberance. Neither were
surprised.
Ciaran noted Deirdre's car behind - warmed to her smile as she braked
to a stop.
Maeve was out and up the companionway in moments.
Nobody expected anything else. She laughed, kissed him and
disappeared. As they gathered in contented reunion, they all knew what
she was doing.
Phil said, 'Believe us, we're glad to be home. I suppose I'll join her
anyway.'
She cannoned into him in the hatchway. They didn't need words. She
kissed him and tore away. The 'family' split, opening passage to the side.
She was over and in.
Each face participated; each shared her laughter.
Donovan met Rod's look. Both shrugged - headed below.
The infection spread.
Deirdre took the parcel Ciaran handed her with smiling bewilderment.
'Wet-suit. Forgotten how to swim?'
'In there?'

'Why not? That's where we're all going to end up.'

She laughed richly. He didn't want to be as dry as he used to be. She kissed him, fingers already unzipping.

Yet another miracle, she thought, catching Rick's broad smile of understanding.

Rick said, 'This Manager has decided he will be damned if he will allow himself to indulge in acts of over-familiarity with non-paying guests that just seem to come and go as they please. I'll put the kettle on.'

He was pointing at his 'stars', the smile giving the lie to everything.

An accurate series of splashes from over the side drenched him... Beak clicking and Maeve's giggling made all three laugh aloud.

Chapter Nineteen -

'IN PODSHERDS' NAMES'

There is a time for harsh judgement, even ferocity for most creatures. Only with strength in trusted comrades, real unity of aim and purpose, does life have meaning - provided that purpose is for the common good; lies comfortably in the cradle of faith and love of a Benevolence from whom all things flow. The compassionate always know sadness in fury.

The facts, surrounding the deaths of two Senior Naval Officers and an unnamed civilian on an Australian minesweeper, were understood completely by only one other person.

She would not explain.

Understanding fully, she would not be heard in any Court.

Knowing and trusting, she knew it no murder. She was as strong as them in her heart...

Seven days after Maeve came 'home', four of them happy and pleasant, cloudshadows grew to stain the sea...

And Maeve went shopping with Phil... he knew exactly how and when it happened, was drinking coffee at the time... Phil, anxious and puzzled, tried to console her.

She grieved for warm friends, forced to shape a safer future - knowing their actions so far from joy in living. Saddest was their firm resolve to banish themselves from those they loved most after what they did...

Maybe dolphinkind could convince them otherwise in time; Maeve could not...

And Ardent's ghostmind, perhaps, too, his dead, great heart, seemed to condemn their intervention...

On the seventh day, in a crowded cafe, Maeve cried... and knew that dolphins cried mindtears too... saw the diffusion of mindlights such sorrowing caused...

They were leaving, they said, for a 'hearts' home'...

Maeve knew where and strove to convince Gaze all their secrets would be safe...

She loved him more for the faith he was demonstrating in her...

Phil would not be told all... not yet, would 'forget' Maeve's tear-streaked cheeks...

Some things she needed to shield from others...

*

Admiral Carson's return was as welcome as a chilly end to a warm spell for young Lieutenant Glynn. Discipline tightened and ratings were barred from free association with the delights of a soft posting. Many wistful glances were cast across dockside waters which seemed grey and flat.

The divers continued to enjoy themselves, Mike full of excitement concerning the remarkable opportunities Rick's 'stars' were affording him. The mess divided obviously into cheerful underwater matelots and another larger group of the 'sullen and shipbound'.

Two things puzzled Glynn greatly. Summoned to attend upon 'Eye-Eye' within minutes of his arrival on board, even before the Naval courtesies were complete, Glynn had been given curt instructions. A heavy steel safe had been man-handled into the sickbay, marine guards stationed outside with medical routines 'henceforth to be conducted in the outer passageway, if needful'.

Carson had emphasised, 'Any medical emergency will be attended by Commodore Dwyer or myself. A rating requiring regular monitoring will be accommodated in your sister ship's sickbay. This ship's medical facility is off-limits to anyone bar the Commodore and myself. A restricted area even to yourself, Lieutenant. Is that clear?'

If that means you keep off my bridge and stay down here, I'll let you lock yourself in and give the door two fingers each time I pass, thought Glynn.

'Perfectly, sir,' he had answered.

'I know exactly what you're thinking, Lieutenant. You would prefer the two Senior Officers on board to be out of your way. Just make sure that if we are out of sight, our presence you hold in mind. Ship's company will continue to function absolutely normally, with no slackness whatever.'

His blue eyes had been cold, fathomless.

'Yes, sir.'

'I wish to see the Engineering Officer, immediately. He will inform you of personnel for whom I have a simple task. You will now ensure the items from the lorry on the quay are unloaded and placed on deck below the bridge. Report when this is done.'

There had been a pause but not long enough for Glynn to be able to frame any kind of question.

'You are dismissed, Lieutenant.'

Mike Saxonby watched the coloured swimhats surface one after the other, absurdly stretched over wet-suit hoods.

Each diver looked puzzled and gave a thumbs down indicating loss of contact with an apprentice. The dive leader raised both hands palms uppermost and he heard the undercurrent of bewilderment.

'It was perfect. Each one could swim through the taped maze on the bottom, obeying the light signals for left or right. One of them even swam the maze in reverse with no signals at all - as if it was too easy? Then they just upped and went. What do we do now?'

Mike could see the dorsals, stationary a hundred yards away from the dinghy.

He remembered Rick's simple conviction that they'd be back when a 'shrimp sale' was over and chuckled to himself.

'Maybe it's a necessary conference or seminar, Bob. Let's head back. Neither of us believe that dolphins go on strike. Let's all take time off. You lads deserve a bit of freedom and I think I can swing that with Dave Glynn - even 'Eye-Eye'. I am a civvy after all. Your bloody stupid regulations don't apply to me.'

He watched the grins grow and hands were already reaching for ropes at the side, eager to buck the system and be seen to be doing so by the minesweepers' crews.

'You don't happen to have a berth for a thirty year old diver at this Navy School of yours, Mike?' Bob asked.

'Piss off. The job's mine, if it's going,' observed someone else.

Blotch, in open mindmerge, said, 'The Abominations are close by, Gaze. We all know it in the mindweb. What do you intend?'

From Dander came, 'They arrived well before vertical sunlight and yet you falter. Why, Gaze?'

White Tip knew Dander would risk any kind of personal danger out of indebtedness to her mate. It was in his nature to act quickly. He trusted Gaze's judgement, acknowledged his superiority. The question was not prejudging Gaze's courage or lack of it. Simply, he could not understand inactivity when dolphinfoe were so close. There were other Bottlenoses and Hump-backs who felt the same.

She realised that for Dander to kill a Splitfluke, as he would undoubtedly seek to do if Gaze asked, it would be uncomfortably close to killing in revenge for the loss of a dam on a bloodstained shore. There were other Hump-backs in whom the motives for assistance were equally muddied. Only love of harmony, belief and faith in a universal purpose in all events - and the lack of any precedent in Hump-back sagas concerning retaliation against Splitflukes - barred action. Dander was bold enough, in his fury, to make a precedent...

Gaze spoke at last. His mindmeet was so quiet and calm.

White Tip realised, from his reefsiding intensity, that he was masking true feeling... Behind the reefside were the mixed glows of orange and red, flickering like fires that would not be put out...

'Cousinkind, you must be patient and strong in heart. Everything you have achieved in this waterspace is a signal of our congruity with the best of Splitfluke heart and spirit. We have to be willing to teach blind eyes to see as we do - to hear the harmonies of co-existence. We have made differences but to change primitive attitudes... and to confront such image-blocking preconceptions as exist in the sagas of the Splitfluke kind... will always be a slow and arduous task... Dolphinkind will have to demonstrate faith that the species divide can be bridged - for Splitfluke conceit is rooted in eons of time and their fear of equals immense...'

He was changing to the voice of command! So subtly, from such quiet beginnings had it been, that White Tip had almost missed it herself... She said nothing...

'These Abominations shall perish. I see no other way but the murder of two to save millions - even the worldspace... Yet I demand you heed our long histories and teachings...

'No Bottlenose or Hump-back here shall offend against their laws of harmony or the White Dolphins of our ancestors in what must be done... No dolphinteeth shall tear Splitfluke flesh save mine - if there is no other way... I forbid cousinkind to jeopardise their own spiritual afterlives...

'If such jeopardy there be, I must answer to the White Dolphins and the Splitfluke God alone...'

And why she did she knew not, but White Tip reefsided and resisted... with greater strength than she had ever known... She heard her mate's mindvoice but suppressed it to a murmur that was an eddy around rock-cliffs of determination...

He must not know that I can resist him, she imaged to herself. Without knowing why...

No... No Gaze, my love, for now and eternity we fluke the waterspace, blue or white together...

If warmstream turns cold and sunbreach ceases...

If we fin infinite darkness in what must be done...

Then shadows in blackness shall we become...

Together!...

She heard him continuing normally and allowed his meaning to filter through...

'No, Blotch, there is no plan yet. These Splitfluke Abominations will reveal more of their strategies in the lightwater next. We are as prepared as we can be. We wait.

'We fishmuster now, if you please.'

Blotch beaknodded. He heard also a mindmerge whisper in confidence...

'Dander needs action of some kind, Blotch. I suggest you delegate fishmustering responsibility to him.'

Blotch beaksmiled, happy to comply. He, too, had the measure of Dander.

As the pod fluked to fishherding stations, Twizzle it was who thought she saw... a lightish dolphin-shape deep below...

But there was no echo return...

Delilah heard and beaktutted.

Feeling foolish, Twizzle kept silence as they began to circle a shoal but she sensed the mixture of fortune and fate which every hunter knows...

Rick wondered what the noise had all been about late the night before. He had seen lights on one of the minesweepers, knew it had been young Dave Glynn's. They'd been using metal cutters and drills and they hadn't finished until five to eleven. Something had been going on below the bridge but it had been too dark and too distant for him to see clearly.

He took an early morning stroll towards the dolphin grotto, refusing to call it 'a chapel' still in his secret self. From the grass bank, staring across the flat divide of the old dock water, he noticed it immediately. The metal and canvas screening below the bridge ruined the vessel's outline.

A minesweeper in silhouette always seemed too chunky - but that screening made it seem ridiculous. Wasn't there enough of the sailor in young Dave? How could he put up with his ship looking that daft?

Rick had it. Of course, that yellow-ringed watersnake called an Admiral had to be behind things. But what the bloody hell was it all about? That sort of thing was put up when the Navy didn't want... eyes to see what was going on!

Unaccountably, a nasty suspicion began to germinate... Was it something Ciaran had said a week or so ago?

He was back aboard 'Fiona' to make the morning brew when Ciaran emerged from the tap-twisting, towel-tugging banter and bustle below.

'This place is getting too crowded. You can't get a shave without risking a wet flannel flung at the back of your head. It's about time you asserted some authority over those boys of yours.'

Flushed and grinning, the Treasurer looked just fine, Rick thought.

He said, 'Well get up half an hour earlier and avoid the crush. It's a bad habit, pen-pushing. Makes you limp and lazy. Seen Dave Glynn's ship?'

'No. Why?'

'Take a walk. Your drink'll be ready when you're back.'

Ciaran's head tilted slightly as he raised his brows. Rick said nothing else so he moved off, puzzling.

Okay sport, let's see what you make of it, thought a practical mind, prepared to invite another opinion. He lit his pipe then reached for the coffee jar.

Ciaran took the mug and sat with him near the rail.

Looking into his eyes, Rick knew the same suspicion was taking root. Ciaran's words confirmed and clarified.

'Someone doesn't want the rest of us to see something.

That someone wouldn't be Dave Glynn. He's acting under orders - just doing his job. Mike's open and friendly and he's enjoying working with the 'stars'... Which leaves the Admiral and his silent sidekick, both medical men. Now one of them is a surgeon and the other a doctor of sorts. Mike thinks this Dwyer knows a lot about decompression procedures for diving and... also more than a bit about anaesthetics...'

They were still looking into one another, almost steadily ticking off the items in a checklist towards an end...

'Whatever the reason, the Navy's very interested in dolphins. Mike says Carson has been doing experimental work in micro-surgery and neurology...'

Ciaran stopped... Then...

'They're going to take a 'star' on board, Rick. They've got some kind of bloody experiment they want to do!'

'Like hell they will!'

He was rising. They both did.

Ciaran barred his way.

'The minesweeper's slipped, Rick. It was heading out. Thought I saw young Glynn wave from the bridge wing.'

There was something between pain and horror in Rick's expression - a wild all-encompassing search for a way to...

His eyes focused on Ciaran's boat...

Ciaran said, 'I need fuel. Sod the Bank!'

Maeve and Phil followed Rod up on deck.

She was somewhere else but still holding his hand firmly.

It was an unusually tight grip. He said nothing. Whatever had caused her to go quiet so unexpectedly, it wasn't to do with the fooling about down below... He knew that...

'Phil? What are the bossmen doing on Ciaran's boat? Expedition or outing day, do you think? Should we get over there?'

It was Maeve who answered as her grip on Phil's hand relaxed steadily to a customary gentle pressure. Somehow, he knew she felt calm and controlled and gave it no more thought,

accepting...

'No Rod, that's not for us today... We're going shopping and it's about time you paid a visit to someone you know, isn't it...?'

That was a bit like having his mind made up for him... and almost a kind of order... but Rod didn't care...

Rod grinned. 'Sounds good to me. Do you think I can take the pick-up?'

'And what do Maeve and I do for transport?'

Phil read Maeve's eyes, or thought he did...

'Okay, brother. Go and be Casanova. We're going to be walking today, it seems.'

He'd expected Maeve's laugh to that - but it didn't come.

She was looking at a minesweeper out in the bay...

Mike Saxonby was a very worried man. He dreaded the next hour or so. This was one of those times he cursed any association between himself and the Navy. They happened rarely - but, this one! This one was a real bitch!

A traitor, that's what he felt like. A traitor to the diving teams, a traitor to common decency and, most of all, a traitor to the dolphin 'apprentices' who were so full of innocent fun. How did he get in this fix?

He caught sight of the small package that had not arrived by post. No, Doctor Bloody Jim Beale had been the hand that had delivered a brother's letter - plus a number of high-level photographs and charts with small crosses carefully inked in - but they had been softening preamble.

He'd drifted across to a bar with Bob, expecting to be pumped for advice about job opportunities. Bob had nearly served his time. Toying around with some options was the least he could do and there was sufficient common interest and basis in friendship to have a can or two -

so they'd gone.

A blonde crew-cut and dark glasses, attached to a lean, fit character had followed them, ordered a drink and opened a newspaper from a smart case. He'd sat in another corner, apparently engrossed in catching up on the news.

The timing had been perfect. After half an hour, when it was Bob's round, crew-cut had drawn up a chair and smoothly handed over a copy of the letter Mike's brother had sent to someone in a Naval College in the States.

'By way of introduction. You wouldn't speak to me unless I could explain how I came to be here. I have some other material for you. Your brother has copies already. We've met and he told me to contact you. May I have a word or two when your buddy goes?' had come a level, friendly voice from under the dark lenses.

'Yes, I suppose so, but just who...?'

Crew-cut had just raised a hand and asked 'Later?' -

phrased like a polite question, but more an emphasis.

Mike had nodded. And crew-cut had risen to return to his reading.

So he'd told Bob about needing to talk to someone else and he'd have 'to cut the evening short'. As it happened, it didn't matter because Bob knew where a number of the other divers were anyway. After a quarter of an hour, Bob had left and Mike approached the man behind the newspaper, knowing the stereotype and wondering what kind of agency he fronted.

The card across the table and the theatrical removal of 'shades' so that a photograph could be checked with face had seemed a bit much; the "CIA" titling the last straw!

Mike smiled. 'You don't expect me to fall for all this crap, do you? Who are you really?'

'Jed Beale, Mike. Just as it says.'

His pleasantness was as hypnotic as snake charming. Mike recoiled, slumped back in the basket chair.

Speechless, he heard, 'You'd better read these and phone the C.O. at Jervis Bay. He is expecting a call. You're going to need to check me out, aren't you?'

There was a letter and a copy of one. Peversely and deliberately, he read the copy first - from a high-ranker in the American Navy to someone obscure in the Agency. Parts had been blocked out but the remaining content was do with Belukha whales, migratory routes and snippets, he thought, concerning shaping or conditioning behaviour in training. The last bit was very heavily censored. The letter - an original - was from the Australian Foreign Office outlining the willingness of the Australian Government to give all assistance possible to 'the said Doctor Beale'!

Mike looked at him, said nothing because it was safer, and got up to make the call. Astonished at just how quickly the phone was answered, he wondered if the switchboard had been bypassed? There was no reason to doubt the voice but he asked what his golf handicap was. As the C.O. at Jervis Bay couldn't stand the game, the sharp retort was confirmation.

Sitting in Jed Beale's car, Mike strove to put it all together. Dear Christ, what was the human race coming to!?

It sounded like some kind of weird science fiction but there were grains of sense and a distorted logical pattern within a maze.

...'In the cold-war period, both the superpowers were experimenting with whales, wondering if they could use them to clear minefields - especially electronic mines. There were no

ways of ensuring regular sweep patterns so the whole project was put on ice. Never widely known, for the 'Save the Whale' campaign was in full swing and steadily gaining support in the world thanks to Greenpeace, it stayed shelved.

...'Armed forces on both sides began to think of ways to couple a computer system to the brains of whales using pain stimulus in micro-circuitry to enforce guidance. Such was sparked by the control mechanisms in the cruise missiles used in combat by the Americans. Unfortunately for the hopeful, potential combatants in East and West, knowledge of whales and

the necessary skills in a mixture of surgery on the large scale - due to the huge, bulk of the 'patient' - and micro-

surgery, in terms of connections to recognised brain centres, was insufficient to make a novel idea realiseable. The end of the cold-war saw the whole thing shelved again...'

The talk of 'surgery' did it... Mike began to leap ahead in thinking even before Beale got the rest out!

'Recently, the Russians lost a Belukha whale from a sea-

aquarium and were very concerned about it. They went to quite

extraordinary lengths to recapture 'a prized exhibit who is a star attraction with the visitors' they said. We don't think such a public place exists,' said Beale, with quiet certainty.

The crunch came...

'I'm in, Mike, from this point on. Your Government and mine want a guidance system, a toothed whale and the whole shooting works. You've been vetted and so has your brother. You're both squeaky clean. Carson and Dwyer have been watched for some time. They slipped up in ordering some cute computer chips from folks Stateside that were too far out of normal requirement. We checked on supply and request.

'You'd better understand that your own Navy could have you replaced easily. But that just might cause a rat-stink and everybody wants Carson and Dwyer to smell only laurel leaves for the moment. You're needed, but we'll play it as clean as we can and ask you to let me assist you. For the record, I can match Dwyer skill for skill and I'm 'Instructor rated' for diving.'

Beale paused and studied him. Mike knew there was the persuasive

DON'T DOLPHINS CRY AT ALL?

way or the coercive way - knew that Beale was waiting to decide if he had to use a 'neat nastiness'...

Beale added, 'We've watched them, Mike. They intend to trade themselves plus 'works' to some dictatorial asshole. Who'd you rather trust? 'Uncle Sam and Waltzing Matilda' - or some 'Maniac in Ned Kelly's backyard'?'

The whole bloody world's crammed with maniacs! thought Mike. As to whom he could trust, he didn't know anymore.

Of course, he'd made the patriotic choice - but there hadn't been any other way to go. Beale was checking the diving equipment with the lads and seemed to be gaining in popularity. But Beale wasn't the one who was going to pass on the orders to have one of the apprentices tranquilised and lifted out of the bay. You'd have thought that each diver had fornicated with a mermaid out here and sired specially gifted offspring. What, in Christ's name, should he answer to the questions that were going to be asked?

Mike doubted that a single volunteer would have come forward from the divers to fire the tranquilising dart...

Beale had had the answer to that as well...

'I guess the Agency's multi-role training steps in there, Mike. You won't have to ask. Another reason to cover my appearance,' Beale had said... and had added, sardonically, 'The Australian Navy works with the same efficiency to small detail as our boys Stateside, doesn't it?'

After two taps at the cabin door, it opened and Dave Glynn leaned on the frame.

'We're going to anchor shortly, Mike. You're needed topside. The chains of command got heavy, didn't they?'

Mike guessed he wanted to say more - but he didn't.

Ciaran eased back on the throttles; allowed the cruiser to creep forward enough for steerage. The minesweeper was a quarter of a mile distant.

'Keep going,' growled Rick. 'What good can we do out here unless we're right under their bloody noses?'

Ciaran asked, 'Can you see any of the 'stars'? Use the binoculars.'

Rick didn't need them. Eyes accustomed to searching the sea's surface, he registered no dorsal or sign.

'Okay, they're not about at the moment but they'll come like lambs to the bloody slaughter. Get closer.'

For the first time, Ciaran asked himself, logically, what they could do legally...? And realised...

'Jaysus, Ciaran, will you get us there!?' came Rick's angry tone.

The knuckles were white in hands gripping a rail.

Carefully, Ciaran said, 'They're free-swimming dolphins, Rick. Does anyone own them?'

'Cut that, mate, they're my 'stars' - in my 'show'!'

'Agreed, Rick. They are. But not legally.'

'So bloody what? Those bastards are going to cut one of 'em about

348

- maybe more! You think I'm going to let that happen? I'm protecting their rights and if you want to get all legal about it, 'I'm protecting their livelihood and my own'!'

'Can we do or say anything until we see something happen? Maybe it's just best to be here... as a kind of deterrent... Nothing much else we can do, if you think about it, instead of being... bullish...' He appeared to struggle for a way to express their folly which Rick would grasp... ''Those bastards' are 'holding all the cards'...'

And further angry words froze in Rick... His eyes took on a thoughtful expression... Ciaran saw the pupils contract to small points as if someone had flashed light into them...

Then a practical common-sense began working...

'Damn you, Treasurer. Okay we wait.'

'Wait' they did... and saw nothing at all unusual...

Gaze had been patterning, urgently... The mindweb had felt it but none save one had any inclination as to what...

None had dared a mindwhisper...

There had been two jolts to the web and they knew that both Gaze and White Tip had leapt to fix in some 'others'...

Reflexively, they separated to fin protective stations,

watchful, alert... as he had trained them...

They felt retractive return much earlier than they'd expected...

Then the Splitflukes' tuneless whistling called...

'Why is the summons loud in waterspace?' mindmerged a few... but Gaze finturned and they flukefollowed...

White Tip knew he had patterned a plan... but he was reefsiding against her...   and it would be too distracting to ask...

She noted his mindglow as fierce pulsing... the exact tempo of the herds' fastfluking...

A hand reached towards a switch; turned a knob too far...

'Not that loud, you dumbarse! Turn it down! Dolphins have big ears and there could be a diver down there.'

The radio room repeater confirmed the underwater speaker was still operating.

Saxonby's 'school whistle' ought to give a few thousand fish migraine, thought Petty Officer Ackroyd. Ah well, so long as those that know blame teacher - it won't matter.

He reported they were 'broadcasting' to the bridge and Glynn acknowledged.

Not his normal perky self, thought Ackroyd.

Dave Glynn was most decidedly not.

There might have been the time he would have felt privileged 'to being put in the picture as far as a superior could allow' - even flattered. But this was different. He'd never liked either of those 'officers?' on board and they deserved a really shitty end to a career. For his Navy to be interested in what they were doing with dolphins - 'because it will be useful as a search aid in finding sophisticated mines' - sounded like half a story... and a whole bookshelf of suffering for one of the apprentices... How many dolphins in the end? Was there something else behind this charade?

Both Eye-Eye and Dwyer were below the bridge checking 'the big-boys' bathroom' - which one of the artificers had called their odd metal and canvas structure. The name had stuck. Power lines and a flexible waterpipe ran into it.

A pipe of larger bore protruded from one 'wall' and was connected to an oil drum. That had puzzled him - until he'd realised that Eye-Eye wouldn't want blood and waste products from his 'surgical investigations' to be immediately visible. Even in the old days, a red deck wasn't a morale-booster.

At least they'll be out of sight, thought Dave Glynn.

Just one hint that they were doing brain surgery on a dolphin, and he'd have a mutiny on his hands! He didn't like it himself but that other Admiral - a sea-going type to boot - had been very, very emphatic. Sometimes the Navy stank to high heaven! And someone had already spelled things out to Mike Saxonby!? With what kind of arm lock? he wondered.

The small cruiser a quarter of a mile away was still bows on to them but with two figures... taking a sounding?

Anglers about to drop anchor, thought Glynn...?

He grabbed the binoculars. That was just bloodee great!

He saw the approach of the dolphins the same time as an excited look-out shouted. They were passing close to Rick and Ciaran on their cruiser... Strange that neither man seemed to give any indication that they were aware of them... Or were dolphins part of the everyday pattern?

No, Glynn was sure that a dolphin would be allowed on board only 'over Rick's dead body'. Happy to bring news of 'an awkward presence' to Eye-Eye, he moved away.

'Ownership, Lieutenant. Mr. Dortmann has no claim of ownership. He has told me clearly that the dolphins in his show are 'free-swimming', that is 'wild'. He calls them for public entertainment. Such is clearly a simple matter of the dolphins being conditioned within a 'Response and Reward'

framework, in psychological terms.'

The bastard's not batting an eyelid, thought Glynn.

'Mr. Dortmann and you are fooling yourselves if you credit the dolphins in this bay with having intelligence or any other kind of human attribute. The fun the divers appear to gain in Mr. Saxonby's experiments is due solely to the novelty of the experience and their own high morale.'

It's just like being lectured and dressed down at the same time by some jumped up schoolmaster, thought Glynn.

Carson finally drew to an end with, 'Fish, Glynn. They are merely trainable fish. There is no legal or ethical argument that precludes the taking aboard of one of the dolphins for experimental research. Fish are taken from the oceans in millions daily and, presumably, you eat fish.'

Your eyes are just as bloody expressionless as a fish too, chum, thought Glynn... and felt like a schoolboy wanting to yell 'Fishface!'.

And then the cold blue eyes... were thoughtful?

'However, to avoid any unnecessary foolishness, the tranquilised dolphin will be loaded from the seaward side.

Turn us, Lieutenant, starboard side facing Mr. Dortmann's craft - we will load from port. Have Mr. Saxonby sent to me.'

'Sir, the crew...'

'Dismissed, Lieutenant.'

'...One of us they intend to lift on to the hardside.

They do not want a Hump-back - they want a Bottlenose for our kind is distributed widely in cold and warm waterspace.'

Gaze paused meaningfully in abbreviated imaging he had taught.

Starkly, he added, 'That Bottlenose will be me...'

Many were the mindgasps. The Splitfluke 'surgery' he had visioned for them had been horror in a darkwater dream!

'They will want a fit 'specimen' to 'tranquilise' and I would not be the dolphin they would select...'

Blowhard felt his fintouch... Unspoken was the warning that he would be the Splitflukes' first choice! His next airsnatch was anger and fear in exhalation...

His airmist hung above his dorsal in uncertain resolution but he mindmerged, 'Me rather than you Gaze? Then... so be it...'

Which was braver than he felt, and not necessary...

'No, Blowhard. We know your courage but no dolphin here will suffer the reality of visioning I have shown. You will be a decoy not a victim...'

And he told them his plan - the part White Tip would play ...never knowing White Tip would do more...

Then, openly and deliberately, they began a slow circuit of the large hardside like Guardians in a distant warmstream Podsherd monitoring everything. Blowhard appeared always to be prominently in view... and in fintouch distance of Gaze...

Ignoring an accusatory silence from the divers a few paces away, Jed Beale settled himself. He drew the support strap snuggly tight around his right upper arm. The thing had more of a recoil than your average dart rifle - understandable when you considered the length of the needle and the size of the syringe! He promised himself he'd never worry about the booster shots to pep up his vaccinations ever again.

Behind, he could feel them watching. He mustn't look too familiar with weapons, he thought. Better they believed this was a first 'real' time for him. That way he could be 'some poor sucker just obeying orders'. It helped the situation if the divers thought he'd probably miss and that the target had 'a sporting chance'.

'Jeez but this thing's heavy,' he sighed, grinning over his shoulder.

'Not as bleedin' heavy as your conscience is gonna be if you hit one of those poor sods,' came back a growled retort.

Which was just fine and dandy, confirming they were viewing him as he wanted. He flicked his eyes to the circling dolphins who appeared to be waiting for something to happen.

They're probably wondering why teacher's late for class, he thought to himself - and then blanked everything else out except that prominent, big bottlenose dolphin...

Yes, Carson, it is... definitely a bottlenose...

'...Dive, Blowhard!'

Gaze's mindurge was an imperative and Blowhard was gone...

Frenzied surface splashing would be what you'd expect as ten inches of metal punctured blubber and flesh. But had he hit the target or missed?

Momentarily, Jed Beale wasn't sure if he'd hit the right dolphin... but only momentarily...

Bob said, 'You've hit one so, from the lads and me, we hope your bollocks drop off for a crab's titbits.'

He wasn't smiling and neither were the rest.

Jed didn't dare a grin, guessing the danger to his front teeth.

Wisely, he said, 'Well let's get in there and make sure the dolphin isn't damaged permanently when it's examined.'

Which was far better than an empty apology in 'following orders' and gave each diver immediate action through which they could save some self-esteem 'aiding a mate in distress'.

Neatly, Jed sidestepped pointed reference as to why the dolphin was being lifted out of the water by implying that trained medical assistance was available on board their ship. He knew it was what people wanted to believe at a given point in time which took precedence in sparking human action.

Jed was first to go over the side, thus, in the Agency's terms, 'giving the lead by example'. The diving group went into action, Bob, as dive leader, not saying a word.

Nobody gave the slightest thought to the possibility of retaliation on the part of the dolphins.

Maeve gasped; leaned forward clutching her side...

Phil was immediately concerned but she straightened...

'I'm alright. Twisted a rib or something. Do you think we could find somewhere soon for a drink? I think I'm going to need a strong cup of coffee.'

There was no laughter in her eyes. That worried him.

He had warned them of his need to check the Splitfluke webbing constantly. He was striving to hold it taut - but not so taut that any became aware. It was too much...

Dizziness was the indicator of the need to limit himself

and delegate... and to do it quickly...

White Tip's response was immediate...

The mixed herd's mindweb shivered and shimmered, but steadied as he withdrew with one Bottlenose...

Better... Blowhard and himself imaged as one...

Almost too late...!

Gaze was too slow leaping; the shock a torment!

Flukethrashing, wide-eyed the sky was blurred in foam and spray!

He was instinct within a breaking wave; mindless in a panic of flukeflight.

Pain saved him. He felt the pain; knew it in mind.

Had Vorg had time to feel the pain? he imaged to himself.

A 'tranquiliser' numbing flukes already...! He leapt...

There? There was her mindmaze he needed, the colouring an unaccustomed blue...? and red...?

The blue was for him and he soothed... but the red...?

Was there fury deep within...?

'Oh, Gaze, my love... Your pain... I knew it...'

Her mindmesh embraced... held his fix far too tightly!

Silently the minesweeper's crew watched the dolphin circling the vessel. The rest were a quarter of a mile away, milling around a small pleasure cruiser. Only a few knew that the manager of the Dolphinarium was on board - and the air they were breathing was salt enough with guilt already.

None aboard needed to be told that the lone dolphin was mate to this one being lifted from the sea on port side - a sense of grievous loss was tangible.

As Jed Beale clambered up the scrambling net, he sensed the walls of boycott being erected.

Dwyer was at the rail.

'Not quite as big as I'd expected, Beale. I'll have to readjust in terms of anaesth...'

Beale's face made Dwyer stop.

Almost too late, Dwyer hastened to say, 'We'll examine the specimen as quickly as possible. It... The dolphin looks fit enough but we'll check it thoroughly and then take a few measurements. The radio antenna might take a little longer.'

His false laugh was convincing enough, thought Beale.

You nearly gave the game away, you asshole.

Dwyer was recovering some poise.

'We have to use thin metal bolts. The sea rusts them in a few weeks and they drop out. But there will be enough time for us to track all their movements. The lads in the radio room should enjoy the next month or so.'

That neat bit of scuttlebutt would rip around the ship like wildfire, thought Beale. Everything back on plan as far as you shits are concerned. And then the Agency steps in and your joyride finishes. A neat block and fumble, our ball and a long throw for Sam's touchdown.

Dwyer made off, to head for the sickbay safe, Beale guessed. I'll wait until you've connected it all up, chum.

Jed Beale turned to Bob who was staring at the circling dolphin.

'Now I feel lousy. Do the Brits drink rum for a bad conscience?'

Bob looked at him. The smile came only very slowly.

'This is the Australian Navy, you bastard, but I might be able to find...'

Ciaran asked, 'Are they all here?'

'Every last one of them,' Rick answered. 'They just seem too quiet.'

'If we headed back, would they follow us?'

Rick looked perplexed.

'I can't read them. I don't bloody know, mate. We can give it a try.'

White Tip knew it all; checked the tightness of tendrils around Gaze's mind... whispered a tenderness and leapt...

He'd expected her to follow retraction to his own prostrate self, a wetted weight on the steel slab on a stout frame within Carson and Dwyer's screening. It was behind the screening walls that the... the killing would be done...

But she did not!

Their leap was her red lightning that horrified...!

Never had he seen her mindlights so vivid in scarlet...?

She was a lioness of landscape... a tigress in pursuit...!

'No, White Tip... It must be me!...' he mindurged.

'And Ardent to haunt a lightwater?... No, not you... White Dolphins shall condemn me! Never ever you, my love...

I will share your pain but refuse you share this guilt...

Her mindvoice was loud, 'For a lost family, Gaze... For the ghost of Bloom... For white bones in whisperless seas...

For this universe songless... Loving you, it will be me!...'

Powerless, he heard the hiss of her fix... within a killer's mind!...

Bob saw the sudden change in Jed Beale's expression.

Later, he would tell a Court of Enquiry how his face had hardened as he had left him at the rail of the ship...

'Maybe the atmosphere got to him. All the lads were a bit angry about him shooting at one of the dolphins but they'd have come round in the end, I suppose. He just suddenly looked furious and went towards Admiral Carson's tent thing below the bridge. We all felt there was going to be some kind of scene and - well we decided to stay well clear of the fall-out. Service life teaches you when to duck.'

Bob Carter saw the merest trace of smiles on two Very Senior Officers' faces.

'He called out and identified himself and then the Marine on guard let him in we guess. That's all I can say, sir.'

'You did not hear Marine Brody's dismissal?'

'No sir, but...'

'Go on Carter.'

'Brody didn't have time to do anything, sir. In less than thirty seconds, he was following us into the mess.'

Bob Carter looked straight at them and added, 'And he had his rifle and bayonet with him.'

'Relax Carter, the look-out on the bridge and Lieutenant Glynn both confirm hearing Marine Brody dismissed by Commodore Dwyer...'

Too bloody quiet, thought Dave Glynn. Whatever those sods are doing down there, I ought to be able to hear something.

Occasionally, the wind would gust and the canvas around the steel frame would flap. Otherwise an unnerving silence had settled forward of the bridge. For half an hour it had been like this.

Why did the American go in? And Dwyer had known him?

There's a lot more to this than meets the eye, Dave old son, he thought. Time for a polite enquiry to see if there's any way you can assist... Any need for another sentry - as a skipper should do...?

Face it, you're just bloody nosey! What are those sods up to? Take someone else as a witness? something cautioned...

I don't want Carson screaming about unnecessary interference with important work. If someone else is around...?

Yes... He made up his mind... He reached for the bridge phone...

The three of them approached the zipped entrance to the screening.

Glynn called out, 'Lieutenant Glynn, sir. Shall I post another guard?'

The only sound was the odd noise of the dolphin exhaling and inhaling. Did it sound drier... weaker...?

Glynn decided.

'Lieutenant Glynn, sir. Permission to enter?'

The silence was almost overpowering.

He reached down and unzipped the entrance on both sides of the large flap...

The First Officer and himself lifted the flap...

'Christ Dave!'

Mike Saxonby peered over their shoulders...

Jed Beale's corpse lay near the entrance with his head resting in his own blood. His open eyes stared straight at them. His right arm lay across his chest, a scalpel clutched in the right hand. Blood had ceased to flow from the deep incision in his neck. Alongside the steel table, upon which the dolphin's laboured breathing was obvious, lay Carson and Dwyer. They were both very still.

It took some moments for them to register the large syringes in a hand of each.

Stunned, they backed away.

Mike said, 'Didn't train you for this, did they Dave?'

'Too bloody right, mate!' was the unofficerly reply.

And then a kind of training reasserted itself...

Dave Glynn watched the dolphin lowered in the sling towards the sanctuary of the sea. He was conscious of the shocked hands gathered at the side to see the reunion as if in desperate need of some reassurance that life had a magic and a wonder - anything but the finality and morbidity of death as it seemed now.

Even as the sling touched surface, reunited, the dolphins were nosing with beaks at each other... one seemingly very impatient that hands should get the alien material off its mate as quickly as possible...

Dave Glynn and his First Officer made for Carson's tent, sombre in duty, trying to forget the nicknames of the dead...

They passed the sentry and dropped the flap.

The small, flattish, stainless steel and glass fibre object, with thin cable and optic fibre connections, was obviously important... Too important to take risks with...

If they used the safe in the sickbay, it just might fall into the wrong hands...

Dave Glynn placed it in a sealed and weighted watertight container as the First Officer carefully recorded the serial number of the disc against their precise position in the ship's log. They had both agreed it would be a lot safer down there than in any other place they could think of...

They would be able to find it easily when they knew who could be trusted in this Godforsaken Navy...

Blowhard and Blotch both pinged to confirm it was dark and deep enough...

Both agreed the place would do.

Blowhard let go and they tracked the Splitfluke container from the lightrays, down the darkdepths. They heard it crush.

It was as Gaze had wanted - and would confirm it so in the darkwater singing of the podsherd's cross when Maeve would join them...

*

As Gaze had requested before his sudden departure, Peen dived as usual to pay her respects to loyal Ardent... and to beaknudge his jade...

In horror and desperation she fastfluked urgently seeking her Gale!

He and the mindweb were already aware - which she should have realised from her son's training if her distress had not been so overwhelming...

Sinu, Tinu, Gale and Beak Spot communed as she finstirred fretfully, only dimly conscious of Gape, Finwarp and Flab at her flanks, soothing, sharing... Fintouching, they sang the songs of consolation as she drifted in their lee through shadowed water...

Peen, ever popular and respected, noted nothing of the mindmerging between Bottlenose and Bottlenose or the deepest
communion between so many minds... Trapped behind cliffsides in her grieving, for much of the lightwater she was totally unreachable... could not have guessed a new patterning in the
large hearts of kith and kin...

In early darkwater, Gale fintouched... Patiently, he finswept her back and sides until, at last, she was aware of his bodybulk close at her side...

He mindmerged soberly, 'Our son is unjustified in the enormity of his

356

shame. Gaze and White Tip have taken lives so that millions might live... They have striven for harmony amongst Splitflukes, most of whom know nothing but discord or

the selfish desire to dominate...

'Dear Ardent was as fearful for Wanderer as he was for Gaze and White Tip. Yet Wanderer was not an Abomination... Neither is our son... And neither, in the Podsherd's opinion, is his mate...

'Some Bottlenoses are special, my love... glimpse a universal patterning from an intelligence greater than any life in worldspace... Special dolphins make new sagas, but always in subservience to something larger than themselves...'

She sensed his great pride and that he was very, very close...

In Merge...? They were in... Merge!...

Fluketrembling, she heard his authority - and the agreed concensus of a much larger podding than the mindweb...

'No son of ours,' Gale said, 'exiles himself from the warmstream for an imagined offence against the White Dolphins or the traditions which Ardent taught well. We are agreed...

'If he will not come to the Podsherd, in His name, Peen - 'The Podsherd of Gaze' voyages in exodus to flukeseek Him!'

In the lagoon, she heard a new song; recognised the clear ping-patterning resonance of... 'His Podsherd's Name'!...

Beyond the Guardian Circuit, she saw the shape of a White Dolphin, the breach to airleap which seemed to pass above the lagoon airspace, descending to disappear in spray at an entrance...

The traditional salute to a new leader from the old... it was also a summons to flukefollow...

There were more white shapes in wave spume - and one flukingpattern she thought she recognised!... So very like that of the old Cleric she knew and loved... but younger and fitter...?

Knowing two White Dolphins' names, Peen was content...

*